A Soldier Far Away

A Historical Novel of the Swedish Campaign of the Thirty Years War

Robert T. Hunting

HOOSICK FALLS, NEW YORK

2017

First published in 2017 by the Merriam Press

First Edition

Copyright © 2017 by Robert T. Hunting
Book design by Ray Merriam
Additional material copyright of named contributors.

The views expressed are solely those of the author.

ISBN 9781576386439
Library of Congress Control Number 2017912778

This work was designed, produced, and published in
the United States of America by the

Merriam Press
489 South Street
Hoosick Falls NY 12090

E-mail: ray@merriam-press.com
Web site: merriam-press.com

The Merriam Press publishes new manuscripts on historical subjects, especially military history and with an emphasis on World War II, as well as reprinting previously published works, including reports, documents, manuals, articles and other materials on historical topics.

There was a soldier, a Scottish soldier,
who wandered far away and soldiered far away.
He'd seen the glory and told the story,
of battles glorious and deeds neforious,
but now he's sighing, his heart is crying
to leave these green hills of Tyrol.

The Green Hills of Tyrol
(Traditional pipe tune. Lyrics added by Andy Stewart)

Note to the Reader

A Soldier Far Away offers an engaging account of a significant phase of the *Thirty Years War,* notably the Swedish campaign (1630-1632).

Perhaps one of the most peculiar and prolonged wars in the annals of military history, the *Thirty Years War* may be considered the end result of both the Reformation and Counter-Reformation movements. *The Catholic League*, under the banner of Hapsburg Austria, Spain and Bohemia, and with the backing of Rome, sought to retake central Protestant Europe. Opposing it (at different times) were Denmark, Sweden, independent principalities—from Transylvania to the Palatinate, and (irony of ironies) France.

Much of the war's savagery took place in what is now Germany and parts of northern Italy. Neither the Catholic nor the Protestant side ever held the moral high ground, yet both insisted God favored them. Those caught between the adversaries held different opinions, perhaps more in line with Shakespeare's declaration, "a pox on both your houses."

The war resurrected the Roman dictum; *bellum se ipsum alet* — war feeds itself. Few nations in the 17th century had standing armies, so relied heavily on mercenaries. Feeding and supplying them frequently fell short of intent. Unable to receive regular pay, food, or clothing, mercenaries took their frustrations out on the civilian population, while those in power turned a blind eye.

By war's end in 1648, the fatigued and cash-strapped combatants reluctantly signed a peace treaty. The major signatories — Imperial Spain and Bourbon France — lost all pretenses of battling for men's souls, and only spoke about political hegemony.

Most of the historical details are accurate. In some places, I altered the story and added characters and vignettes to enhance reading enjoyment. If I've missed or overlooked something historians, fact-checkers or re-enactors catch as erroneous, my apologies, and please remember I only set out to entertain.

Chapter 1

THEY'D traveled by night, these reivers, border raiders, on thick, sure-footed Highland ponies, from the market town of Doonhamers. Their destination, the fishing village of MacQuoid; their prey, the crippled Dutch cargo ship, the *Gray Valk*.

The bright half-moon made traveling easy. Halfway up the small mountain overlooking the River Nith they crouched and peered through the darkness at their prize, the ship. A reddish-orange slash in the eastern sky gave notice of the sun's approaching return.

"You'll stay back, Lee, until everyone's down?" the craggy-faced Aiken Raeburn, the band leader, said in a hushed tone to the only member who refused to wear the flat cap. "Keep an eye on things. Observing."

Observin' wot? a nettled Ainslie thought, swallowing his disappointment. He saw no reason to be left out. *Why do I have to always come up last? It's not fair.*

Raeburn ignored his nephew's long face and pointed to three raiders. "Off now. Walk your ponies down; last thing we're needin' is a fall."

"Right," the portly Diarmad Fraser answered. "We'll wait a wee when we get there. Come when I whistle."

"We'll do tha'," Raeburn replied. "See you at the bottom."

Fraser led the other two reivers down the steep, loose incline. The peninsula's lone fishing village remained in deep slumber as the scouts searched for signs of danger.

"You hear anything?" Sionn Moffett whispered to Fraser as he stared at the outline of the village.

Fraser shook his head. "No. Nothin' 'cept tha' dog barkin.' Otherwise, quiet as a grave."

The barking stopped. The two Scots gazed at each other. "Wot you make of it?" Moffet whispered. "Dog gettin' wind of us?"

Fraser again shook his head. "Thinking we're alone." He turned and placed his fingers to his lips and let off a soft whistle for Raeburn.

Moments later Raeburn and the remaining men arrived. No one spoke but all eyes took in the Valk as it bobbed beside the pier.

Fraser leaned closer to Raeburn. "The dog, Aiken?"

"Ay. Wot of it?"

"Think we should be mindful-like?"

Raeburn's eyes searched for anything amiss as he considered Fraser's suggestion. "It's no barking now, but let's hold back a wee more."

They waited. A few watched the village; others, the approaching light of day. Nothing suggested danger.

Raeburn at last signaled to mount up. "Remember," he warned in his soft voice; "in and out. Fast-like. We round up everybody and take wot we come for. Gone afore the world's the wiser."

Misfortune struck. Noises; the screech of protesting shed door hinges pierced the night. Lanterns appeared. Men whooped.

"Horses!" Raeburn cried out at the heavy, dull sound of hooves on wooden planks. "Run for it, lads."

In panic the Scots raced away, knowing their smaller animals were no match against the larger English steeds.

Ainslie followed Raeburn to a thicket. Three pursuers overtook them; two pulled in front and blocked their way while the third moved behind them. The abrupt cut-off forced them to the left.

"Stop, ya Scottish sons of whores," a voice called out. Its owner held an imposing round-barreled cavalry pistol at arm's length. "Stop or you'll die in your cheap saddle."

Lacking any alternative, Raeburn and Ainslie reined in and tossed their hands in the air. Worry etched itself on Raeburn's face. By contrast, his young nephew's face suggested wonderment at their plight. In dumb awe he gaped at the man with the pistol and disregarded the butt end of a swing from the side. The hard blow snapped Ainslie's head to the side. He toppled out of the saddle and onto the dew-filled grass.

Darkness claimed Raeburn's nephew.

"Lee!" Raeburn's voice rose to its highest pitch as Ainslie hit the ground. He dismounted. A soldier rode closer, sword drawn. "Back on your little horse."

Raeburn ignored the command and stared up at the soldier. "Why'd you go and do tha'? He already gave up. You may've killed him."

The Englishman tossed a glance at the prone body and snorted. "Good. Save the Crown the bother of a hanging. Something tells me he'll live long enough to dance at the end of a rope. I won't tell you again. On yer pony."

"Come on now," Raeburn implored. "Will you not let me help the laddie up? Where's your decency?"

The Englishman snorted his contempt. "Decency? You, a no-account making his living thieving—talking about decency? Leave it to you Scots to preach." He gave a dismissive shake of his head. "Least heeded when most needed."

His companions laughed at the retort.

Others arrived with their captives, and Ainslie's slack body was hefted across his pony, Duff.

Straps dug into the wrists of all the prisoners, binding them tightly and cutting circulation. The posse made its way to Carlisle.

A sizable crowd met the riders at the city's western gate and followed the captives to the courtyard of the Great Gaol. More than a few heaved spoiled food, dried animal droppings. Others restricted themselves to venomous language as the column proceeded.

A line of gaolers pulled the reivers from their ponies. Yelling, pushing and cuffing their charges, the gaolers herded them to a heavy oak door. Two gaolers held each man's arms while a third unlashed the straps.

Heads forced down, the prisoners shuffled along a narrow passageway with a musty odor. Rush lights in iron holders cast long shadows. From somewhere distant came the soft drip, drip, drip of water.

The guards moved their prisoners down well-worn granite steps to a dungeon corridor. After a short march, they stopped before another thick, wide oak door. One of the gaolers swung it open. Two others guided each prisoner in and shoved him down two steps to a large, empty, reeking cell.

The reivers listened as the sound of a metal bolt slid into place with finality. All eyes remained fixed on the door.

Scant light meandered through the bars of the small underground window as the prisoners took in their surroundings. Their eyes scanned the thick, quarried limestone, coated with black mold. In places, the stone wept runnels of water.

An offensive stink assailed their nostrils — the smell of old, rotting and damp straw infested with feces, urine, dried vomit, blood and who knew what else. The smell forced them to breathe through their mouths.

Sitting on the black slime floor proved a problem. Each man used his boots to scrape a clearing. With reluctance they sat against the walls. At least they'd have support for their backs. Two placed themselves on either side of a still-senseless Ainslie, chin on his chest, and kept him from toppling sideways.

Soon the prisoners discovered a new worry.

"Creepy-crawlies," a revolted Dusty Laing shouted as he scrabbled about in his beard. "Jay-suz! There's somethin' in me beard." He pushed himself up onto his feet. "God almighty Himself, hangin's better than this."

Almost as one, the others rose and madly brushed away at real or imaginary body lice.

A dazed Ainslie stirred. A man crouched in front of him. His uncle.

"How you feeling, laddie?"

"A cadger's curse, eme," Ainslie croaked. "Fearful headache, sick to me stomach, and a powerful thirst." He glanced around at his surroundings. "Prison?"

"Ay. But there's still hope."

Ainslie recalled what happened. He used his fingertips to probe the welt on the side of his head. "Englishman landed me a good one, eh?"

Raeburn nodded. "Afraid so. For a while I thought he'da killed ya."

"Feel's worse than being dead," Ainslie muttered as his chest heaved, ready to vomit. "This smell's no helping."

"Your mouth," Raeburn advised: "breathe through your mouth. It's wot we've all been doing."

Ainslie obeyed. "Water, eme; water," he said through parched lips. "I've a powerful thirst."

Raeburn shook his head in dismay. "None to be had. Doubt any'll be coming anytime soon." He turned and pointed at a wall. "There's a wee bit coming down there. See if ya can trap it in your hands."

An unsteady Ainslie rose and staggered to the wall. The water tasted rusty, but he didn't care. He couldn't get enough.

The tramp of marching feet reached the bandits at first light. The cadence stopped at their cell. All turned their eyes to the door and listened to the unlatching of the metal bolt.

The door swung open with a querulous creak. Two armed gaolers with rush lights walked in and moved to either side of the top step. A moment later the High Governor entered. Short, double-chinned and bow-legged, feet apart and fists on hips, he considered the prisoners before he spoke.

"Ya sorry lot of sheep shaggers." With the judgment offered, he shook his head in disapproval. "This'll teach you to come up against the might of the Crown. You'll be sorry you ever crossed our border."

He drew in a breath of air. "You're to appear in front of a magistrate day after tomorrow, it being Sunday. Make your peace with the Lord God because it won't go well for you after."

He stopped and let his words have their effect before he continued. "Now, to show you we're civilized men, you'll have two buckets — one with water, and the other for your business."

He glared at his audience once more, shook his head, turned and exited.

At trial, the raiders presented themselves as misunderstood.

"Innocent, Your Lordship," Fraser called out from the prisoner box. "You caught the wrong men. You've to believe us. We wouldn't as much rob a widow for a beer, and there's your truth."

His comrades called out their agreement, but the magistrate dismissed the account. "You'd lie till your dying breath, the lot of you. You'd take an old widow's underskirt if you could manage it. Do not tell this Court you are innocent. You're reivers — every last one of you. First, we are made to suffer the wash of your beggarly kinsmen flooding our good lands. Not content, you Scottish toads repay us with thievery. No, you had your eyes on the cargo ship. It's the Lord's blessing we caught you first."

No spectator doubted the outcome. The magistrate sentenced all to hang. "Be a lesson to others like you," he concluded and moved on to the next case.

Back in the enclosure, some of the raiders appealed to a higher power in hopes of intervention. On their knees, they clasped their hands and recited every prayer known to them. The rest resumed their places against the walls and stared into empty space, lost in some other time and place.

Ainslie's eyes rose as his uncle approached. "Nothing you could have done, eme," he said in a low voice without much conviction. "You've gotta stop blamin' yourself. Who knew the English, would be lying in wait for us?"

"Easier told than done, laddie," a dispirited Raeburn replied.

Ainslie rubbed the wan and pitted scars on his cheeks. The small, tight mouth held oversized and already yellowed teeth yet flashed a quick smile at his uncle. "You're no listenin'. You've no cause to say it like tha'. It's no one's fault." He rotated his broad shoulders as if he might work out stiffness, and considered the man he held in high regard, who never quit on him or his mother. It wasn't Raeburn's obligation, yet he had taken in both Maisie and Ainslie, when Nial Souter left.

Word had it Ainslie's father, Nial, lived in Jamaica, shacked up with a mulatto. Ainslie didn't care. Meant nothing to him. As for his mother, Maisie, she'd suffered long and hard with constipation, diarrhea and bad humors before she died in Saint Kentigern's.

The door unlatched once more. Two armed gaolers entered the cell and stepped aside for the Governor. A contemptuous sneer on his face, he declared, "Right then, you lumpish hedge-born lot, your time's at hand. Work it out who meets his Maker first, next, and last. I'll be back soon, so get on with it."

Satisfied with his message, His Majesty's High Governor of Carlisle Gaol spun about and left.

No one spoke until Fraser said, "Likes to throw around the insults, our fat Governor. Could throw a few words his way — startin' with his ma's chest hairs. Pobably looked better than those sittin' atop his swag belly."

The humour eased the tension. For the briefest moment the reivers forgot their troubles and chuckled at the retort.

Silence again settled over the men. They turned to Raeburn and waited for his advice. "Draw straws, laddies. It's the best way. I'll go first. I led you into this. Only fittin' I hang first. Be brave. Let's show these bastards how good Scots die."

All agreed to Raeburn's wish, but insisted Ainslie go last.

Weighed down with regret, Raeburn approached Ainslie and removed his surcoat. He held it out for his nephew. "Brave now. I've no need for this; you have it for however long you can. I'm sorry, I am, I wasn't a better parent — but I want you to know I loved you like me own son."

He gazed at his nephew with tenderness, and drew him into his arms. His mouth close to Ainslie's ear, he whispered, "In case you survive, you know where I keep the gold."

He kissed his nephew's cheek a final time and broke away.

Ainslie felt tears form as the band of men surrounded Raeburn, patted his back, and offered kind words.

Moments later the gaolers returned. Ainslie peeled off his mantle and slipped on Raeburn's surcoat as his uncle turned and faced his executioners. "I'm first to go."

The High Governor and a priest stood in the corridor with six gaolers. One moved to either side of Raeburn while a third bound his hands behind his back. The task complete, he turned Raeburn toward the stairs.

All remained still until the Governor cleared his throat. With the practiced signal given, the gaolers, a priest and the condemned man followed. In a slow, dignified manner the retinue made its way up the cold granite steps, past the soldiers at the courtyard door and into the bright sun.

Raeburn squinted as he met the cheers, jeers, and colorful invectives of a mob ready for entertainment. Soldiers held the crowd back as Raeburn's gaolers jostled him forward.

The crowd started its chant. "A-hangin', a-hanging, it's time we had a hangin'."

Raeburn did his best to block out the noise and hold his head high.

The procession marched for another three hundred yards until it reached the T-shaped upright gibbet on a small platform. A thick rope attached to an iron loop on the cross beam swung in the breeze, its noose full of fearful meaning.

Surrounded by the blood-thirsty crush of citizens, the Governor turned and gave the slightest of nods. In turn, two gaolers rough-handled the weak-kneed Raeburn up the two steps of the wooden frame to his place of execution. He endured more catcalls, whistlings and the odd pieces of flying food.

Public hangings always drew large crowds, but none like this. No one remembered so many felons hung in the same day. To maintain peace and order, the Governor limited the number of spectators in the courtyard itself. Those inside waited with great anticipation while vendors sold ale, meat pies and trinkets. Cutpurses worked the crowd — by day's end many a man found himself without a purse.

The executioner stepped closer to Raeburn. "Cap off," he ordered, and swatted at Raeburn's headgear. The action drew cheers from the crowd.

Priest and executioner traded places. The clergyman opened his bible and peered into Raeburn's face. The Scot met his gaze. The two stared at each other as the crowd's noises intensified and swirled around them.

Raeburn spoke. "Presbyterian then, is it?"

The priest shook his head. "No. Church of England."

Raeburn's response surprised the cleric. "Then fuck off, you blaspheming papist," the condemned man spat out in a defiant manner. "I'll no' have some bloody antichrist prayin' over me."

"I'm not a pap..," the vicar began, but a fast punch to Raeburn's kidney doubled Raeburn. He fell to the platform. His head bounced off the hard surface as the crowd roared its delight. Waves of pain and sickness washed through Raeburn.

The executioner pulled him to his feet. "Insolent Scottish bastard," he growled. "You'll keep a decent tongue in your head against your betters, and respect a holy man."

The pain receded but Raeburn's mouth and throat grew dry. He wished they'd offer him water but knew otherwise.

His legs shook and he pressed down hard, hoping to stop them. His eyes found the heavy upside-down wooden bucket before they settled on the oxcart. *No doubt to toss our bodies*, he thought.

The trembling increased and moved north into his torso.

The crowd took up a new chant. "The rope, the rope; you'll have a lovely burn."

To distract himself, Raeburn gave his full attention to the sky. He found a pair of guillemots, his birds — Scottish birds — flying northwest. They came to boost his morale, he told himself, and drew some comfort from the thought.

The executioner threw a black sack over Raeburn's head and tightened the drawstring while two gaolers guided Raeburn to the bucket. "Keep still," someone ordered.

The heavy noose came next. Raeburn felt it slip over the sack and above his collarbone, then someone tightened it. He prayed for his young nephew as the hangman made his final adjustment. Raeburn sensed him move away.

The agitation in the crowd rose as Raeburn offered up a prayer. "The Lord's me shepherd. I'll no' want. He makes me lie down in pastures green, he leadeth me. The quiet wat..."

He never finished his song of praise. The executioner kicked forcefully at the bucket several times. It wobbled, and Raeburn with it. He adjusted his stance, but the final kick sent the bucket backward, and left him dangling in mid-air. He bit his tongue in reaction.

No long drop, sudden death and breaking of the neck for Raeburn. He received nothing less than a slow, tortuous strangulation as the rope tightened violently and held him suspended less than two feet above the platform.

A powerful burn tore into his neck as he sought air—any air. He moved his neck to and fro in an effort to get air, but to no avail. The noose stiffened even as his legs gamboled in a macabre end dance and the mob cheered its delight.

Raeburn stayed alive and suffered for yet longer, drawn-out moments. Fatigued, denied air, he at last blacked out, unaware of time or place. Even then his body sought to maintain a life no longer possible.

It proved worse for the others when they spied their comrades' bodies on the ox cart.

The frenzied, blood-lust noise of the crowd seemed to grow with each hanging. The mass demanded its entertainment.

Chapter 2

ECHOED sounds of laughter reached the last two reivers as they awaited the gaolers.

Ainslie paced as he touched and re-touched his bump. Stopping in mid-stride, he cocked his head and listened before he turned to his companion. The other man leaned into the corner, eyes closed and arms folded high on his chest.

"Ho, Dez. Listen. Outside — they're gettin' all liquored up."

The scraggly bearded Derek Penny cocked his head. "Ay, you're right. They're having a fuckin' holiday over this. Wot kinda people are these English?" He moved closer to the door. "Bettin' the gaolers are drinkin' as well." Outraged, he hurried up the two steps and yelled, "Hey, you eejits; have a care. We're to hang, so shut the fuck up."

He followed his harangue with a furious kick to the door. It gave. Mouth agape, Penny turned and gawked at Ainslie, who was every bit as dumbstruck.

Penny moved with care and pushed the door. It creaked. He drew back and turned to Ainslie. "You think they heard us?" he whispered.

Ainslie hurried up the steps and matched Penny's voice. "Don't know. Not sounding like anyone coming. You catch anything?"

Penny listened. "Nah." He held Ainslie's gaze. "Ready?"

"Ay. Damned if I stay here."

Penny opened the door and stuck his head out with caution. No hand slammed on him, no cry of alarm sounded. Bolder, he pushed the door farther into the corridor.

Ainslie followed. Distant laughter echoed down to them. Penny turned to Ainslie and whispered, "Somebody gave us a gift, eh? Let's take a run at the guards. Better be dead on our feet than swingin' from our necks."

"Ay. Stop your blathering and get on with it."

Penny gave Ainslie a fast once-over. "You'll be fine?"

Ainslie pushed Penny. "Will ya get on with it afore it's too late?"

"Right."

They crept out into the corridor. Penny turned, shut the cell door and slid the bolt in place. A malicious grin appeared. He leaned close to Ainslie's ear and whispered. "We get away with this, this'll have 'em scratching their heads and sayin', 'How the fuck did these bandits get out?' Wish I was here to see the look on their faces."

"You'll see it fast enough if we don't get moving," Ainslie hissed and again pushed on Penny's shoulder. "Go."

They edged along the corridor, ready for anything. No one opposed them. Better still, no one guarded the passageway, stairs, or the landing. Two astonished reivers walked through the gaol door, into the courtyard, and melded into the crowd. Strong drink made much of the mob forget its true purpose for attending the event. People yelled, smiled, danced, and sang. Twice someone pulled Ainslie closer and offered a drink. *If I didn't know better*, thought Ainslie, *I'd swear they're having a Twelfth Night festival.*

The men worked their way through the crowd and came upon the cart with their comrades' bodies. Ainslie stopped and stared. Blood drained from a face full of hatred. Penny moved closer. "Do no good starin', Lee. Can't help 'em now." He pulled on Ainslie's sleeve. "C'mon."

They at last arrived at the main prison gate. A man asked about the hangings. Penny did his best uncaring imitation and shrugged a shoulder, worried his speech might give him away.

Outside the escapees made their way into a warren of small lanes and stopped. "Make sense to you our ponies are here somewheres?" Ainslie asked.

"Ay," Penny said. "Has to be a horse barn 'round here."

A quick search resulted in the discovery of a stable. Inside they found two seated gaolers already full of ale, along with a stable boy.

Ainslie spied Duff about the same time a gaoler recognized them, and rose to his feet. "What the fu..."

Ainslie charged.

Already full of ale, two besotted gaolers and a stable boy proved no match for the hostile fugitives who had surprise and desperation on their side. Ainslie drove a hard fist into a gaoler's face. He crumpled. Penny rushed at the other man.

The wide-eyed boy cowered as Ainslie's foot shot out and kicked the prone gaoler in the face.

Penny gave the other gaoler a pummeling. The man's arms flew up to ward off the series of blows that brought him to his knees.

The reivers kicked and stomped with abandon. When they were finished and heaving with exertion, they gave the boy their attention. "You didn't see a thing," Penny warned.

The trembling ten-year-old's head shook in a hurried response.

Ainslie pointed. "Go sit in th' corner," Ainslie demanded. "And don't leave until we tell ya."

The boy obeyed.

The reivers bent over their victims and searched for anything of value. Both discovered heavy purses and pocketed them. "Best get moving," Penny advised. "Someone's bound to come at any time."

"Ay. Been here long enough. Let's get the ponies. I'm no' leaving me eme's behind."

"Wot 'bout Duff?"

"Wot of 'him?" Ainslie challenged. "I'll ride him and take Caillen."

Penny gave him an all-the-same-to-me shrug. "Do wot you think's best." He pointed at the small bulbous stove. "Wot say we burn this place to the ground? Won't be hard."

"Fine by me," Ainslie said as he hurried to saddle Duff.

While Ainslie readied the ponies, Penny found a hand-held shovel on a post near a small stove. He opened the cover, pushed the shovel inside, angled around and pulled out some red pocket-sized pieces of coal. He tossed them into a stack of hay. Smoke rose, followed soon by an orange flame.

Ainslie rushed about and freed the remaining horses before he opened the double outside gates. "Get a move on, will you?"

"Comin.'" Penny climbed into his saddle and kicked his pony. He glanced at the boy. "Now, off ya go."

The boy ran outside as Penny glanced over his shoulder at the flame and yelled to Ainslie, "Tha"ll give these bastards something else to think about." They tore off down the overcrowded narrow streets. "Time the English bring it to order, we're far-n'-gone," he shouted to Ainslie. Both knew an out-of-control fire proved more dangerous than any approaching enemy.

Penny spied the western gate. He pointed. "There."

"Think those two back there'll make it out in time?" Ainslie called out.

Penny turned his head and hollered, "Couldn't care less. Wouldn't give any of these bastards the steam of me piss."

Few took heed of the two men as they approached the gate. A guard, his thumbs tucked into his wide belt, stepped up and nodded. Ainslie stopped his pony. With a fast movement he yanked the guard toward him and slashed down with his dirk. The blade cut a diagonal line across the guard's face, from his eyebrow to the edge of his lip. He screamed and threw his hands to his face.

Bystanders gaped as the man crumpled to the ground and the reivers rode into the countryside. Half a mile out of the city the escapees stopped and turned. Black and gray smoke twirled into the sky over Carlisle. Ainslie dismounted as Penny stared off into the distance.

"Glorious sight, tha'," Penny said.

Ainslie paid no attention. Instead, he cleaned his blade on the tall grass. "Better, if the whole fucking city went up."

"Be grand," Penny agreed. "Wonder how long before our friends send the militia after us?"

Ainslie climbed into the saddle and kicked his pony. "No friends of mine."

Penny moved beside Ainslie. "Funny thing."

Ainslie regarded him. "Wot's funny?"

"Us getting away. Thankful, I am, mind, but I can't work out where all them gaolers went to. Not so's it matters, but strange."

"Suppose, but I'm glad tha's the way it went. Wot's the saying, 'danger and delight grow on the same stalk'? Just wish we'd all got away."

They rode for a while in silence.

Dead, Ainslie thought. *All ten dead except for Dez and me. How'd we deserve to stay alive?* Deep in thought, he didn't at first catch the sideway glances Penny tossed at him. He frowned at Penny. "Out with it then."

"You're readin' me mind."

"Not hard."

"Never seen you doin' the likes of tha' before."

"Seen me doin' wot?"

"Slice a man."

"Never had the need," Ainslie replied.

"'Pose."

They stopped often and checked for signs of pursuit. Nothing but a few shepherds and a family of tinkers. Both relaxed as they crossed onto Scottish soil.

Late afternoon found them eating with enthusiasm in the comfort of an alehouse. They shook the coins out from their newly claimed purses. Penny whistled in appreciation. "Fair lot here. You'd'a thought gaolers wouldn't have much on 'em. Is it a good livin', bein' a gaoler?"

"Askin' the wrong feller, Dez, but I wouldn't guess it. Must'a bin up to something else to get this kinda coin."

The money divided, they fell into silence.

Late evening found them at the edge of Dumfries. They bade each other farewell. Ainslie felt certain they'd never meet again.

A SOLDIER FAR AWAY

Chapter 3

A medieval track led Ainslie to his village, Mosstone, located a mile from Dumfries' old city walls.

His uncle's whitewashed croft cottage came into sight. In truth it belonged to Cormag Raeburn, Ainslie's grandfather. A most desirable cottage, everyone agreed, one of the few with cut and polished flat stones in place of beaten-down earth and straw.

Ainslie had never known another home but this cottage. He lived there even after they took his mother, Maisie, to Saint Kentigern's. His grandmother and Aunt Skeena, came daily to fuss over his main meal.

He led Duff and Caillen into the corral and entered the small house. His eyes swept the cottage for signs of trespass. Nothing appeared amiss. Satisfied, he crouched close to the fireplace and strained with the task of prying an embedded stone tablet free from the surrounding clay. It took a while before the tablet loosened. His fingers scrabbled about in the moist soil. He at last found what he sought. A few moments later he withdrew a leather pouch. It bounced in the palm of his hand.

He set the little sack on the floor, pushed the tablet back in place with all his weight, to embed it once again. He untied the straps of the pouch and shook out twenty gold half sovereign coins. "Rich," he whispered, "I'm rich." He'd never held so much money. The memory of his uncle final words came to him — "In case you survive, you know where I keep the gold."

"How'd ya know, eme?" he whispered to the cottage. "How'd ya know I'd survive?" He answered his own question with a shake of his head. "Nah. Not possible. Couldn'ta bin. It's just me luck, and his bad, is all."

Even so, Ainslie marveled at whatever brought him to safety. He returned the coins to the pouch and added the ones he'd lifted from the gaoler in Carlisle, retied the strings and moved to the cedar chest.

Lid up, he spied his uncle's favorite blue-dyed cotton Jacobite shirt. Sadness overcame him as he brought it to his nose and inhaled the faint whiff of his beloved uncle. A curious man in many ways, Raeburn — a bachelor who liked women and drink — who suddenly found himself with a family.

Ainslie recalled the man who believed in weekly washing when everyone else bathed once per month. The village grew accustomed to seeing him haul water from the well for his bathing. In the summer he'd place his wooden tub outside the house. He'd scrub his naked skin with soap and water. Should a village woman be a passerby, she'd scurry past and shade her eyes.

Maisie felt certain her brother took leave of his senses. Many a time she protested his washings. "Wot's the point, Aiken?" she'd ask. "How many times have ya heard Pastor Wallace tell us washing weakens the skin? It's no good for you, and there's the bald truth."

Ainslie's uncle simply batted aside her arguments.

Other enduring memories crowded in on Ainslie as he stood and clutched the shirt to his breast. His uncle held opinions not always in step with others.

Ainslie's mother once said, "The village is talking about you, Aiken."

Raeburn tossed a shoulder in response. "Is it now? No matter. Empty barrels make the most noise. If they're not talking 'bout me, they're talking about somebody else then."

Raeburn insisted Ainslie learn his letters. Maisie put up another of her protests. "It's just givin' him airs, Aiken. Where's the sense in tha'?"

Raeburn waved her away. "Not a bit of it, Maisie. I'm the laddie's male parent, and I say he needs an education. Can you no see? A new age's comin' and he better be part of it. Time's soon done for raiders the likes of me. The boy's to have some advantage."

Every day Ainslie rode or marched off to Duncan Carstarphen's cottage for lessons. The teacher found this pupil different from Lord Carrigan's two simpletons at Ellesmere Castle. Ainslie fidgeted, true, but enjoyed learning.

The white-haired Carstarphen, with tufts of hair growing out of his ears, not only taught Ainslie to read, but also instructed him in Latin. "Don't fool about," the lean, round-shouldered tutor warned, "and pay attention, because you've to understand Latin and Greek roots. If you've got them down, you've a fair taking with any language."

Carstarphen let Ainslie borrow books. At night Raeburn rocked in his chair and Maisie knit while Ainslie read aloud stories from faraway lands.

Raeburn's nephew sniffed the shirt once more, then himself. He wrinkled his nose in disgust. Best to have a quick wash. He lifted the lid from the water bucket and dipped his fingers in it; it held enough water.

The cottage grew darker. Soap and washcloth nearby, he stripped down to his bare skin and gave himself a good cleaning. He lathered the strong soap to his face and by feel, used his dirk to scrape away the growth of facial hair. He hoped to avoid nicking or cutting himself. Under the nose held the greatest challenge. His hand proved steady; no cuts or skin burn.

When Ainslie finished washing, he toweled himself, lifted the basin and opened the door. He tossed the water, then slipped on his uncle's shirt. He found it a bit long, but didn't care. He laced the leather cording and shoved the ends of the shirt into his breeches.

A final tour of the cottage summoned up boundless memories of his uncle. "Sleep well, eme," he whispered to the room. "I'm sure you're not in hell. Somewhere nice with ma, and no doubt she'll have you feeling right at home."

With tightness in his chest and his eyes moist, the young Ainslie stepped out the door and divorced himself from the last of his childhood.

Darkness settled over the land as Ainslie made for Cormag Raeburn's stone cottage. It held the same outward features as its nearby neighbors and offered no clue its tenant owned wealth the equal of many a minor nobleman. Hidden wealth, but wealth nonetheless. Cormag Raeburn still lived when most his age had passed away. His word remained law. As the local clan leader, he settled arguments and shared in profits from stolen goods, cattle and sheep-thieving, and counterfeited coins. He also served as the village's memoirist and keeper of legends.

Ainslie guided the ponies into his grandfather's paddock. He walked to the front of Cormag's cottage, knocked, and waited. The stooped, grey-bearded village elder opened the door and peered out into the night. His eyes took in the young man. "Och, Lee," he said as he let out a plaintive sigh. "Bin expectin' ya."

"I've no doubt of it, granda," a long-faced Ainslie replied.

Cormag rubbed his hands as his wife, Edine, and daughter, Skeena, peered over his shoulder.

"Lee," Edine said and stepped up beside her husband. "When we saw you come back alone, a deep gloom come over us. It's bad, isn't it?"

"'Ay, nana. The worst."

His grandmother turned to Cormag. "He's gone," she moaned and raised her hands to cover her face. "Our Aiken's gone. Wot'll we do without him?"

Afraid he would lose control, Ainslie turned his attention to Cormag. "I need to have a word with you, granda."

"Oh, ay," Cormag said and stepped aside. "Come in."

Ainslie entered the cottage with its flat, polished stone floor. Flames in the hearth danced with delight. A large, fat beeswax candle flickered on a stand in one corner. A brass oil lamp sat in the middle of the kitchen table.

He gazed at his grandmother. The low-set and plump Edine always wore the tenderest smile, but not this day; grief clouded her normally cheerful face. It took some doing to remind himself of the woman who'd often tickled him as a child and say, "Och, Lee," you're needin' some fat on them bones. Here, I've your favorite..." She moved toward Ainslie, followed by Skeena, and pulled him into her embrace. The three stood in their tight circle as tears fell. Cormag stood aside and stared at the floor, his face contorted with misery.

Long moments passed before Ainslie pulled away and calmed his breathing. Edine wiped at her face with her fingertips. "I don't want to hear, Lee, but I have to anyway. You've to tell us how your eme died."

Cormag agreed. "Ay. Sit and tell us what you must." He directed Ainslie to the kitchen table.

Ainslie sat. His eyes moved to Skeena. Widowed six months after her marriage to Ewan McKenzie, his aunt found herself alone and without children when the reiver took a musket ball during a cattle raid.

Feeling an outcast in a village with few unmarried women her age, Skeena took comfort in her parents' company. Tall where her parents were short, the smooth-faced Skeena showed little similarity to them. Village gossip often wondered how Cormag and Edine Raeburn turned out one as fine as she.

His aunt twisted and re-twisted her hands in anguish as Ainslie drew in a fresh lungful of air and said, "Nothing' but rotten is what I've to tell you. The English caught us trap-like. Took us to Carlisle." He stared into his lap, pulled in another deep breath before, exhaled, and began again. He gave them a general account of what happened. "Hung us all 'ceptin' me and Derek."

The sound of the women's sniffles filled the room as Cormag muttered, "Worthless bastards."

Ainslie shook his head and continued. He told them how he and Penny escaped. Finished, he trained his eyes on the fireplace as Edine spoke. "Our Aiken; our poor darling Aiken." She turned her gaze onto Cormag. "Maisie, and now Aiken. We've no mercy in life — great Jesus help us."

Ainslie played with his nervous fingers. "I blame myself for this."

"Rubbish."

Ainslie's head shot up as he heard the annoyance in his grandfather's voice.

"Get tha' idea outta your head," Cormag commanded. "It's foolish, is what it is. Nothin' you coulda done woulda changed wot happened."

"Your granda's right," Edine chimed in. "You're way too young to have any fault in this."

Her husband drummed the table with his forefinger. "Luck it was you an' Penny got away," he said.

Ainslie searched Edine and Skeena's faces for additional proof. They rewarded him with fast nods.

"It's our way," Cormag continued. "It's who we are and wot we do. One time or other, the Lord's bound to ask us to pay the bill."

"A sad amen to tha'," Edine answered.

A long silence followed before Cormag rose and moved to the hand-carved sideboard. He picked up a bottle of a woody-looking drink. "We'll no doubt need a dram or two ta brace ourselves."

Edine shook her head. "Not me. I'm no wanting drink at this time. Won't stay down. Need to get out; clear me head. I'll go and pay a visit to Maisie."

"Can I come with you, ma?" Skeena asked.

"Course."

The two women reached for their shawls. Edine stopped and turned. "He's dead, Cormag; our lovely Aiken's dead. Nothin' we can do about it now, but I want his body back. Here. You'll see to it."

"Ay, woman; I will."

The exchange finished, Edine opened the door and stepped out into the night, with Skeena behind her.

The two men retreated into silence as Cormag brought the malt whisky and two small shot glasses to the table. He sat and poured. The glasses full, he studied Ainslie. "Och, see you're wearing your uncle's favorite shirt."

"Ay, I am granda."

Cormag nodded his approval. "Loved tha' shirt, he did. Course I told him to be careful wearing it. Sets the English off, seeing our laddies with the Scottish color." He pushed a glass toward Ainslie and raised his own in toast. "Bad luck to the English, and good health to ya."

Ainslie brought his glass up in response and accepted the salute. "Health forever."

Grandfather and grandson tossed the drink back. The whisky burned as it made its way to Ainslie's stomach. He disliked it, but didn't want Cormag to see. He smacked his lips and banged the glass with too much drama.

"So," Cormag said. "I'll be hearing anything you left out fer the sake of the women. Go on with it."

"Ay, granda." In detail Ainslie told of the escape, the assault on the gaolers, the bodies piled on the oxcart, the fire, and cutting the guard. Cormag didn't interrupt but poured himself a second drink as Ainslie finished the tale.

"Tha's it, granda. Derek and me...we're home."

"And he's gone back to Doonhamers?"

"Ay. Says he's thinking 'bout catching a ship to the New World."

"Suppose it's wise. You've to leave too. They'll come — the English. No mistake about it. They'll want their revenge and they'll put a reward on your head."

"Thinking the same thing myself."

Cormag tapped his fingers on the table and peered into Ainslie's face. "Off with you for a while. If you want, come back when this passes — and it will, some day. I can't say when."

"Ay, granda. I'll stay the night in our cottage with your blessings."

Cormag waved away the asking. "Don't give it another thought. It's your home."

Pleased with the response, Ainslie shot Cormag a fast smile. "And in the morning, can you have someone ride with me to Glasgow and bring the pony back?"

"Glasgow's where you're off to? Ay, I'll have Blaine go 'long with you."

"Thanks, granda. Glasgow for now. I'll hide in the crowd until I figure out wot comes next."

"Good a plan as any."

"I put Duff and Caillen in the corral. You're welcome to 'em, course. And anything else in the cottage."

Cormag blinked several times and spoke again. "It's a sad day it's come so. Your eme Aiken ...we'll no see the likes of him around here again. He'll be sore missed, he will, especially by grannie and me. Had some fancy ideas, he did, but ya'd never find a better and truer son of Scotland."

He stopped and stared off again. "Rotten bastards."

A weighted silence passed before Corgmag spoke again, "Your gran's right. Your eme will not lie in some unnoticed grave. We'll have to pay a pretty coin to get him, but get him we will."

Ainslie straightened in his chair as a sense of relief washed over him at the news.

"D'ya have money?" Cormag asked.

"Ay. You wantin' it?"

Cormag threw back his head in reaction. "Don't be daft. I only care you have enough. Do you need any?"

Ainslie shook his head. "I've plenty. Took eme's if it's all right with you?"

"Course. What'll I be needing it for?" The old man stretched out a veined hand and patted Ainslie's. "Let's cheer up and toast to the future, especially yours, with 'nother dram."

Ainslie thought it best to offer no objection and let Cormag refill their glasses. The old man raised his glass. "To them tha' loves us or lends us a lift."

Ainslie brought up his glass in unison, and both men tossed the fiery drink back. "Ahh," Cormag said as his watery eyes glistened. "You're to remember, no matter wot; no matter when or where, you're always kin. Our door stays open to you. Always. And your eme's cottage, it stays the way you leave it, waiting for your return."

Heaviness settled in on Ainslie. He felt his eyes moisten. "Thank you, granda, but will you do me one last turn?"

Cormag gave a slow nod of his head. "Ay."

"Will you say a prayer for me at eme's funeral?"

"Tha'? Glad to. You've no to ask."

A Soldier Far Away

Chapter 4

EARLY the following morning, Ainslie and two of his childhood friends made the long trek to Glasgow. They reined in at the village cemetery. Ainslie dismounted and stood at his mother's grave.

"Oiy, ma," he whispered. "Haven't been here since they brought you from Saint Kentigern's. Isn't tha' I dinna want to, ya understand, but it was hard to get to come."

He raised his head and took in the cemetery. "Lovely place, this. You'll no be pleased to know eme Aiken's dead, but pleased he'll be near ya. Granda's promisin' to bring him back."

His voice cracked as he took several deep breaths and at last finished with, "I'll be sayin' goodbye to you, and sweet dreams, ma. Pray for me if you think of it."

They arrived in Glasgow mid-morning the following day.

Ainslie dismounted at the park opposite the medieval cathedral and handed Duff's reins to Blaine. "Bye, then," he said as he shook his friend's hand. "And thanks for coming along."

"No bother," Blaine answered. "Take care of yourself."

Ainslie also shook hands with Conan. Next he moved to Duff and fed him an apple. "I'll be missin' you," he whispered into the pony's ears as it enjoyed the treat, "but you'll be well taken care of. In case I don't see you again, have a good life."

He stepped back. "Bye again, fellers, and safe trip home."

The other two wished him well, turned and led Duff down the avenue filled with dirty puddles, horse droppings and a dead cat.

A wave of sadness overcame Ainslie as he watched the pony turn a corner and disappear. His uncle gave him Duff as a gift when the world seemed more certain. He blinked away the moisture in his eyes. It took another moment before he felt convinced he wouldn't make a spectacle of himself. *Stop feeling sorry for yourself*, an inner voice grumbled. *Life's not easy; get on with it.*

Can't argue tha', a less critical voice replied. *But what should I do?* He had no immediate prospects.

Start somewhere, the first voice insisted. *Can't do much standing here wasting time.*

Ainslie glanced both ways along the street and hoped a solution might present itself. None came. He tossed a shoulder as if to some imaginary companion and walked toward the commercial district. This, his second trip to Glasgow, didn't impress him any more than the first. He turned onto Argyle and spat out a harsh taste — one he remembered only too well.

He jostled through the mob on the street. *How do people stand it here, everybody pushing every which way? Doonhamers was bad enough, but nothing compared to Glasgow. Cities. Why would anyone live here?* No, he decided, as he walked past shops and hovels alongside half-timbered houses—he'd never be a city boy.

A casual walk down any city street involved risk. His uncle had taught him the trick of keeping to the middle and staying alert. "No one'll give a care", he warned his nephew as they made their way down Bath Street, "if you're a soft touch to a cutpurse or run over. You understand?"

"Ay, eme," a wide-eyed Ainslie assured his kinsman. "I think I do."

"Good then. Stay alert and keep to the middle, away from the buildings. Never can tell when some idiot housewife chucks her pot of kak. They don't look; just toss. Your bad luck you happen to be below."

The constant noise of metal carriage rims and horseshoes clanking up against cobblestones set him on edge. Other strident, rough sounds of daily street life bothered his ears as well. Ainslie dodged and weaved around horses, carriages and wagons, and paid attention to those near him. Every so often his eyes checked the upper floor windows.

"Will you be stayin' with us long, then?" the sturdy innkeeper's wife at the tasteful Harp and Thistle Inn asked as Ainslie handed over the coins.

His eyes narrowed at the question. "Why?"

"Why?" she repeated. "Just askin' the gentleman; making conversation, like. Didn't mean nothin' by it."

"I see," Ainslie replied. "Don't know at the moment, but won't be stayin' longer than I havta. Oh, and I'll be needin' a pitcher and water basin in me room."

Her brows furrowed. "Wot for?"

The manner in which the question arrived annoyed Ainslie, but he thought it best not to show his displeasure. He forced himself to smile. "For me own use, you understand."

Whether she did or not, she replied with, "Cost you more. Can't have people walking off with our property."

"Right. How much?"

"Bawbee."

"Done." He fished out the coin. "'I'll see it in me room when I return, then?"

"Ay. Ya've paid for it. I'll make sure it gets there."

He turned and made for the front door.

His stomach growled. Time to eat. The inn's posted menu didn't appeal to him, so he decided he'd wait. His nose led him to *The Fox and Furrow*. Inside the Public House he ordered the day's special, mutton with carrots and onions. Lovely, he thought as he imagined the meal set in front of him. He'd wash it down with some good ale.

He ate well and ordered extra bread and butter. Stomach full, the reiver ventured outside again. Conditions remained wet, chilly and miserable. Even so, he felt adventurous and wandered freely along both wide avenues and narrow streets.

The long walk around the city fatigued Ainslie. By late afternoon he made his way back to the inn. He passed a few buildings with tall, majestic columns. They looked familiar, or was it just his imagination? Had he been there with Raeburn? He couldn't be sure.

He dodged puddles of rainwater and detritus. Wind and rain increased in strength. His clothes soggy, he sought shelter. He spied the body of a bloated dog, its fur ripped open and the inner skin exposed. A rat stopped its feeding, looked around for signs of danger, and then scurried away.

It thundered — deep clapping thunder, followed by brilliant lightning bolts. The streets emptied of the few remaining pedestrians. A squeaking sign over a Public House caught Ainslie's attention: *The Rose and Anchor*. It might do. "One port inna storm's good as the next," he muttered to himself as he rushed for the front door and made his way down a wide flight of granite stairs.

It didn't surprise him to find the cavernous alehouse filled with customers. They crowded the fireplace in the center of the room. Its heat competed with the musty smell of wet clothes. Men drank, talked and ate in the cheerful atmosphere. No one appeared drunk, rude, or loud-mouthed.

The room with its thick beams had a cheery feel to it. Overhead, wooden wagon wheel chandeliers held candles in wrought-iron holders; the flames flicked back and forth with the movement of air, and cast mysterious shadows onto the walls and ceiling. Rectangular tables and benches filled much of the room, all darkened with age and smoke. Fat, thin, and in-between bottoms took up all the seating near the heat.

Ainslie claimed an empty table. He waited for service. It took a while coming. When it did, it arrived by way of a pretty, bare-headed girl with a long, green kirtle and a half-apron tied around her waist. A small purplish-red shawl, fastened at her chest, draped her shoulders.

She stepped close and said. "'Lo."

Ainsley glanced up at the smiling face.

"Wot'll you be havin', then?"

"Gotta wait out the storm," he said, "so, ale for now, and wot's turning on the spit?"

"Ale we've plenty, and nothin's turning at the mo', but we've some leftover herring pie inna kitchen. You can have it with neeps and tatties. And if you've a bit of a sweet tooth, we've some hasty pudding as well."

Ainslie considered the offering. He knew he'd be there for a while. He ordered both the pie and the scoops of mashed turnips and potatoes. "Extra butter on the neeps and tatties."

"Cost you a bit more."

"Fine."

"Butter it is. Back inna wee." The girl spun away only to return a few moments later with his ale, then bent low and set it in front of him.

"Oiy, Elspet," a heavy male voice shouted out; "'careful dere. Any closer and they'll be in the man's beer."

The remark earned the voice's owner a few laughs.

Not to be outdone, the girl rose to full height, placed her hands on her hips and turned to face her flouter. "Can ya no behave yerself for once, Kendrik, you big hill of dung." She shook her head dismissively. "Dunno why yer always tryin' to be clever. Yer no bright enough to see through a ladder."

The room roared its approval as patrons slapped the table, stamped their feet, and whistled.

Ainslie couldn't be sure, but thought the shaggy-haired man reddened as those near him thumped his back and pushed his shoulders playfully.

The room calmed and the serving girl turned her attention back to Ainslie. "Not a day goes by somebody don't...." She let the sentence trail and hurried away.

The pie turned out better than Ainslie expected.

More patrons arrived, friends and strangers alike. Some crowded in next to Ainslie. The room buzzed with conviviality; voices rose and fell, and men argued or roared with laughter.

Ainslie contended himself with listening as his new bench mates discussed high taxation, Scotland's parliament, The *Kirk*, the Church of Scotland, and the false king — James. He heard talk of crops, opinions about Jacobinism and something new — a bank run by London's Royal Exchange.

He considered the owner of the news, round-shouldered Hamish. "Hard to believe, wot you're sayin'—this bank thing."

The lawyer tossed a shoulder in indifference. "Believe what you will, but it keeps your money safe. They vouch for it too."

"Never heard of something like tha'. Who come up with it?"

"The English. Been around for a while. Hard to do better. Even pay you a bit of interest if you keep your money there."

"No."

"Ay."

Ainslie shook his head. "Something, tha'."

"But true," Hamish assured him. "You got anything to deposit?"

"I might, but wot happens if this bank thing's robbed?"

"Like I told you, nothing to concern yourself with. Your money's still there. They vouch for it."

Ainslie shook his head in wonder. "Amazing. Giving your money back even after somebody runs off with it." The idea intrigued him as Hamish belched and set down his tankard. "New times coming to Scotland. A branch of The Exchange here in Glasgow. Not much good to say about the English, but there's one of 'em."

Ainslie decided he might go and see for himself one day. Not now.

Conversation drifted onto other matters. "Take heed, laddies."

The table turned to Hamish and waited for more.

"Take heed of wot?" Bean Stenhouse, a blacksmith, asked.

"The English. They're startin' their nonsense again; impressing men onto ships. Heard some awful tales, I did."

"Now if tha' ain't a thing," Stenhouse said. "They don't like us crossing into their lands, but they've no cares about stealin' our laddies for their ships."

"Another reason not to be wandering down 'round the piers," Hanish replied.

"What's 'impressing?'" Stewart, the oak barrel maker, asked.

"You never heard?" Hamish asked.

"It's why I'm asking."

"All right then. Navy toughs grab you, truss you like a calf and haul you onto their ships. Next thing you know you're in the Royal Navy, like it or not, and on the high seas. Won't see hearth or kin for a few years—if you're lucky enough to get back home."

Calum, the loose-jowled silversmith, set his tankard down, wiped his mouth on his sleeve and belched. "Bastards. Bad enough we have to pay ship taxes. Won't catch me down by the water—not unless I got a lotta company around me."

Ainslie learned yet something else —a Swedish king wanted men for his army.

"Now there's a thing?" he said to Calum, a milliner. "Wot's it all about then?"

Calum wiped his mouth with the back of his hand. "Haven't the details. Only heard they're paying out more'n the English army. There's posters all over the city. Can you read?"

"Ay."

The expression on the milliner's face suggested surprise.

"Read? 'Imagine. A young one the likes of yourself. Well, then, if you can make sense of the words, have a see for yourself."

"I may," Ainslie said, ready to add something else when, with great flourish, the door flew open and four men entered.

At once the room fell silent and all activity ceased. Eyes turned to the intrusion. Each of the four strangers wore clothing one might find on the street any given day; only their wide belts with short swords and scarves of reddish color identified them as members of the English army.

The soldiers moved to either side of the door and allowed an officer in a cocked, three-cornered hat to make his grand entrance.

Fear gripped Ainslie. Had the hated English found him? How? His eyes scanned the room, searching for escape or a place to make a stand. His finger gripped his dirk.

A second look told him the officer appeared too lofty with his preening—one hand on the hilt of his rapier, one knee bent—to bother with the likes of him. *Maybe it's something else*, Ainslie told himself as he made himself relax. *Wait and see.*

He took in the man's clothes, the well-tailored dark gray tunic with large gold buttons. Each piece said expensive. His tunic, split in the back to allow proper motion for his straight saber, fell below the knees. Red thread sewn into the hem matched the red of his hat, and adorned the broad, folded-over sleeve edges. Underneath his tunic, the Englishman wore a red velvet waistcoat. Dark blue breeches offered an impressive contrast.

"He does command attention," Calum muttered.

Legs apart, chin held high, the Englishman's eyes swept the room. *Snot-nosed bastard*, Ainslie thought. Anger replaced fear, and the memory of Carlisle returned to him. His eyes narrowed as he regarded the trespasser who pulled air into his lungs and called out, "Right, then; which of you men will step forward, do his duty and join His Majesty's army?"

Fixed eyes considered the officer in sullen silence. No one stirred. The room remained silent.

The Englishman spoke again. "Up now," he said with the confidence of one used to giving orders. "Come on, fight for your King and country. Who'll step forward and sign up?"

"Me country's Scotland," Ainslie heard Calum whisper, "and you're no it."

Faced with a sour audience the Englishman's mask of confidence slipped, replaced by the hint of agitation. A slight but hurried shifting of feet and small nervous movements betrayed his earlier confidence. He sniffed and at last said, "Typical. Twelve *teuchters*, highlanders, a bagpipe, and damned if you don't have yourself a rebellion."

Satisfied with his authoritative last word, the man spun around and left the room. His soldiers close behind him, left the door ajar following their departure.

Everyone heard them stomp angrily up the stairs. A long moment or two passed before someone shouted out, "Give him this, leastwise he's learned our sayin.'"

The room howled as the portly ale house owner walked forward, shut the door, turned to his patrons and said, "Blockheads."

"Mad," Hamish offered to the table, "if the English think any Scot worth his salt would join their army of illegal occupiers."

The unpleasant intrusion gone, the room once again came alive. Yet an intense anger remained in Aiken Raeburn's nephew. He felt it in his muscles and the fluttery, uncomfortable feeling in his stomach. His face took on a grim expression.

It had always been so with Ainslie. Well known for acts of kindness, Ainslie could also quickly lose control of himself. Unlike his uncle, he couldn't be said to have a relaxed manner. He felt things intensely — especially negative things, and brooded over them long after others put them into perspective.

He once overheard his mother say, "It's good the laddie stands up for himself, Aiken, but I fear he carries too much bad temper in him."

Ainslie's uncle dismissed the charge. "Maybe, and maybe not. If he does, time's bound to take care of the problem — don't worry none."

Ainslie left the alehouse, ready to walk off his tension. He looked skyward to study the dark clouds break and the sun make a feeble attempt to reappear.

Foot and horse traffic reappeared on the street. He wondered which way to go, and decided to continue in the direction of the inn.

No one paid attention to the square-shouldered young man in fast stride who made his way down the narrow street. No one but the gangly cutpurse, who lingered for a moment too long in the archway of a small church.

His eyes followed the country bumpkin with rough clothes. *This should be easy pickings*, he told himself. He had a sense of things, and felt certain there'd be something to be had from this prey.

He quickly fell behind his quarry, careful to get neither too far nor too close. When the time came he'd pounce and push the mark into one of the many alleyways. Quick it'd be — like always.

The shorter man surprised him with his fast pace, and the cutpurse had to pick up his own pace to stay near.

The clip-clop of heavy hooves accompanied by ironclad wheels jostling over uneven and slick cobblestones drew the attention of both men. They turned to see a heavily laden wagon full of bales of cotton rumble after them. The noise echoed loudly in the narrow and near-empty street as the wagoner kept close to the right side. Every so often a spark from the wagon flew off the cobblestones.

Ainslie's senses went on alert at the lone man behind him. Vertical frown lines deepened between his eyes. He sensed danger immediately. He silently spoke to his pursuer. *You're trying too hard to go unnoticed, but I've spotted ya. You've evil in your heart, I'm thinkin'.*

The wagon almost caught up to the two men. Both stepped aside to let it pass, but Ainslie had other plans. At the last moment he dashed ahead and tucked in front of the lead horses. The wagoner shouted a curse and a warning.

Ainslie's stalker lost sight of him for a moment. *Here, what's his game?* A hand on the grip of his dirk, he moved out into the street and sprinted forward only to have his progress slowed by two wellborn who rode toward him side by side.

No other choice, the thief tucked back in behind the wagon. His agitation grew with each second. *Get a move-on, willya*, he mentally commanded the riders, his muscles tense with anticipation for the assault. He'd always prided himself on his abilities to survive and prosper in the unsafe streets of Glasgow. Pay attention to everything and you'll do well, he liked to say. This time he failed to follow his own advice.

Ready to bolt out from behind the wagon, he never expected what followed as he came up to a narrow alley. A lunge. Powerful hands seized the thief by his sleeve and spun him into the debris and piss-filled alley. He issued a small yelp of surprise as his shoulder and head slammed into brick. Pain shot up and down his numbed arm. He released his knife and winced.

"Got ya," his would-be victim said as he drove a fist into the cutpurse's kidney.

The air left the thief as he crashed to the packed earth, bits of glass cutting his arm on impact. Pain, nausea and fear all competed for his full attention. His assailant stood over him for a minute before pulling the Glaswegian to his feet. Strong fingers found the back of his neck and forced his head down. His attacker led the thief deeper into the alley. "Farther in's best, so's we don't attract attention."

The cutpurse sought desperately to think his way out of this danger. What should he do? He had no plan. He'd never been in this position before; he'd become the soft touch.

"Let's stand ya up and have a better look at ya," Ainslie said.

Stunned but thankful for the release of powerful fingers dug into his neck, the cutpurse straightened. He wasn't prepared for the blow to his soft stomach. He doubled over as hard bone from an upward driving knee met his nose. Both men heard the crack.

Blood splattered from the thief's nose. His assailant stepped back. The thief crashed to the ground. Rough hands again pulled him up, turned and pressed him against a wall. A forearm constricted his windpipe. He fought for air and attempted to wrest the arm away.

Three hard, fast rabbit punches doubled the cutpurse again. He felt a rib break as he dropped to the ground once more.

His assailant stepped back. Tears trickled down cutpurse's nose. A soft plea whispered into the packed soil, "Mother, mother; please help me."

Ainslie stood over the prone man. "You'll not bother innocents again. I've a feelin' some of your victims would buy me a drink if they saw this. The next time you'll think twice before you try anything like this."

Ainslie brought the heel of his boot down hard on the thief's knife-wielding hand. His victim let loose a soft scream, followed by plaintive moans.

Ainslie glared down and took several deep breaths. "Ye shall know 'em by their fruits.' It's the Bible I'm quotin'— something I'm guessin' you've no knowledge of. Best to remember it for the rest of your days."

He bent and searched the powerless man, and found the purse. "The weight of this," he said as he jingled it in his right hand, "should make up wot you intended. You owe me it."

Ainslie slid the purse into his shirt, rose, straightened his clothes and left the helpless thief on the ground. He moved to the edge of the street. Empty, except for a manure wagon. The driver barely gave him a second glance. He hurried into the street, hoping he hadn't drawn attention. Twice he glanced over his shoulder, but no one paid him any attention.

His attack on the cutpurse drained much of his anger, yet a measure of remorse quickly replaced it as he walked along. *Lookit me*, he scolded himself, fightin' in an alley, *not bothering with who comes along. I coulda bin caught and they'd toss me into gaol again. Yet here's me walking aloof when I should be running like I had the back door trots.*

The debate raged on as he moved down the street. *The man had it coming*, he told himself. *Still, he might call the authorities and give a description. You never know.* Maybe he should change his clothes, get a different look?

His eyes searched the wrought iron signs over the shops in hopes of finding a clothier. He spotted one but decided against it. Too fancy. He'd keep looking. Soon enough he saw a merchant's sign—*Samuel Goldfarb. Tailor.* It might do.

He approached and stepped inside the cramped, narrow shop. A little man with a brimless cap on the crown of his head looked up from his work. Ainslie offered a fast nod of greeting.

"Beholden to you if you can fix me up with some clothes. Don't have to be brand new."

The tailor rose. "With wot will you pay, sir?" he asked.

Ainslie understood: the man doubted his ability to pay. "Whatcha think I'm gonna pay with — the bloody Crown Jewels? Why'd I be visiting your wee shop if I couldn't pay?" His eyes swept the small store. "No much to rob here, so I must be a customer, eh?" He paused and stared at the tailor. "Ya want me as customer or no? If you need, I'll show you me purse."

The tailor held out his hands in supplication. "Pardon, sir. I meant no offense. What does the gentleman need?"

"Wait on," Ainslie said. "I'm a 'gentleman' now? "Fast improvement." He took a breath and told himself to take the edge out of his voice.

The tailor spoke again. "I beg the gentleman's pardon, sir."

"So you'll show me something?"

"The tailor raised his eyebrows as he nodded. "Ay, sir; of course. If the gentleman would like to see, I have some clothes in the back, behind the curtain. They may do — if we can find a fit. Worth a look."

"All right, then. Let's seem 'em."

"Fine enough," the little man said and pulled back the flimsy curtain of the recessed room.

Ainslie examined them carefully. Good quality. He asked how they got there.

"Customers," the tailor replied. "Didn't return." He swept a hand toward the clothes. "I keep them sixty days, and then sell them. Give the gentleman a good deal, if he likes something."

Ainslie picked up a pair of knee length breeches. He set them down and the tailor handed him several more to consider. "Got some fine stockin's ta go with 'em, sir." He retrieved two linen shirts to be worn under doublets and jackets. "The latest fashion in London, sir."

The mention of London caused Ainslie to snort. London. Why would he care what those devils in London wore?

He inspected the rest of the offerings. *Nice. Very nice*, he thought as he tried on a pair of durable tan breeches and hose, a light brown shirt under a green doublet, and a black three quarter length cape tied across his upper chest. He felt guilty at the thought of parting with his uncle's shirt, but reasoned he'd understand.

The tailor gave him an approving look in the new clothes. "It's not a bad fit, sir."

Ainslie agreed and said he'd take the clothes, but wasn't quite sold on the cape. "A bit too much for the likes of me."

"No sir," the tailor argued gently. "Keep ye warm, it will, when you're needin' it, and you can take it off fast-like."

Ainslie thought for a brief moment and changed his earlier opinion. "All right then, I'll have it too."

"A fine decision, sir."

A thought came to Ainslie. "Ye don't think I'll be lookin' like some cockscomb, do ya?"

The tradesman shook his head. "None of it, sir. The gentleman has the appearance of a well-respected man going about his business. Nothin' more, nothing less."

Satisfied with the answer, Ainslie said, "Good then. I'll be taking these and leave me old ones here."

The former reiver left the tradesman, pleased with his new clothes, his set-to with the cutpurse all but forgotten.

Chapter 5

AINSLIE headed out to find the posters Calum spoke about. He walked three blocks before he happened onto one, glued to a church column. He drifted over and read. *Soldiers. His Royal Majesty, King, Gustavus Adolphus, offers handsome pay for service in the German lands. He seeks hearty men, preferably with fighting experience, but welcomes all comers. Interested parties should report to the signing officer at number eight Convey Lane.*

Ainslie read the poster again. He weighed the advantages against the disadvantages of signing up. Military order and discipline — would those suit him? What of Sweden or the German lands? He knew nothing of either, but supposed he could adjust. He had no other prospects at present. Being in the army might lead to adventure. As well, there'd be no militia on his tail.

He arrived at a decision, but had no idea how to get to Convey Lane. He asked seven or eight passerby; no one seemed to have heard of the Lane. He finally found a gong farmer who stunk to high heaven. Ainslie kept as far back as possible as he asked his question.

"Convey Lane," the toothless, ponderous man said. "Hold a wee. Lemme think." He set his empty waste bucket down and rubbed his chin in thought. Yes, he knew where it was, he said, and gave Ainslie a quick inspection. "Ya sure you're wantin' ta go down there, a young one like y'self."

"Ay."

"Yer funeral. Wouldn't go m'self 'less I have ta, mind. Danger's afoot I hear."

"Heard likewise, but I've no much choice. Can ye tell me the way?"

The farmer pointed a crooked finger westward. "Down at the docks." He offered specific directions and finished with, "Mind ye now; stay clear of them lousy sailors."

"I'll be sure of it," Ainslie said and walked away.

It took a while but he at last found the lane and the address, a near-empty shop on the waterfront. He entered. The interior held a beat-up desk and a few chairs. Three clean-shaven, burly men occupied the chairs and passed the time in idle talk.

Conversation stopped as Ainslie shut the door and approached the desk. The dusty wooden floor groaned with each step. Ainslie took in these foreigners in their finery—nicer than some of the local nobility back home. All three men wore leather vests laced tightly over rough-cut crimson shirts and grey breeches. He noted the carefully bundled dark gray capes and wide-brimmed matching felt hats on top of the desk, stacked one atop the other.

Aware he might appear the fool if he stared too long, he forced his gaze toward the man in the middle, the one with a pointed chin and inquisitive eyes.

"Have the right place, then? You wantin' soldiers?"

The man smiled. With care he said, "Goot Morgon. Ja, our king is looking for men."

Ainslie returned the smile. "Are you interested in the likes of me?"

The Swede considered the prospect in front of him. "Ja ...yoo can fight?"

It took Ainslie a moment before he understood the question. He tossed off a fast nod. "Me? Ay. No interest in joining the English army, mind, but I'm ready for some adventure. Maybe with you." He raised his fists in demonstration. "With these and any weapon I get me hands on."

"Ja?"

Ainslie replied with a quick nod. "Ay."

The soldier stroked his chin. He turned his head and spoke to his comrades in their own strange language. When the exchange concluded, they focused their attention back on the Scot.

"Ja," the soldier said. "We take yoo." He pointed to a sheet of paper, leaned forward and slid it toward Ainslie. An inkwell and quill pen followed.

Ainslie had no idea what to expect, but thought enrolling might be more complicated. They only wanted his signature. He picked up the feather and read the document in English. It advised the signee, without duress, consented to join the Royal Swedish Army in return for the monthly sum of four pence, payable at the beginning of each month.

Everything seemed straightforward. Ainslie dipped the feather into the inkpot, signed, and handed the pen back to the recruiter. The man turned the document back and studied Ainslie's name.

"Goot," he said as he blew on the wet ink. "Yoo come beck in four deys." He let go of the paper, held up four fingers, and repeated himself. "Four."

Ainslie nodded his understanding and waited for more. It arrived fast enough. "Am. Söndag. At ten hour in de morgon."

Once more Ainslie took a moment to understand. He brightened. "Right. I'm understandin' your meaning. You're wantin' me here at ten...in the morning, Sunday?"

The other man's forehead wrinkled up in response

"Yoo go too fast."

Ainslie pointed to himself and sounded out each word "Ah. You'll have me back in four days." He splayed his fingers to show four. "Ay?"

A nod and a smile let Ainslie know the Swede understood.

His patience won him quick smiles and more head-nodding. "Ja. Goot," the spokesman said. "Sondag. We take yoo to de Tre Kroner."

The Kroner, thought Ainslie. It must be a ship. To leave nothing to doubt, he asked, "It's a ship, this Kroner?"

"Ja," the Swede said with haste. "Yoo come to Kroner."

Ainslie beamed at the man. "Good. I'll be there. See you then."

The matter settled, three Swedes and a Scot grinned foolishly at each other.

Ainslie gave a formal bow and left. In the lane he drew in his breath, retraced his steps, and whispered, "Well, you've found your calling, Lee. You're off to fight in some strange land for what you've no idea, and for men you can't understand."

It all happened so fast. Earlier in the day he had no prospects; now a signature changed everything.

Full of excitement and amazement, Ainslie walked along, giddy at his new prospects. "Well, eme," he said under his breath, "what do you make of me now? It's a right adventure I'm off to."

His thoughts sobered as he remembered the warnings about that part of the city. Head up, eyes alert for trouble, Ainslie kept a hand on his dirk and picked up his pace until he felt certain he'd cleared the dockside area.

In the commercial district he remembered Hamish's comments about the bank. He had plenty of time. Why not go and see for himself? He found the branch of the London Exchange and spoke with the manager. He opened an account.

Time on his hands, Ainslie wandered idly through the streets of Glasgow. He passed a boney mother barely into her twenties, in a short, tattered blue cloak with snug padded sleeves. Two children trailed behind her. Hand out, she approached. "Please, guv, sir, will you no help us? It's me an' the wee ones, and we've nowhere to go but the Poor House. It'll be me death sir, if I go dere."

He ignored her, continued on his way as she aimed her pleas to his back. No, he decided; he would not allow himself to be disturbed by her request for help. He was but one man. What could he do? Yet the image nagged at him, especially the resigned look on her face. He surprised himself, turned and retraced his steps.

She saw him approach and averted her eyes. He stopped in front of her. "Look, lassie, no point in me givin' ya money if you're goin' be out here tomorrow doing the same thing. I'm guessin' ye've nowhere ta go. What're your plans—where you bound?"

A faint ray of hope came into her eyes. "Aberdeen, sir. If I could git me n' the wee ones dere, I'd go to me brother's. He'd be glad to have me back." She shook her head. "I'll no go to the Poor House."

"So you're on the street?"

She nodded in defeat.

A story here, Ainslie thought, but chose not to hear it. He exhaled vigorously. "Don't call me sir. I'm no old enough."

His eyes traveled from her to the children before he spoke. "Here's what I'm considerin' doin.' I'll give ya the money for a coach in the morning. Tonight you and the whelps eat with me and share me room. An in case yer wonderin', I want nothin' from ya. Ye needn't worry."

She looked at him dumbfounded. Her mouth opened and her hand flew to it. Tears formed as the two children moved closer.

Even distraught and dirty, Ainslie considered the woman's attractiveness shone through. He could only imagine what she might look like free from dirt and with a little more meat on her bones.

He brought the three back to the *Fox and Furrow and* let them eat. Something about the woman reminded him of his mother. Maybe she'd smile at his act of kindness. Besides, he reasoned, he still had most of the cutpurse's and gaoler's money.

"What's your name?"

"Ann, and me bairns are Dorrel an' Parlan. Dorrel's four and Parlan's three." She peered into his face. "And what am I to call you?"

"Ainslie."

She repeated it. "A good name." She hesitated before she said, "I've a question."

"Which is...?"

"Ya said we could sleep in your room. Where?"

"On th' bed. The three of you. I'll make do somehow. Ye've no to worry."

But something in her eyes told him she would.

After the meal he led them to the inn. Ann looked nervous as they approached the stairs, her eyes darting around.

The innkeeper's wife saw them, cluck-clucked her tongue, hurried over and intercepted them. "Word, sir, if I may?"

She took him aside and out of earshot of Ann and whispered, "We run a respectable 'stablishment, sir, and can't have a streetwalker come in. Bad for business, ya understand?"

Ainslie did, but chose to bristle anyway. He drew himself up to full height and said, "Take a care. You're talking 'bout me cousin callin her a 'streetwalker.' She's a lady come down on some hard times, is all. I'm here to fetch her and the wee ones back to Aberdeen."

He hoped to appeal to the woman's motherly instincts as he continued. "What kind of eme would I be if I let the wee ones loose on these dangerous streets?"

The woman looked from Ainslie to Ann, and back. She placed an open hand over her heart and smiled at him. Ainslie noticed the canine teeth on the left side missing.

"Ay, these are terrible times," she said. "Well, then, ye'll forgive me the mistake, sir, an' I'll wish ye and the lady a good evenin.'"

He did his best imitation of a gentlemanly bow, smiled and wished her a good evening in return.

Ainslie let mother and children play on the bed while he sat in the chair and watched the rains outside. Darkness took over the room, and he lit the kerosene lamp. The children sleepy, Ann whispered. "You're sure now ya want us to have the bed?"

"I am, ay."

"But ye've only the floor."

He dismissed her protest with a whispered, "It'll do fine. I'll take a blanket and a pillow."

"And ya want nothin' else?"

"I've nothin' else I could want."

She looked overcome by his generosity, her eyes wide, and managed a soft, "Good night, then."

"And yourself."

"I can turn the lamp out?"

"Ay."

He watched her move beside her children, utter a satisfying sigh and put out the lamp. Only then did he climb out of his clothes and slide under the blanket, purse and dirk next to him.

He slept deeply.

In the morning mother and children watched as Ainslie cleaned himself at the basin. Self-aware and awkward he begged them to turn their heads while he finished. He heard the little girl ask her mother why the man did that.

"'It's not for us to tell others what to do with their lives, luv," Ann replied. "We're his guests, so let's just leave him to his labors."

Ainslie remembered one of his Uncle Aiken's favorite lines — them that smell least, smell best. He kept the quote to himself.

Downstairs, a quick breakfast of cheese, black pudding, rye bread and beer, and they found their way to the coach station. Ainslie paid for the tickets and handed Ann two sixpence coins "for food and such. It'll last you until you're in your home."

Ann clutched the money to her breast and said, "You're most generous...very. I'll never ferget ya. Never. I'll pray you stay safe and well night an' day. At's a great kindness ya did for us. We cannot thank ya enough."

Ann reached for his hand, raised it to her mouth and kissed it. Embarrassed, Ainslie pulled it away and feigned great interest in the activities of the children.

The coach arrived. Ann bade the kids to kiss their Uncle Ainslie.

Passengers settled, the driver flicked the reins, yelled out a command and the horses moved off.

Ainslie waited until the coach disappeared from view. He stood for a few seconds longer and wondered why he didn't ask Ann what brought her to Glasgow in the first place. Too late now. He turned and walked away.

The peal of church bells woke him. At last, he thought: the day's arrived. He bounced out of bed. Downstairs, he again ate cheese, black pudding and rye bread, all washed down with ale. The morning meal completed, he headed to the pier. He retraced his earlier steps, again mindful of anything suspicious. His hand never left his blade as he wandered along the narrow, barren cobblestone streets until he reached the empty store. No evidence of life this early in the morning.

He tramped on and reached the pier. Twelve men stood beside a ship. A blue flag with a yellow cross fluttered from its mast. Confident he'd found the right ship, he joined the others. None showed more than a passing interest in him. "This the Kroner?" he asked one of the men.

The man answered with a curt head nod.

Ainslie stood and waited along with the rest. Others arrived and fell in with the small assembly. In hushed tones, a few engaged each other in conversation. Most kept to themselves.

He shifted from foot to foot as his eyes swept the area. Three Swedes in grey capes and hats moved into his line of vision. With them came a fourth man, wide-bodied but as tall as his companions. A yellow-and-black woolen cap, a rough-cut greyish-brown shirt and a belted yellow-and-black plaid kilt betrayed his origin. A broad over-the-shoulder belt supported a sheath for his rapier.

The four stopped in front of the recruits. The Scot spoke in his thick highland accent, "Mornin' laddies, an' welcome."

A few men, including Ainslie, returned the social greeting. He decided he liked the fellow with the groomed salt-and-pepper beard, asking the recruits to gather around him. Both light and heavy wrinkles, as well as dark shadows beneath his eyes, made him appear old, perhaps older than his true age.

"I'm Sergeant Fergus Donaldson," the Scot said. "As you might be able to tell, I'm of clan Donald, up around Glengarry way. Any of you laddies up from there?"

Two hands rose. Donaldson acknowledged their presence. "Good to see you, and all the rest as well."

He glanced around at his audience. "Now, onto what we've to do. I'm here on behalf of the King of Sweden, his Majesty, Gustavus Adolphus. You're his business from this moment on."

He stopped and pointed at the Swedes. "We'll be taking you to Stockholm. You'll have training an' then it's off to the Duchy of Pomerania. Ever hear of it?"

He studied the faces and waited. No one answered.

"Right, then; you'll come to see it by and by." He paused, took a breath before he continued, "You'll no doubt have lots of questions, but save 'em for the ship. Ready then?"

All were and answered with nervous shuffling of their feet.

Donaldson turned to his companions and spoke in their native tongue. They answered, spun around, and headed up the ship's gang board. Donaldson waved the recruits to follow as he hurried to catch up.

Ainslie watched as sailors ran along the Kroner, loaded cargo, and checked the rigging and dock lines.

Donaldson called the recruits to gather around him.

"This is it, laddies," he said. "Time to say good cheer to your homeland; take your last, long whiff of blessed Scottish air."

The Kroner cast off. By mid-afternoon she entered the North Sea. Sailors scurried up the masts and jabbered in their strange tongue.

An excited Ainslie watched as men yelled back and forth along the foot ropes. *Wouldn't catch me up there, no matter how much they paid me.*

Sails unfurled, the Kroner welcomed the inviting southwest winds. In no time her sails billowed out and she readied for her homeward passage.

They passed outlying islands. Ainslie saw a few villages hugging the western shore. He wondered who lived there, and why.

The waters proved bumpy as they lost sight of land. Ainslie turned to the man who stood next to him on the rail. He gave him a fast nod of greeting. "You ever get seasick?"

"Ay, I have," the affable man answered. "First time I set foot on one of these things. They say if you look at the far distance, where sky and sea meet, it'll help." He shook his head. "Dinna do me a lick of good, but even if you get seasick, you'll get used to it." He scratched under his heavy beard. "Off to the king's army?"

"Ay. And you?"

"Coming back from a bit of leave."

"So you've been in the war?"

"Have, aye."

"What's it like?"

"'Like,'" the portly man repeated? "I've naught to compare it to, and I call out the man who says different. One time you damn near shit yourself, and the next you find out you have pluck. But the best thing is the comradeship." He stopped, stared out at sea, and returned his gaze to Ainslie. "You'll have to see it all for yourself, is the best I can answer."

Ainslie peppered the heavily-bearded man with more questions about the war, but only received vague answers. He gave up and returned his attention to the sea.

Chapter 6

A INSLIE stared in awe at the flat, vast seacoast of the Pomeranian Duchy, as he and others waited for the lowering of rowboats. His eyes traveled along the white sloping beach, unlike any on the Scottish coast; here, the sun's bright rays bounced off the fine white sand and made him squint.

A light hand slapped him on the shoulder. He turned. Paolo. Ainslie reminded himself to smile at his new friend. Tall and bone-thin, yet knotted with sinewy muscles from a life of hard toil, the Italian from the Duchy of San Giulo pushed back a strand of dark brown hair. His stretched, clean-shaven face, with its sunken cheeks and thin nose, slightly curved, reminded Ainslie of a Roman portrait sketched in one of Duncan Carstarphen's books. Paolo as a Roman senator, Ainslie thought. Yes, he could imagine it.

Paolo followed Ainslie's gaze to the beach. "Is good, yes?" he asked, pointing his chin toward land.

Language proved a small challenge for the two, but both had a natural skill for it. Ainslie silently thanked Carstarphen for introducing him to Latin and Greek. As a result Ainslie understood much of Paolo's intent. In turn, his newfound friend proved better at catching onto English than Ainslie to Italian.

Ainslie returned his attention to the beach. "Ay, Podo," he said, using his new friend's nickname. "It's good. Never thought the sight of land would be *so* good." With slow and careful deliberation, he continued. "Il relativo molo bella." Pleased with himself, he switched back to English. "Did I say it right?"

Paolo winked and followed with his rich, deep laugh. "Perfetto. Italiano with Scozzese accento."

Ainslie chuckled. "Ay. A Scot having a go at Italian."

The sail in the Atlantic proved pleasant enough, but the Baltic itself had instilled the greatest terror in Ainslie. With little warning, the sea, known as for its calmness, turned angry even before the Kroner lost sight of land. Huge swells tossed the ship from side to side.

A grateful Ainslie gave thanks when he at last stepped onto the Swedish shore in Stockholm.

Donaldson gathered his charges around him once more.

"Hush now, and give a listen. You're in a new land with different customs. It'll take some getting used to, but it'll come fast enough. You may well get homesick. It'll pass."

He waited to let his works sink into the recruits. "Mind too, you're not to be foolish. Don't do nothin' to put the locals or the Royal House in bad temper. It'll go merry hell for you if you do."

He explained they'd be billeted in homes.

"You'll sleep and take your meals there. We expect to see you at the back of eight tomorrow morning. You're in the King's army now, and when you're called to show at eight, eight it is. Sharp. Not a moment past eight. Clear?"

Heads nodded and ayes filled the air.

Ainslie, the last man to be billeted, tagged along behind Donaldson. The sergeant headed along a narrow, uneven, cobblestone street, and up to the second floor of an apartment house. He knocked.

The door opened. A short, fleshy woman with two children behind her stood in the doorway and considered the arrivals.

Donaldson spoke to her in the strange new language. Ainslie found it amusing whenever Donaldson didn't know a particular word he substituted an English one in its place—with a Swedish accent.

"Ja! Ja," the woman said when Donaldson finished. She peered past him and smiled at Ainslie as Donaldson addressed him.

"Right then, laddie, welcome to your new home." He gestured to the woman. "This is Stina Andreasson, the woman of the house."

Housewife and mercenary offered each other tight smiles as Donaldson spoke again. "Remember, we'll have your presence at the parade ground tomorrow at eight. Any questions?"

Ainslie had never heard of a parade ground. What could it be? Maybe just another odd custom the Swedes had? He wanted to ask but couldn't bring himself to do so for fear of looking the fool.

Donaldson interrupted his thoughts. "Now, here's how you get to the parade ground." Twice, with considerable patience, he gave Ainslie directions as mother and children watched with curiosity. "You have it?"

"I think so, sergeant."

"You think so?" Donaldson repeated with full mimicry in his voice. "Thar's only two answers to the question; yes and no. 'I think so's not one of 'em. I'll ask again — you have it?"

Humbled by the crushing response, Ainslie mumbled, "Ay. Have it, sergeant."

The answer satisfied Donaldson. He slapped Ainslie's shoulder and said, "Good. Had faith in you, I did. Once more, repeat where you'll meet me."

Ainslie complied and Donaldson rewarded him with a fast smile. "You'll do fine, you will."

The matter settled, Donaldson turned and headed down the stairs. The socially uncomfortable Ainslie and the Swedish housewife stared at each other until she gestured for him to enter. Ainslie wondered if the couple offered to share their accommodation, or if they were somehow pressured to do so.

Stina did her best to make Ainslie feel at home. Curious about the new city, Ainslie gestured he'd like to wander around a bit. Stina smiled and bobbed her head up and down, and pointed for him to return.

Ainslie explored the city center, amazed and delighted by the differences from his homeland. Clean, spotless, and everywhere people smiled and made eye contact. *Strange*, he thought; *smile like this much in a Scottish crowd, and fast enough you're in a punch-up.*

In the evening Stina made up a comfortable-enough bed on the floor. He barely felt the hard surface beneath him.

Stina's husband showed himself to be an even-tempered man with a quick smile.

Language remained the great barrier. The parties smiled and gestured a lot, but managed for the most part to convey their intentions.

Afraid to be late for his first morning and face a possible scolding, Ainslie left the Andreasson home with plenty of time to reach his destination. He found the parade ground and discovered it belonged to something called military grounds. The grounds, largely an open plain, sat near the Jönköping Castle and encompassed a dozen or more acres.

Various maneuvers were in full progress. Ainslie saw a company of soldiers march in close order formation as a sergeant yelled orders. He couldn't understand the words but from the soldiers' response guessed they meant, "Forward march," "Right turn," "Left turn," and "About turn."

He had his first introduction to horsemen called hussars. Splendid in their plumed helmets and silk tunics, they held themselves in a stiff and correct manner as they raced on light horses up and down the field.

Unaffected, Ainslie turned away, snorted and muttered, "Tittups. If I was born high-and-mighty, I'd have a fine horse and be all fancy too."

Farther away other horsemen lined up in their practiced charge-the-enemy formation. He learned these were the famed cuirassiers, with their polished coats of mail.

Once more Ainslie stopped to gape as the morning rays beamed off their polished upper body armor.

Four perfect ranks of cuirassiers sat like statues on their warhorses and stared at distant posts with cabbages on top. A single call rose from somewhere, and the first rank answered with a deep, virile roar and charged at the posts.

Rapiers, held ready at forty-five degrees, the horsemen approached the imaginary enemy, readied their blades, and dealt the cultivated plants decisive blows for King and God.

Appreciative *oohs* and *ahhs* followed the clapping from an audience of females who stood off to the side and watched as the next rank readied to charge. Foot soldiers rushed forward to replace the severed cabbages.

The morning held more wonders. Ainslie got his first look at musketeers.

Each musketeer cradled a long-barreled weapon, and wore a leather coat and broad over-the-shoulder belts with pouches.

Ainslie couldn't help but gape; so many weapons in a single place.

Like the cuirassiers, the musketeers stood in perfect ranks as a sergeant kept an eye on them.

Every so often a sergeant barked out orders. In response, the men opened lids to their small charging pans, called bassinets, near the sights of their muskets, and poured in gunpowder. Done, they blew away any extra powder and closed the pans. Next, practiced hands reached into pouches and took out stiff, cylindrical paper packets.

Each man used his teeth to tear open a pre-measured packet of powder and a lead ball. The ball held between his lips, he emptied the packet down the barrel of his weapon. He then dropped the ball down the barrel's opening and pushed it farther with a long scouring stick.

Ainslie couldn't understand why the men held the lead balls between their teeth. Days later he would learn the answer in an alehouse. A sergeant from Paisley set down his tankard, wiped the foam from his mouth and said, "Easy answer. Have to do it in the right order, otherwise it won't work. They're holding those those god-awful packets they've ripped open, so where else they going to keep the black balls? Between the front teeth's the only place. You do it enough and your teeth take on a color not natural to them." He tipped his tankard back, took a long pull of his beer, and finished with, "Makes you thirsty as hell too."

Weapons loaded, the first rank jammed their fourquettes, prop staffs, into the ground. They next rested their twenty pound muskets in the crooks of the prop staffs, and waited for the command. It arrived soon enough.

"Set up."

The first line aimed at some distant place while the next stood behind, weapons pointed to the sky.

Another command barked out "Make ready to fire."

Each musketeer reached for a thin, twisted cord of slow-burning wick called a match-cord. He blew on it to brighten its brilliance.

"Fire."

Smoldering cords entered tiny holes at the sides of the weapons' pans where they made contact with gunpowder.

The contact caused a small internal explosion. Its fiery release tore down a pathway to the barrel and set off the main charge, causing the musket ball to fly.

Nearby birds scattered from the noise, and a cloud of smoke hung over the foot soldiers.

Noise from discharged muskets proved nothing compared to the thunderous clamor of large-wheeled artillery pieces. The deafening noise unsettled Ainslie even as he watched with fascination.

After every round, two soldiers rammed a corkscrew-like pole down the cannon. Ainslie later discovered this cleaned the artillery piece of any left-over debris from the inner walls of the barrel.

Once finished, a second team rushed forward and inserted a long wet mop into the barrel. No sooner had they finished than a third team inserted a long dry map into the cannon's opening.

Next, soldiers raced for leather canisters as their comrades produced different wooden poles with metal scoops. With care, the canister-bearing soldiers tipped gunpowder into the mouths of the cannons.

Others then pushed the gunpowder in deeper with their poles. They jiggled the poles several times and pulled them out.

A cannonball came next. Once in the mouth of the cannon, two-man teams returned the rag-covered pole and pushed. Satisfied powder and projectile sat in the bottom end of the cannons, they signaled to the soldiers who stood near the touch holes. They in turn lit the cannons' slow burning wicks.

All stepped away from the carriage as the wick burnt down. A moment later the cannons discharged, issued their fearful noise, and the carriages jumped from the discharge.

It took Ainslie a while to find Donaldson among the hundreds of men spread over the vast grounds. "Sergeant," he said as he stopped in front of the man, "Hope I'm no late. Had no idea the size of this place."

Donaldson seemed unconcerned. "Important thing is you're here." He studied Ainslie. "Souter, right?"

"Right, sergeant."

"Where from?"

"Near Doonhamers."

"Doonhamers," the other man repeated. "Good town. Been there many a time. Met a few Souters in Dundee. Any kin of yours?"

"Can't say for sure."

"Ah." Donaldson's arms shot out and he squeezed Ainslie's biceps. "Supposin' you'll do fine." He stepped closer to Ainslie. "Pike man."

"Beg pardon? I don't understand."

"Not much to understand," Donaldson answered. "You'll see in short time." He wheeled around and in quick step led Ainslie to a group of men who practiced formations with long poles boasting spear tips at the ends. All wore curious uniforms with metal conical pot helmets.

What had he got myself into, Ainslie thought as he took in the men in their peculiar helmets? The hot sun would beat down on them, sure to bring misery to the owners. *And to think, I never took to wearing the cap eme and the others wore.*

In time Ainslie came to discover the pot helmet also caused muscles in his neck to bunch up and bring on tremendous headaches.

In addition to the helmet, each pikeman wore a metal breast and back plate under a thick, brownish-orange flax shirt, thick leather thigh guards, gloves and a sheath with a short, slender two-edged sword.

A heavyset man stood off at a distance and watched the men in idle boredom. He turned his head as the two Scots approached.

"What've we got here?" he asked in English, his eyes lighting on Ainslie.

"What you've got, Sergeant Harris," Donaldson replied, "is Ainslie Souter." His eyes left Harris and turned to the recruit. "Ainslie's your Christian name?"

"Ay."

Donaldson returned his attention to Harris.

"Private Souter comes all the way from God's country and not the miserable excuse of land your lot calls home."

Harris made a show of snorting his contempt.

"Ah, God save us from you heathens. Scotland, land of shepherds and nervous sheep. Nothing ever good comes from Scots, and you expect me to train this one?" He threw a glance at Ainslie.

Donaldson chuckled at the reply.

"Och, listen to ya; this coming from a people who think tripe and onions make a fine meal. Never got over William the Bastard getting the best of you, did you? Course you'd a thought a Frenchie'd bring some decent food with him, but wasn't to be. We all know what you ended up with. No matter — I've no more time for idle chatter. Do what you can with the laddie then."

He gave Ainslie a quick pat on the arm and left him alone with Harris. Unpleasant memories of Englishmen still fresh in his mind, Ainslie didn't care to be around Harris, but decided to make the best of his situation.

Harris gave him a close inspection. "So we're to make a pikeman outta you?"

"I suppose," Ainslie answered.

"Do you know anything about it, being a pikeman?"

"Sorry, no; can't say I do."

Harris spoke again. "Then let's find out what you're made of. Come with me."

He led Ainslie to where a large group of men practiced with long wooden shafts, iron spears attached to the ends. Ainslie guessed the shafts to be at least twelve feet long.

Harris pointed. "You're gonna need a lot of muscle to be a pikeman. No good to me if you haven't got 'em. Now pay attention to what they're up to."

Ainslie watched as the men formed three lines. The first line bent one knee and held their pikes skyward. The second moved behind and positioned their pikes straight out and to the left of the men in front. The third line raised their pikes over the shoulders of the second line.

"See the formation?" Harris said.

"Ay."

"Ay what?" Harris demanded, censure in his voice.

"Och, sorry. Ay sergeant."

"Good lad. Anyway, the pikes scare the living shit out of cavalry horses. Horses are smart enough to know they don't want their chests lanced with these nasty things. They get one good look, panic, and run."

Ainslie nodded his understanding as a command filled the air. The pikeman regrouped and formed a circle — all facing outward.

"This formation," Harris advised, "is when danger comes at us from all sides."

Sergeant and recruit watched as the formations went through their drills.

At last someone called the men to rest.

Harris took the opportunity to walk over to the men. He relieved a soldier of his pike and returned to Ainslie. "If we're to make a pike man out of you, let's see what you've got."

Ainslie didn't know what to expect as Harris held out the pike. Ainslie took it. Harris backed away. "Hold it out at me — up at eye level — as if you'd stab me from there."

Ainslie obeyed.

"Now keep your arms stiff," Harris ordered.

Ainslie complied.

Harris moved closer and corrected Ainslie's stance. Done, he stepped back.

At first the task appeared simple enough. Time passed and the first signs of tremor appeared in Ainslie's arms. He felt as if he held up heavy bags of sand.

He motioned as if to lower his arms, but Harris called out, "I didn't say you could do lower it. Hold your position."

Sweat collected on Ainslie's forehead and trickled down his temple. The muscles in his arms begged for release. He gritted his teeth. You're a statue, he told himself. A statue. Ignore the pain.

His arms trembled noticeably. The wobbly shaft gave further proof of his fatigue.

Harris, weight on his right foot, stood unmoved and watched. At last he spoke. "All right; enough. Bring 'em down."

Ainslie almost wept with relief. He dropped his tingling arms, certain they'd never perform another function.

"Takes work," an encouraging Harris said. "You'll do. We'll make a pike man out of you."

For the next seven weeks Ainslie and others were drilled and redrilled in the fundamentals of pike man maneuvers, proper positioning, moving as one — forward, backward — as well as trained in the cut-and-thrust maneuvers with swords.

Ainslie came to respect Harris as a man smart but fair. Maybe they're not all bad, the English, he told himself. After all, the worth of a thing is what it brings.

Ainslie found it hard to break the habit of using his left hand. The Swedish army frowned on left-handedness, considered it a tool of the devil. Even the hint of being left-handed resulted in punishment.

The recruits learned the importance of marching in step and taking their correct places on the field, musketeers to either side.

At training's end, they received their uniforms.

In full uniform, pikes in the air, Ainslie and Paolo, considered one another in their coats of dullish brown-grey and hose of dark blue. Both broke out laughing.

"Have to say, Podo, we look the fool."

Paolo responded with a quick nod. "L'abito non fa il monaco."

Ainslie shook his head. "Not sure I make it come out right, so tell me what it means."

Paolo pointed to himself and said, "Clothes, yes?"

Ainslie understood. "Ahh — got it — clothes."

"Si, the covering...this is the word?"

"Ah. I suppose, ay."

"The covering, it does not make the friar. No, like uh, uh, magistrato..." He imitated a judge with a gavel.

"Uh, is it judge?"

Paolo's index finger shot out in response. "Si. The covering is not the friar."

Ainslie raised his eyebrows. "I get it. We have somethin' like tha' in English — don't judge a book by its cover."

Paolo pointed. "Si. Is good."

"Got you. You're sayin' we're better than what we've got on. All-righty. But best we don't fall into a river. Sink like rocks."

Later Paolo made a face as he examined his sword. Ainslie under-stood. In a low voice he said, "No, I don't like it either. Cheap steel. Won't last in a fight. Me dirk's better."

Chapter 7

THE Christian Konungen bobbed in the calm waters on the coast of Pomerania with its complement of soldiers and officers, all waiting their turn to go ashore.

Ainslie watched with amusement. Officers in proud, lofty gaits stood and preened as they waited for the rowboats. All wore the obligatory white powdered wig under gray, three-cornered hats. All conformed to the latest fashion — ruffled silk shirts under matching blue, loose outer coats, split in the back to allow free movement of swords. Blue or dark green knee-high silk breeches set off the surcoats.

Broad, green sashes finished off the ensemble.

Ainslie shook his head slowly. *An eyeful, actin' all superior-like in their finery. Och, who cares? Long as they feed and pay me, all's right.*

On land he gaped at the full regiments fitted out in the matching colors of their officers — green, red, or blue. "Time'll tell," he said to Paolo, "if we're to be the best army around, but you have to admit we're bound to be the loveliest."

Paolo chuckled at the remark.

The pikemen gathered and waited for someone to take charge. More soldiers in different uniforms passed; it surprised Ainslie a single war could involve so many nations.

A bow-legged, barrel-chested sergeant, eyes almost hidden in his moon face, approached the pikemen.

"I don't think he's carryin' loose body fat," Ainslie whispered to Paolo, as the newcomer, with his thick bluish-black beard, swung his stumpy arms widely and came closer.

Paolo nodded his head in agreement.

The sergeant stopped in front of the men. He regarded the arrivals with the expression one might give a proper cut of beef. He drew in air and bellowed in perfect English, "Fall in."

Long pikes pointed at the sky, the men hurried to place themselves in military lines. The sergeant spoke again in a deep, hard-edged voice likely of a battle-tested warrior. "You are pike men." All waited for him to continue. He obliged. "You are given to me. I am Sergeant Dritan Geiger from Canton Thurgau."

He spoke English with too much care and gave each word careful attention. Ainslie sounded the name out silently. Thurgau. Funny-sounding. He'd never heard of it. Where was it? For sure not in any English-speaking country. He leaned to his side. "Psst; Podo, what's this Thurgau place?"

"In Switzerland I am thinking."

Ainslie furrowed his brow. "Not helpin' me any. Never heard of it either. Might as well be out in space somewheres."

Geiger drowned out any response. "In quick step, by twos, follow me." He turned and headed off.

Flax kits banging against hips, the men followed. Each kit held a metal dinner plate, a large spoon, and anything of personal use.

Soon enough the new arrivals came upon their first evidence of war. Five men and two women dangled from a rope on a fat limb, their hands bound behind their backs, their faces distorted and white. Their tongues lolled out of their mouths.

With his own mouth open, a dumbstruck Ainslie gaped at the gruesome sight. Who were these people? What had they done to deserve their fate?

Geiger marched on past an empty, scorched field, ash everywhere. He took his men through a hamlet where the houses had been put to the torch, past an abandoned farmhouse, and made for a pond. At their destination, musketeers, pike men and cavalry lolled around makeshift fires. Here and there the scarred remains of felled trees gave evidence of recent cuttings.

Geiger approached an officer in a three-corner hat and blue outer coat who idled by a campfire. He rose and revealed a long torso and short legs. Hard-bitten, the shaved face suggested a man who'd already seen too much. Permanent narrow lines forced his eyes into a squint, but the curving lines of his mouth hinted they were newly formed.

Ainslie guessed him to be about four and thirty. Could this man be their commander?

The officer tugged at his mid-thigh surcoat, placed a hand on the hilt of his sword.

Geiger saluted as the other man's eyes took in the arrivals. The sergeant moved beside the officer and turned and faced the pikemen. Nearby soldiers broke away from possible tedium and crowded around to watch.

The officer spoke. A short moment of silence followed before Geiger translated. "Soldiers, here is Kapten Kristofer Bjorkman."

Ainslie's eyes went from Geiger to Bjorkman and back. He decided the sergeant had to be older than his superior.

"Kapten Bjorkman," Geiger said, "instructs me to tell you to make yourselves as comfortable as you can. We will have our marching orders as soon as they arrive. Fall out."

The men left their formation.

Ainslie, Paolo, and a few others hung back to ask Geiger questions about pay, sleeping arrangements, and meals.

"Sleep anywhere," Geiger advised. "Summer is here; you won't freeze. Sleep under a bush, tree, whatever suits you." He waved his hand toward the house and barn. "Too dangerous there. For blankets..." He shook his head. "It is war. In war there is always shortage. About food." He drew in a lungful of air. "Supplies are leaving the ships. Soon you will eat. In the meantime walk to the fires; see what's in the pots, and who will share."

None of the recruits dared to ask questions, yet Geiger did little to calm their worries. They hadn't expected this, they muttered as they broke away; all through training they rightly assumed the army would take care of them. Now this new reality.

Ainslie shook his head. "Queer this, Podo. What kinda way is this to do things? They can't think soldiers'll be runnin' 'round, expectin' to find their own way."

Paolo shrugged. "Comporti come se tutto dipenda da voi e sappia che tutto dipende dal Dio."

Ainslie frowned. "Wot's it mean?"

"It is saying, behave as if everything depends on you, and know everything depends on God."

It took Ainslie a while to get the meaning of the proverb. "Och, ay; kinda like God helps those who help themselves." He puffed out his cheeks, blew out air and said, "Right. Let's see if we can make the best of it."

He again reflected on his new friend. Cut from different cloths, we two, he thought. Paolo presented himself as cheerful, whereas he leaned toward brooding. Paolo could easily be described as naturally optimistic, whereas Ainslie always braced himself for something to go wrong. Paolo favored a practical approach to life; Ainslie, a doubtful one.

"You've a plan?" he asked as he followed Paolo around the campfires.

Paolo continued to walk. He approached a pit with a small fire and a four-foot, bark-stripped and seared tripod balanced over the pit. A rope darkened by smoke hung from the tripod and supported a black cast iron pot.

Something in the pot smelled delicious. Ainslie and Paolo hadn't eaten since they'd left Sweden.

Three musketeers and two pike men sat around the pit. Four stared into the coals, and the fifth busied himself sharpening his dirk against a ceramic stone.

Ainslie judged them to be nearly ten years older than him. Three were clean-shaven, one wore a long beard, and one favored thick, tawny-brown mutton chops.

The two newcomers' arrival offered a diversion to the veteran men. Paolo halted and delivered a disarming smile. He pointed to Ainslie and himself and said, "Buongiorno. We are not long. You speak English?"

It awed Ainslie how easily the Italian engaged others. Left to his own, he doubted he would have stopped here.

A clean-shaven soldier with an ugly face and raspy voice spoke first. "We do speak English, but I can tell you don't. As for me, I'm the king's servant, the English king, mind, not like some of the rabble here." His eyes took in the stone whittler before they settled on Ainslie and Paolo. In a low voice he said, "The Swedish king has my loyalty, but it comes with terms."

Ainslie didn't know what to make of the man as the fellow bore on. "Blackpoolian, myself. I come from God's good country." He gestured with an open hand. "Take a seat if you've a mind, and join us."

A Lankie, thought Ainslie as he and Paolo struggled to get out of their helmets. The man's accent should have given him away.

Ainslie and Paolo set pikes and kits next to helmets and moved closer to the fire. Ainslie's mind still on the Blackpoolian, a new voice—Scottish—almost startled him. He searched for its owner and found him, a bearded soldier who held his gaze.

"How's it going there, young one? Scot?"

"Ay. You can tell?"

"You've the look." The fellow pointed to the Blackpoolian, "Do yourself a good turn and pay no mind to his nonsense. Can't help himself. Something in the water makes the English a wee daft, if you take me meaning? Anywho, always good to see another countryman."

He called over to the knife sharpener. "Keeps a man sane, eh, Gisis?"

"Och, ay," the clenched-jawed and equally bearded other man muttered, as he continued with his task.

The first Scot directed a quick, mischievous grin at his comrade before he turned his attention back to Ainslie. "So, where you calling home then?"

"Down near Doonhamers way," Ainslie said. "Self?"

"Isle of Skye's me home. Name's Sloan Lang. Folks call me Jigs."

Ainslie introduced himself and Paolo. The others did as well.

Ainslie discovered the Blackpoolian was Devin Skinner. Cecil Corey, the other clean-shaven man, hailed from Norwich. Cadman Moxley called Stoke-on-Trent his home. Of the two Scotsmen, Gillis Morison lived in Starrier, a day's ride from Belfast.

Conversation fell off for a moment. Ainslie's eyes returned to the Blackpoolian again. The man's face called forth revulsion. A beard would do him some good, thought Ainslie as he took in the scar that ran from his upper chin to his temple. In places, angry reddened islands, varying in sizes, distinguished themselves against his pale skin. The near-hideousness of the fellow didn't disturb his companions. A kindness, thought Ainslie; they're likely used to him.

Ainslie's curiosity about the men didn't match theirs about Paolo. They fired questions at him: what language did he speak, why did he join the Swedes instead of the Imperialist army, was he Catholic, and so on.

The questions died off. The men watched Skinner poke the fire for a few moments. He at last spoke to Paolo. "So what are you not long' for?" he asked. "This world? Bit early, what, leaving it so soon, seeing ye just got here."

His companions laughed without much enthusiasm.

Ainslie and Paolo glanced at each other, unsure what the man meant.

Morison spoke up. He tossed his head in Skinner's direction and said, "He's picking apart your friend's words about not being long here. Made it sound like he was ready to die, see?"

Ainslie and Paolo nodded politely. "We've not been long off the landing ship, a heap of us," Ainslie said.

Skinner jumped in. "Zat so? Well, here ye are now, in this foreign war; it'll fast enough make ya long for the place ya call home. Can ya fight?"

Neither of the friends found the chance to answer; the cleft-chinned, mutton-chopped Moxley spoke instead.

"Well, they'll learn fast enough, won't they, Dev? Gotta start somewhere. You did. Best they can hope is they don't get killed. No different from the rest of us."

"Voice of experience," Moxley's fellow Englishman, Corey, added. He let his eyes sweep over the newcomers. "They look fit enough. As long as they have heart, what else matters?"

No one challenged the statement.

Ainslie turned to Lang. "Ask you a question?"

Lang poked the fire with a stick. "Suppose. What's your question, then?"

"How'd you get the name Jigs?"

"Easy. Never could sit still as a child. Jiggy-like. Better now. Me ma gave it to me and it stuck."

Chapter 8

PAOLO'S stomach noises caused all eyes to turn his way. Embarrassed, he offered a feeble smile.

Lang responded to the growl. "You've not eaten, I take?"

Paolo shook his head and Ainslie said, "Been more'n a while."

The long-limbed islander from Sky pointed to the pot. "Suppose we can make it stretch for a Scotsman and a good Eye-talian."

"Kind of you," Ainslie said, "but don't want to put you out."

"You'll eat," Lang cut in. "Not a feast, but what we give you will keep you alive. We'll be all right, long as no one else comes along."

The stew dished onto their metal plates, Ainslie and Paolo tucked into the food.

"We'll pay back the favor soon's we can," Ainslie said between bites.

"See ye do," Skinner said.

The stew filled them; it only needed thick bread to soak up the gravy.

Ainslie guessed the meat might be rabbit. He pointed to his plate. "Can I ask how you put this together?"

Corey spoke up as he set down his plate. "Pot's ours." He rubbed the stubble on his lantern jaw before he bore on. "Goes in the wagon and follows us when we move out. Food—hmm, we do what we can."

Paolo furrowed his brow. "What is this meaning — what you say?"

Skinner answered. "It means, our papist friend, we've been going on our own for quite a spell now. Us and the other men you see 'round here." His finger waggled among the other groups nearby.

No holding him back, thought Ainslie, as Skinner continued.

"The five of us come with Gustavus the Great last year. Fed us good in them days, but now the meal wagons' gone, goodbye. We're mostly all of us on our own for food. It's a big problem."

"So what do you do?"

"'Do'? We buy food when we can, and the rest of the time we take it."

A shadow crossed Skinner's face as he stared into the fire. He shook his head as if to rid himself from some thought. "We've done some terrible things, we have, and if Christ Jesus wasn't who He was, and we didn't ask for His forgiveness, we'd for sure burn in eternal hell."

The men fell silent for a moment before Moxley said, "Nice going, Dev. Those words will cheer them up."

The combative Skinner rose to the challenge. His head shot up and he said, "I declare my faults and ask for forgiveness; you on the other hand..."

The two began an argument.

Morison gave them a dismissive wave of his hand and turned to Ainslie. "The good thing is we come up to help bring supplies back. Soon we'll have something better in the pot."

Morison's assurance brought Ainslie some comfort, yet he returned to Skinner's words. Not feed the troops? How could the Protestant forces defeat the Catholics if troops went hungry?

Skinner lost interest in his argument with Moxley. He pointed to the blackened pot as he spoke to Ainslie. "Ya not curious how we got what's in this pot?"

"Dev," Morison cautioned, a note of warning in his voice. "Shut it!"

"Have to learn sometime," the Englishman answered.

Morison exhaled in dramatic fashion. "They just arrived, man." He shook his head in disapproval. "You're liking this too much. Just stop it."

Skinner ignored the reprimand and again spoke to Ainslie. "What did ya think we had in the pot?"

Ainslie dared a guess. "Rabbit?"

Something like a prankish grin appeared on Skinner's face. He licked his lips and said, "Kitty-cat."

"What?"

Ainslie couldn't believe what he heard. His face tightened, his eyes narrowed, and he turned to Paolo to judge his friend's reaction.

It came fast enough. "You are making fun, yes? It is not so?"

Skinner shrugged. "Believe what ya will, but it's what ya ate. Not as good as rabbit, I'll wager, but it fills a man's stomach fast. Lucky we wuz, to get it." He jerked his thumb in the direction of the farmhouse. "Except from some vegetables we found in a root cellar, everything's been ate long time back."

Disgust swept through Ainslie. Eating a cat — his aunt Skeena would never forgive him. He searched the faces of the others. "Why's it come so?"

Moxley answered. "Like Dev said, nothing to eat." He too pointed toward the farmhouse. "Farmer cleared out before we got here. Or the bastard Catholics killed him. No chicken, no pigs; nothing." He paused. "You saw Geiger?"

"Ay."

"Hard to believe, I know, but he's thin compared to before."

Lang spoke. "Corey and me caught the puss in a trap in the woods. Hissed and scratched a powerful lot before we killed it. Sorry we had to do so, I'm partial to cats, I am, but I'm beholden to it for giving us life."

"It ran out of its ninth life when you caught it," Corey added.

Ainslie turned to Paolo. "You following this?"

His friend, jaw clenched, ignored the question and stared into the distance with controlled anger.

"For sure, all this will lower your spirits," the dark-skinned Corey with the fierce eyes and hollow cheeks said, "but you'll learn what the rest of us had to learn. You two know any Latin?"

"Sì."

"Some."

"Good," Corey answered. "I have some myself." He sounded out the Latin phrase '*Bellum se ipsum alet.*'"

Paolo responded first. "Da war, it gives...." He gestured wildly in the air with his hands; at last he found the word. "Itself."

Corey pointed a finger at Paolo. "Good lad. A little off but you get it. War feeds itself. When we first came, we had food aplenty, and they paid us on time. Now we're cadging for food and worse, and making a cry and hue for our pay. It didn't take long for things to get so."

"How?" Paolo asked.

"Ay," Ainslie piped in. "Eager to hear it m'self."

Corey's eyes surveyed his companions. In answer, Skinner gave an exaggerated bow. "Its' a tolerable pulpit ya have, professor. As it's yours, why not keep going?"

Corey ignored the remark and again searched the others' faces. He received nods to carry on. Satisfied, he turned his attention back to Ainslie and Paolo.

"War's expensive," he said. "Our fighting's funded by Sweden, a small country with two problems: one, not enough men and two, short of money. The king took care of the first problem by renting us."

Corey waved his arm around in an arc. "Go to any of the fires; for every Swede you find you'll see ten men from different lands."

Ainslie nodded and remembered the many languages spoken at training camp and at Peenemunde.

Corey gave him no time to dwell on it further. "Money's harder to get than men. The froggies send Gustavus some, but he needs more. You think we're eating cat because we want to?"

No one spoke.

A new thought came to Ainslie. "Wait a wee. So, the French are helpin' to pay for this war?"

"Right."

"But France's a papist country."

"Right again—as far as it goes, but they have their own plans."

"Makes no kind of sense. France goin' to war with the empire; they're both papists."

Corey shrugged in response. "All we know is what our glorious Captain Bjorkman tells us. France is nervous about Austria and Spain. Bjorkman says France thinks they're getting too big in their boots. Worried the war'll spill over into her borders. So Catholic or not, the froggies have a stake in this."

Ainslie shook his head and turned to Paolo. "What've we walked into, Podo?"

Corey answered instead. "What've we all walked into, you mean? Right now Gustavus' feeding — if you call it that — and arming us, but I don't see him continuing both. If he's forced to choose, guess which he'll pick?"

Lang pointed to Corey. "Nicely said, there, Cec. Gave a good 'count of things."

Corey acknowledged with a mock bow. "Good of you to say."

"It's true. Ya've the gift of the gab. Should take up something like being a pastor."

Corey chuckled. "Imagine me, a man of God."

"Why you not leave?" Paolo asked.

"What?" Skinner demanded.

Paolo pointed to the ground. "Leave. Why do you stay?"

"Not an easy answer," the weedy Corey replied.

"Cec's right," Moxley said. "Pay's mostly late or has trouble findin' us, and the food...." He pointed to the pot. "Look what we ate"

He broke off as if to collect his thoughts. "I can't speak for the others, but I fight for my mates."

"Rightly put," Skinner added, "but I also fight for the cause of freedom against Imperialist papist forces." He glowered at Moxley and added, "'*And they shall mount up with wings as eagles; they shall run and not be weary.*' Isaiah forty, verse thirty-one."

Moxley snorted a response. "Devin — you and your religious piety."

The other man waved the remark away. "Surprised you even understand the word, piety. At any event, I'm quoting the Good Book."

Moxley gestured with a shake of his head and returned his attention to the newcomers. "We fight for our comrades, and to stop creeping papism. There's nothing else left"

Morison joined the conversation.

"They're right; all of 'em. Some days I think about chucking it, but somethin' happens and, I'm still here." He bunched his shoulders let them drop and said, "Respect n' honor is it for me."

A lot to think on, Ainslie decided. A lot. Things showed themselves to be different than what he first imagined.

Paolo changed the subject. "Where is the sleeping?"

Moxley jabbed a finger downward. "Here — around the fire. You won't need a blanket — you're fine here. Fire keeps lotta the mosquitoes away."

Supplies arrived the next day. Cod, salted meat, turnips, and potatoes filled pots. In addition to dried fish and meat, the men received eggs, bread, cheese, and even fruit.

A general sense of well-being returned to the soldiers.

Moxley used up the last of their pilfered flour. "What's a stew without gravy, eh?" he said with a mischievous grin.

Ainslie and Paolo stayed with the others and soon became part of the little group.

"Good choice, Podo," Ainslie said as they wiped their plates after a meal- "you pickin' this lot to chum with. How'd you know?"

The Italian chewed and swallowed. "I am not knowing. I am making a congettura."

Ainslie shook his head. "Sorry; stumped. Wait a wee. 'Guess.' Is guess your word? You *guessed*?"

His friend smiled. "Perfetto. I make the guess."

"All right, then. A guess, and a good one."

Cadman bit into an apple, chewed and swallowed. "Good strong drink and everything would be put to right."

"Ay," Jigs agreed. "Been so long since I had a drink of wonderful tartan pleasure."

"I take it he means beer?" Cecil said to no one in particular.

In reply Lang waved him away as a simpleton.

Ainslie addressed the others. "I have a question."

"Out with it," Jigs said.

"Why's everything put to the torch?"

"Ah, you noticed," Cecil replied. "Blame the Imperialists. Our Gustavus gave them a black eye before kicking them out of Pomerania. They had no choice but to run. Burned everything they could. Poisoned the wells too. Hardly find any peasants left around here."

"Mostly true," Cadman chimed in. "Peasants high-tailed it. Can't blame 'em. Probably gone east or west; can't go south, Catholics there. Froggies, they're Catholic, but better ones than the Imperialists."

"What is next?" Paolo asked.

Corey answered the question with his own. "What do you mean? Don't understand."

"To go?"

"Ah. The Englishman said. "Get you now. We'll leaving with the supply train. Heading south, and with luck we might run into the shit, Conti. You know about him?"

Ainslie and Paolo shook their heads.

"One of your countrymen, Paolo," Cecil said with disapproval.

"I am not knowing this man," an incensed Paolo said.

"Not worth knowing. Villagers call him 'The Devil.' Black as the Earl of hell's surcoat, him. His troops make us look like angels. Would have killed the whole damn civilian population if we hadn't come along."

Ainslie changed the subject. "Do you speak German?" he asked Cecil.

"I do," the Englishman said. "Decided if I'm here, might as well learn."

"Will you teach us?" Ainslie turned to Paolo. "You interested?"

"Si. Yes."

Cecil thought on it and said, "Why not?" He pointed to the others. "They don't much care."

"Hard enough learnin' Swede," Devin broke in. "Why bother with German?"

Late in the afternoon captain Bjorkman sent sergeant Geiger around to announce they'd break camp in the morning.

"I'm ready to march again," Cadman said. "If I had drink and women, then everything'd be perfect."

"Ya'd rather do drink and whore," Devin challenged, "than bask in the fierceness of the on-going fight for righteousness?"

Cadman swatted the accusation away. "Speak English, you barmy Blackpoolian. Something in your mother's milk makes the lot of you annoying as hell. And if you want to know, no self-respecting soldier anywhere turns his back on women and drink."

Ainslie noted the two men were often at each other, yet in spite of their bickering he sensed a mutual fondness.

Chapter 9

PAST first light, bugles woke Ainslie. Muskets in hand, men raced to fall in formation. Geiger's voice commanded his men to hurry along. All waited for their seventy-six-year-old commander. He at last rode up on his gray-and-white Andalusian war horse, aware all eyes were on him. A detailed and polished cuirass hid most of his resplendent, blue, embroidered silk coat. White-maned and arthritic, Herre Baron Colonel Reine Carlquist's joints hurt and almost brought a tear to his eye. The heavy body armor didn't help. He did his best to sit spine-straight on his grey-and-white Andalusian horse.

He sighed at the prospect of a long day ahead. *Be forever before we strike camp for the night. Nothing to do but endure until then.* He comforted himself with the thought of a few good shots of akvait. He'd hurry into his tent, and climb under his soft comforter. No useless officers' banter for him. Sleep and freedom from discomfort would be welcomed.

Carlquist well knew war was a young man's calling, but duty and honor demanded the family always lent their swords to their sovereigns in times of need. A pity Carola had never delivered him a son. His daughters were wonderful, but daughters nonetheless. It thus fell to him to ride into battle and fly the Carlquist pennant.

Another sigh escaped him. *Put your fusses away. The war's still going the king's way. The enemy's military posts on the Baltic have fallen. Our armies now control the Pomeranian shore and much of the North German plain. Dutch and Swedish warships see to it no ships of the Catholic League dares sail Baltic waters.*

Yes, he had reason to believe the war would be short. He'd do his part; make a good enough impression, and then return to his estate.

Carlquist regarded the profile of his second-in-command's handsome features. *No doubt a ladies' man.* No military experience, Lovgren, but Carlquist felt certain it wouldn't hinder the man from rising fast through the ranks. He didn't care. By the time Lovgren took over, he'd be back on his estate playing cards and enjoying his grandchildren. No unnecessary heroics, he reminded himself; focus on staying alive.

The colonel moved about to get comfortable. The damn cuirass chaffed. He shifted and felt a sharp jab to his hipbone. He winced and hoped no one took notice. It wouldn't do to have his underlings think him a weakling. *God's Misery, There is no comfort for old age.*

The pain wouldn't let him be. Think of something else, he told himself, something pleasant. Carola's body. Yes, the memory always brought delight. He'd chuckle when she insisted a man his age shouldn't be so randy.

The horse moved and brought him back to his present state. He considered Lovgren again—a man who seemed born to the saddle. He reminded the baron of himself at a much younger age.

Carlquist adjusted his three-cornered hat, turned, and took in the drawn-out line of soldiers. All waited for his command. His gaze lingered on the line before it turned to Lovgren. With an almost imperceptible nod he signaled his readiness to begin. His deputy spurred his horse, moved beside the colonel and called across to Sergeant-Major Borje Sahlstein. "Begin."

Sahlstein pointed to the buglers. With great ceremonial blasts, they sounded the make-ready warning. No sooner were they done than the two drummers in front of the cavalry beat out a marching tattoo. Sahlstein took off his cap, raised it high, and barked out, "For Christ and Crown, soldiers, onward."

The column answered with a raucous cheer and moved forward.

What a pair we are, Anders Lovgren thought as he rode alongside the older man, at least twenty-five years his senior. Sometimes he wondered if Carlquist knew what day it was, let alone what century.

Anders Lovgren had Carlquist's full measure long before the battalion boarded for Pomerania. His commission in hand, he found himself seconded to Carlquist. His father had made discreet inquiries about Carlquist. They discovered the man gave a good account of himself during the Polish War. Such a long time ago, Lovgren believed.

"Like it or not," Justus Lovgren advised his son over dinner, "Carlquist's your commander. Nothing you can do about it. Do his bidding and make sure he doesn't get you killed. I have it on good authority His Majesty will withdraw him in a month or two. Bear up until then."

The senior Lovgren sipped from his glass of port wine. "It falls on you, Anders, to advance our family name. This war will provide opportunities to get His Majesty's attention. The highborn already have it; now our chance has arrived."

One of the richest families in Stockholm, the Lovgrens wanted nothing more than entry into the well-guarded upper class. Significant interest-free loans and lavish gifts to the Royal House brought them closer. As did Anders' recent investiture to the *Order of Swedish Knighthood*. Honor on the field of battle promised to do the rest.

The younger Lovgren smiled to himself. The future belonged to him. He remembered his vow to his father. Yes, he'd be sure to prove himself and bring glory to the Lovgren House.

In double line, the soldiers marched behind the artillery pieces.

"So, we're finally off?" Ainslie asked Devin and Cadman, who paraded ahead of Paolo and himself.

"We are," Cadman said, over his shoulder. "Back into the thick of things. If you're itching for action, you'll have it soon enough. Trust me. But in the meantime we march. No idea where the battle front is now, but we'll find it soon enough."

"Right," Devin agreed, and turned to glance at the two friends. "Battle front keeps a-shiftin'. One time our side's on top of things; next theirs."

Ainslie found it cool for mid-summer. *If I didn't know better, I'd guess it felt like early autumn.*

The column continued south. By mid-morning the skies opened. At times the rains came down hard; other times they lessened, but they never ceased.

Sodden and grim, made worse by wet feet, soldiers limped along behind officers and cannons. Thoroughly wet, they suffered worse during the night. No one slept; at best they shivered and napped, only to wake to their cold reality, wipe their noses and sneeze. Cooked meals were out of the question. Men ate soggy bread, cheese, and salted fish and meats as they marched. They complained of swelling in their legs, pain, and lack of sensation in hands and feet.

Heads down, the column trundled on in the mud and cursed the rain, the war, their officers, and anything else they found displeasure with.

The situation worsened. Artillery pieces bogged down in the muck of roads long neglected. Shouts of "Put your damn shoulders to it," almost became a catchphrase as soldiers grunted, swore, and flopped into mud, pulling horses and pushing artillery pieces.

The first casualties came without an enemy in sight. Eight soldiers fell, victims to lung illness. Carlquist ordered them removed to the wagons. None lingered long.

A platoon of men grumbled as they dug a communal grave by the side of a road. Considerable straining and cursing accompanied the shoveling of heavy, sodden soil. Chests heaving from exhaustion, the men hollowed out a sufficient hole to place the dead.

The pastor moved up and flipped through the wet pages of his Lutheran *Book of Worship* while the column waited, sniffled, and shuffled from foot-to-foot. Quick benedictions, and they pushed on.

More soldiers fell to illness. Carlquist summoned Lucas Gedda, the physician. He reported things would worsen if something wasn't done.

"With respect, Colonel, I have no medicine for this. Dry socks and boots is the best cure, but nothing is possible under these conditions. We have to get out of the rain. If we don't things will only get worse."

"Easy for you to say, doctor," a frustrated Carlquist shot back. "Where do you suppose we go to escape the rain?" Quick to remind the physician he too suffered, he added, "I cannot stop it. It falls on all of us. There is nothing to do but tough it out." He wiped the rain off his goatee and went on. "If it rains another five days I'll take it as a sign, and have the men build an ark—assuming we find any trees."

If intended as humor, his medical officer failed to see it. All well and good for Carlquist to tell them to tough it out, the rather small, middle-aged man thought. The soldiers couldn't pull thick gabardine coats like his over their silk coats. Or sleep under the protection of a tent. Instead he said, "Yes, of course, Colonel." His face grim, he continued. "I suggest, Colonel, at the next town we stop and quarter the troops no matter what. If we don't, we'll have men digging more graves."

Carlquist turned to Lovgren to judge his reaction. His second nodded to signify agreement.

Carlquist returned his attention to Gedda. "I suppose you're right." He hoped he sounded like a man in control. Others were watching. With effort, he straightened. "So be it." He turned to Lovgren. "What's the next town?"

"*Hochland*, I believe."

"*Hochland* it is. We stop there."

Fast enough, word passed down the line: they'd sleep under roofs instead of open fields.

Ainslie and Paolo kept their heads down to let the rain pelt off their helmets. The Scot didn't know how much longer he could go on. Everything ached, especially his feet. He felt like an old man. He sniffled as he muttered, "I miss granda and nana. Shoulda stayed home. The English come pokin' 'round, sure, but they'd tire soon enough. Could be in a better place than this, but nah, fool, this is where I find m'self."

He let out a plaintive sigh as another wave of shivering came over him. Water from the heavens mingled with his tears of self-pity as he listened to the squish, squish of his water-laden boots.

The rains at last eased up as deep, wet coughs echoed up and down the column.

Church steeples of a fortified town came into view. The column moved closer to the town wall. The broad and massive oak gate gave evidence of damage. Pulverized pieces of it lay outside the wall.

A shout followed by a trumpet came from the battlement. Ainslie caught sight of men on the wall point at them.

In short time a small line of civilians rode out of the archway, led by a soldier bearing a white flag on a stick.

Ainslie hacked deep, wet coughs. He nodded toward the delegation. "What'd you make of it, Podo?"

Devin answered instead. "Town government from what I can see. Gotta be. Powerful lot of finery sitting on them horses."

"And with any luck, will soon be getting as wet as the rest of us," Cadman added.

"What do ya have against them, other than they're foreign?" Devin asked, hawking a green gob of phlegm. "Never did ya any harm."

Cadman shook a dismissive head. "I'm in a foul mood, Devin, all right? If I feel like being unrighteous, so be it. You, you keep busy praying for my miserable soul." He used his right forefinger and thumb to blow out his nasal passages, wiped his nose on his sleeve. "Besides it's us, not them who are foreigners. This is their country, remember?"

"Sill, no call wishing them ill."

"Wishing them ill, Dev? They're not the ones I'm wishing ill at the moment."

The column halted while Carlquist and Lovgren rode to meet the deputation. Ainslie watched as both sides gestured wildly — either toward the town or to the column. They heard Lovgren's voice rise. More yelling and gesturing until, at last, the leader of the deputation held his hands up to suggest resignation. A moment later Lovgren turned his horse and made for Sahlstein. They spoke. Sahlstein saluted, rode several steps away from the column, turned and bellowed, "Soldiers, we camp here, dry out and have a rest period."

A mighty cheer rose from the ranks, all gladdened by the tidings. Moments later the men marched through the archway with newfound enthusiasm. Inside the town walls they halted. Sahlstein called for the column to break up.

Bjorkman summoned his men to gather around him. Deep bags under his eyes, he spoke to Geiger. The sergeant listened and translated to the men.

"Kapten Bjorkman instructs me to tell you the town is half-empty," he said, as he scratched three days of facial growth. "Imperialist forces came through a while ago. The citizens are still recovering. Not our problem; shelter is."

He caught his breath. "Colonel Reine Carlquist has given his word as an officer and a gentleman we will not rape or loot while we receive their hospitality."

Geiger turned and spoke to Bjorkman again. More words passed between them before Geiger spoke to the men again. "I repeat: no raping or looting. Are I clear?"

A murmur of agreement reached him.

"Louder," he demanded. "I can't hear you. No raping or looting. Do you understand me?"

The men assured him they understood.

Satisfied with the answer, Geiger said, "Good. I'm wet, tired and cold. God help the man brought in front of me because he couldn't follow a simple order. Keep your dicks in your breeches, and your greedy hands to yourself while we're here."

He finished, turned and gave his attention back to Bjorkman. Another sing-song exchange passed between the two before Geiger nodded, turned, and once more faced his men. "The captain will pick us a street to stay in," he called out. "We march."

Bjorkman kicked his horse.

In single file his men followed him down narrow cobblestone lanes.

"Raping and looting," an astonished Ainslie grumbled as they moved off. "Who's got strength for it — or anything else?"

Another bout of coughing seized him. He felt dizzy and used his pike to support himself. The fear of disapproval from his comrades worried him more than his sickness. Best not to show any sign of weakness.

Bjorkman chose a narrow lane for his men. They searched the houses and found most abandoned.

Moxley claimed a house for the friends and waved them in. "Let's go, lads. Get outta this rain once and for good. Hurry."

"Don't have to convince us," Cecil said, as the others rushed into the small, half-timbered structure.

"Fine choice, this," Devin offered as he scanned the interior. "Small, mind, but bound to keep the rain off."

"Good," Cadman said, as he strung a rope near the fireplace, "cause we're gonna stay here whether you agree or not. We can dry our clothes on this line. Now, let's go find some wood."

"Soon we'll have our boots in front of the fire," Jigs added. "I'm afraid to find out the state of me feet. Me socks been swimmin' in water for these last few days."

The room held almost no furniture, but no one cared. All hurried into the lane to scavenge anything capable of burning. They found coal; not much, but enough to get a fire started while they searched for more wood.

Other soldiers also scurried up and down the lane in search of anything capable of burning. They returned with splintered parts of wood, and set about feeding them into the fireplace. Next each man stripped and crowded around the welcoming heat.

"The blessed Lord in His Heaven," a naked Cadman said as he warmed himself in front of the fire. "I thought I'd never get warm and dry again." His eyes narrowed in a warning for Devin, perhaps anticipating the other man might say something. "Not a word out of you, hear? I'm cold, wet, and God made me in His image. You have a problem with that, take it up with Him. I'm staying here in my altogether until my clothes dry."

Devin's frown in evidence, he said, "Even so, Cade, you must fess you're indecent. Why not cover your privates?"

Cadman ignored him and turned to Corey. "Help me?"

Cecil took up the cause. "Let up, Devin. No one's in the mood."

The fire crackled and sizzled and their clothes began to dry, the moisture releasing as steam. Some time passed before any of them chanced to climb back into their garments.

"You are not so good, no?" Paolo told his friend as he pulled on his boots and listened to Ainslie's cough.

The comment made the others give Ainslie a closer inspection.

"Ay," Jigs agreed; "It's so." He moved closer and studied Ainslie. "Feeling powerfully ill, I'm betting."

Ainslie licked his lips. "Something, but I'll be fine in a bit." The room swam. Ainslie worried his legs wouldn't support him.

Devin approached and felt Ainslie's forehead. "You've a heavy fever. A bad one. Come and sit." He led Ainslie to a chair, changed his mind and direction, and stopped at the edge of the only straw bed. With gentle pressure on Ainslie's shoulders he managed to guide the young Scot to a sitting position.

"Someone, anyone," Devin called out to the room; "come and give me a hand and get him on his back."

Paolo approached. Together he and Devin helped Ainslie lie down.

The Scot shut his eyes. He felt a covering placed over him as his body increased its uncontrolled shivering. He heard a distant voice say, "He's bad. We best send for the doc."

Ainslie saw shadows of forms hover over him. Hands prodded and lifted him. He heard snatches of voices, including what sounded like a female voice.

"Sweat it outta him is what we need ta do."

"All right, then; keep the damn fire going."

"Get this down him. Come on lad; drink up. No, no, no. All of it."

"Gem-u-lick. It's a German word."

"Wot's it mean?"

"This. Cozy-like. We're warm, dry, and got food. If we had more female companions like Ute here...and some drink, we'd be set."

"Are ya on with this again?"

"Good thing we didn't see action. Gunpowder's all wet. Couldn'a did a thing with it."

Four days later the fever broke and Ainslie became aware of his surroundings. He opened his eyes and saw Devin, who offered up his own version of a smile.

"Give thanks, lad. You're up and ya've conquered Satan. He wanted ya badly he did, but God's mercy stayed Beelzebub's hand."

"What're you bothering the lad about, Devin?"

Cadman's welcoming voice filled the room as he moved beside Devin. "Leave him alone, can't ya?" The Englishman gazed at Ainslie. "Not enough he's sick, but you've got to make him worse with your religious gibberish."

He bent and patted Ainslie's shoulder. "Welcome back. We thought we'd lose you. Fact we didn't, you can thank the kind hands of a local angel of mercy, a Fraulein."

"Angel of mercy, indeed," Cecil agreed as he stepped up beside Cadman; "but it took some doing to get her to come here. She and her mother were sure we'd rape or murder her. Had to bribe them."

Ainslie offered a weak nod, unable to grasp what he heard.

"And ya've Doc Gedda ta thank as well," Devin added. "He won over the Colonel. Said we need to get the likes of you back to health."

Cadman chuckled at the remark. "I don't think it took much — heard the old man's not feeling too fit himself."

Ainslie still had the cough, but nothing as before. Back on his feet, he and Paolo wandered into the town square to find a long line of citizens lining up and advancing to a table. Sahlstein sat behind it and wrote in a ledger as citizens handed him monies.

Dragoons and soldiers stood nearby.

Ainslie noticed the women in the line sniffle and wipe their eyes while the men made hard faces. More than a few raised their voices and pleaded some case or other with Sahlstein. Those unable to hand over money were taken aside harshly by soldiers and hurried out of the square.

"What're they up to then, Podo?" Ainslie asked. He failed to receive an answer and turned to see the Italian's grim profile.

"Is not right."

"What's not right?"

Paolo pointed with his chin. "What they are doing — making pay. We have this in my country. People do not like. We call it rapina."

Ainslie raised his eyebrows. "Rape?"

Paolo hurriedly shook his head. "No." He brought his arms up and clenched and unclenched his hands. "Taking what is not belonging to you." Paolo's eyebrows furrowed together — a man in search of a word. The eyebrows loosened and he added, "Like criminal."

"Robbery is wot you're sayin'?"

"Si. We should not do like this."

No one in authority appeared to share Paolo's views. Citizens continued to stand in line; soldiers continued to lead some away.

Gisis moved up beside them. "What're we lookin' at?"

Both turned and acknowledged his presence. Ainslie pointed. "The line and what's going on with some of the people."

"Oh, right," an untroubled Gisis said. "Happens pretty well everywhere. Collecting taxes."

"Where they are taking those people?" Paolo asked, again pointing with his chin.

The Scot followed Paolo's gaze. "To their homes to see if they can get anything to pay for the taxes."

"And if they can't?" Ainslie asked.

"Depends. A beating; sometimes a hanging."

"This is not, how you say, a trouble to you?" Paolo asked.

Gisis shook his head. "Not causin' me much hand-wringin'; no. It's war. You've to expect this and worse in war. It's not pleasant, but you'll soon catch on what to bother about, and what's not worth your time."

The column left *Hochland* in an orderly fashion on a sunny morning five days later.

Ainslie couldn't help but wonder if the townsmen held an equally poor opinion of them.

Two days later they approached the medieval city of *Rothenberg on the Tauber*. Carlquist collected another levy. In spite of it, the city fathers supplied the soldiers with beer, glazed and knotted bread and wurst.

"Not bad," a grateful Moxley said as he bit into a pretzel. "Could get used to this. Can't let it fall into enemy hands."

Chapter 10

THREE days after departing *Rothenberg* the column arrived in the king's camp on the Leipzig plain.

Tents were crowded together. Beyond them, scores of horses, wagons and cannons covered the distant field.

The supply wagons moved off and joined other wagons; dragoons rode to join their fellow cavalrymen, and foot soldiers searched out any vacant spot they could find.

Gustavus' pavilion earned its fuss as the eye-catching centerpiece of the camp. Ainslie and the other recruits gaped as they marched past the proud and majestic shelter done up in the royal colors of blue and gold. The House of Vasa standard flapped in a slow and lazy manner atop the tent.

For weeks the Swedish king, Gustavus, met and reviewed battle plans with his Grand Council of War. They readied everything and everyone for upcoming clashes with the enemy.

Ainslie marveled at the languages he heard and the different uniforms of the Saxons, Swedes, Dutch, Croatians, Silesians, and numerous armies who served under the Swedish flag.

At night men sat around fires, cooked, talked and waited for the call to battle. Ainslie glanced up to the large number of stars and back to the field, certain the fires made an equally impressive showing.

To their delight, Ainslie, Paolo, Devin and Cadman, along with six others, received their first lessons in the use of muskets.

Geiger translated for Bjorkman. "Consider this an honor. You are pike men but in an instant you may be called upon to be musketeers." Without another word he turned and led the ten to the far end of the field.

"Training us to be musketeers," Cadman whispered as they followed their sergeant. "A lot of musketeers go down in battle, so they want to have enough musketeers at all times."

"What if we go down in battle?" Ainslie asked.

Cadman answered with a vague shrug. "The hazards of war."

Geiger turned them over to the training instructor who lectured the men on the heavy, three foot weapons, and on musket maintenance, then repeatedly took them through the drill of loading, aiming and firing in unison.

Ainslie caught on fast, even as he found the twenty pound musket cumbersome, and the fork staff unreliable. He recalled the maneuvers at Jönköping Castle. Do what they did, he told himself.

Close to sunset, the men wandered back to their fires. They smelled of gunpowder. All repeatedly spit to rid themselves of the aftertaste of musket balls.

"'Musketeers,'" Devin later said as they ate their evening meal. "They'll have me as a musketeer. Imagine. It's a miracle."

"This time I have to agree with you, you barmy Blackpoolian," Cadman added.

In return Devin made an annoyed face, and Moxley grinned.

"Make fun of me if ya will, foolish Englishman," Devin said. "Dead papist bodies have more brains than you at the best of times."

Cadman chewed, swallowed and replied, "Not very Christian of you. What's more, you calling me an Englishman? What are you then?"

"A Blackpoolian, is what. A Blackpoolian whose people have the right bad luck to be swallowed up by land-grabbin' Englishmen."

"You don't say? What happened to 'proud to be a patriot, the king's servant,' and all your other nonsense?"

Devin batted away the counter charge away with, "I don't discuss gov'ment and politics with my social inferiors."

Cadman tossed back his head and snorted. "'Social inferiors'? Someone's been listening in on intelligent conversation. Here's something for you to think on..."

For the next few moments the two friends had the others in fits of uncontrollable laughter while they gave themselves over to another senseless argument.

Ainslie and Paolo smiled at each other and enjoyed the devil-may-care argument. He now understood the close bonds that grew out of good fellowship. These were his friends.

A new intensity swept through the camp —everyone aware of an impending battle with Imperialist forces. The order arrived: pack up, we're on the move.

Like all young men eager for action, the order lifted Ainslie's spirits.

"Had enough drilling, marching and sittin' around," he said to Paolo as they soaked their feet in a nearby stream at day's end. "Not seein' a thing since we left Peenemunde. I've blisters on me blisters. Drillin' and marchin' is all we do."

Devin overheard him. "Stop your bellyaching." He picked at the dead skin from the soles of his feet. "You'll see action a-plenty — more than ya ever wanted, you can bet."

Ainslie turned and said, "Fair's fair, but I didn't sign up just to march around the bloody continent."

His argument won no favor with the Englishman. "Right then; be in a big hurry to get yourself put in the ground."

"Why does it have to be one or the other? Just wanna do what I signed up for, is all."

Gustavus' advance scouts returned to camp and reported the enemy a half-day away from the village of *Breitenfeld*. King and his Council took great interest in the report. They reasoned the battle would happen at Leipzig, not four miles from it. "This changes things," the short, plump king said. He turned to the scouts and demanded particulars. What cannons did the enemy have — light or heavy? Where were they positioned? And the main army — what of its size and strength?

Thrown somewhat into confusion by the many, hurried questions of their sovereign, the scouts appeared anything but confident.

"Well?" the impatient Gustavus asked. "Are we to receive an answer?"

"Yes, of course, Your Majesty," Olaf Hambourg, the captain, said. "I cannot say definitively at the moment."

His lieutenant nodded in agreement.

"Pray," the monarch replied, ice in his voice, "when will you be able to offer an assessment with more authority?"

Hambourg opened his mouth but Gustavus shut him off. "No. You are an intelligence officer and your monarch relies on you to favour Him with correct information. Go back and return with such detailed information."

"Yes, of course, sire," Hambourg responded.

Both men bowed low, executed smart turns and hurried out of the tent.

Gustavus waited until they left, turned to his Saxon allies and French advisors. "We can only wait until they return with something helpful." He moved to a side table, picked up a wine goblet, and drank heavily. "Luck, gentlemen," he said to those around him, "she only lends but never gives her favor entirely. Let us hope she continues to smile at us."

The two scouts returned and reported the enemy made camp in the undulating hills on the edge of the plain.

"We also saw movement, sire."

"Be specific, man," Gustavus demanded. "What kind of movement?"

"Of course, Your Majesty," a subdued captain Hambourg said. "General Field Marshal Johannes von Tilly leads them, his advisors and marshals close at hand."

Gustavus repeated the Catholic general's name. "So he calls himself Tilly? Easier than his real name to pronounce, one supposes." He turned to Hambourg. "You are certain you saw him?"

"Yes, Your Majesty. Through our spyglasses."

"Give us more."

"Yes, of course. The enemy knew we were there because they watched us watch them."

"Ahh," Gustavus said and stroked his moustache with a velvet glove. "The fox invites us to approach his lair."

"A trap, you think, Majesty?" Gustav Horn, Count of Pori asked.

"No doubt, my dear, Gustav," the king said. "All the more reason for us to be doubly careful." His eyes returned to Hambourg. "Now, Captain, you think Tilly is moving his men onto the plain?"

"I am certain of it, Your Majesty."

Gustavus' right eyebrow shot up for a second before he turned to his French advisors and exchanged smiles. "Good of the Field Marshal to accommodate us."

He returned his gaze on Hambourg. "What else?"

"As to numbers, as best as we can tell, Majesty, we place them somewhere between high twenty thousand to low thirty."

Gustavus grunted an answer, waited for a moment, then said, "And artillery?"

"Their pieces are heavier but match ours in number."

"And the small hills — who has those?"

"No one at the moment, Majesty."

Gustavus clapped and rubbed his hands together in glee. "Excellent. Then we shall have them. Luck does seem to favor us." He tossed a fast nod to his scouts. "Very well. Dismissed."

Both captains again bowed and left the tent.

Gustavus turned to the French military advisor, Comte de Archibeque. "We are not daunted, Edgar. This could work to our advantage."

Archibeque responded with a small bow and said, "The House of Bourbon has every confidence *The Lion of the North* will continue his sweeping successes."

"Yes, yes, of course," Gustavus muttered, impervious to the flattery. He turned his attention to his Saxon allies to discuss further strategy. Long moments later the Council resolved the army would break camp first dawn. "If Field Marshal Tilly awaits us," Gustavus said, "let us not disappoint him."

Gustavus placed his cannons on the western hills sloping down to the open plain. "Delighted to hold the advantage," he informed his marshals, "We are certain to have better range and accuracy there." He moved in the saddle and glanced at the others. "Their folly; our gain. At this rate we can march into Leipzig in time for bratwurst and beer."

The comment brought genuine laughter from those around him. When it vanished Gustavus spoke again. "Move the infantry forward."

The blare of trumpets gave notice for all to fall in. Men ran to their assigned positions. Drummers beat out staccato time. Full and deep shouts from sergeants ensured all formations conformed to the king's standards.

A voice from the front bellowed. "By the left, quick, march."

In colourful and tight formation, banners and pennants aloft, the steady tromp of marching feet shook the earth and the fife and drums sent notice Anti-Imperialist armies were on the move.

Goosebumps rose on Ainslie's arms as the army advanced along the levelled open land where the enemy awaited.

Before noon the two warring sides stared at each other across a distance of no more than four hundred yards. The only sounds in the Swedish camp came from the creak of saddles, the jingle of bridles and halters, and the strong breeze.

Gustavus opened his spyglass and trained it on his nemesis, who sat on his mount in a proud, disdainful manner. His *famed Tercio Espanola*, formations of foot soldiers, pike men and musketeers waited behind him.

Imperialist forces copied a Swiss model in which pikemen organized themselves in squares, with swordsmen, cuirassiers, and officers in the middle. Musketeers with their long-barreled weapons guarded the outer edges and offered extra protection against onrushing enemies. The Tercio earned a fearsome reputation, matched only by the janissaries, the merciless foot soldiers of the Turks.

Gustavus took his time inspecting the enemy even as he spoke to his confident, Duke Bernhard of Saxe-Weimar.

"Johann."

Bernhard considered Gustavus' profile. "Your Majesty."

Gustavus handed over his spyglass and pointed. "Have a guess, Johann; how many artillery pieces do *you* think we are up against?"

Bernhard accepted the field glass and spent several long moments moving it back and forth before he spoke. "Less than two thousand I would offer; perhaps in the range of fifteen to eighteen hundred."

"Yes," Gustavus agreed. "Close to what I would have guessed." He held out his hand for the spyglass, again trained it on the opposing force, flags and pennants waving in the sharp breeze. "Impressive, but not enough to worry us. God will lead us to victory."

Across the field and aware the Swedish king observed him, the Imperialist Field Marshal gave a stiff nod of recognition before he lost interest and spoke to the man beside him. The other turned his head and shouted something. At once the first line behind the Field Marshal opened and widened; he and his officers turned and rode through.

The line closed. Long moments passed before six teams of oxen arrived; each pulled a heavy siege artillery piece on wooden carriages. With the oxen unhitched, the men readied the cannons.

"He intends to flatten us," Gustavus said as he continued to watch. "We won't give him the opportunity. Pull back and spread out."

Catholic bombardment began at mid-day.

Ainslie found it hard to believe a warm, bright, and pleasant day could bring such a hellish din. Had devils escaped their infernal region and caused this? "I thought Jönköping cannons were loud," Ainslie told Cadman. "They're nothin' compared to this." The noise proved deafening. He placed his palms over his ears to seek as much relief as possible.

The air cracked with the loud, deep boom of cannons. Large chucks of soil flew high. Craters and pockmarks appeared in the once-level field. The few trees in the area bore the worst of the carnage. None survived. Cannonballs turned them into ugly splintered stumps.

Ainslie found it hard to stay in control of himself. *I don't think I can stand it much longer.*

No choice presented itself; he and the rest covered their ears and endured the barrage.

Catholic forces continued to load, discharge, and reload their cannons. "Soon," Gustavus remarked to his marshals, "the ground and trees will sue for peace."

Long shadows made their appearance as cannon fire slowed and at last ceased.

Ainslie removed his tired hands from his ears, "Thank God. It's over."

"Don't be so quick," Cadman advised and pointed. From both hills and plain, teams of horses pulled lighter cannons forward, soon unhitched. Moments later Swedish cannoneers delivered their own response. Each artillery piece fired three rounds before it moved elsewhere.

The Swedish barrage proved more accurate and devastating. It disabled two of the enemy's six heavy siege-gun carriages, and destroyed five supply wagons. Catholic cannoneers became the battle's first casualties.

On the Catholic side a grim Count Tilly watched the carnage.

"I don't know if the Swede's lucky," he growled to Graf, Count Pappenheim, his second-in-command, "or I underestimated him. He has my attention. God favors us, but if we don't act soon the Swede is sure to win."

Swedish cannon fire continued until Gustavus waved his hand and signaled an end. He lifted his spyglass and studied the enemy. "What are they intending next?" he said to himself as the Tercio Espanola reassembled. A few moments later the middle of the Tercio's front line opened and horse cavalry rode through. "Curious strategy," Gustavus said, "bringing out the horses so early. Is the Tercio there for show?"

Marshal Horn followed his king's gaze. "I cannot say, Majesty," he said as other lines formed behind the first.

Gustavus seemed unable to contain himself as he bounced about in his saddle, a smile playing on his lips. "So, a heroic charge. How magnificent."

"It does play into our hands, Majesty," Horn answered.

Gustavus lowered his spyglass. "Hmm, yes, and if glory they seek, glory they shall have—all the way to their graves. Let them come."

In answer, Horn turned in his saddle and shouted, "Musketeers, ready."

Scores of musketeers, including Ainslie's friends, ran forward and surrounded the king and his entourage.

"Best we get out of the way, Majesty," Horn advised.

Gustavus replied with a quick nod. From farther back, he again raised his spyglass and his attention was directed to a nobleman in a fine plumed helmet.

He lowered his spyglass and handed it to Horn. "To the right of Tilly. Who is he?"

Horn took the glass and trained it on a man who held his flintlock pistol in an upright position. "I'm quite certain it's Count Pappenheim, Majesty." He said as he continued his inspection. "Tilly's second-in-command. A dragoon."

Gustavus repeated the name. "Indeed. Is he the....?"

"The very one, Majesty," Horn said, anticipating the question. He handed back the spyglass. "The butcher of Magdeburg. They curse his name forever. Said to be reckless."

"Well, well. Doesn't take a great feat of the imagination to guess he'll lead the charge. Let's hope he's reckless today."

The king and his Council remained on their horses and paid close attention as the Spanish lines of dragoons readied themselves for the charge.

Horn spoke out. "Say what you will about them, they have the look of confidence."

"More like overconfidence," Gustavus corrected as he kept his spyglass on the enemy. "Overconfidence is an unreliable feeling. Nothing takes it away from a man like a knockdown. He maintained his inspection of the Catholic lines. "Are we ready to cut them down?"

"We'll give it our best try, Majesty."

Gustavus lowered the field glass and offered up an exaggerated sigh. "My dear, Gustav, 'best try' won't do. It amounts to second-rate. I'll ask again. Can we get the better of them?"

"Yes, Majesty, we can."

"Better," the self-satisfied king said. "Think positive."

"Yes, of course, Your Majesty."

Chapter 11

A deep cheer rose up from the front rank of the Imperialists. Horn's steed danced sideways. He took a moment to settle the beast before he said, "We should move back farther yet, Majesty."

Gustavus agreed and allowed his marshal to lead him through the parted lines of musketeers. King and nobility through, the Protestant lines closed again and faced the enemy. The first line rammed their fourquettes into the ground, and set their muzzles into the tines of their prop staffs. They tightened their grips on their weapons and waited for the headlong charge.

A strident voice from the Imperialist side called out, "*Jesu-Maria.*"

Scores of Catholic riders repeated the cry. With impressive precision, three solid lines of Catholic hussars, Count Pappenheim in the lead, trotted fifty yards closer to the Protestant side. Without delay, Pappenheim spurred his horse to a gallop. He bent low over his steed, with his pistol ready to fire, and charged. A wave of riders behind him, the resounding cry of *Jesu-Maria, Jesu-Maria*, filled the air.

Protestant musketeers took aim.

Hazardous, uneven ground denied the Catholic hussars their full and glorious charge. Four horses stumbled on the mangled field; one fell and broke its leg. Undeterred, the others came on.

"Aim," Geiger shouted to his men as the riders drew near. "Aim for the horses — horses go down, so do their riders. A cavalryman without his horse is a pathetic thing, one at your mercy. Show him none. Hold until I say fire."

The shooters waited for the call.

"Fire."

The simultaneous discharge let loose its accustomed noise along with an unmistakable acrid smell. Through the acrid smoke, the shooters strained to see what damage they caused while they made room for the next line.

Less than half of the musket balls found their target horses. Of those they felled, the fortunate ones died. The rest, riders and beasts, screamed their agony as they collapsed on the undulating ground.

Fallen riders, able to stand now, faced twin dangers—uncaring, murderous musket balls from the Protestant side, and frenzied riders who charged up from behind.

Mouth open, his hands gripping his pike harder than he realized, Ainslie watched as lead balls flew by the Spanish leader, who fired his pistol and wheeled his horse about. "Fella's born under a lucky sign," Ainslie shouted to Paolo.

Geiger thought so as well. "The lead man," he barked. "Bring him down. Shoot him, shoot him!"

None managed; their quarry moved out of range.

"Jackasses, you ask me," Cadman said as another charge bore down on them. "To have so little regard for life. What are they thinking, rushing like mad men at us?" He shook his head. You'd never catch me doing tha'"

Or me, thought Ainslie. I wouldn't throw my life away for so little. He remembered the earlier unrealistic notions he had about warfare back in Glasgow. None matched this mindless savagery.

"Now what?" he asked Devin. "D'ya think we'll charge?"

"Don't be daft," the Blackpoolian rebuked. "No need at the moment when the game's going our way. Can ya not see our lads handing out a beating to those foreign, idol-worshipping papists?"

A beating? It didn't look like much of a beating, but Ainslie wasn't in the mood to argue.

The next wave of Catholic hussars charged and suffered the same fate as the earlier one. Struck by musket balls, some riders slid out of saddles; others remained upright and lifeless as their confused animals pulled up, unsure which way to move.

Some hussars rode as close as they dared, discharged their pistols and rushed back to their lines.

Pappenheim cheated death but not injury. A musket ball singed the side of his neck. The loss of blood forced him to retreat.

On the Protestant side, a lead ball struck Geiger in the upper thigh. His men pulled him to the back where a barber-surgeon stopped the blood flow with a tourniquet.

A bugle from the Catholic lines called the horsemen back. Strewn corpses and the wounded were left where they fell. Except for those screaming in pain and calling for help, a state of inaction settled over the field.

Ainslie stared at the open land. "Wot's botherin' me the most about all this," he said, as he stood with Paolo, Cadman and Devin, "aside from the fools who ordered it, is the poor innocent beasties lying out there, dead."

Cadman agreed. "Know what you mean. No animal ever fired a musket or cannon. War's ugly enough without bringing animals into it."

Ainslie's eyes flitted to Devin, a man given to opinions on most things. This time the Blackpoolian held his tongue.

Conversation turned to Geiger. All four wished him well. "Not good, what's happened to him," Devin said. A bugle drowned out the rest of his comment.

The pike men stiffened, ready for another charge by the enemy.

On the Catholic side the Tercio again parted; more horsemen came through — different ones, heavy cavalry and cuirassiers in their polished body armor.

Ainslie turned to see Gustavus but too many men and horses blocked his view. "Wonder wot the king'll do now," he said to Paolo.

The answer arrived a few moments later. Protestant lines opened to make room for Swedish cuirassiers, who rode in single file through the middle, led by Marshal Banér.

A cheer rose from the Protestant side, at first low in volume but growing as more riders moved forward. By the time the cuirassiers fanned out in front of the musketeers, the cheer grew riotous and was accompanied by clapping and whistling.

"Can ye believe it?" a joyous Devin shouted. "We're to show the papists what true bravery's like. It's a blessed day, it is."

Ainslie, Paolo, and Cadman offered each other slow, knowing smiles. A rare sight, they knew, to see a gleeful Devin.

"But when's the king using us, his pike men?" Ainslie asked.

"Don't know," Cadman answered as he shifted his weight and gave his attention to the riders. "Not in a hurry to die, are you?"

"Course not."

"Then be glad you're only standing and taking in the show. If they want to kill each other without me, you won't hear me complaining."

In elegant dress of deep purple beneath polished body armor, black thigh-high riding boots and broad-brimmed hats with feathered plumes, each Protestant cuirassier drew admiring glances as he rode to the front.

The lines remained open. Moments later, lightly armored Finnish cavalrymen in their distinctive powder blue jackets rode forward. The riders crowded together and made it impossible for Ainslie to see anything but the backsides of their horses.

Catholic and Protestant horsemen glowered at each other across the divide.

The Catholic side again took up its battle cry, *"Jesu-Maria."*

Banér's men answered with *"God with us."* He tapped his horse on with his spurs. It moved in a way suggesting its owner intended to take the air.

His legs tapped the animal again. It picked up speed as he brought his curved sword to the forty-five-degree position. The riders behind him imitated the action.

Carcasses and a rough, pockmarked ground denied either side a full charge or the opportunity to crash into each other. The steeds barely managed a trot as the two sides met in the middle of the field. Instead of pistols, swords and knives became the weapons of choice.

Banér and a Spanish officer locked eyes. He leaned forward in his saddle and swung his basket-shaped sword. With ease, the Spaniard angled away and avoided its arc. Both horses danced to and fro as their riders sought to find the decisive blow.

Combating riders from both sides crowded around the two men.

Farther back, opposing foot soldiers took in the sights and sounds and shouted encouragement to those caught up in what soon became a medieval melee. Men tumbled from saddles, horses pushed with shoulders and chest.

The more adept riders used thigh-muscle strength to remain in their saddles, and relied on the intelligence of their steeds to stay alive.

Advance and retreat strategies proved impossible, as did well-practiced swordplay. Few sword-yielding horsemen had the chance to use wide sweeping strokes or downward stabs. Punches, kicks, the skills of street brawls likewise found favor.

A Spanish cuirassier's longer reach allowed him to grab his Protestant counterpart. He punched the Swede in the face and pulled him out of the saddle. Not satisfied, the Spaniard turned his horse in an attempt to trample his opponent, but the narrow space denied him the opportunity.

Alert, the fallen Swede jumped to his feet and plunged his dagger into the horse's fleshy hindquarter. The animal screamed its pain and threw the Spaniard. He tumbled backward and landed hard on his shoulder.

The Swede raced to the stunned cuirassier. A roar escaped him as he yanked the Spaniard's head back and plunged his dagger into the man's throat. The Spaniard gurgled and twitched in a wild manner, and died.

A Saxon tucked up behind a Bavarian. The Saxon leaned forward and with ease slid his dagger under the Bavarian's breastplate and into the soft, exposed flesh. The Bavarian stiffened, released the reins of his horse and whipped his head around as his assassin grunted and recovered his blade.

With eyes wide in terror, the Bavarian shouted, "Mother of God, I am wounded." Blood seeped out from his slashed flesh. He made an awkward attempt to clamp his hand over the wound.

A light-headedness and whirling sensation from rapid blood loss caused the Bavarian to totter in his saddle. He pitched forward.

"Die, you misbegotten whoreson," a Spaniard yelled as he thrust his dagger into the throat of a Finnish rider.

Elsewhere, a Swede invited his opposite to copulate with his favorite mule as he smashed the guard of his rapier into the man's collarbone.

Words themselves held no importance. Few on either side spoke the other's language. The emotion and transmission of hate was what mattered — nothing else. Horses stumbled and lost their footing, taking their riders down with them. Few who tumbled, survived.

Little by little, chaos gave way to order. More Catholics than Protestants fell. No one sounded the retreat but Catholic riders retreated to their lines. Protestant yells of excitement grew more thunderous in response.

Gustavus' eyes never left the struggle. Determined not to let victory slip from his grasp, he shouted, "Release them."

Again the middle parted as a thousand hackapelites, swords drawn, rode forward and hollered a different battle cry, "*Hakka Paalle*! Cut them down. As fast as they could, the newcomers rode across the chewed-up field to aid their brethren-in-arms.

"Christ's balls," a worried Spanish cuirassier shouted as fresh enemy riders descended on him. A moment later he met an inglorious death as two hackapelites slashed and stabbed him.

Protestants cheered themselves hoarse when Banér waved his sword at the Catholic side and shouted, "At them."

Hakka Paalle drowned out Jesu-Maria. Battle-crazed Finns rushed for the Spanish Tercio. To Protestant surprise the mixed formation of pike men and musketeers did an extraordinary thing — broke the Catholic line. It turned and ran.

Farther back, Tilly and his commanders watched in disgust as enemy riders cut and rode down Spanish foot soldiers. He handed his spyglass down to his aide, Count von Wallenstein, who sat in his purple, silk-covered sedan.

Wallenstein's peers secretly mocked him. Not fit for duty, they said of the man who arrived at battlefields in an open litter, carried along by four men. For years, Wallenstein suffered from gout, and could do little more than keep his left foot raised to relieve the pain.

Tilly didn't care much for Wallenstein, but thought him an excellent tactician, and so overlooked his weakness.

"They're now having an easy time of it," he said. "Our cannons are our last hope. Prepare them and ready the musketeers. If we can't hold back this onrushing horde, retreat is our only option."

Wallenstein gritted his teeth. "Let's pray it doesn't come so."

Protestant Marshal Banér signaled his bugler to call back the men and regroup. He turned and raised his arm to the king. *Come, hurry,* the gesture said.

Gustavus understood. He turned and glanced behind him. A sharp command, and a moment later the lines opened again to let more knights through, including Carlquist and Lovgren.

"We've no time," Banér roared to his commanders as he reined in his horse. "Any moment they'll fire, so seize the cannons." He filled his lungs with fresh air. "Many of you will not return, but songs and stories will honor you to the ends of time. Are you ready?"

As one, the cuirassiers roared their approval.

Banér had his answer. With frenzied cheer ringing in his ears, he kicked his horse and made for the enemy.

Tilly's side replied with cannon fire.

Undeterred, the frenzied Protestant side came on.

Catholic cannoneers aimed low and released both stone and iron projectiles. Many struck the ground and bounced upward. A three pounder caught Carlquist and separated his head from his body. He died before his panic-stricken horse bucked and threw off the headless body.

Carlquist's second-in-command, Lovgren, escaped cannon fire only to receive a different death. Something struck and burned his forehead. In response, his hand moved to the hole. Fifteen feet later he toppled from his saddle.

More cavalry fell but Banér's men reached the cannons, rode past and changed direction. Using their advantage of height, they slashed down at the men who worked the heavily-wheeled guns. Open terrain and lack of adequate arms to defend themselves gave the artillerymen no chance at survival. Most ran, only to be cut down. The few who fought made valiant efforts to stab the horses or pull the cavalrymen from their animals. In short order they too fell to the overpowering riders.

Banér reined in his horse, locked his arm, and pointed his sword at the Tercio. Farther back, Gustavus understood the gesture. He lowered his spyglass and ordered his infantry to move forward.

Musketeers, pike men and foot soldiers set forth in their orderly, quick trot. The devil-may-care hackapelites gave them no chance to participate in the rout. Bellowing out their murderous *Haakaa Paalle, Haakaa Paalle* battle cry, they indulged themselves and cut down remaining artillerymen, and then turned their horses to the Spanish Tercio.

Something unexpected occurred. Discipline broke in the Catholic lines. Protestant footmen, cheered by their cavalry's success, broke rank, spread out and raced to join the Finns. Soon enough, soldiers rushed past musketeers, all yelling at the top of their lungs, eager to be part of an anticipated rout. None heeded the pleas of the wounded lying on the ground, the rapid swishing of tails or the groaning and squealing of injured horses.

The Tercio squares lost their practiced shapes; gaps appeared. Pike men left their formations. Many dropped their pikes and ran as the horde of Protestants approached. In some places, Catholic musketeers managed shots and toppled a few hackapelites, but the riders kept coming.

Commanders shouted for order but the fighting force splintered and made it easier for the Finns to penetrate.

Ainslie kept pace with the others. Excitement and a feeling of unease coursed through him. He now became part of a life-and-death struggle. He hoped he'd prove himself and not falter. Pikes lay everywhere, abandoned in favor of swords or knives. Ainslie similarly cast his off, pulled out his sword and followed Devin and Cadman as they made for a small group of Tercio in striped gold and crimson breeches.

Four Spaniards surrounded a Finnish cavalryman, whose horse moved back, forth and sideways, attempting to avoid Spanish blades. Its rider slashed down to keep the soldiers back.

Cadman, sword in hand, reached the first Spaniard who changed direction abruptly and faced him. With feet spread apart and knees bent, the short sword pointed at Cadman, the soldier dared him to attack.

Cadman made his first feint. His opponent parried the lunge and easily sidestepped it. In return, the Spaniard brought up his sword, but failed to see Devon throw his shoulder into him.

The sheer force and weight of the crash caused both men to topple. Devon had the advantage of anticipation. He rolled as the Spaniard's sword flew from his hand, and his helmet struck the ground hard. No chance to recover, the ill-fated soldier threw his hands up in defense and hollered a plea as Cadman's sword plunged into his chest.

Ainslie rushed an opponent. Legs apart and bent slightly, his weight balanced, right foot a bit behind the left, the Spaniard waited for Ainslie.

Ainslie swung his sword. His opponent stepped back and out of the blade's arc. Fast enough it became clear to both, Ainslie faced a more accomplished swordsman. He easily fended off the Scot's thrusts, wild swings and awkward techniques. Ainslie wasted far too much energy with these actions. Both heard his loud huffing and puffing as the Spaniard pushed him backward.

The sweat on the handle of his blade forced Ainslie to hold it tighter, to secure his grip. Fear, along with a loss of confidence, now overcame him. He's going to kill me, Ainslie thought as he glanced at the leer on the other man's face.

Desperate to save himself, Ainslie stepped closer and took another haphazard swipe. The Spaniard easily sidestepped it, but caught his heel on a partly buried rock. It caused him to lose his balance and tumble backward with his full weight.

The abrupt change in fortune resulted in a euphoric Ainslie rushing in and slashing down. No second chance, he thought, make it count.

The blade angled in and cut deep into the artery of the soldier's inner thigh. He screamed and stared at the harm Ainslie inflicted. Ainslie pulled out his blade. At once blood poured out, covering the gold-and-crimson breeches. The man moaned, turned his gaze on Ainslie and muttered something in Spanish.

Long moments passed and at last the man lost awareness. The Scot gawked at his defeated foe. *How'd I manage this? By rights, should've been me lying there.*

"Stop standing there with your mouth open, like you've just won first prize at the county fair," someone shouted at him. "Get a move on. There's a battle on, or haven't you noticed?"

Catholic forces fled. The Swedish king showed no interest in being part of a happy celebration. He rode out much like a man ready to take the air. He took in the captured artillery pieces with a broad smile. His gaze next moved to the distant enemy as it hurried to safety across the Weser River. "Splendid, splendid," Gustavus declared, "but let's give the Roman a taste of what's to come."

He pointed to the captured cannons. "Turn these around and fire them at those fleeing dogs. We'll add insult to injury."

Officers barked out orders and cannoneers sprang into action. They repositioned the heavy Catholic cannons. The large guns roared, but the king soon lost interest. He rode off a small distance, dismounted and fell to his knees on the empty field.

Officers and soldiers surrounded their sovereign as he gave in to grand theatrics. He clasped his hands in prayer, raised them high above his head and stared up at the heavens. Surrounded by privates and generals, he prayed aloud for guidance and continuous victory.

His Grand Council dismounted and joined their king. Other men stood nearby and wept.

Protestant troops gave glory in the victory. Voices grew raw, until at last soldiers drifted apart and returned to camp where sergeants counted heads and chose men for work duties.

Intelligence estimates later put enemy losses at a third of his weaponry, dozens killed and hundreds lost to desertion.

"You see," the chubby-cheeked king crowed at the sumptuous dinner table laid out for his marshals. "There is much to celebrate." He held up a piece of a drumstick and waved it toward the battlefield. "The Roman is no longer invincible. How can he be, when his foot soldiers break and run?"

Ainslie and his friends settled themselves around their campfire. A sergeant, Naullan Saynsberry, a man whom God made ugly, joined them. His face full of massive wrinkles, cavernous eyes, and veins on his forehead, the easy-going Saynsberry said, "Strange how I even got into this war. Don't have the constitution for it, but here I am."

A cow set events into motion for Saynsberry. Prank or not, he'd remained far too drunk to remember marching down the muddy street of his hometown, Taunton, with a rope around old Bessie, a local farmer's cow. The farmer and a few members of the militia caught up with him, gave him a sound thrashing and threw him in the county gaol.

The regional magistrate wasted no time in passing a harsh judgment; he sentenced Saynsberry to the next caged ship bound for Australia. Only late night intervention by Saynsberry's brothers and cousins put him on a different ship — to the Baltic.

"Anything new with sergeant Geiger?" Cadman asked as Saynsberry stood over the fire.

Saynsberry shook his head. "In a bad way. The ball didn't smash the big bone, whatever the name is. Course they have to dig it out." He grimaced at the image. "We're hoping he'll pull through. But what I'm here for — two of you have to come with me. Work detail."

His eyes swept over the men. "Best way to do this —I'll have the two juniors."

The others turned to Paolo and Ainslie. Resigned to their fate but with no enthusiasm for speed, both rose, passed a quick wave to their friends and followed the sergeant.

"Don't wanna do this," Saynsberry said as he moved along, "but it's part of being in the army." He offered no further information as he led them to a circle of men gathered at the edge of the battlefield. All gave their attention to a small-framed corporal named Pierce Hand, from Waterford, Ireland.

Ainslie and Hand already had a brief first time run-in when Ainslie saw the ill-tempered Irishman kick a fellow soldier to the ground. Hand only ceased kicking after Ainslie yelled out a protest.

The Irishman had turned and faced the young Scot. "B'jesus, what the fuck you staring at then, you Viking reject?"

Never one to back down from a fight, Ainslie squared his shoulders, narrowed his eyes, and said, "I'm feastin' me eyes on you, since you asked. Wot's it to ya? You stupid, on top of being blind?" He pointed to the prone man. "Ya hit him when he wasn't looking, didja?"

Hand responded to the taunt with impulse. Fists bunched, he charged. Almost upon Ainslie, he pulled his right shoulder back, ready to deliver the quick, decisive blow. It never reached Ainslie. Gifted with a longer reach, and the skills of a capable boxer, thanks to Raeburn, Ainslie knew hooks, straights, rabbit punches, overhands and rounds.

He let Hand's forward motion work against him. At the last second he sidestepped Hand's rush, and with a twisting force landed a hooking punch to the Irishman's jaw. The quick blow took the Irishman off his feet even as Ainslie thought he broke his own hand.

Hand lay on the ground and moaned; meanwhile, Ainslie opened and closed his fist and whimpered quietly in pain.

The commotion attracted attention, but the fight ended almost as fast as it began. Hand's jaw and cheek swelled.

A sergeant Ludvik Andreasson demanded to know the cause of the disturbance. Hand massaged his jaw, pointed to Ainslie and made his case to Private Nansen Bosse, who acted as interpreter. "Sure," he said, "with no reason this fool decides to give it out to me. I didn't do nothin' to bring it on. If he says other, he's a liar."

Ainslie gave his side of the story. He kept his voice calm and his eyes on Andreasson as he recounted the events.

The sergeant's eyes went from Ainslie to Hand. He exhaled and ordered the scrappers to keep out of each other's way.

The order fell on deaf ears. No sooner had their superior moved away than Hand glared at Ainslie.

"Your thinkin' this is over, so you are, you shite. Long cry from it. Mother Mary, first chance I have I'll bloody well square things with you."

Ainslie answered with a taunt. "You've got to be joking. I've stood up to bigger and better than the likes of you. Move along now unless you want more of the same."

Still full of bluster and aggression, both men eyed each other with further antagonism but thought it best not to engage in another fight.

Saynsberry made his way into the circle with Ainslie and Paolo behind him. He gave a cursory nod to Hand and said, "Here you be then; two more." His mission finished, he left.

The Irishman followed him with his eyes before he set them on Ainslie. He held Ainslie's gaze for a moment before he turned away and said, "Right, lads, make room for the new men."

The others shuffled and let Ainslie into the group.

"Come in tighter," Hand said, "She's a soft old day, she is, but your work won't be. You've all been picked for this task. We've to do it, so no use sittin' on our arses an' whining."

He took a breath and exhaled before he started anew. "We're to move out to the field and count the bodies, and report any useful information we find."

"What kind of useful information?" someone asked.

"Mary and Joseph," the irritable Irishman cursed and gave the man a withering stare. "May you fall down and not rise again. Information. Information to help us. You'll know when you see it."

Now what's his problem? Ainslie asked himself. It wasn't hard to see why the Irishman's face' had been punched in so many times.

"We've not the time or means to heal the wounded," Hand said. 'Some may still be breathing, but it's not possible to do anythin' for them. Give them the kindness and slit their throats, and may the Good Lord not weaken your hand."

Ainslie's words poured out before he knew it. "So, they're to have no medical help?"

Hand tensed at the question. His eyes narrowed and his chin jutted out. Red-faced, he marched from the middle of the group and poked the sturdier Ainslie in the chest with his forefinger.

Ainslie bunched his fists by his side, ready to spring.

Paolo's hand shot out. He held onto Ainslie's sleeve. The warning had its desired effect.

Hand caught the gesture. With scorn in his face and voice he said, "Best pay attention to your friend if you're thinking of takin' a swing at me."

Ainslie stayed in place, brought himself under control and settled for glaring at the Irishman.

His tormentor moved closer. "Am I to be cursed with fools the likes of you?"

Almost nose-to-nose, the two men glowered at one another. Hand broke off the contest first and stepped back. He exhaled, inhaled, and then trained his eye on the larger group. "Back to what I said...there are still some on the field dying. Either ignore them or put them to death. It's a mercy death you'll deliver, but watch you don't get blood all over you. Now, let's get on with it"

Ainslie followed the others as they moved toward the field of corpses. He seethed; worse yet, he sensed another confrontation with

Hand was inevitable. *Whatever it is, I hope it'll go bad for him and not me.*

They spread out across the compact battlefield strewn with bodies.

Already the stink of death, of spilled blood, organs and fecal matter, hung over the field. The same foul odor gave way to a greater stench — rotten flesh, both human and animal.

As long's I live, Ainslie told himself, I'll never forget this smell, and never get used to it. Never. He vomited three times. Nothing left in his stomach and still unable to bear the smell, he resorted to theft to help him through his task; he removed a blue embroidered neckerchief from a dead hussar, sniffed it, decided it would do, and tied it over his nose and mouth. Better, but not perfect.

Breathe through your mouth, he told himself, reminded of the gaol at Carlisle.

It took a while to work out a system for counting bodies. On several occasions Ainslie couldn't be sure if he counted one man or more.

It weighed on him, the gruesome carnage and the vague body messes he knew were once human. Those still alive writhed, moaned, and begged for water or relief. Some whispered for their mothers, loved ones or a god indifferent to their plight.

At first Ainslie did his best to block out the pleas, to avoid the beseeching eyes, but he eventually arrived at a different resolution after he saw Paolo stoop and drive his dagger into a man's neck.

Ainslie gawked as his friend wiped his pointed blade on the man's tunic and straightened. No words passed between the two, yet the quick eye contact spoke more than words. Both recognized their mutual distaste for the deplorable chore.

Paolo shrugged and moved on with his duties.

Maybe Hand, was right, Ainslie thought. Paolo seemed to think so. If he had to, it might be best to help somebody into the next life quickly.

It took practice to bring about a fast, clean death. Even wounded men chase life, and intended to cling to it. More than a few held up feeble hands to stay his knife. In the end he settled on the technique of bending, grabbing a man's jaw and a fast slice to one side of the neck. Victims offered up a quick gurgle and convulsion. Death arrived at once.

"I'm goin' to hell for this," he told himself every time he wiped the dagger on the dead man's clothing. "Hell."

Horses with their sad, pleading eyes bothered him the most. He begged forgiveness each time he made a fast slice of a tormented animal's jugular vein. Why did horses bother him more than men, he asked himself, as tears streaked down his cheek? It shouldn't be. They had no souls.

Scores of crows arrived, attracted by the stench. Sea gulls too, followed by kestrels, common buzzards, field rats and even feral cats.

Cats, Ainslie, thought as he glanced around at the barren landscape. Out in the middle of nowhere? Where had they come from?

The scavengers all ignored their natural enemies, aware of the bounty scattered across the field. They pecked, bit, tore flesh, and gorged themselves on this unexpected feast.

The crows annoyed Ainslie the most; they struck at the vacant eyes of men and beasts. He threw whatever he could at them to chase them off, but couldn't scare them away from their meal.

Paolo called over and told him to save his energy. "It is the natural thing of the birds. They go to find food."

"You're right," Ainslie said and rubbed his eyes, "but I hate the bastards."

He again felt certain he'd lost count, but didn't care. He wanted to be done, done with this field of horror.

Just ahead he spied the remains of a decapitated corpse. He moved closer and stared. He recognized the expensive garb of Colonel Carlquist and recalled the man with the kind face.

Unable to explain his own actions, Ainslie searched about for the head. Five feet away he spotted it — eyes and mouth open wide as if in amazement. He picked it up and placed it atop the body. "For all your finery," Ainslie said to the corpse, "you still met a bad end. Terrible to die like you did, but you likely dinna suffer."

They stepped off the field and gathered around Hand, all affected by their day's work. None cared to meet the others' gaze.

A benumbed Ainslie pulled off his neckerchief, his eyes unfocused and his face vacant. Conflicting emotions roiled deep inside him — feelings of some unnamed guilt, anger, and sadness.

Hand tallied their numbers. Seven thousand dead, most of them Imperialists. The numbers found its way to Ainslie's awareness. Seven thousand. Was it even possible? God help all of them.

Hand praised their day's effort. "Sure, you've done grand work, lads, so you have."

None of the weary men responded to the flattery as he continued. "We'll have ta pile 'em up soon an' burn 'em. Carry disease, those corpses, but listen, lads, it's for 'nother day." His eyes settled on Ainslie as he readied to dismiss the men. The two held each other's gaze for a long moment before both moved off.

Ainslie silently spoke to Hand. *I ever get the chance to give you the beating you deserve, count on it.*

He slept poorly. Full of agitation, he tossed and turned fitfully. Much of his waking hours focused on Hand, but eventually he turned to a new matter — life and death. So much death around him; impossible to really understand it all. In a single day, thousands perished — men Ainslie never met raced toward each other with murder in their hearts. Cannons roared, muskets fired, rapiers slashed and daggers were thrust deep into bodies. Where was the sense of it all, he asked himself? There couldn't be any sense in it, only the random, organized violence of two armies throwing themselves at each other.

It led him to consider death. Death stood off to the side, like a spectator, so close, and watched everything.

It brought a first-time awareness to Ainslie about how fragile and precious his life, any life, could be — able to be snuffed out at a moment's notice. What did it all mean? He failed to answer the question. Sleep claimed him at last.

Chapter 12

THE next morning, with great ceremony and accompanied by a continuous drum roll, the Protestant army lined up to receive medals and awards from the king.

Field Commanders Banér, Horn, and the rest of Gustavus' inner circle received their *Orders of Chivalry*. Junior officers received *Badges of Honor* and *Ribbons of Distinction*. Each man knelt in front of Gustavus, who placed the bronze, coin-shaped medal attached to a yellow-and-blue ribbon around his officer's neck.

Common troops accepted yellow and blue ribbons, secured by brass mounts.

Those who fell received posthumous recognition.

Major Dolp Halvorsen moved to the side of his sovereign, cleared his throat and read the names of the dead. Finished, he asked for a moment of silence. All bowed their heads.

A moment later the ceremony continued.

"I'll send this home to me ma," Devin later said, after the ceremony ended and they walked to their fire. "Like the last one. She'll be proud of her boy, she will. Better than gold — for bragging, anyways."

"Ay," Jigs agreed. "'Tis an honor."

Paolo also seemed favorably influenced. Ainslie didn't hold the same regard.

Paolo considered his friend. "You do not like?"

"It's all right."

"You are sick?"

Devin jumped in before Ainslie answered. "Yes. All's well with ya?

"I'm fine," Ainslie insisted with too much agitation. "Just thinking what we had to do with the dead. Not brimmin' with human kindness at the moment."

"Ye've changed," Devin said. "Getting all sour-like."

Ainslie might have let the remark pass if Pierce Hand hadn't walked by. His jaw tightened. He turned to Devin. "Ah shut your mouth. I'm in no mood to listen to your blathering." He drew in a rush of air and walked off in the opposite direction of Hand.

His friends discussed Ainslie's feud among themselves.

"Doesn't take much to see the little weasel brings the worst out of our Scot," Gisis said.

Jigs nodded. "What else could explain it?"

None knew, but all felt certain another punch-up or worse would come.

"If I've ever seen murder in anyone's eyes, it's in theirs," Cecil commented.

The walk helped Ainslie calm down. *Gotta take it easy on me friends. Not their doing I'm tensed up. Gotta mend me ways.*

He returned to the fire and spoke to Devin. "Ho,' Dev, you're sending your medal home. Ya want help writin' the letter?"

Devin stared at Ainslie for the longest moment until Ainslie felt certain the Blackpoolian intended to reject the offer. He didn't, but instead gave a curt nod and said, "Kind of ya."

"Right then," Ainslie said. "I'm off to see about writing material."

The following morning, Saynsberry arrived at Ainslie's tent with quill, paper and a bronze inkwell. He held them out with a warning. "Treat this as gold and return it in the same condition."

"Ay, sergeant," a grateful Ainslie responded, and wondered how such fine paper and inkwell came into Saynsberry's position. "I' will."

"Good."

Ainslie followed Devin's lead and mailed his ribbon along with a letter to Mosstone. In it he detailed his trip to Stockholm, his training, the long marches and the recent battle.

The letter proved an unexpected surprise. The more Ainslie wrote, the more he felt a sense of release. Words tumbled onto the page. Penmanship suffered in his hurry to get them down, and from time to time he flexed his stiff fingers, then kept at it. He finished the letter and considered it. Who might read it to his grandparents? Most likely Duncan Carstarphen. He imagined them around the fireplace, discussing the letter's contents.

Finger and thumb stained, Ainslie enclosed the ribbon and signed off with, "My love to all of you. Until I see you next, Lee."

He found Saynsberry and handed over the writing material and the two letters.

Two weeks later, chilly winds swept the land. Rumors of winter plans spread through the camp.

Saynsberry, who filled in for Geiger, spoke to his men.

"King's heading southwest to the Rhine; plans to make the city of Mainz his winter quarters. Splitting his forces. A detachment's to stay behind."

"So, sergeant," Ainslie said, waving his finger around to his friends. "Are we part of the detachment leavin'?"

Saynsberry opened his mouth to answer but Ainslie pressed on. "Wouldn't mind having a look at one of those big German cities. Supposed to be somethin' to behold."

Saynsberry shook his head. "Sorry to disappoint you, lad, but 'afraid you're not going. We're off to Altenburg."

"Altenburg," Gisis repeated. "Wot's doin' in Altenburg, and why're we to be placed there?"

"You're asking the wrong man," Saynsberry said. "I'm following orders, and you're to follow them too. We're off to Altenburg."

Ainslie's mood worsened when he discovered Hand was part of their detachment.

He tried to work his way out of his state. Nothing to be done. He reminded himself to make the best of it and just stay out of Hand's way.

Devin commented on Ainslie's mood. "You should see your face," he said as the mile of soldiers and materials moved past on their southwest journey. "It's not the end of the world. Cheer up."

"Ay, but I wanted to go."

"Thought ya didn't like cities?"

"I don't, but I've heard a lot about German cities, so..."

"Aw, don't give it no mind. This Mainz, it's nothing' special, so I'm told. No need to mope about it."

"Wot's in it anyway?"

Cecil pointed to Devin. "He's right. Just a city on the Rhine."

"You mean with big churches, castles, taverns, and women?"

"It's generally how they come," Cecil said. He paused. "Wait. Altenburg's got churches, women and taverns. Won't be so bad. Better than sleeping in tents, come winter. Market town from what I hear. About thirty miles south of Leipzig. Do us fine." He gazed up at the sky. "Won't be long before snows come, you mark my words."

"Why not just bring us to Leipzig?" Cadman asked. "Bigger town; not far away, and probably more conveniences."

Cecil threw up his hands in resignation. "Nobody bothered to hash it out with me."

They broke camp and arrived in Altenburg as the sun set. Almost immediately following their arrival, the locals made it known they resented the new occupiers as much as the old.

Hard-headed Colonel Eloffson, who led the detachment, did little to endear himself or his troops. No sooner had they arrived than he evicted the town's sole nobleman, Baron Grawitz and his family, from their small castle overlooking the town. Proof positive, townsfolk griped, these Swedes were no better than Catholics. The Grawitz family has called the castle home for more than eighty years. Now the Swedes toss them out like dogs. Shameful.

Eloffson further raised the town's hackles when he announced he intended to billet the troops in citizens' homes without compensation.

The town fathers asked for an audience and tried to dissuade him. He wouldn't budge. "I need to house my troops," he said through his interpreter. "In war, sacrifices must be made. Yes, it costs the town something to have us here, but be thankful we've saved you from those vile Catholics."

Grumblings in the shops, market, and taverns increased.

"Them being here is bad for us," someone said. "There won't be enough food."

Others again took up the refrain the troops would make indecent advances toward the womenfolk.

Weeks after the troops arrived, opinion of Eloffson reached a new low when he nailed a notice of his new "exigent tax" to the massive town hall doors. "The tax," it read, "helps offset military expenditures for maintaining peace and order in and around Altenburg."

The townspeople despised the tax but the troops praised it. As a result, all received back pay. Their pay fast enough found its way back into the coffers of the local taverns and Frau Zumpt's house of prostitution, just outside the town walls.

Chapter 13

HOW'RE ya makin' out with your living arrangement?" a disgruntled Ainslie asked Paolo, as they drank in the tavern.

He cursed his bad luck for weeks now — stuck with a dour, corpulent grain merchant with foul breath named Viktor. At least the man's wife, Gabi, proved a treat for the eyes. He wondered what the old fool did to get her. It had to be money, he told himself. What else?

Paolo's eyebrows furrowed. "'Making out?' I am not understanding this question."

Ainslie laughed in reply and followed with a fast upward eye shrug. "It means is everything all right with the widow you're staying with."

"Ah. Si. Widow and the mama. Is good."

Paolo again considered his friend. He'd changed since Breitenfeld. Paolo couldn't quite name it, but knew the man sitting opposite him wasn't the same one who stepped off the ship at Peenemunde. Gifted with a natural ability to understand things others missed, Paolo saw the frequent blank, confused stares, the long bouts of brooding, the forced smiles, and the unexpressed pain hidden behind Ainslie's eyes. There is much hurt in Lee's heart, he told himself.

Twice he broached the topic of the battlefield; twice Ainslie changed the subject.

Paolo got the message.

"She a looker, the widow?" Ainslie asked with a grin, and brought Paolo out of his thoughts.

Palo played along and made a lewd face. "Bello! She arouses the desire." He held out cupped hands to imitate a man holding a woman's breasts. "She has much religion. She is praying all the time. It is not for me."

He set down his beer mug. "And you — you have the same in your house. You are making the sheep's eyes at her?"

Ainslie snorted. "The hen's young and comes with a whole set of problems wrapped in one fat husband. Hard to take, him; always bellyaching about his hardships since we come." He lifted his mug and poured more beer down his throat, wiped his mouth with his sleeve and said, "But ay, I suppose I do 'make sheep's eyes' at the wife."

"It holds the attention, does it not," Paolo said. "We have beautiful women, but not for us?"

"Ay," Ainslie agreed and smiled. "It does hold the attention. Maybe I can try out my German on her. 'Sie sind eine schone Frau.'" *You are a lovely woman.*

Ainslie would have asked for other arrangements earlier, if not for the pretty wife. The ill-humored merchant took every opportunity to make life irritating for his unwanted guest.

Mealtime were especially awkward. The merchant's main contributions to conversation were to bark at his wife and make sour comments.

Essen, nicht fressen — eat like a human, not like a pig, Ainslie thought, recalling the oft-used German insult. He watched with disdain as Viktor lowered his head and shoveled food into his mouth. *Doubt the pig's even chewin'. Even snorts like one.*

Viktor's wife jumped at her husband's every command. When seated she kept her eyes downward. On occasion Ainslie caught her sneak a glance his way. Twice he held her glance; she blushed and looked away.

But for the torturous snoring from behind the heavy drapes of the merchant's canopy, Ainslie might have slept well enough. The noise bothered him so much he finally pleaded for a different home. To no avail.

He avoided the house as much as possible. He spent much of his free time in the tavern. Stupefied from drink and exhaustion, he'd plod back to the house and manage to sleep through the merchant's rattling noise, as well as his ugly grunting when he furrowed into his wife.

"I'll slit the man's throat, I will, Podo," he warned his friend. "If I don't have me sleep, I'll kill him."

"The sergeant is finding you a new house?"

"Lieutenant now," Ainslie corrected him. "Been promoted, remember, since he took the musket ball."

"Lieutenant?" Paolo said and raised his eyebrows. "Is good."

"Ay, but wot I don't get, if he's crippled why're they keeping him on?"

"Maybe they hope he is getting better?"

"Ay, possible. Anyhow, I tried to talk to him about me arrangements. Not in the best of spirits since he took the ball. Says I'm fine where I am, and to consider m'self lucky to have a roof over me head."

One evening, when cold winds whistled down narrow lanes and into the market square, Viktor, Gabi and Ainslie sat down to dinner. Viktor's eyes moved from his plate and he tossed Ainslie a dismissive glance before he returned his attention to his food.

Moments later, Ainslie felt a foot rub his. At first he assumed it belonged to Viktor and drew his own back. The foot found him a second time. He glanced at Viktor, then over at Gabi, and found her wide, sky-blue eyes staring into his. She offered a speedy smile and returned her eyes to her plate.

Bewildered, Ainslie bunched up his forehead and returned to his meal. What was her game? She'd never been rude like her husband; then again, she never invited him into conversation or been overly friendly. Now this. It didn't make sense. Yet the touch excited him.

He cut into his sauerbraten and let his mind drift to her sensual mouth, lustrous yellow-brown hair, tiny body, and provocative hips. He felt himself getting excited.

Gabi cleared the plates and refilled Viktor's beer, but not Ainslie's. The merchant drained his goblet and set it down with a bang. He belched, rose, and made for bed. Gabi stood, followed her husband, and refused to meet Ainslie's eyes, even as she pulled the drapes around the canopy bed.

Ainslie endured sounds of coupling and muffled sobbing from behind the drapes of the canopy. He cursed himself for being in the room.

A week later the winds brought the first snow flurries. Snow or not, Ainslie decided he'd make for the tavern rather than spend another unpleasant evening with Viktor.

Gabi tossed logs into the fireplace and set the table as Viktor ranted about the needless presence of troops. Ainslie stared out at the dark lane and tried to disregard Viktor's claptrap. In turn, Viktor's voice rose. Ainslie noticed the spittle form at the edge of Viktor's mouth.

"You're all the same," the merchant insisted as he jabbed his finger in Ainslie's direction. "You and the Catholics; you both pick on innocent, hardworking Germans and bleed us dry."

Ainslie held his silence even as he imagined breaking Viktor's nose.

Halfway through his meal, while Gabi directed a forkful of meat to her mouth, Viktor ordered more bread.

"In a moment," Gabi said. "Let me finish this."

"Now," a stern-faced Viktor ordered and pounded the table.

Gabi jumped along with the cutlery. She set down her fork, took a deep breath, pushed her chair back and rose.

Ainslie listened as she fussed about before she returned.

They continued their meal. Nothing but the sound of cutlery against pewter plates came from the table. Then the next command. "More beer."

Shoulders drawn back, Gabi rose with slow deliberation, reached across Viktor and took his goblet. She moved to the beer barrel as Viktor sopped gravy with the heel of his bread.

Ainslie let his eyes follow Gabi as she bent over the barrel, lifted out the golden liquid and slid the tin back in place. He shifted his gaze to Viktor, almost finished with his meal, then to Gabi, who stood behind him. She pulled a small jute pouch from her apron pocket. In haste she shook something into Viktor's beer and stirred it with her forefinger. Her eyes met Ainslie.

"What's keeping you?" Viktor demanded, half turning in her direction.

"Coming," Gabi said, holding the goblet out over his shoulder, her hand trembling.

Viktor took the goblet and drank deeply. He held it at arm's length and gave it a long suspicious look. "Tastes queer," he said and made a face.

"Probably going," Gabi answered as she returned to the table. "Almost bottom of the barrel."

Viktor sniffed the liquid, took another drink and turned his attention to Ainslie.

"You think I'm blind," he accused Ainslie as his eyes narrowed. "I see you leering at my wife. Soldier or not, I catch you doing anything, anything improper, I'll shoot you like a dog. The law will be on my side."

Ainslie blinked several times, reddened in embarrassment and stared at his plate as Viktor brayed on. *Ay, it's so, but if you saw wot I saw, unless I guessed wrong, you're about to have a heap of trouble.*

Viktor wouldn't stop his rant. "It's not enough you eat my food and drink my beer — now you want my woman. You're all alike, you soldiers. Nothing good comes of you."

He's out of his mind, Ainslie thought, but not far from the truth about Gabi.

Viktor kept on. "Believe me; I'm onto your ways."

Ainslie gave him a dismissive wave and shook his head. Best not to say anything. What had she put into his beer?

Viktor turned his head to Gabi. "Cake."

Gabi took his plate and stood up.

Viktor returned to his bombastic rant. "Bah! I curse all of you. Nothing but trouble to our peaceful town. Worthless — the lot of you."

Ainslie's couldn't take it anymore. He met Viktor's gaze and glared back. "Ach, halt den mund!"

His jaw clenched. He watched and waited for a reaction. It arrived fast enough. "What! What did you say to me?"

No going back now, Ainslie told himself as Viktor tried to stare him down even as beads of sweat appeared on his crimson face.

Gabi intervened and set a large slice of cake in front of her husband.

"Don't want it," Viktor said.

The words spilled out almost with a thick tongue. He pushed the cake aside. "My face — it feels odd." The fingers of his right hand kneaded his cheek.

Gabi sat. Her eyes darted from Viktor to Ainslie. "Odd?" she repeated. How? It has to be the beer. Wait a bit; it will pass. Do you want a lie down?"

Viktor nodded but didn't move. She tried to help him to his feet, but his weight made it impossible.

Ainslie rose and came around the table. Together he and Gabi hefted the large and unsteady man by the elbows and guided him to the bed. They set him down and struggled to get him out of his clothes and into his nightshirt.

Gabi pulled back the featherbed cover while Ainslie hefted Viktor's legs and swung them onto the bed. He puffed from the exertion.

Viktor's speech grew slurred as he complained about numbness and tingling in his arms and feet. "My stomach hurts, and I have to use the toilet table, but I can't move. Get help. Hurry."

Gabi didn't move.

Ainslie stared down at Viktor's blue-gray face. "You've poisoned him," he hissed. His breath came hard and fast as his eyes widened. "How long have you planned this?"

Both stared down at the dying man. Eyes unfocused, Viktor issued soft moans of distress. Gabi pulled the drapes around the bed and beckoned Ainslie to follow her across the room.

"Answer me," Ainslie demanded. "How long have you planned this?" He gave her no chance to answer. "You could have done this when I was out, but now — now look, you've dragged me into it, and I had nothing to do with it."

He turned to the bed. "He's going to die."

"Yes, soon," Gabi whispered. "Please, please. Can I explain?"

"No. While you're explaining, he's dying. We have to get help." He turned to the door, but she ran forward and barred his way.

"Viktor's beyond help now — even if you find it."

Ainslie wouldn't listen. "They find out you poisoned him, they'll hang you — and what's more, me."

"No, no, please," she said as she moved closer. "They won't find out. You have nothing to worry about." She glanced at the bed before she spoke again. "He's beaten and raped me. I can't go on like this. One way or another, tonight everything has to change."

Ainslie couldn't find an appropriate response.

Gabi took control of the situation. "Close the shutters," she said, "and I'll tend to the fire."

As if someone else inhabited his body, a compliant Ainslie obeyed and returned to her side. She sat at the kitchen table and patted Viktor's chair. Ainslie obeyed.

Soft, plaintive moans came from behind the canopy drapes.

"Can you believe what I did?" she whispered.

Yes, probably. If her story was to be believed, one way or another Viktor would have sent her to an early grave. She simply beat him to it.

He rubbed his face with a hand and said, "From what I saw, couldn't figure you having any kind of life with him. What I'm mad at is you dragged me into this. What if I didn't agree?"

"I hoped you would. If you turn me in now, they'll hang me."

"Yes, but keep you forgetting mine will be the same fate, no matter what I say. No one will believe me. They'll think I was part of this."

"No one will suspect us," she assured him. "I've thought this through long and hard. They'll think Viktor died of a heart attack."

"Us?" an annoyed Ainslie spat. "It's us now? When did it become us? I didn't poison your husband. You did."

"Please calm yourself," she begged and offered him a soft smile. "You have no need to fear. All you have to do is leave and come back later — much later. When you do you must give a believable showing of a drunken soldier. The rest will fall into place."

Her argument sounded convincing. "Are you not curious about the powder?" Gabi asked.

Ainslie offered a fast shake of his head. "No. Don't want to know anything about it."

They listened to the crackling of the fire. Ainslie waited for her to decide what to do next. Instead, she complimented him on his German.

She's just poisoned her husband, he thought; and here she is making small talk with me. Fine, he'd go along — for now. No other logical plan of action made itself known.

"You think so?"

She nodded. "You are mostly foreign troops. We did not expect many of you to have our language."

"Not simple to learn," he said. "It's like English, but different. Easier than Swedish. I get confused sometimes, and have to sound things out a lot. I'm getting there."

"Yes, you are."

"Thanks. I'm told what we've been speaking is Low German."

"Plattdeutsch," she supplied.

He sounded out the word with care. "Can't wait to find out what High German's like."

"Not so hard. It's what most of the country, except the north, speaks."

"Huh. Anyway, I practice with a friend."

Neither heard further noises from behind the drapes. Their eyes met; as if by silent agreement, they moved to the bed. Gabi pulled back the drapes. Both stared down at the dead man, his eyes raised to the top of the canopy.

"Face is wrong, frightened," Ainslie said.

Gabi studied her husband. "You're right. We should do something." She climbed onto the bed beside Viktor and bent over the body. She worked her fingers to massage Viktor's face, raised herself to study her efforts and said, "There. I think he's better. Don't you?"

Ainslie offered a tepid agreement, unsure what Viktor should look like dead. "I suppose."

Gabi climbed down and again pulled the drapes around the bed. "Throw a few more logs in the fire," she said, "and come join me at the table again."

With a good flame in the fireplace, Gabi turned to Ainslie, "Here's what I think we should do."

Ainslie let her speak.

"Go to where you drink," she said, "and let people remember seeing you there. Me, I'll play the surprised widow who's found her husband dead. I'll call for help."

She stared into the fire for a moment before she said, "Don't show up for quite a while. We don't want people connecting any of this to you. And remember to look unsteady on your feet."

Ainslie couldn't remember when time hung so heavy on him. He sat with his friends, barely heard a word they said, and flinched every time the door to the tavern opened. Were they coming to arrest him?

The others tossed him occasional glances before they returned to their own conversations. They made allowances for his conduct, aware he wasn't one to chatter, but also recognized the change in him since Breitenfeld. He'd lost some of his moodiness and standoffishness, but the old Ainslie hadn't yet returned.

They decided to leave him be. Whatever bothered him, he'd sort it out.

Most of the regulars of the tavern left. Ainslie decided he'd stayed long enough. He rose, said farewell to the table and returned to the cottage, wobbling and hoping he looked convincing enough as a drunk.

A few neighbors milled about outside in the cold air. They shot hostile stares at him as he entered the cottage. Inside, two women and a pastor sat at the table and consoled a grief-stricken widow who did her best to present herself as an anguished widow.

All but Gabi turned their fixed gazes on the besotted intruder. He made a grand gesture of bowing and moved to the fire.

The grizzled pastor spoke with a screechy voice, "So sudden, Frau Hoffmeyer. I only just yesterday saw your husband in the Market Square. He looked in fine health."

Gabi continued to gaze into her lap as she wrung a kerchief.

The room remained quiet for a few long moments. The pastor spoke again. "Unseemly, Frau Hoffmeyer, for you to stay here by yourself with this...this intoxicated soldier. You should find somewhere else until we get another place for him."

Annoyance crept over Ainslie as he poked at the logs in the fireplace. *Are they dense? Can they not see I'm in the room — drunk or not? Unseemly? She poisons him, and you'd think I was the killer.*

Gabi swallowed, took in a breath of air and said, "Yes, a good suggestion, Pastor Schweissguth." She fixed her attention to the woman on her right. "Can I stay with you, Josefina?"

"But of course. We'll collect a few things and leave at once."

Ainslie watched Gabi move hurriedly around the cottage while her three companions let their feeling known to Ainslie with sour, disapproving facial expressions.

Moments later he found himself alone. He barred the door, moved to the bed and drew back the drapes. Gone. Someone took Viktor away. Only the indent of his body and the telltale sign of a soiled sheet were evidence of his recent presence.

"Won't say I liked ya, Viktor," he told to the empty room, "and Gabi would probably have come to a bad end at your hands. Maybe it's all for the best this way. Only God knows I've no blood on me hands over you."

Used to his nightly routine, he set down the three sheepskin rugs, shook a blanket over them, and placed two more thick ones over those. He readied himself for sleep. "Best I can tell," he whispered to the empty room, "our Frau Hoffmeyer's gettin' away with murder. At least I won't havta worry 'bout any of it landin' on me."

His last thoughts were of Gabi's body. Would he ever see it?

Grawitz Castle summoned Ainslie the following day. A deputation of Pastor Schweissguth and Gabi's family and in-laws pressed Colonel Eloffson to remove Ainslie from the cottage.

Their bad luck Eloffson disliked Germans in principle, and almost never agreed to any of the town's requests.

"She is young, comely and vulnerable, Colonel." Schweissguth said. "She cannot be left alone and taken advantage of by a soldier with baser needs.

"Come, come, you exaggerate," the ruddy-faced Eloffson said. "Have any of my soldiers raped any of your women? Have any of my soldiers stolen or murdered? The answer is no. Why would this man be any different?" He waved a hand toward Ainslie. "The widow is bereaved, so let her be comforted by your spiritual guidance. As for the rest, well, my dear Pastor, if she's as young and as pleasing to the eye as you say, who are we to stand in the way of nature? It behooves those two to work out their living arrangements, wouldn't you say?"

His audience jumped to its feet in righteous indignation. They left the Great Hall mumbling, crying, and vowing to write to the Swedish king.

Viktor's corpse lay on display in the cottage the following day, while Gabi received visitors and accepted condolences. Ainslie whiled away the day as best as he could before he returned to the cottage.

His friends teased him about his good fortune.

"She's a beauty," Cecil said. "You've got her all to yourself now, lucky dog."

Jigs agreed. "As close to heaven as you'll ever get with the likes of her. Be daft not to have a go. I'd no let the chance pass me by."

Devin offered his opinion. "Fine thing, she is. I'd hurry her into bed to..."

Cecil cut in. "What happened to your morals, Dev? Thought you'd disapprove."

"God bears our imperfections," Devin shot back, "but asks us to strive for better."

"Listen to you," Jigs said. "In the end you're no better'n the rest of us —happy to play 'bury the bishop' with the ladies."

They carried on at Ainslie's expense. Later he and Paolo discussed his situation in private.

"She will invite you to her bed soon?" Paolo asked.

"No idea," Ainslie said. "And listen, wot of you? How're you making out with your widow, um, wot's her name?"

"Jutta."

"Fine-soundin'. You making any headway?"

"We had our first kiss."

"Oho! Was it lovely?"

"Si. She gives a pleasure."

"You dog, you."

Ainslie asked for more details. Paolo threw up his hands to suggest lack of progress.

Ainslie didn't know what to expect from Gabi. The first few days after the funeral she received numerous visitors and kept him at arm's length. On the fourth day, Gabi prepared the evening meal. Neither cared to mention Viktor. They ate without hurry and told each other stories of their past.

A week later, Gabi took Ainslie to her bed.

Chapter 14

HAS *the Blessed Lord abandoned us and our cause?* Fra Hippolito Costello asked himself as he hurried to the church in the little town of Saint Leonhard.

The cold wind tugged at the Dominican's black mantle and blew his hood against his neck. He shivered as he arrived at the thick oak door of the old Franciscan church once known as Saint Basil, and hurried inside.

Inside the narthex Hippolito caught his breath, grateful to be out of the wind. He stood still and let the life principle of the church speak to him. Could he feel it — the presence of holiness, of priests and churchgoers past, feel their piety as they worshipped in the bosom of the Holy Mother Church, representing God on earth?

He thought he could, and inhaled deeply. God be praised, the little church had been returned to its rightful possessor. Only yesterday Hippolito re-consecrated it and said mass. Few of the locals showed up. In time the faithful would return.

Comforted by his conviction, Hippolito stepped into the nave, prepared to endure the desecration his eyes beheld earlier. Why had these loathsome Protestants brought so much infamy to God's House, he asked himself? He shook his head in profound dismay as his eyes found the outlines where statues of the saints and the Blessed Virgin Mary once stood.

Idolatry, these Protestants called it; idol-worshipping. With glee they smashed all representations of Blessed Jesus, his mother Mary, Joseph, and the saints. Did defiling God's sacred images bring these transgressors closer to God? No. They failed on every level and only managed to deprive God's church on earth of its full sacred character.

Hippolito moved to the center aisle, knelt, and crossed himself before he took a seat in one of the pews. His mind returned to these so-called champions of the Reformation. In rejecting the magnificent mysteries of God, the best they could manage was to splinter, unable to agree with even each other.

He snorted his contempt. Luther, Calvin, Zwingli — false prophets, all; and none able to lead their flock closer to the Divine. Malicious destruction coupled with harsh and unfair judgments was the legacy of these reformers. Topple statues and destroy paintings, spiritual tools to tell stories to the ignorant and gave solace to the brave of heart. Holy Mother Church in her wisdom made them part of a judicious ecclesiastical tradition.

Hippolito bowed his head, reached for the rosary around his waist and kissed the beads. He crossed himself and started with the Apostles' Creed, then he moved on to Our Father, Hail Mary and Glory be to the Father.

With repetitious veneration, Hippolito worked his way through each decade of the string of beads.

His devotions finished, the small-shouldered priest with the closely-trimmed beard stood, crossed himself and returned to the question of whether the Lord had abandoned them.

He considered the evidence as he scratched at a small rash at his groin. Things hadn't gone well of late, true, but Almighty God had a plan, and Hippolito believed it would reveal itself soon enough.

He heard grumblings around the Imperialist camp questioning the Grand Count under Tilly's leadership. He dismissed these talk as defeatist. *I, Hippolito Costello*, he chastised himself, *indulge in such defeatism whenever I wonder if the Almighty has forsaken us.*

He reminded himself all must remain steadfast in the Faith. Setbacks should be expected from time to time, but God is ever truehearted and would never lead Catholic Forces to real defeat.

The last of three children, Hippolito arrived in the world twenty-four years earlier in Oviedo, Asturias. His parents, Miguel and Teresita Costello, enjoyed the boy's keen mind and firmness of purpose. Yet they also sensed intensity and an offensive boldness. It in turn resulted in more than a few bloodied noses for Hippolito during his childhood.

"He has spirit, Teresita," Hippolito's father once commented to his wife as she pressed a damp cloth to Hippolito's bleeding nose.

"Spirit," the senior Costello later went on to say after Hippolito left the room, "but unlike Alejandro, he lacks the muscle to back it."

"True," Dona Costello whispered. "He is our son, and has an intensity one so young should not have. I sometimes wonder if he really enjoys life."

The senior Costello had held a prestigious position at the university. Hippolito's mother volunteered in the Parish Council. Both were highly devout Catholics.

Hippolito's oldest brother, Alejandro, whom he worshipped, left home at eighteen to join Philip IV's army in the German lands. His sister, Iniz, took Holy Orders with the Carmelites.

"I've often asked myself if joining the army would be good for Hippolito," Miguel said to his wife, "but then I think maybe there's something else in store for him."

"Yes, and what, husband?" Teresita asked. A thought came to her. "Do you think the priesthood holds any interest for him? He has a fine heart and a good mind. It might suit him."

Don Costello admitted the idea had certain logic. The Church: why not? The last child, Hippolito had no prospect of inheriting anything, and given his disposition, service to the Church might well be an excellent career choice.

To both his parents' surprise, Hippolito didn't reject the idea, and even admitted he'd narrowed his career path to administration in South America, or Holy Orders. He at last selected Holy Orders. On his father's advice he chose the *Society of Jesus*. He enjoyed the classes and the tutors, but failed to fit in well with the other students. Something about his bearing annoyed them. They often played mischievous pranks on him.

It proved too much for Hippolito. Twice he approached the Monsignor of the seminary and begged to be released, convinced a different calling might be for him. Twice the good-hearted priest listened to his novice and kept him from a rash decision.

"Do try to get along with others," he advised, well aware of criticisms leveled against Hippolito. "Give the other students the chance to see the real you, and above all, try to see their points of view. Do so, and they will soon enough find you to a pleasant companion."

A good idea, thought Hippolito, yet aware the deed would prove more demanding than the intent. "I'll try, Monsignor," he promised and left the room.

He did try and had a small measure of success, but could never quite check his dominating ways.

An unexpected surprise awaited him: he fell in love. He hadn't anticipated it, but had had enough life experience to realize no one chose to fall in love. It happened, but until then, not to him. He'd watched others — his brother, Alejandro, for example — rise to love's glorious heights, only to later crash in despair.

The handsome yet frail-looking visiting tutor, Alberto de Gongora, turned on the charm with Hippolito, using flattery to its fullest advantage. His fingers did light, furtive dances over Hippolito's arms whenever he stood close. A soft touch here, a quick stroke there — all intended to seduce the young novice.

Hippolito basked in the attention and the positive feelings toward him. He hungrily absorbed and savored every moment of the tutor's company.

The affair ended almost as fast as it began. The tutor grew tired of the novice and turned his attention elsewhere. A confused and crestfallen Hippolito sought to find an explanation — any explanation — for this sudden rejection.

Students arrived one afternoon for Latin class, only to discover a Brother at the front of the room in place of the tutor. He made no mention of the lay tutor, and inquired about their last lesson. When someone dared to ask after the tutor, he simply said, "Senor de Gongora has taken a sudden leave from this seminary."

A disconsolate Hippolito fell behind in his studies. He made frenetic efforts to locate his lover. All were useless; it seemed the earth had swallowed Alberto de Gongora.

When another student made a cutting remark about Hippolito's affair, he charged. The two traded punches until the floor monitor rushed in and pulled them apart.

Once again, Hippolito found himself in the Monsignor's office.

An exasperated Father Munoz felt torn between disciplining and consoling him, and chose to steer clear of the well-known affair. Munoz spoke about Hippolito's "loss of friendship" and directed the unhappy novice's attention to the future.

For weeks thereafter, Hippolito played his sudden loss of de Gongora over and over in his mind. *Gone like a puff. One day Alberto is here, the next day he's fled somewhere, and I'm stuck with nothing but memories.*

He couldn't have known de Gongora left him with more than memories. Deep within Hippolito's body, a silent battle raged—pitting tiny, unseen-to-the-eye invaders against ever-on-guard natural defenders. The invaders brought their poison. The defenders countered and attempted to suffocate them. Neither side gave at first, but bit by bit the invaders overpowered the defenders and claimed the first round.

A SOLDIER FAR AWAY

Hippolito came down with a severe fever. Six days later he awoke in the infirmary, several pounds lighter.

He returned to his studies and noticed the small aches in his body, along with the arrival of sores around his mouth.

Slowly, Hippolito reconciled himself to the loss of Alberto, but his battered mental state soon wrestled with shame and guilt — in equal measure. He professed his remorse at weekly confessions. He vowed never to give in to baser needs again. In penance he made himself say silent prayers on the cold marble floor of the chapel.

His confessors reminded him his God was a forgiving God. If the Almighty could offer the magnanimous gift of forgiveness, who was he, a mere mortal, to ignore it?

Hippolito heard but did not heed. Perhaps he needed a more demanding Order, he thought; one with the strictest discipline over all his actions, and bring him to deeds worthy of redemption.

It took time, but he searched and at last narrowed his choice to the Dominican Order.

In audience with the Monsignor of the seminary, Hippolito again begged his release.

"It's clear, my son," Father Munoz said, "you wish a different Order, but tell me — why the Dominicans?"

"God calls me to it, Holy Father," Hippolito responded.

Munoz doubted the claim and waited for more, but nothing further came. He held a deep disdain for the Friars — preachers, torturers whose reputation damaged the good, pure name of the Church.

With his voice low and calm, Munoz did his best to talk Hippolito out of joining the Dominicans. Hippolito would not be swayed.

Father Munoz listened and resisted the urge to shake his head in dismay. Join them, Munoz thought as Hippolito took his leave. Join those torturers who bring dishonor to our Holy Mother Church. Join the Hounds of the Lord, if you like, but you may regret this decision for the rest of your life.

Shaped by loss and a measure of continued self-loathing, Hippolito took his place in the new seminary. He ate only enough to sustain himself, wore his hair short and scrubbed the hall and dining room tiles for a month after his arrival. In spite of his self-mortification, shame remained with him.

A new father-confessor offered Hippolito a ray of hope to salvation.

"The oil of good deeds," he told Hippolito, "can, in the right circumstances, make the unclean, clean. Seek out what God favours."

Encouraged by those words, Hippolito wondered what deeds might redeem him in God's eyes.

By chance, his own father soon provided the answer. At a family dinner he said, "You'll be ordained in two years. I've heard Philip IV's soldiers are enjoying victories over the heretics in the north. If such a thing interests you, perhaps I can put in a good word for you with the Archbishop, to join them when the time comes."

Hippolito nodded as he swallowed. "It does interest me, papa."

"Excellent," the senior Costello said as he sliced into the fish on his plate. "A stint as a chaplain with the Catholic League will give you world experience, and who knows, it might even help you move up in the ranks of the Church."

Hippolito acknowledged the comment with a fast nod. The idea of joining his brother appealed to him more than his father knew. He believed Protestantism to be the work of the antichrist. It had to be ground into the dust, and he could be a part of bringing it about. The Lord God needed help in the destruction of the iniquitous.

"You are a true messenger of God, papa," an excited Hippolito said. "I think serving our troops may well be my destiny."

Two years passed.

Hippolito reminded the senior Costello of the earlier promise to speak to the Archbishop. Several weeks later the newly ordained Father Costello received an invitation from Grand Field Marshal Tilly — with one condition. The Field Marshal insisted all of his chaplains undertake a study of languages, particularly Flemish, Tilly's Belgian-Dutch language.

Eager to be in the army, Hippolito applied himself with energy to his new task. In addition to studying German and Flemish, which he enjoyed, he had to study English, which he found difficult.

"Why," he asked his tutor, "do I need to learn English?"

"For many reasons," his teacher replied. "One is we have Irish, Scotsmen, and Englanders who serve under our banner. It will be useful for you to speak to them in their language."

Hippolito couldn't find fault with the reasoning.

Father Eugenio Ordóñez stopped at Hippolito's cell as he packed.

A SOLDIER FAR AWAY

"We wish you well, Father Costello." He studied the young priest before him. "A new calling awaits you. Our work of combating heretical perversity will still be here when you return. Until then, we will take pride one of ours rides with our glorious troops. I have every confidence Catholicism will triumph in this war against Protestant impurity, and you will be part of the victory. Now, bend your knees and I will give you a blessing."

Hippolito obeyed.

Ordóñez raised his hand over Hippolito, made the sign of the cross and said, "The Blessed Lord protect you in your work of the destruction of those who follow a false idol. We pray for your safety and anticipate your eager return."

He again made the sign of the cross and commanded Hippolito to rise.

"Thank you, Monsignor," a humbled Hippolito said, as he shoved the last of his belongings into his canvas bag. "I promise to make you proud of me."

"Hmm, yes, of course," the aged man said, his mind already elsewhere.

Three months later Hippolito and his parents stood beside a caravan readying to head to Count Tilly's headquarters.

Hippolito couldn't wait to get going. He imagined great deeds for himself, and good conversations with Alejandro.

"You'll go far," Don Costello promised his son, as they waited for the escort to arrive. "Rome keeps a close eye on the war. Make us proud."

"I will, papa," Hippolito responded. He wished his parents a final farewell and hurried to climb next to the wagoner. A company of hussars moved to the front of the caravan. A moment later they rode off, followed by the lead wagon. Hippolito's mother wiped her eyes as his father shouted, "Keep an eye out for your brother."

Reality clashed with Hippolito's fantasies fast enough. Morale suffered as the Catholic League staggered from loss to loss. No one remembered when the desertion rate ran so high.

Tilly's camp grew tense and agitated. Even Hippolito's generally unperturbed brother drank and cursed too much.

"I don't know what we need to do to drive those dogs back into the North Sea," he said as they sat in his tent at their last meeting.

A well-intended Hippolito sought to cheer his brother's spirit. "Keep a good heart, Alejandro; things will get better. They're bound to. God wills it."

"Grow up," his brother spat out in reply.

Unprepared for the sudden and explosive outburst, Hippolito jumped.

Alejandro wouldn't meet his brother's eyes and glowered at the ground.

He's changed, Hippolito thought, wounded by the crushing and unexpected remark. They had always been close; they never kept secrets from each other, and rarely spoke an unkind word. Now this.

He took his time and studied his brother's face. Why hadn't he noticed the restive eyes, the deeper vertical lines between Alejandro's brows, skin washed-out, pale? And Alejandro's disposition — when did he become so snappish?

Unable to find the proper words to console, Hippolito blinked several times. Then he rose, patted his brother on the shoulder and left Alejandro's tent.

Eight days later Alejandro died in a run-in with Protestant hussars. When Catholic troops retrieved the fallen and returned them back to camp, someone recognized Alejandro's body and sent for Father Costello.

Hippolito gaped with open mouth at the ashen-colored, stiffening corpse of Lieutenant Alejandro Costello. He noted his lips had drawn back in a grisly half-smile and no longer held their natural color, but a hue of blue. Already a thin, cloudy coating slicked his unseeing eyes.

Hippolito reminded himself to breathe. He moved closer and spotted the hole at the side of Alejandro's neck. Caked blood surrounded it. *He's dead. My dear brother, my friend, Alejandro is dead.*

He fell to his knees beside the corpse, bowed his head, clasped his hands and murmured, "Grant him eternal rest, O Lord, and let Your Perpetual Light shine upon him. May the soul of the faithfully departed, your servant, Alejandro Javier Costello, rest in peace through the mercy of God. Amen."

He made the sign of the cross over his brother's body, rose and allowed himself a final look at the shell of his brother, Alejandro. Hippolito turned and went off in search of Father Wouters.

Two days later Hippolito accompanied the wagon as it carried the hurriedly assembled casket of Alejandro to Oviedo. Lost in his gloomy thoughts, he barely remembered the trip home.

His mother came out of the house when she heard the wagon and two riders pull up. Her eyes darted from Hippolito to the wagon and back. With an open palm pressed to her chest, she hurried and peered inside. Her eyes widened as Hippolito climbed down. Her hands flew to her face and she shook her head. Hippolito threw an arm around her and guided her back into the house.

He sent a servant to fetch Miguel Costello. His father surprised him when he caught sight of the coffin; normally the elder was overly concerned with proper decorum, but now he issued a loud cry and pulled at his hair.

"No, No. This cannot be. No."

The family summoned Hippolito's sister, Inez, home from the convent. Neither she nor her brother could comfort Miguel Costello. At the Requiem Mass he collapsed in the front pew. Men hastened to his aid while a startled priest and church dignitaries looked on.

Miguel later returned to the church, held up by Inez on one side and Hippolito on the other.

At the graveyard, he again collapsed.

Inez volunteered to escort her father home while Hippolito and his mother remained behind.

The senior Costello worsened.

"I've never seen him like this, brother," Inez said to Hippolito in a private moment. "He was always the strong one. I understand grief, but I cannot understand the level of papa's despair. It seems..." she struggled to find a word. "I don't wish to be insensitive, but it seems, almost out of proportion. Mama grieves, but nothing like this."

Hippolito nodded his agreement. "Yes, but remember Alejandro was always papa's favorite. Always. He tried to hide it, you recall, but we always knew."

Miguel Costello refused all comfort. At night, when fitful sleep finally claimed him, he called out his dead son's name. During the day he sat on a bench beside the house, warmed by the sun, and stared out toward the sea, imprisoned by his grief. And so they found him — collapsed on the ground, a spilled bowl of yogurt and peppers at his feet.

Three days later the remainder of the Costello family held a second funeral.

Hippolito stayed behind for another week before he announced his intent to return to his duties.

"Will you be all right, Inez?" he asked.

She stepped closer and peered into his face.

"I will be fine. So will Mama. I'll find her a room in the convent. She will be fine too. You can visit us any time you like." She stopped for a moment before she continued, "I must say, you don't look well. Are you...well?"

"Nothing to worry about," he assured her. "The strain of all everything during this last little while. I'll write to you in a few weeks and let you know how and what I'm doing."

Two days later Hippolito took a coach to Barcelona where he joined a supply column on its way to Tilly's camp.

Did the Almighty God take Alejandro's life because of my actions, he asked himself? Is Alejandro's death on my hands? He shifted on the wagon bench, his mind fluttering between his father and brother. He recalled a story Alejandro once told the family.

"You'd think I had some magic power. My comrades like to ride close to me. They believe I'm protected by a shield, able to deflect musket balls."

The story finished, Alejandro set down his goblet and chuckled at the image while the rest of his family smiled with pleasure at the warrior who made everyone so proud.

A long, suffering sigh escaped Hippolito. The wagon driver stared at him.

He tried not to fidget on the hard wooden bench, but the itch bothered him. Not the first, but this time it established itself around his bottom. Maddening! He longed to scratch, but he didn't want to draw attention to himself.

The supply column at last arrived in camp. A stiff, sore Hippolito climbed down, grateful to be on his feet again. He didn't know how he survived the trip, especially traveling with the unpleasant wagoner.

He borrowed a small mirror, returned to his room and flopped on his bed. He gave himself a careful inspection and saw the angry rash. Worse, he couldn't believe what his eyes observed — ugly, small, flesh-colored anal warts.

He stared in horror at this malady.

Chapter 15

Count Tilly's forces regrouped. Spanish reinforcements insured his army remained formidable. The setbacks didn't trouble him too much. In war battles were won and lost, and soldiers died. Understandable and to be expected, this warp and woof of life.

He accepted setbacks, but financing—an entirely different matter. He needed money, and lots of it, to purchase supplies and to pay his troops. The emperor either failed to understand this or thought it of no consequence.

For the past several weeks Tilly sent dispatch after dispatch to Vienna and begged for more funds. A long time passed before he received a reply.

"We have your letter at hand, good Count Tilly," the emperor wrote. "We call on you to do your best for the time being."

The letter went on to assure him he remained foremost in the emperor's thoughts and prayers. "We engage in urgent meetings with our most excellent cousin, Philip of Spain, and His Holiness, Pope Urban. Both are aware of your financial plight. Both assure Our ambassador they will do their best to find additional monies."

Tilly snorted his displeasure. 'Aware of my financial plight?' How long have I complained to all three, and for what? I don't see any mule wagons laden with silver and gold.

He read on. "Even so, Philip is weighed down by the loss of the Netherlands, and Pope Urban points to the Plague on the Italian Peninsula."

Tilly paused and glanced up from the letter. *Puffs of air. Nothing but puffs of air. I cannot fight and win this war on good wishes.*

He shook his head and returned to the last of the letter. "Take heart," the emperor advised, "and as always do your best. God will provide."

Tilly crumpled the letter into the brazier. "God may provide," he muttered to an emperor hundreds of miles away, "but He needs a little help from you."

Out of nervousness, Tilly stroked his closely cut and oiled beard. If the emperor didn't send him what he needed, victory would go to the enemy. *I sit on the field of battle. I fight Ferdinand's war, and all I get is this.*

He squeezed his eyes shut as if to block out the abrasions of life. There's little to *be gained by feeling sorry for myself.*

He rose and pulled his thick fleece-lined coat around his neckpiece ruff. It grew colder every day. He'd have to find shelter soon. If he didn't, the troops would freeze. But what would he do about food and supplies?

No answer presented itself. Somehow he'd try to manage and hold on until spring. By then the emperor might come to his senses. Full coffers would allow Tilly to mount a major counter-offense against Gustavus.

Again Tilly played with his beard. His eyes moved to the map on his desk. With full concentration he bent forward and stared at the markings of the front lines. His gaze settled on something — a small city, *Rothenberg on the Tauber.* It appeared sizable enough and not far away. He searched his memory. Who held Rothenberg?

Tilly turned and bellowed. "Wecelo."

A moment later his adjutant, the low-set Captain Wecelo von Durin, rushed into the tent. Tilly took in his assistant's dark-spotted doublet sleeves with their wide openings, red velvet breeches and boots with generous fold-over cuffs his assistant. *He may be fat, but he's always better dressed than me.*

He stared at the man's girth. Hoarding had to be the only explanation for Wecelo's condition— especially when everyone else scraped about for food. *Ah well, let him be. It isn't worth the bother to say anything. He has his faults, but he's loyal, competent, and makes me laugh.*

"Herr General," von Durin said, as his superior continued to study the map. "You called me?"

"I did, Wecelo. What do we know about Rothenberg?"

Von Durin thought for a moment, and then replied, "Not much, sire, other than it holds a Protestant garrison."

"How many?"

"I cannot say."

"Then send men to find out and come back and say. I want to know who's there and what strength they have."

"Of course, Herr General," von Durin responded. "I'll send scouts immediately." He turned and rushed off.

By eventide he stood back in front of his superior, who cut into the last of his boudin sausage.

Tilly's eyes rose as he chewed, swallowed, and dabbed his mouth with a table napkin. "Well?"

"Herr General," von Durin said; "the city is, as we suspected, defended by a small contingent of Swedish soldiers. Not enough to cause us concern if your intent is to take it."

Tilly reached for his goblet of wine. "'How many?"

"A local woodcutter puts them at around sixty. Light horse cavalry, commanded by Conrad von Ritenberg.

Tilly allowed himself a brief smile as he thought on von Durin's words. "Hmm. Very good. Sixty men can only be for show. The Swede doesn't think the city's important enough to defend. Not important to us either, other than shelter." He ran a finger around the rim of his goblet. The hint of a smile came to the Field Marshal's face. "We'll take it and tweak the Swede's nose in the bargain."

"Very good, Herr General. I'm certain you have a sensible plan."

Tilly dismissed the empty compliment with a wave of his hand and considered the situation further. Reports had the Swedes settled down in Mainz for the winter. Word of Rothenberg's fall would put him in a foul mood, but Tilly doubted Gustavus would risk his troops if cold and snow appeared early, as they might.

The more Tilly thought about it, the more he liked the idea. He had everything to gain and nothing to lose. He returned his gaze to his assistant and said, "Call my generals."

"At once, my Lord."

Tilly watched Von Durin leave the tent. One problem solved. Now for the next.

Everyone in the Catholic camp delighted in the sudden shift from chilling cold to sweltering heat. Has to be a sign, the Spanish troops said. We fight better in warm weather.

Rumor tore through the camp they'd soon be on the move.

In his tent, the highly devout Tilly reconsidered taking Rothenberg. Maybe Gustavus would send troops to repel Catholic advances.

An hour at prayer brought him back to his original position. He crossed himself, kissed his beads, thanked God for these welcoming conditions, and climbed to his feet. The Lord Jesus had answered his prayers. *I worried we'd have to tramp through snow, and here God provides. No, the Swede has settled in. Excellent chance he won't challenge us.*

He gave Count Pappenheim the task of taking the city. "You shouldn't need more than half a dozen field pieces, Gottfried. If Rothenberg fails to surrender, you know what to do?"

"Of course."

"I'll join you shortly. You think they'll put up a fight?"

"Not if they're as small as you say."

"Good, but take enough men for the assault. Oh, and ladders to scale the walls."

"Sound idea," Pappenheim said, as he fussed with his sword belt.

Heavy horses pulled cannons along the Tauber Valley as Pappenheim followed the river and arrived at the city gates on a balmy morning.

Guards around the city walls spotted the Catholic invaders and sounded the alarm. Within moments church bells pealed the call to arms. Soldiers rushed to bar the city gates.

Von Ritenberg and his men hurried up the stairs to see the enemy unhitch its siege cannons.

"God Almighty," a defender shouted and pointed to enemy soldiers pushing, pulling and guiding the heavy artillery piece in place.

"We're in for it," the hardened campaigner, von Ritenberg said, as he stared at the enemy.

"Don't worry, sire," a captain of the local militia said. "We have seven hundred men, plus your men. We can hold."

Von Ritenberg rewarded him with a dismissive glance. *Fool.*

A solitary rider bearing a white flag rode up the hill and stopped twenty yards from the city gate.

"State your business," the burgomaster shouted from the parapet.

Disdain appeared on the rider's face. He turned behind him to the cannons, then back up at the parapet. "You jest, Mein Herr, no?" he called out. "Unconditional surrender. Do so and no one will be hurt. Refuse and suffer what follows."

"Impossible," the scrawny, wrinkled burgomaster shouted back.

"This is your final word," the rider asked?

"It is."

"Then accept the same fate as Magdeburg. You did hear of what happened, did you not?" He didn't wait for an answer. "Explain it to those who expect better judgment from you."

Earlier in the campaign Catholic forces overran Magdeburg. They slaughtered, raped and looted the town. Those who survived watched as Catholic forces torched the city.

The messenger turned his horse and cantered back to his lines.

Von Ritenberg stared at the burgomaster. "You put everyone in peril with your foolish bluster," he growled, yet never took his eyes off the rider. "Magdeburg? Does the word mean nothing to you? It's not too late to change your mind."

"No," the defiant old man spat. "Never. We will not give in to the unrighteous. We take a firm stand. Better the city burn."

Von Ritenberg squeezed his eyes shut, opened them, and muttered, "Age doesn't protect a man against foolishness."

Big Felix, the invader's massive cannon, boomed with its first launch. Catholic soldiers cheered as the cannonball fell short of the main wall.

"They're finding their aim," Ritenberg said to those nearby. "Bit of guesswork for the moment, but not for long."

Five shots later, a projectile flew over the stone wall and hit the Roderturm Tower. Those crouched on the walkway turned to see where it landed. Fear and awe swept through them as bits of the tower flew into the air.

Other Catholic League cannons opened up beside Big Felix. As fast as they started they fell silent.

With caution the Protestant defenders on the walkway raised their heads.

"What are they doing?" the aged burgomaster shouted up the steps.

"Repositioning their cannons," Ritenberg hollered down. "My guess is they've found something." He removed his helmet, ran his fingers through his hair and stared across the field at the cannons. "We had our chance," he told his lieutenant. "There is no dignity in being dead."

Shelling resumed, this time targeting the northeast corner of the granite wall. Large pieces tore away and tumbled into the moat; bit by bit holes appeared.

"It's only a matter of time before the whole thing crumbles," von Ritenberg bellowed.

By sundown, a third of the corner wall and the adjacent parapet were gone, but the enemy stilled his cannons again.

Night fell as the defenders finalized their strategy. The enemy would breach the gaping hole, everyone agreed.

At first light cannon fire resumed. Women moaned and prayed; children cried, and men waited for the inevitable assault.

Moments later the barrage ceased. All remained quiet on both sides until a cry arose from the Catholic invaders. It floated over to the city. *"Jesu-Maria. Jesu-Maria."*

The defenders raised their heads to see a wave of foot soldiers rush the northeast corner. They hurried down the dry moat with ladders and scaled the city wall, only to meet an annihilating fire from the city militia and von Ritenberg's men.

Women and boys joined the defenders with slingshots and stones. The few enemy soldiers who dodged those missiles and climbed the rubble still faced musket balls and more.

Try as he might Pappenheim could not take the city; an uncountable number of his soldiers lay dead or dying in the moat or at the opening in the wall. He sent for reinforcements.

The defenders passed another quiet night and wondered what the morrow would bring.

"Think they'll quit?" a young militiaman asked his sergeant. "I mean, they saw what we did to them."

"It'd be nice," an old hand said, "but don't count on it."

Mid-morning the next day the city's defenders stared across the walls at hundreds of Catholic soldiers, ready for another assault. Once more Catholic forces sounded the battle cry; once more they charged toward their prize.

Men with ladders rushed ahead of the musketeers who aimed their weapons up at the walls. Others attempted to scurry across the rubble. More than thirty men made it through, only to meet the stiffest resistance yet. Protestant soldiers, militia, women, children and even dogs attacked them.

One invader crossed the rubble only to lose his footing. A dog bit his leg as a sharp stone caught and tore the skin beneath his eye. Women and children surrounded the prone man; they kicked, hit, bit and stabbed him to a painful death.

The defenders fought well. Pappenheim again pulled his troops back. Taunts rose from those gathered atop the wall.

A hurried meeting was held in the city hall. The room was packed with scores of citizens who listened to speeches about their noble efforts at holding back the enemy. A cannon's boom interrupted a councillor's speech. Everyone crouched on instinct only to hear an earsplitting explosion. All rushed into the street, pushing and shoving, to locate the source of the noise.

A cannonball struck the tower of the exterior wall, the repository for the city's gunpowder. It grew into a massive orange fireball. The force threw the thick double gate doors outward and sent fiery debris into the sky. Three adjacent houses went up in flames. Thick, black smoke followed the violent release, and as the air began to clear, a greater horror was revealed: a hole — a huge, gaping hole in the city wall.

Raucous cheering beyond the city wall reached the defenders.

"Lord in His Mercy," a councillor moaned. "We're finished."

A bucket brigade ran to snuff out the fires, even as more cannon balls pounded the wall.

Not long after, a Catholic League lieutenant spotted a white flag being hoisted above the main gate. By nightfall Catholic Forces roamed freely throughout the city, a boyish-looking Dominican priest among them.

The victors allowed von Ritenberg to leave unharmed. The Prussian offered a stiff, short bow and mounted his horse. In perfect military formation he and his men rode out the main gate.

Tilly watched them depart while his own soldiers raced down twisting lanes and into timbered, gabled houses to seek the spoils and find their pleasures. They pillaged and raped at will. An indifferent Tilly beckoned his aide.

"Sire?"

"Wecelo, seize and execute the city fathers. We need to make an example. They had their chance and dared to thumb their noses at us. Hang them in the public square."

Random citizens were pressed into service to build scaffolding.

A last-moment change of heart saved the city fathers from the noose. Still, Rothenberg paid dearly for its insolence. Tilly imposed a heavy taxation on the citizens and seized the granary and every source of available food.

By the time his forces left, hundreds perished from cold and starvation.

An ecstatic Hippolito fell to his knees and delivered a short prayer of praise to Almighty God. At last — victory; the forces of righteousness had triumphed.

He rose, aware the taking of Rothenberg was only a small success. But still, one success would build upon the next. In the end they would triumph over all iniquitous forces.

He wished Alejandro was alive to see it. Alejandro —his beloved Alejandro, whom he worshipped since childhood, how he would have laughed and reveled in this victory.

The memory of his brother brought on an ache. Hippolito sniffled, wiped his eye, and forced himself to think of something else. Work; he knew there'd be much work ahead. Soon the small band of priests would start re-consecrating churches. He hoped he might be given an honorable role in the makeover.

He sat, crossed his legs, winced and rose again at the pain of an open sore in his genital area. Something inside was wrong. Had been for some time, but he couldn't bring himself to go to the infirmary. The mere thought of it frightened him.

He exhaled and decided he'd go for a stroll. A chance encounter with Captain von Durin near the Town Hall made Hippolito forget about his malady.

"Father Costello," the captain said, "what a fortuitous run-in. I was coming to find you."

"You were?" an excited Hippolito replied, waiting to hear what came next. "How can I help you?"

"Yes...the Field Marshal remembers your brother who died valiantly for our cause. In memory of him, I am to extend to you a noble charge—the task of restoring the true faith to Rothenberg 'by all means possible.' Are you up to the task?"

Hippolito could barely believe the words. Him? Nine other priests and Tilly chose him. If not for his sores, life would be perfect. He sought to put the sores out of his mind and focus on von Durin's words — "by all means possible." It could only mean complete freedom to act as he pleased.

"So, Herr Captain, do I understand correctly I am to return the true faith to this city — *with full freedom*?"

Von Durin acknowledged the question with a slow nod. In turn Hippolito bowed. "Please thank our glorious Field Marshal, Herr Captain. I will do everything in my power to make the wrong right."

His peers peers offered congratulations, yet none silently approved. All felt the Field Marshal's selection would result in a bad end. Hippolito's too dictatorial, too unbending, they whispered among themselves.

He visited and inspected the churches, even the sole synagogue. He closed all until he formulated a proper plan. Righteousness must prevail but how? How would he bring it about in this city? Returning the misguided to piousness would take more, much more than the simple matter of re-consecrating physical buildings.

A plan hatched itself: bring in the evangelical leaders. Convert them, or as Jeremiah urged, strike them down with the sword.

Hippolito chose an Italian musketeer, Erasmo, as his assistant. He instructed Erasmo to round up all clergy and hold them in the city prison. Next he had Erasmo search for a suitable place to question the captives. They settled on a dimly lit kneipe — tavern.

"Does our task trouble you?" he asked the Italian. "This is no place for anyone disturbed by, shall we say unpleasantness. We do God's work — you, me, all of us — even if it causes pain and distress to others."

"No, Father," the soldier assured him. "You have the education and know these things. Do what you think is best."

"Then let's begin; but remember, the devil is at hand. He will not let go so easily."

Soldiers paraded the first Protestant clergyman through the main square and into the kneipe. Loved ones and supporters trailed behind with fear and worry etched on their faces.

Inside the tavern the captive sat and faced Hippolito. If first impressions proved true, the friar seemed a man humble in spirit and manner. However, the captive didn't trust first impressions, and he searched the friar's face. His eyes took in the priest's roughened forehead, an indication of tension, the large brown eyes, and a mouth suggesting, what, caginess? He couldn't be sure.

The Black Friar knew none of this. Dominican training taught Hippolito to perfect a serene countenance. Let those accused of witchcraft and sorcery believe you are compassionate and understanding; create a false sense of security in the quarry before you strike.

He met the gaze of the seated, pinched, deep-eyed and bent sixty-four-year-old across the table. He tossed a fast smile and made a show of reading a document in front of him. At last he raised his eyes again to Pastor Gerhard Scholz, with his tufts of white hair and thick bushy eyebrows.

The elderly Scholz couldn't stop trembling. Rumors swirled around the Catholics intended to use torture to get their way. He licked his dry lips as the friar spoke.

"Calm yourself, Brother," Hippolito advised. "There is no need to be excited."

Scholz offered no good response, beyond a nod.

Hippolito opened the interrogation with, "Tell me who you are and what you do."

Hands pressed into his lap, Scholz tried to still himself. His voice quivered.

"Yes, of course, but before I begin, pray, do I address you by the honorific, Father?"

"Yes. Father Costello."

Scholz drew in another mouthful of air. "Very well, Father Costello. I am Gerhard Scholz, Senior Pastor of Saint Wolfgang's." He paused to allow moisture to gather in his mouth before he continued. "As a man of God, you will understand I and my Brethren in Christ are charged with many responsibilities."

Hippolito let Scholz talk and waited for his moment.

Scholz pressed on. "In my capacity as the Shepherd of Saint Wolfgang's. I try to lead by example, preach our Almighty God's Word, pray for triumph over the devil, visit the sick and the infirmed, and make decisions about doctrinal disputes."

Sweat trickled into Scholz' eyes, down his face, and onto his collar. In spite of his discomfort, he made himself focus on the priest. "Perhaps I could have a drink of water?"

"Water," the priest called to someone behind Scholz.

Heavy footfalls pounded on the wooden floor. Scholz heard the sound of water being poured into a cup. More steps before a hand appeared over his shoulder and proffered a tin cup. He thanked whoever held it out, and drank.

The tightness in his chest lessened somewhat.

His questioner spoke again. You believe —your faith believes — in personal conversion and the infallibility of the Bible, namely the four canonical gospels."

"Correct, Father, though we refrain from using the word canonical."

"Yes. No matter for now." The young priest threw a brief glance at the paper and back up at Scholz.

Something told Scholz the questions would increase in scope and strength.

"You reject our Holy Mother Church's assertion of good works leading to salvation?"

"A different emphasis, Father. Grace through faith alone."

"I see. Let me ask you this: do you accept the Holy Roman Catholic Church is and will evermore be a perfect society?"

Scholz shook his head.

"You'll appreciate, Father, I cannot. It is one of the dividing issues between Rome and the rest of Christendom, including, I believe, the Eastern Orthodox Church."

The priest's face clouded.

So, thought Scholz, beneath the exterior lurks something more. This is when the devil shows himself, when his mask slips.

"Apostates, all," Scholz' questioner shot back. "You profess to be a theologian so you will know in Matthew sixteen our Blessed Lord Jesus says to Simon Peter 'You are Peter; upon this rock I shall build my church. The gates of hell shall not prevail against it.'"

Scholz offered Hippolito a kind smile and corrected Hippolito.

"I'm a pastor, Father; not a theologian. Theological fine points are beyond my reach." *Keep your gaze on him. Do not waver.*

The priest sniffed and carried on.

"What I have told you is indisputable proof the earthly successor to Christ Jesus was Saint Peter. It follows then apostolic authority evermore belongs to those who walk in the Shoes of the Fisherman. Only the insane or twisted can deny the Roman Catholic Church is a perfect society."

The words didn't reach Scholz. He closed his eyes and tried to will away a pressing dizziness and pain in his chest. He gulped air, and made an effort to speak as his right palm moved over his heart. His eyes flitted to his questioner.

"Good priest," he gasped, as he rubbed his chest, I..." The cup left his hand and fell. He leaned forward and tumbled out of his chair. His head stuck the floor. A brief moment passed and Scholz ejected the contents of his stomach.

Hippolito flew to his feet and moved around the table. Erasmo and others stood over the dying man, unsure of what to do. The pastor made horrible sounds as he gasped for air. Everything spun. Pain tightened in his chest and in his arm. Panic seized him as he thought of Clothilda. *Merciful God, please...*

Scholtz tried to think, to pray, as men hovered over and around him. Everything became a blur. He heard voices, words, but nothing made sense — not even his own state. His stomach disgorged itself again as men yelled and he tried to draw in breath.

A moment later Gerhard Scholz passed from the physical life. The living gaped, unable to move or act. They stared with revulsion at the mess on the floor, stunned by the pastor's sudden demise.

Erasmo bent and searched for a pulse on Scholz's neck. He stared up at Hippolito and shook his head.

They remained in a small circle around the dead man.

A soldier spoke to Hippolito and pointed to the corpse. "Father, shouldn't you...you know...say something over the body? After all, he's a priest — well, kind of."

Hippolito gave the man a stern glance. "Absolutely not! He professed to be of the cloth, but he was of the unfaithful. He rejected the true religion. The best his soul can hope for is purgatory. Now, no more talk of this kind of nonsense." He pointed to the corpse. "Pick him up and let the locals dispose of him."

He watched as they carried the body into the street. Hippolito wondered if the pastor's death might work to his advantage. *If word got back to the others, it might instill the right amount of fear.*

Word did spread but the outcome proved different than Hippolito hoped.

Emboldened by Scholz's fine courage, evangelical and Lutheran pastors resisted all efforts to renounce their faith. A few suffered broken arms, splintered lips and the loss of teeth, but Hippolito failed to bend a single clergyman to his will.

Frustrated, he returned them to the tower while he sat and brooded. He re-consecrated the Catholic churches and named the seized Protestant ones after saints.

He held Mass each Sunday. Almost no one attended; most citizens remained loyal to their faith and pastors.

Word of the pastor's death and of Hippolito's failure reached the Field Marshal. He sent von Durin to meet with Hippolito and let it be known he took the dimmest view of the recent turn of events.

"There are words, Father," von Durin said as the two men sat in the kneipe and shared a glass of beer. He set his glass down, wiped his moustache and continued. "Unkind words to be sure, but words, snickers and whispers this task entrusted to you is beyond your capabilities. I don't wish to be the bearer of bad news, but I am instructed to say you have one more week to prove yourself — or you will be replaced."

One week, thought Hippolito, as von Durin left. What does the Field Marshal expect can be accomplished in a week? These things take time.

It astonished him how quickly his circumstances changed from jubilation to despair. He folded his hands, closed his eyes and prayed for Divine Guidance. Nothing. Only silence, the sound of men moving about outside and the faint scurrying of a mouse across the wooden floor.

Eight days later the Field Marshal made good on his threat. He removed Hippolito from the post and gave it, along with the position of head chaplain, to Father Christof Wouters.

Hippolito seethed at not only the loss of prestige, but also the loss to Wouters of all people. He despised the smug, know-it-all Belgian. He recalled a German word: schadenfreude, finding satisfaction in another's misfortune. He, Hippolito, would stand back and watch Wouters make a colossal mess out of re-converting the populace.

The mere thought of Wouters in charge made Hippolito snort. Wouters; the man would have trouble finding his way out of a root cellar. The saints and angels weep.

"Your face betrays you, Father Costello," Wouters said in a loud voice as he watched the low-in-spirit priest enter the dining room. A self-satisfied smile on his face.

Wouters bore on. "As the Blessed Saint Matthew said, 'For the called are many, and the chosen are few.'"

Gas and nausea roiled through Hippolito. Food was the last thing he wanted. He wouldn't have come to the dining room at all, but Wouters insisted on it. "We all eat together, Father," he told Hippolito earlier. "No exceptions."

Enjoying my public humiliation, Hippolito thought as his eyes met Wouters — his own filled with bitter anger? He squared his shoulders and shook his head.

"With respect, Father Wouters, the St. Matthew quotation refers to salvation, and does not suggest promotion or stoppage. Yes, I was relieved of my charge, as you or anyone here might be. As to my successes or failures, I will only quote a different saying: 'Even to the best scribe comes the smudge.'"

The room remained in stunned silence as eyes flitted between Wouters and Hippolito.

Hippolito poured himself a glass of wine, feeling certain Wouters' eyes were boring into the back of his neck. He set the wine pitcher down and searched for a place to sit, and found old Father Bohumil busying himself with a bowl of stew. The priest gestured for Hippolito to sit. He did, offered a fast bow of acknowledgement and set his wine down. Hippolito then made the sign of the cross, clasped his hands and in a low voice said, "Bless us, O Lord, who bless Your Holy Name, and by this food, feed us for your holy service. Amen."

Hippolito liked the Bohemian priest, one of only two who in turn enjoyed his company.

Bohumil winked at Hippolito and in a low voice said, "Don't be too hard on Father Wouters. He tries his best — as you do." A soft chuckle followed. "But I have to admit you had an excellent riposte. You should teach logic at a university somewhere."

The elder's words made Hippolito feel a bit better. He took a sip of wine and said, "Thank you, Father. It's been hard."

"I have no doubt," Bohumil replied, "but you know, failure isn't always such a bad thing. Only time will prove if Father Wouters can succeed. As for the Protestant conversion—me, personally, I cannot agree great ferocity is the answer. It only brings death and injury and creates more ill will. What I say may shock you, but they are also holy men, these Protestant men of the cloth. God loves them just as much. Their..." he snapped his fingers, "What is it these Germans call it? Oh, yes, weltanschauung, world view, is different. If we could only find the middle ground..."

Hippolito gazed at the old man and shook his head.

"I like you, Father Bohumil, but I cannot agree with your under-standing. Let's move on to something else, shall we?"

Chapter 16

WOUTERS made every effort to humiliate Hippolito further. He assigned him to menial tasks, forced him to write Wouters' sermons, and barred from attending strategy sessions.

Hippolito endured all, and repeatedly reminded himself he would outlast this unpleasantness.

More troubles rained down on Hippolito. Fatigue sapped his strength. He lost weight he could ill afford to lose, and suffered from an unquenchable thirst. New abrasions appeared on his penis and a nasty rash took hold on the sole of his right foot.

Wouters addressed him after morning devotion. "Look at you, Father. You're ill and can barely walk. The Blessed Lord expects better from you."

Does He? Hippolito thought. He wondered what God expects for donkeys who fail to control their incessant braying.

Wouters waved his hand in front of Hippolito. "Father?"

A sigh of defeat escaped Hippolito as he gazed into the unpleasant face of Wouters.

"Apology, Father... a headache. It is hard to concentrate."

Wouters dismissed the excuse. "Yes, you seem to have a lot of these 'headaches' of late. It is time for you to visit Brother Francis at the infirmary and find out the cause of your ailments."

Hippolito soon found himself standing in front of the former Francis Muñoz, a one-time tanner, and now Brother Francis, in charge of the infirmary. Good-natured, and a man of sincere piety, the Augustinian friar from Cadiz immediately recognized Hippolito as a fellow Spaniard.

In their native tongue Muñoz said, "If you will follow me, Father, to the examination room...." He noted Hippolito's limp.

Inside the barren room, Brother Francis listened to Hippolito's complaints. He stroked his beard thoughtfully, and asked Hippolito to remove his mantle and lie on a table.

Hippolito tugged at his black cloak as Brother Francis took his own large cross from around his neck and set it on a chair.

Naked and uncomfortable, Hippolito hurried onto the sturdy, low table. Eyes on the ceiling, he stretched out, shivered, and covered his privates. He listened to the splash of water in a tin basin.

A moment later, Brother Francis said, "Father, I understand your discomfort, but I need to examine you better. Please, remove your hands so I may carry out my examination."

A reluctant Hippolito complied.

Francis bent forward and studied Hippolito's groin. At once he spotted the open sores.

He pointed. "How long have you had those?"

Hippolito raised his head and followed the Augustinian's line of vision.

"Several weeks, and you'll address me by my proper title, Brother. I am an ordained priest of Holy Mother Church."

"Yes, yes, of course, Father; my apologies. May I return to the examination?"

"You may," a nettlesome Hippolito answered.

"Thank you, Father."

Francis' eyes returned to Hippolito's torso. "You say you've had these sores several weeks, Father?

"Or thereabout."

"Ah."

Nothing in the emotional response betrayed an opinion.

Francis moved to the end of the table, pried Hippolito's legs farther apart and continued with his examination. He lifted Hippolito's left and then his right foot. "And this rash, Father — how long?"

"About the same time."

The Augustinian had more questions. How long had Hippolito been feeling so? Any irritability? The symptoms...were they constant or did they come and go?

Francis at last completed his examination. Hippolito pulled on his mantle in haste, stood and waited with disquiet for the portly friar's findings. Francis took his time. He adjusted his cross and chain, intertwined his fingers, and faced a sitting Hippolito.

"I regret to tell you, Father, but you have *morbus gallicus*; otherwise known as the French disease."

He paused to let his words sink in before he spoke the one dreaded word. "Syphilis."

Hippolito gaped at the Augustinian friar. A moment passed before he recovered, able to compose his face. In truth, he'd suspected this — believed for some time this might be the case. Even so, he couldn't bear to hear the word spoken. He squeezed his eyes shut. Syphilis. Now, here, someone gave voice to his deepest fears.

What have you done to me, Alberto de Gongora, a bitter Hippolito thought? What did I do to deserve this?

Syphilis was almost always a death sentence. In parts of Christendom the disease took as many victims as the Plague. He, Hippolito, found himself stricken with the same disease that felled so many others. The bony old man with his scythe and cowl now cast his fiery eyes on him. *Kyrie elision.* Lord have Mercy.

Brother Francis watched as the Dominican opened and closed his mouth like a fish on land.

The Augustinian's voice broke through his thoughts.

"You are aware, Father, of what I refer to, are you not?"

Hippolito acknowledged the question with the slightest nod.

Francis spoke again. "It is not for me to judge the reason for your condition. For me, the issue is how we make you better." Francis continued to talk but Hippolito's mind slipped away. The French Disease. Unbelievable.

"Father Costello?" Francis asked in a soft voice.

Hippolito pulled himself out of his self-absorption. "Yes?" he whispered.

"Father," the Augustinian said, "what I am about to tell you — I beg you to attend to every word." He peered into Hippolito's face.

"Of course," a benumbed priest admitted. "I drifted off. Continue."

"Thank you. I'm afraid I must tell you few survive what you have. You may be one of the fortunate ones. For treatment there is only quicksilver applied to the skin. It shows promise to hold back the disease. I must order it for you."

"Yes," an absentminded Hippolito said. Sleep. He wanted to lie down and sleep, to be away from all of this tragedy.

"Do you know of sarsaparilla, Father?"

"No."

"Its roots are shipped from the colonies. They are said to also have beneficial properties. I will order those too. It may be a few months before I can get any, and I will summon you when it arrives."

Hippolito stared at him, a blank look on his face.

"Your sores, Father. As much as possible let the air at them, and keep them dry. I suspect they will heal on their own." Francis stopped for a moment before he added, "And the rash you have—I will give you something for it."

Hippolito wanted to flee. He suddenly yearned for happier times, for his childhood in Oviedo. It took all of his willpower to concentrate on the friar's words.

For the headaches, Francis advised Hippolito to wrap cool, damp cloths around his head and lie in a darkened room.

"I will give you some herbs of lemon to also help calm your nerves. Drink lots of water and take cool baths for the fever you describe."

A few moments later, a fatalistic Hippolito limped out of the infirmary.

In the spring, when the sun at last melted the snow and the ground became firm, Tilly, feeling generous in spirit, released all of Rothenberg's prisoners. Next, he called his generals and planned his spring offensive. The army packed.

With a nod, the fife-and-drum struck up a tune and marched out the city's main gate, the cavalry behind them. In perfect precision, line after line of foot soldiers followed.

Rothenberg's citizens had no interest in cheering the invaders' departure.

"Good riddance," a councillor stated, as he stood on the city wall and watched the troops make their way along the Tauber Valley.

"We survived," someone else added, "but at great cost. We have to take heart we out-lasted them."

No one disagreed.

Weary and broken, the city set about to return to its former self. Farmers headed out to the fields to sow what seeds they had. Tradesmen planned how to replace looted stocks, and the city council again turned its attention to offering good administration.

Church bells pealed and called the faithful to Mass to give thanks for deliverance from the hated enemy.

Chapter 17

WORD spread through Altenburg: wolves were seen roaming lanes and alleys. Panic set in. How did wolves get past the city walls, people wondered?

House cats disappeared. Few citizens ventured outdoors without being armed or in the company of others. Even soldiers didn't walk alone.

"Gonna be a long winter," Gisis grumbled, as he set down his beer. "Nothing to do but march 'round the city, and sit and drink."

"You complainn'?" Jigs asked.

Morison gave him an uncharitable stare. "Course I'm complain'n. Ya deaf? I've much to complain about. It's colder outside than the old one-tooth hag I'm living with. She's always at me about something or other. I'd put up with her nagging if she was a beauty, like Podo here's got, and our friend, Lee. Me own bad luck I get stuck with an ugly crone."

Devin signaled for the waiter to bring more beer. The man shot him a disapproving response and ignored him.

"Oiy," Devin shouted after him, drawing the eyes of the other patrons. The waiter trained his eye on the table of men.

"Mehr bie," Devin called out in bad German, pointing to the steins on the table.

With an emotional appeal to his fellow Germans, the waiter offered up a dramatic sigh, came to their table, and removed the empty steins.

"What's his problem?" Cecil asked as he followed the man with his eyes.

"He is thinking the same as the people," Paolo answered.

"What — they don't like us?"

"Si. They are not liking we eat, drink, and do not pay much."

"Terrible lies," a falsely outraged Devin proclaimed. "We pay; we pay in coin and more — with our lives. We protect their town, women and children, the thankless wretches. It's plenty enough. Me, I think they'd do proper to give us a parade, and stop whining about what we owe 'em."

Cadman rolled his eyes.

"A parade? You batty, Lanky? The only parade they're bound to throw us is when we march out the front gate and never come back. Assuming they don't string us up beforehand. Weren't you listening to Podo? We eat their food, drink their beer, sleep under their roofs, and who knows what we do with their women?" He tossed a fast glance at Ainslie. "We've not made ourselves popular here."

Jigs pointed to Devin.

"Alla same, he's a point. We're the victors, their protectors, and they best be happy with things. Let's see how they like it when they've no got us, and the papists come back. Be whinin' an' screamin' for us to free em', they would."

Two weeks before Christmas, senior Lieutenant Geiger died.

The castle ordered a dignified service. Soldiers packed the church. Later, they took the body in its oak casket and stored it in an empty warehouse until spring.

"I don't want to end up like him," Ainslie whispered to Paolo as they left the church. "This is no land for a Scot to die in. Not saying it's a hard place, but it's no Scotland."

Paolo offered no response.

"You reckon they'll bring his body back to his homeland?"

Paolo tossed off a shake of his head. "I am thinking it is not so. I think they bury him when it is warm." He stabbed toward the ground with his finger. "Here."

Ainslie left the tavern and made his way to Gabi's house, his thoughts turning to his relationship with her. It still amazed him he could sleep with her every night — and get away with it. Worst kept secret in town, yet no one dared to do anything about it.

Still, it wasn't all peaches and cream. He'd seen another side to her — calculating and moody at times.

They'd come on suddenly, these moods, and she'd pull into herself. Speaking to her only made things worse. He just had to wait her out. And truth be told, he wasn't a stroll in the woods himself.

The worst times came when their ill moods overlapped.

It wasn't long before she grew more critical of him. Arguments over the smallest things arose. She mocked his obsession with cleanliness, and thought him too controlling. "I had enough of it with Viktor," she would say.

He retaliated and complained about her nagging and changing disposition.

More complaints sprang up, and along with them came deep, cutting remarks. Both knew to keep their voices low, lest someone passing by overheard, but the fights continued. Days of wretched silence often followed.

One evening Ainslie arrived at Gabi's to find her at the dining table with a heavyset man. Both jumped as Ainslie shut the door and took in the scene.

With brows knitted together, Ainslie studied Gabi and then turned his attention to the stranger, who rose and removed his broad-brimmed hat. Ainslie considered the man. Hairy; blue-black hair seemed to grow everywhere — even on his knuckles. One of Duncan Carstarphen's books came to mind. It was set in Africa, about gorillas. Here in front of him stood a close imitation of one.

He put the thought out of his mind. An inch or two taller than Ainslie, the man's eyes were sunk into the folds of his face. Ainslie thought they were gray, evasive. Twin, deep, indented vertical lines ran down from his eyebrows to a wide, unremarkable nose.

Gabi fidgeted and announced, "Oh, you're back." Drawing in a fast breath, she bore on, "Ainslie, this is Herr Ebbe Schlup. He is head of the Masons Guild."

Schlup offered a curt bow as Gabi turned to the German and said, "Herr Schlup, here is the soldier quartering with me, Herr Ainslie Soutar."

Something troubled Ainslie. It came to him proper; too proper. Gabi's voice lacked its normal softness, naturalness. It seemed jumpy. All his senses told him she'd been up to something.

"So you like our town, Herr Soutar?" the German asked in a high-pitched voice at odds with his girth.

"Like it well enough," Ainslie answered with no warmth, as he held the other man's gaze.

The two men stared at each other until Schlup re-directed his gaze at Gabi.

"I have been visiting with Frau Hoffmeyer, but I best be off to my own home." He cast a fast look at Ainslie, broke off, and turned his eyes on Gabi. "I bid you farewell, Frau Hoffmeyer."

"Of course," Ainslie agreed. "You don't want to be caught in the curfew. Only soldiers are allowed."

Without another word Schlup took hold of Gabi's hand, proffered a dry kiss, released it and offered Ainslie a cursory bow.

He left.

Ainslie slid the crossbeam across the door as Gabi poked at the fire. "My turn, is it, now Viktor's gone?" he said to her back. "I see you like the fat ones. Or is it they like you?"

The hurtful shot hit its mark. Gabi turned, pulled back her arm and swung a poker with full force.

With ease Ainslie eluded the arc and stepped in front of her before she could wind up again. He seized her by the neck and drew her onto her tiptoes. Through clenched teeth he hissed, "Go easy now. Take nothing to kill you. Let it fall."

Her eyes wide and filled with fear, Gabi let the poker clatter to the wooden floor. She tried to draw breath into her lungs as the fingers of one hand scrabbled to remove his tight grip. She used her other hand to scratch at his face.

Caught up in his emotion, Ainslie held on until she almost lost awareness. He relaxed his hold and pulled away.

A fit of violent coughing seized Gabi. Long minutes passed before she made an effort to speak.

"We've...been...at each other for...a while...Lee. It shames us."

She had him there, he admitted. He'd nearly killed her. But then didn't she try to brand him with the poker?

In a raspy voice, Gabi kept on. "I'm sorry it came to this. Can we talk?"

"A little late for talking, isn't it? You treated me badly, especially considering what you did to Viktor."

She coughed again, cleared her throat, and sat at the table.

Tired of standing, Ainslie took a chair opposite her. Neither spoke; both stared into the fire.

More coughing as Gabi held up her hand. He waited and let her catch her breath. She cleared her throat and croaked out, "Can I tell you something?"

"Yeah, what?"

She launched into a story about how the Hoffmeyers and others were trying to force Ainslie out of the house.

"I said nothing for a long time, but people kept at me and asked me why I'd let you continue living under this roof. I didn't have a good enough answer."

"You could have said you had no choice; no more than anyone else."

"You're right" she said, "but people still talk. They thought it indecent for you to be here with me. They said I didn't try hard enough to get you out."

She chewed on her lower lip.

"I'm sorry for what I did — whether you believe me or not. I grew angry, angry at the soldiers, angry at rationing, and at people pressuring me, even angry at me."

Her fingers played with the strap of her apron. "I...I can't put it into words."

Ainslie remained silent.

She dropped her eyes. "Herr Schlup; he's just a kind man, a kind, married man." Her lower lip quivered and her eyes filled. Two plump tears made their way down her cheeks. She swiped at them with her fingertips.

Ainslie softened his position and reached for her hand. She accepted the gesture. Hands entwined, they sat in silence, neither willing to speak. The fire turned to embers when Ainslie at last rose and added more wood.

Food rationing ended with the arrival of spring. Almost at once cheeses, hams, eggs, loaves of bread, salt, fish, beer, geese in crates, livestock, and trussed-up chickens appeared at the market — as did honey and other sweet goods.

The transformation astonished Ainslie. *If I hadn't seen for myself, I wouldn't believe it.*

Along with better selections of food, the surliness disappeared. Friendly, competing calls from vendors filled the air, uplifted by the notion hawk-eyed town officials no longer watched over their shoulders.

"Best buy here! Best choice," a vendor shouted. "Trust me, you won't find better anywhere."

"Only two things you can count on in life," another called out, "your mother and what I sell."

In the taverns, men thought back on the winter. Damndest thing, some said — what we put up with. At least the winter's behind us.

A harsh winter, all agreed. Has to be better days ahead.

In early April the land still wet and cold, Colonel Eloffson received orders to pack and link up with the king.

Townsmen and troops alike reacted with jubilation at the word of their departure.

Away from prying eyes, Ainslie and Gabi said their final farewells in her house. "We had some good times," he told her as he stood with his back to the door. "And some rough ones."

Gabi made a remorseful face.

"True, but nothing we can do to change it now." She moved closer. "Let's not dwell on it. We part as friends, yes?"

"Yes. Hope the rough spots will be forgotten soon enough. Take care of yourself. I'll think about you to the end of me days."

"All good, I hope," she teased.

"Nothing but," he assured her. "When your name comes to mind, I'll smile."

Ainslie approached Paolo.

"Sergeant Alberti," he said to his newly commissioned friend, "it's time. I've a yearning to see me family, so I'm wanting to make me way back. Can you help me get it done?"

A hint of sorrow appeared in Paolo's eyes. The corners of his mouth tightened. "I am missing you."

Ainslie chuckled and slapped his friend's shoulder. "Fine, but I haven't gone yet. Anyway, I know what you mean, and I'll miss you too. So can you help me get my leave?"

"Si."

"What of you, Podo — will you stay on?"

"Si. They are my comrades. Is not soft, but I remain."

"'Soft,'" Ainslie repeated. "A good word. Ay; it's not soft."

Paolo stepped closer. "For you, Lee; you are coming back?"

"Fool like I am, I think so, ay."

"Good."

Paolo interceded on Ainslie's behalf with Michiel Piersoin.

Paolo bowed and approached the Huguenot, Captain Pierson. Born to Flemish parents who settled in Liege, Pierson had studied theology and languages under the Jesuits at Heythrop College. His English suggested only the faintest hint of an accent.

Pierson listened to Paolo and asked to speak to Ainslie himself.

"I'm owed leave sir," the Scot said, when Pierson interviewed him. "Come with sergeant Alberti when we landed in Peenemunde, so it's been almost a year."

"Yes," Pierson answered. "Sergeant Alberti speaks well of you, and recommends you. I see no reason to deny the request, Private Soutar. The spring offensive hasn't started. Your leave is granted."

Finished, Pierson took in his subordinate's reaction.

Ainslie offered up a full smile. "Great, Captain, but will I get paid?"

"We will make this is a lucky day then, Private. You will be paid, and we will see what we can do about getting you to the Baltic. Find out when the next supply column is heading up."

Excitement rolled through Ainslie. "Ay, I will, sir. This is getting better and better. Had no idea how this would go. Almost have to pinch myself."

"Well, now," Pierson said. "We have done you a good turn. You can do one for us."

Ainslie arched his eyebrows. "What?"

"Come back and finish the fight."

"You've no need to ask, sir. Once I've done with me visit, I'll be back."

"Excellent. Be safe, and Godspeed."

The meeting over, Ainslie saluted and left Pierson sitting alone at the long dining table in the Town Hall banquet room.

Outside he picked up his pace and headed to the business district in search of a gift. He found something better than he expected — a pale purple silk doublet, widened at the bottom and embossed with a scene of dogs in pursuit of a stag.

He examined it with a critical eye. It might fit Paolo and give him freedom to swing his arms. *Yes*, he decided he'd take it.

The eager tailor interrupted his thoughts.

"I made this for a wellborn who told me he didn't like it after all." He held out a sleeve. "Feel the luxurious material. I can let the gentleman have it for a good price."

"Lovely. What're you asking for it?"

"The gentleman can pay?"

Ainslie snorted. "Course."

The German drew back. "I'm sorry, Mein Herr. I mean to give no offense."

Ainslie waved away the apology. "Forget it. I'll ask again — what do you want for it?"

The price settled, Ainslie took the coat and went off in search of the metzger. Since the rationing, the butcher always had fresh cuts of meat on display.

"Do you know Frau Hoffmeyer on Lutherweg?" Ainslie asked.

The butcher said he did.

"If I order, will you deliver?"

"Certainly, Mein Herr."

"Venison steak," Ainslie said and pointed. "These two. If the Frau isn't home, go back later, but I want them in her house today."

"Jawohl, Mein Herr."

Paolo seemed almost speechless when Ainslie presented him with the jacket. He insisted it was too grand a gift.

Ainslie batted away the objections and helped him into the jacket. It fit to perfection.

"You've to look heroic, Sergeant Alberti," Ainslie said as Paolo tried to get used to the gift. "Who can say, you might be Lieutenant Alberti someday. A jacket the likes of this is fitting for someone of your station."

That evening his friends took Ainslie to a tavern. Almost everyone seemed determined to get blind drunk. And of the civilians in the tavern, none glowered at the friends; bygones were bygones. On more than several occasions a townsman paid for their drinks or toasted them.

"I'd be buying, too," a chipper Cadman slurred out, "if I was local and knew we'd soon be gone."

Gisis pointed an unsteady finger at Ainslie. "You be sure you come back now," he slurred. "It's no a good fight 'less'n there's a Scots in it to make it interestin.'" He glanced over at Cecil. "More Scots, the better. Fucking English can't tell their arse from their teeth."

The others laughed at his quick wit and insolence.

"It's why we always have you Scots around to tell us which is which," Cecil said, and belched, "when we clean those teeth."

The men threw their heads back, roared and thumped the table at the retort.

A melancholic feeling came over Ainslie. He'd miss his friends. All thoughts of past depravation and difficulties vanished as he considered this special group around him.

To great cheer, Eloffson's troops marched out through the town gate the following morning.

Ainslie kept an eye out for Gabi and spotted her just inside the gate. She waved. He returned the wave. She'd do fine, he told himself; with her appeal and property, she'd not lack for suitors.

A SOLDIER FAR AWAY

Chapter 18

HIPPOLITO'S breath stank. He became aware of its offensiveness when others pulled away from him as if he stood too close.

He also developed a peculiar metallic taste in his mouth, and felt certain it contributed to his foul breath. Leave it to smug, ignorant Wouters to draw attention to his breath, he thought. He narrowed his eyes in annoyance at the unpleasantness in even thinking about Wouters. Typical. What could you expect of someone from the mendicant order anyway? Lacked refinement, they did.

A few days earlier in Nördlingen, after the priests had finished evensong, Wouters held him up and again said in a voice sure to be heard by others, "Your breath gives great offense, Father."

Hippolito decided he'd had enough. His body hurt, and he had no patience for more of Wouters' hostile outpourings. He took a deep breath and said, "'Ezekiel seven, verse twenty-seven, Father, 'I will deal with them according to their conduct. By their own standards I will judge them.'"

He watched the Benedictine's thin, boney face comport itself. The eyes widened and the furrows deepened. "I beg your pardon."

"I think the meaning is clear enough, Father," a determined Hippolito said. "At every turn you humiliate me. 'Give and it shall be given to you.'"

"Using Holy Scripture to make some petty point," an indignant Wouters asked as he glanced about to see who might be listening. "Shameful."

Hippolito ignored the censure. He felt a newfound confidence. The Order had renewed his request to remain with Imperialist forces for another six months. Cheered by this recent news, Hippolito drew in a breath and said, "Perhaps it is not for you, of all people, Father, to judge. Mark my words, the day will come when I return favour for favor."

"You," Wouters huffed. "Are you threatening me?"

Hippolito's eyes held the Benedictine's for a moment. "I am, but you will have trouble proving it as there is no one about." He tossed off a careless shrug. "Your word against mine."

Shock replaced indignation on Wouters's face. He hadn't expected this, Hippolito thought, aware Wouters wouldn't hold his gaze.

Hippolito moved closer. "Bad breath or not, Father, attend my words. I have it on good authority the Grand Field Marshal recently received a letter from my Order. I am told the letter spoke well of me."

No stopping me now, Hippolito told himself as he gave in to his full anger.

"You're well aware, Father, I'm sure, the Holy See holds the highest regard for the Supreme Sacred Congregation— deplorably called 'The Inquisition' by its enemies. Among its many charges is to root out those in Orders whose beliefs are — how shall we say? — not in full and harmonious agreement with Rome's dogma."

He paused for the briefest moment to let his words sink in, and then continued.

"Full and harmonious agreement, well, those things might be open to interpretation, but not after someone is brought before the Congregation. And lest you forgot, Father, the reach of the Congregation is long. Those who come to its displeasure are never the same afterward. Sadly, sometimes the reach catches those undeserving of punishment."

The threat hung in the air. Color drained from Wouters' face.

Pleased with the effect, Hippolito pressed on. "About my undertaking in Rothenberg; it is true the Field Marshal relieved me of my duties, but I will report to the Congregation I did not have enough time to achieve my end results. I will further argue your results may have worsened the situation. Rothenberg remains Protestant, and you, Father, were last in charge of spiritual change when we left. Perhaps the Congregation should ponder this fact. Who knows, they might see it as a breach of full and harmonious agreement? If you're called before the Congregation, they'll no doubt wish to hear from me."

Hippolito saw a flurry of emotions charge across Wouters' face as he attempted to bring himself under control. Disbelief, disdain and anger appeared to clash with good judgment. Twice Hippolito took note of the loud snorts; twice Wouters' eyes met Hippolito's before they turned away.

A dramatic exhalation, a deep inhale and Wouters said, "All right, all right, on reflection I may have uttered a careless word or two, Father, but all can be remedied, do you not agree?"

He offered Hippolito no chance to comment. "The Sacred Congregation does such important work. I am certain they are overstretched. No need to bother them with unnecessary work. We are, after all, brethren in Christ."

Hippolito watched with satisfaction as Wouters transformed himself from haughty to fawning. He immediately lost interest in vengeance. Weasel. Let him scurry back into his infested hole. He simply wanted to be done with him.

"You are correct, Father. Things sometimes happen and cause misunderstandings. It is best we get on with the matter of inflicting the most serious blows on our enemies, the heretical Protestants."

Thus Hippolito won on a measure of freedom from his tormentor. His own exaggeration and lies caused him no concern. He came out on top and doubted the frightened Wouters would challenge any of his claims.

His state of health once more took his full attention. In addition to his foul breath, his gums bled and his teeth loosened; he could actually wiggle a few.

One ailment after another: his skin turned rough; he becoming plagued with unsightly pustules, and suffered from bouts of chest pains. On top of everything else, his bowel movements became watery.

Hippolito searched out Brother Francis shortly after the quicksilver treatments began.

"Look at my face," he moaned. "I've turned into a *lupus nature*."

The kind and patient Francis listened with care to Hippolito's complaints.

For his part, Hippolito had developed a liking for Brother Francis and desired his good opinion. He hoped the Brother wouldn't see him as vain. "It is not about conceit, you understand, Brother, but one's face inspires either confidence or dread. I fear the latter."

"This may not be as big a concern as you fear, Father," the barber-surgeon assured his patient. "Your face has these blemishes, true, but it will get better again. I cannot explain why, but it happens. God's Mystery I suppose."

Hippolito craned his neck toward Francis. "You don't think I got this from the quicksilver?"

Francis shook his head. "I have no reason to think so, Father. No one else has made this conclusion. Still, let's hold off using it for a while."

Their eyes met for a quick moment before Hippolito glanced at the floor.

Francis spoke again. "Besides, your other symptoms — the ones you saw me about earlier — are all but gone."

Hippolito agreed, then added, "But I have these new ailments. I cannot help but wonder if I've replaced one set of problems with another." He let out an exasperated sigh. "What have I brought onto myself?"

Francis continued to listen to Hippolito's complaints. When the priest finished, Francis turned to the matter of treatment. He recommended oil of clover for Hippolito's gums. "Not pleasant, but your breath should improve. I'll give you some. Use just a little on a regular basis. As for your face, I could try bleeding you, Father, but I must say I do not have much confidence in it. Let's wait a bit and see what happens."

"Wait? A frustrated Hippolito asked. "How long?"

"Two weeks. If there are no changes, come back and see me again."

Hippolito's face did clear up, and he felt somewhat better. His gums ceased to bleed. Better yet, once again his teeth felt firm and reliable when he chewed. Francis hadn't done much for this recent turnaround, he knew, therefore all credit had to be God's. Nothing else but the Almighty's intervention explained his sudden recovery.

The Lord favored him again, Hippolito told himself, and likely forgave him for his past transgression. Or perhaps He never held him as accountable in the first place. Perhaps Hippolito failed to give Him proper credit for His benevolence.

He knelt in prayer and vowed to be both a better man and a better spiritual leader. *I will re-dedicate myself to the task of bringing light to the darkness in northern Europe, this I vow.*

He next prayed for his dead father and brother, as well as his sister and mother, and asked his Savor to watch over them all.

With his heart lighter, Hippolito entered the dining room. By chance his eyes lighted on Wouters. Both offered each other the tight-lipped smile of two people wary of each other.

"Father Wouters," Hippolito said and nodded.

"Evening, Father Costello. Hope you had a fine day."

"I did, yes, thank you," Hippolito said and moved to the sideboard to help himself to cheese, veal and sauerkraut sprinkled with bits of dried, smoked pork.

He cast about and spied Father Bohumil in conversation with Father Ibanez, a fellow Spaniard. Hippolito didn't much care for Ibanez, but felt generous in spirit, so set aside his personal feelings.

"May I join you?" he asked as he approached.

Both glanced up.

"Please," Bohumil replied, and held out an open hand. Ibanez offered a fast nod and returned to his conversation with Bohumil.

Hippolito set his plate down, crossed himself and offered up his quiet grace. With the ritual completed, he tucked into his food.

Ibanez waved a forefinger at Bohumil.

"It cannot be, Father. The devil brooks no compromise, and neither must we. This is a struggle for the heart and soul of Christendom. These Protestants, beholden to the devil, cannot and will not see the goodness and truth of our one true faith. At their worst they wage war and murder those of our faith. At their best — assuming one is generous and can describe it as so — they degrade and humiliate our teachings. Where then can one find a place for compromise?"

Bohumil stroked his gray-bearded chin as his eyes traveled left, down to the table and up again to Ibanez. He pursed his lips, inhaled and said, "A deft but unconvincing argument, Father... But our discussion wasn't whether one side is good, and the other bad. We discussed compromise. I uphold there is or should be room for compromise. It might bring us to a position where we can both learn from each other. I draw your attention to the fact our Lord Jesus taught us to seek compassion for our fellow men. Compromise and compassion must at some point go hand-in-hand."

Ibanez turned to Hippolito. "What do you think, Father Costello?"

Ah, Hippolito thought; so you're going to pull me into this. The old Bohemian seemed in clear need for an ally. He did agree with Ibanez, and secretly thought someone needed to tone down Bohumil's more progressive views.

On another day, at another time, Hippolito might well have indulged his appetite for delivering moral judgment. Not this day. Imbued with a happier heart, he wasn't about to say anything uncharitable about the good Bohemian priest.

He set down his fork and said, "Father Bohumil expresses views not entirely in keeping with Rome, and likely at odds with most of his equals, but those views are his and come from his personal experience in the world."

Serious shock registered on Ibanez' face. It took him a long moment to recover. When he did, he hurriedly returned his attention to the last of his meal and ate in silence. Finished, he muttered a fast good evening and left the table.

As for Bohumil, his face betrayed his bemusement.

"You surprised me, Father Costello," he said. "I'll have to re-think my full sense of you. I could not have foretold, ever, this kind of reply would come from your lips."

Hippolito waved off the comment. "Be careful, Father Bohumil," he cautioned. "Not all will tolerate your views in perhaps the correct spirit."

Tilly longed for war — to take the fight to Gustavus. Thoughts of the Swede sitting on his horse in a haughty manner at Breitenfeld made his heart race.

So many good men, Tilly thought as he remembered the battle, so many cannons lost, and "the Lion of the North" still struck fear and worry into the Holy Roman Empire.

He snorted his contempt. Lion of the North indeed. More like flea-infested alley cat. Still, you had to hand it to him; he was anything, if not innovative. Early March and the man's army sat on the edge of Bavaria.

March. Who mobilized troops in March? One man. Gustavus.

Full of the deepest frustration at not having yet bested his hated rival, Tilly pounded the armrest of his chair. "Goddamn the man."

His outburst surprised even himself; he prided himself on his sangfroid and avoidance of vulgarism; he wasn't a man to take the Lord's name in vain. This wouldn't do. He'd have to say an extra rosary tonight. Besides, history proved the best field generals were always pragmatists.

He turned his attention back to the problem. Think like Gustavus, he ordered himself; reason out — what he's after. Why is the Swede sitting at the edge of Bavaria?

It came to him. *Divide et imperia.* Divide and conquer. Nothing else made sense. Attack Bavaria. If it fell, the Swede could march to Vienna without challenge. Ferdinand would run like a rabbit; if he did, he'd lose the confidence of the German princes. They'd abandon him and make their separate peace with Gustavus.

The more Tilly thought about it the more he understood Gustavus' plan. "You still have to deal with me," he whispered to a far-away enemy. "I intend to see you don't succeed."

Yes, but how? How would he outfox the fox? Nothing came to him, nothing beyond the obvious — a solid victory, one worthy of a legend; something the League could build on. All well and good to dream, but what victory and where? He needed something big, something to catch Gustavus by surprise.

Try as he might, Tilly failed to come up with a plan. He'd pray something would come to him. He had faith. All in good time. God provides.

The following day a rider came into camp with a dispatch from Munich. Duke-Elector of Maximilian of Bavaria ordered him to Bamberg.

Tidings of the most urgent reached Us, the communiqué read. *The Good Bishop of Bamberg, Gottfried von Dornheim, has fled from the Protestants who intended to murder him. He is currently safe in Amberg. You are closer, so give him succor, and deliver him to Munich with an escort.*

Tilly read the dispatch twice. Von Dornheim — he'd met the man, and didn't like him. He thought him Janus-faced, a double-dealer.

Remember what you thought earlier about being pragmatic, he scolded himself? What you think of von Dornheim shouldn't matter. He's Catholic, important, and may be of some help to you.

He rose and moved to the large table to study his map. His finger traced the lines of the warring sides until it stopped. *There...Bamberg. In Swedish hands, judging by the duke's dispatch.* A new thought came to him. *Perhaps not.*

He stared at the map as an idea formed. Of course! God spoke through the dispatch. Why didn't he see it? He would rescue von Dornheim and draw the Swede into a trap at the same time.

Elated, Tilly bent on his knees and gave thanks to his Saviour for showing him the way. Last year Gustavus had had his way; this year belonged to him.

He crossed himself, rose, and opened the door to his suite. "Wecelo," he called out as he returned to his desk.

A moment later his aide hurried in. "Herr General?"

Tilly turned. "Wecelo, I want intelligence on Bamberg — its troop strength and weaknesses, if any. Get it to me as fast as you can; no excuses."

Von Durin saw the determination in Tilly's set jaw. He bowed and sped off without a word.

He returned much later with his report.

"From what I'm told, Herr General, Bamberg is firmly in Protestant hands. They aim to hold it. They've dug deep trenches around key parts, in anticipation of a possible charge by us."

He broke off and waited as Tilly crinkled his brow.

"Go on."

"Yes; yes, of course. The city is defended by Marshal Gustav Horn, the man who showed exceptional courage at Breitenfeld. He..."

"Wecelo," an impatient Tilly interrupted.

The aide stopped in mid-sentence and stared at Tilly.

"Herr General?"

"Wecelo, spare me the exaggeration. I am aware of the Marshal you so flatter. I remind you you're my aide-de-camp, not his sloganeer. Whose side are you on anyway?"

Von Durin reddened.

"'Side,' sire? How can I be for anyone but 'Papa Tilly'?"

At the mention of the popular name his men had for him, Tilly softened his scowl.

Von Durin continued. "I mean your side, our side, of course. I intended no disrespect to your excellent leadership." He wiped at his well-groomed moustache with nervous energy. "Shall I continue, sire?"

Tilly gave a restless wave of his hand to signal his assent.

"At any event, sire, Marshal Horn and his hackapelites — I'm not sure I'm saying this correctly..."

Tilly frowned. "Wecelo. Don't show off. You know quite well I have no idea what hackle...whatever you said...is."

"Of course, Herr General."

Von Durin hurried on. "Horse cavalry; I believe it means horse cavalry. A Finnish word, I'm told, from some province in Sweden."

"Does it now? And you expect me to be familiar with what some backward province in Sweden calls its horsemen?"

"No, of course not, sire; I suppose it is of no consequence. These — shall I call them dragoons, sire?"

"Yes. Dragoons will do nicely."

"Very well, then. These dragoons are backed by foot soldiers. All in all, it's estimated the combined strength is about two thousand men."

"Two thousand men — you are certain?"

"No, Herr General. With respect, we cannot be sure. It's our best guess, but I imagine close enough to the real number."

"And Amberg?"

"Yes...Herr General?"

"It's in our hands?"

"Exactly so, sire. In our hands."

"How far is the distance between the two?"

"Maybe a full day's march if conditions are right, sire. A quarter of the time if by horse."

Tilly drummed his forefinger against his chin as he stared off at a painting on the wall, beyond von Durin.

He glanced at von Durin. "Wecelo."

"Herr General."

"Correct me if I'm wrong, Wecelo, but isn't Bamberg in Bavaria?"

"Yes sire."

"And you say Amberg belongs to us?"

"It does, Herr General. The situation is fluid there. A small area; some towns belong to us; others to the Protestants. Bamberg is in their hands"

"I see. Hmm."

Von Durin had no idea what 'hmm' meant.

They remained silent for some time. Von Durin's eyes flitted about, and he wondered what his commander plotted. Tilly broke out of his trance. "Summon my generals. Tomorrow at noontide we break camp. It's time for the enemy to feel our presence."

He stopped, drew a breath, and said, "We will take Bamberg. A small victory, but we will build onto it."

Chapter 19

FEW of Tilly's soldiers knew their next destination; few cared. They took it on faith Papa Tilly had a plan to smite the hated Protestants.

A general sense of cheerfulness moved through the long column as it marched along the riverbank. No more defeats, they said; success called them to battle.

The sun warmed them. Men sang, and priests shouted out prayers and biblical passages as they passed through villages and hamlets.

Wouters pressed Tilly to stop and question the inhabitants about their religious convictions.

Tilly considered the request. "I suppose, Father, although I see little value in it. We all know there is no road to Heaven for these misbelievers and their narrow ideas. In any event I doubt we'll find many people. I suspect most of these villages sit empty by now."

Wouters bowed and said, "It may be so, my Lord, but we cannot and should not leave degenerate free-thinkers who mock true ecclesiastical authority behind. Left alone, they spawn, grow, and spread. Best we root such heresy out now as we pass through."

"What do you mean to do, then?" Tilly asked, as he watched the priest from his saddle. "Hang them all?"

"No, my Lord, but perhaps the ringleaders, to set an example."

Keenness at the idea failed to appear on the Grand Field Marshal's face, so in haste Wouters added, "If necessary, of course."

"'If necessary,'" Tilly repeated. Intense little man, he thought.

"I fail to be convinced this will do anything to change the situation, but ah, well, it's a fine enough day. I suppose it can't hurt to wait a bit."

Tilly shifted in his saddle, gazed at the horizon, and said, "As you wish."

Tilly guessed right; most villages and hamlets proved shells of their former selves. All the same, Wouters rounded up more than two dozen peasants and had nine swinging from trees.

Each priest had his own way of selecting a victim — a feeling, a wrong word, insufficient deference. It took nothing more than a pointed finger or a few short words and soldiers seized the wretch. Guiltless men, women, even three boys dangled from lynching trees.

"Dramatic, I admit, sire," an unmoved Wouters said to Tilly, as the Field Marshal sat in the shade of a tree and nibbled on a chicken leg. "It does put greater fear into our enemies."

"If you say so," Tilly said as he licked his fingers.

Three peasants held his immediate attention as they gamboled from ropes on thick tree limbs. A fourth, on her knees, begged for mercy from a priest.

Women wailed and tore at their hair, children screamed, and men wrung their caps in helplessness, their faces contorted in anguish.

Tilly took a final sip of wine.

"We've a full day ahead of us, gentlemen," he said to his generals. "Let's finish this and be on our way. Best not to tarry."

Hippolito disdained Wouters, but the cold-hearted attitude Wouters displayed surprised him. *I wouldn't have thought he had it in him to be so hard-bitten.* On this single issue the two shared the same opinion. God alone saw into the hearts of men, and knew Protestant hearts were black. *Perhaps I've judged him too harshly. I must make an effort to be more charitable toward him.*

His eye briefly met the Field Marshal's as he walked from the hanging tree. The memory of the humiliation he endured still rankled. He put his head down and hurried away until he stopped next to a peasant hut.

Brother Francis moved beside him. Heaviness in his voice, the Augustinian said, "It saddens the heart and troubles the mind what we do, does it not, Father?"

Hippolito's eyes narrowed at the remark. "I gather you refer to the hangings, Brother. Be careful. Such talk is dangerous and questions Divine Wisdom." Hippolito pointed to the strung up peasants and continued, "Beelzebub welcomes them home."

Francis' face grew solemn. He muttered something under his breath, turned, and walked away.

It took a moment before Hippolito realized what Francis said. "The price of wisdom is above rubies." He thought about the quote. Where had he heard it before? It came to him. Job; the Augustinian had quoted Job.

Annoyance welled up in him. Impudent man, lowly Brother, suggesting priests were harebrained. What next — sheep judging their shepherd?

Should he give Francis a good bawling out? He decided against it. The Augustinian worked hard to help him with his disease. He'd overlook the affront, but should it happen again, the Brother would suffer for it.

To great cheers, Tilly arrived in Amberg. He dined with the prince-bishop. Over sauerbraten and potato dumplings served with Riesling wine, von Dornheim regaled Tilly with the horrors his Protestant captors heaped on him.

Tilly offered his best condemnation and focused on the food. Unlikable, this jowly man, he thought, but he set a good table.

Von Dornheim brayed on.

Tilly endured the gassy little man. He'd only have to put up with him until tomorrow. Afterwards, the man could bend the ear of Maximillian as much as he liked. He swirled a dumpling in the rich sauce. "Must be put to right," he said, popping it into his mouth. He chewed, swallowed and followed it with a drink of wine.

With horse cavalry surrounding the bishop's carriage, von Dornheim's retinue headed for Munich. Tilly waited until they were out of sight and then stationed a battalion to remain in Amberg. The remaining twenty thousand troops marched out of the city gate and into the misty dark morning, with clergy at the rear.

A little past midday, they rode into the Protestant town of Elrich. The town offered no resistance. In turn Tilly spared it, taxed the townspeople and took what supplies he could.

Tilly summoned his favorite dragoon commander, Colonel Bonifaz Traugott.

"Bonifaz, we're quite close to Bamberg. Take a battalion and scout what we're up against. Don't, unless absolutely necessary, engage the enemy. Best he doesn't see you. I want our cannons here before we assault Bamberg. I intend surprise."

Traugott gave a curt nod and said, "I'll see to it, and report back." He offered a short bow, spun and left.

The ride went well for Traugott — the distant spires of Bamberg's cathedral came into view. They approached a bend at the Regnitz River. So far no sight of the enemy, and Traugott thought it best to turn back.

Bad luck arrived as they rounded the bend and met a platoon of hackapelites recently arrived from Peenemunde. Both sides, taken by surprise, reined in their horses and gaped at one another.

The battle-hardened Imperialists broke the trance.

Traugott, a veteran of Breitenfeld, reached for his sword, raised it high, and bellowed, "Jesu-Maria!" Caught up in the moment he either forgot or shrugged off his orders from Tilly. He kicked his steed into action and charged at the Finns. Unwilling to show any less bravado, his men followed.

The untested Finnish hackapelites watched them come. Their commander, a fresh-faced and quick-thinking lieutenant, saw Traugott bear down on him. He calmly drew his flintlock pistol, placed the brass-barreled weapon in the crook of his arm, and took aim. The pistol gave off a spark and discharged.

A single lead ball changed everything. The missile left the lieutenant's pistol and tore into the Imperialist's neck. Traugott's sword flew out of his hand. He tottered in the saddle and slid sideways.

With concern for their beloved commander, Traugott's men did the unthinkable: they reined in, neglected the enemy and stared down at his lifeless body.

The Finnish lieutenant used the precious time to shout "Quick! Back to our lines." They turned and rushed back to the town's main gate.

The action brought the dragoons out of their reverie. "They're getting away!" someone shouted, followed by, "After them. Avenge Colonel Traugott. Cut the bastards to the ground!"

Full of bloodlust the dragoons tore after their quarry.

The Finns charged for the city's main drawbridge, past the newly dug trenches manned by foot soldiers recently arrived from Peenemunde.

With eyes wide in astonishment, the soldiers looked on while the Finns, in their blue coats, raced toward them, a horde of enemy in pursuit.

War cries and pistol shots filled the air. More seasoned soldiers would have let their own men through and sent a volley of lead balls at the pursuers. The recruits only stared on as a hackapelite toppled from his saddle.

Finnish riders tore past, a furious enemy in pursuit.

Panic set in among the foot soldiers. They rushed out of the trenches and raced across the bridge, behind the hackapelites.

Encouraged by the sight, the Imperialists came on strong. "We have them on the run, boys!" a dragoon shouted.

Twenty yards or so and Traugott's men would be on the bridge. Their horses thundered toward the open gate. Excitement and revenge filled their hearts. If they made it through the gate, they might well hold off any retaliatory charge long enough to send for reinforcements.

The hackapelites dismounted, turned and faced the oncoming dragoons.

"Pistols ready," the lieutenant called out. "Shoot the horses. Bigger targets."

Feet pounded on the cobblestones behind him. Someone shouted, "Over! Over! Move over."

The lieutenant and his men crowded together near the wall of a counting house. The line of men behind readied their weapons.

The lead Catholic dragoon crossed the bridge, his horse's hoofs clomping along the cobblestone. The Finnish lieutenant could make out a sneer on his face. He heard a voice cry, "Fire."

Sparks ignited, quickly followed by puffs of smoke. The unmistakable smell of gunpowder filled the air.

Two horses fell and took their riders with them.

In the narrow confines of the street, the Catholic riders became easy prey. A few fought well, but most fell to the larger numbers.

More foot soldiers appeared. Blood soaked the gateway bridge. Men and horses slipped and fell. Soldiers yanked the dragoons out of their saddles, and they had no chance against the pummeling of heavy stock butts.

Other infantrymen stabbed horses with swords and knives; bleeding, the animals grew mad with terror and sought escape.

Catholic dragoons in the rear at last turned and raced back across the bridge, afraid a musket ball might catch up to them.

"Addle heads!" the usually placid Tilly bellowed at two officers whose eyes flitted back and forth in nervousness. "I have addle heads fighting for me. I'm beginning to understand why victory escapes us."

He clenched and unclenched his fists as the two men shifted in quiet agitation in front of their commander, fire in his eyes. "I gave strict orders not to engage the enemy."

Hands behind his back, Tilly paced in front of his lieutenants and muttered, "So close; too close to the enemy. I thought I could count on Traugott." He pounded the outer side of his thigh. "Am I cursed?"

He glared at the two cavalrymen. "What fool came up with this idiotic and impulsive idea to charge the enemy?" He held up a hand. "No. Let me guess—Colonel Traugott?"

Both men had enough sense to keep their mouths shut when Papa Tilly was on a tear.

Tilly gave his back to them, aware he was losing control. *I'm surrounded by fools.*

He took a deep breath, followed by yet another, and then allowed himself to continue, in a controlled voice.

"Gentlemen, I brought some twenty thousand men with me. Now thanks to your idiocy, you've advised the enemy of our presence, and given him good reason to crow. In future, you will be more circumspect. Do I make myself clear?"

"Yes, of course, Herr General."

"We'll make sure it doesn't happen again, Field Marshal."

"Henceforth, if any similar incidence occurs, the enemy will be the least of your worries." He shut his eyes in disgust, opened them again, and waved his hand. "Dismissed."

They saluted and left. A heavy sigh escaped Tilly as he watched the men go.

For their part, the men thought Tilly had overreacted.

"What's he expect?" the bushy-browed and taller of the two whispered as they walked away. "It's war. Men fall. It could have all gone our way."

"I agree," his companion replied. "No point in being bold if this is what we get? If Traugott hadn't been cut down, Papa'd be toasting us."

Chapter 20

TWILIGHT arrived as Protestant forces blew Bamberg's two major bridges. Catholic scouts who sat beyond musket-range later reported great cheering when the bridges buckled and fell into the river. They also told of seeing teams of horses pulling heavy artillery pieces.

"They kept working in the dark, Herr General," a captain said in his clipped German. "You could see hundreds of rush lights — like fire-flies."

Tilly glanced at von Durin after the scouts left.

"What are they up to, eh, Wecelo? Only one bridge left and they know we can't charge it without a blood bath." He tapped his teeth with his fingernail. "Maybe it's time to move on. I'll have to figure out some other way to trap them."

Hippolito's thighs and behind chafed from so much time in the saddle. For some thirty miles, the Field Marshal's army had been following the Main River in pursuit of the hated Protestant enemy.

A new town came into view — Schweinfurt. He sighed with grateful relief to discover Catholics held the town. No fighting; they would simply get a well-deserved rest.

The next morning Hippolito watched a company of dragoons tear off. He offered up a quick prayer. *I hope they smite twice their numbers.*

The mere thought of Protestants — killers of his brother, murderers and blasphemers all — moved him to anger. Hell awaited every one of those misbegotten evildoers.

The regiment returned later with three captured prisoners on foot, behind a dragoon. The sight of them brought a crowd of spectators. Everyone wanted to see for himself those who fought at Breitenfeld.

The bound prisoners tried to keep up to their captors. One stumbled and fell. The cavalryman stopped, turned, and waited for the captive to regain his feet. Aware the prisoner couldn't keep up, the horseman slowed to a walk.

Covered in dirt, ingrained by sweat, and with their shirts and doublets in near tatters, the three did their best to appear stoic. They moved through a gauntlet of Catholic soldiers who spat, kicked, slapped and jeered at them.

"Don't look like much, if you ask me."

"Hey! Lookit this one; ugly brute if I ever saw one."

"Not so almighty tough now, are they?"

"Whoresons. They'll learn they can't stand up to us."

Drawn by the noise, Hippolito rushed to learn what had caused the commotion. He took particular interest in inspecting the captives. He'd never seen any enemy soldiers this close. Very ordinary, he thought, but then had he expected cloven hooves and horns?

The dragoon broke away from the mob and led the prisoners to a stone house. Hippolito guessed it to be the local gaol. He glanced around and found a soldier.

"My son, do you know how these men were captured?"

"I don't, Father. All's I can say is they were cut off from their main body. Our dragoons found them. Good enough for me."

"You don't say. Away from the main body? How?"

"Happens," the soldier answered, his body already turning to leave. "The army's stretched. Men get lost." He offered up a crooked smile "Happens to us too sometimes."

Tough, the Field Marshal thought of his captives. Tough-minded. Neither would give up the information he so desperately wanted and needed.

Tilly sat in the burgomaster's chair. "We're not getting anywhere with those captured prisoners. I need to know what the Swede's up to."

"May I make a suggestion, my Lord?" von Durin asked.

Tilly leaned back in his chair, closed his eyes and rubbed his temples. "And what is it?"

"Let that Dominican have a go at them."

The Field Marshal's eyes opened in disbelief.

"Are you mad? We've already had a sample of what he's capable of." He shut his eyes once more and worked his fingertips on his temple.

Stay quiet, von Durin told himself as he waited for Tilly to speak. He counted by one-thousands. *One thousand and one, one thousand and two.*

At one thousand and eleven, Tilly spoke again. "All right, tell me what you're thinking."

Von Durin didn't dare smile lest the Field Marshal open his eyes and catch him in the act. Inwardly, he felt smug. So often he had planted an idea and waited until Tilly claimed it as his own.

He began. "Perhaps the interrogation needs more finesse."

He waited and saw Tilly open his eyes. "I'm not saying, sire, our men can't get the information out of them, but we already lost one prisoner."

"Yes, go on," a curious Tilly said. "I'm waiting."

"Well, Father Costello is schooled in these things. Has to be. The Grand Inquisition does well in extracting information."

Tilly's eyes never left von Durin.

"Perhaps it's the manner in which they're questioned," von Durin suggested.

"I think I see what you're driving at," Tilly said. "You believe our little monk can succeed where our soldiers couldn't."

"Yes, sire."

Tilly shifted in his chair. "You favor this priest. Why?"

Von Durin raised a shoulder. "He reminds me of someone I once knew."

The Field Marshal appeared to consider von Durin's words.

"Well and good, I suppose. Just don't let it cloud your judgment. In any event, let me think on it further."

After evensong Wouters crooked his finger at Hippolito and beckoned him over. The Field Marshal's portly aide-de-camp stood beside Wouters.

Hippolito at once felt a sense of dread. What did this mean?

He approached and gave a curt bow.

Wouters spoke "Father, Captain von Durin has something important to discuss with you. I will leave you to it."

Without another word he turned and left.

Nervous, Hippolito waited for the other man to begin. The captain smiled.

Hippolito returned it. So, Captain, he thought as he waited for von Durin to explain the reason for their meeting. What's behind your smile, eh? What's in store for me this time?

Von Durin cleared his throat. "Father."

"My son."

"Bygones are bygones, Father Costello."

Encouraged by the remark, Hippolito offered up a nod of agreement.

"Of course, Herr Captain. Time takes care of most things, does it not?"

"Just so. Now, to why I am here...we have need for your special talent — a need vital to the success of our spring offensive. This might be the perfect chance to redeem yourself with our Field Marshal."

A fresh chance, Hippolito thought, barely able to control himself. A chance he wouldn't waste. He threw his shoulders back and said, "Of course, Herr Captain; happy to do anything to benefit our holy war."

"Exactly so. Time is a problem and here is what we need..." He explained the matter and finished by asking if Hippolito spoke English.

"I have some, Captain. It is not polished, but it will no doubt do. Tell me again what particular information you seek."

"Anything to let us know about the Swede, what he's up to; troop strength, formations, anything to help our cause. You can order the prisoners' termination afterwards if you wish. I trust you aren't squeamish about such things — given your, um, previous line of work."

"It is God's necessary work, and does not bring the damnation of Eternal Judgment."

"Exactly," an indifferent von Durin said. "I'll leave you to see to all of this, then. Good evening, Father."

He wheeled about and returned to his superior.

Darkness fell just as a worked-up Hippolito entered the front door of the dank jail. Four sets of rush lights did their best to brighten the room. He sniffed and wrinkled his nose at the musty odor. *My chance, I will not let this opportunity slip through my fingers.*

In the middle of the room two prisoners sat adjacent to one another, tied to high-back chairs.

Three soldiers rose from benches. One, a tall gangly man with a hard face, moved toward Hippolito. "Father, I'm Arnop MacRaghnaill."

Hippolito guessed the man to be in his late twenties. He acknowledged MacRaghnaill with a curt nod and asked,

"You are English?"

"Beg pardon...Father?"

Hippolito repeated himself.

"Ah," MacRaghnaill said, "Got ya. Yes, all three of us are English. Me, I'm a Dorset man, but my father's Irish."

"I see, and you do not object to this — what we do?" He pointed to the prisoners.

"Nah, no bother. No countrymen of mine, the likes of them — fightin' for the Swede an' all."

"You are ready?"

MacRaghnaill nodded. "Am, Father. Go ahead."

Hippolito approached the bound prisoners. He scowled at the man on the left. Hideous might be too strong a word, he thought; perhaps repellant would be more accurate.

Hippolito turned his attention to the other captive. The long-faced man held Hippolito's gaze. It surprised Hippolito. From his experience captives rarely did this, preferring to stare at the floor or over his shoulder. This man had resolve. Well, he'd lose it soon enough.

Hippolito's eyes roamed back and forth between the men before he spoke.

"You will tell me of your army. How many men you have, and what is the plan of your generals."

The captive with the ugly face angled his head and said something to his comrade. Hippolito couldn't follow it. He turned his head and spoke to MacRaghnaill.

"Tell to me what he is saying."

"You're sure, Father?"

"Yes."

"All right. He said, 'Well done, Cade. Don't let this frocky court-card get the better of you.'"

"What is this court-card? Give me what he says."

"Has its own meaning, Father; an insult."

"Yes, but give it to me."

MacRaghnaill's face suggested puzzlement as he sounded out Hippolito's last word.

"Meaning? It means you don't look very scary in your dress. Like a girl."

Hippolito flushed with anger. "What are their names?"

MacRaghnaill pointed to the prisoners. "This one is Devin Skinner. The other's Cadman Moxley."

Hippolito sounded out their names several times. Queer language, English; hard on the tongue. He cast the thought from his mind and said, "We are going on."

His eyes settled on the man called Skinner. "You must give me information about your army."

Skinner turned his head to his comrade. "He just speak English, Cade?"

"None like I've ever heard."

MacRaghnaill stepped forward. "Don't be a smart ass."

"Or what?" Skinner challenged. "You'll give us a beating? Already done."

"Can be done a lot worse yet," MacRaghnaill shot back.

Hippolito tensed up, already feeling the interview slipping away. MacRaghnaill and Skinner behaved as if he wasn't in the room. He, Hippolito, needed to be in full charge, to inject a stronger bearing.

He yanked on MacRaghnaill's sleeve, pulled him back and stepped closer.

"You give me information about your army."

Skinner frowned for a moment before he said, "There's nothing to tell, ya understand? We were two innocent lambs, takin' the air, whistling our song, see, when your strong-armed men seized us. Shameful, it was, and you're wasting your time with the likes of us."

"It will go bad for you if you do not say."

"'Bad,'" the prisoner mocked? "Can it get any worse than now?" He turned to his companion. "What'ya think, Cade?"

Cadman shook his head. "Hard to imagine."

Hippolito stared down. "This is your answer?"

Both men let the silence speak for itself.

Frustrated, Hippolito exhaled noisily and turned his gaze up at the thick, dark, hand-hewn beam. He spoke to MacRaghnaill.

"Get rope; long rope to lift these men." He pointed to the captives and waited for the sergeant to acknowledge his understanding. It came with a quick nod of the head.MacRaghnaill turned to the other two men. "You heard him. Blake, get some rope."

The soldier moved off; the rest of the room remained silent, each man in his own thoughts. A noticeable amount of time passed before the soldier returned. He held the lengthy coil of rope to Hippolito. "What do you want done with this?"

Hippolito pointed to the beam. "Throw over this wood."

The soldier made several efforts to toss the rope before it cleared the thick beam.

Hippolito again turned his attention to Skinner. "It brings, how you are saying, bad pain, what we do. Better if you tell me."

"I've nought to tell ya."

Hippolito nodded and walked to one end of the dangling rope. He signaled for the soldiers to bring Skinner. Two dragged the bound prisoner to his feet.

"Be brave, Dev," Cadman shouted.

MacRaghnaill answered with, "Shut your lousy ungodly mouth!"

Hippolito spun the prisoner around and tied the rope behind his back. He inspected his work, stepped back, and gestured for the soldiers to hoist the man in the air. It took three men to lift Skinner off his feet. He winced as his tormentors raised him higher.

Hippolito approached the hoisted prisoner.

"You will give me the information."

The man inhaled and exhaled through his mouth. Arms forced over his head at an unnatural angle, his upper body thrust forward, he groaned and squeezed his eyes shut.

Hippolito motioned for the soldiers to jerk the rope. Skinner screamed in agony.

Hippolito spoke again. "The information, yes?"

Skinner would not answer.

Hippolito signaled for the soldiers to raise him higher. They pulled Skinner upward. He screamed again.

Hippolito waited until the screams lessened and became plaintive moans. "The information."

Skinner continued to moan.

"Remove the hand," Hippolito said.

"You want us to let go?" One of the soldiers asked.

"Yes."

The soldiers released the rope. The heavy thud of Skinner's body bouncing off the unforgiving floor made all but Hippolito wince. Dead weight, the prisoner's knees hit the floor first. The unmistakable sound of bones breaking echoed through the room. The skin on his forehead split open; blood seeped out. He released an anguished moan into the floorboards.

Hippolito hurried over to the prone man, bent low and said, "You now will give me the information." He saw the slow, feeble shake of the man's head. *Stubborn, this one.* Once more he signaled to the soldiers to hoist the prisoner higher. Blood dripped onto the floor. Aloft, his face etched in great torment, Skinner screamed but still refused to speak.

His comrade answered for him. "Have mercy, willya? This is evil, what you're doing. You're a man of God. Stop!"

Hippolito ignored the entreaty.

The hoisted prisoner surprised everyone as the rope pulled him off the floor. Blood flowed freely from his mouth. He coughed his words but managed, "Bye Cade I'll wait for ya in Heaven. Ya've been the finest of friends."

Hippolito turned to MacRaghnaill for an explanation. He shrugged. "Some Protestant gibberish, is all."

Hippolito instructed the men to jerk the rope. Their victim only moaned softly this time. In frustration Hippolito had the men pull the captive higher. Still nothing but deep moans.

Hippolito again demanded information. The captive remained silent. Again Hippolito signaled for the men to release the rope.

All heard the unmistakably sickening thump, like two large overripe melons, followed by a low groan.

Hippolito waited a few moments, stepped closer, but avoided a pool of blood. "You have information," he asked the face-down body?

It remained still.

MacRaghnaill approached and bent over Skinner. He felt the prone man's neck for a pulse. A moment later he straightened, and said, "Close to dead as you're going to get, Father. Won't get nothing from him no more."

Hippolito's face remained expressionless. He pointed to MacRaghnaill's belt.

"You have knife."

"I do, yes."

"Kill him."

"Kill him?"

"This is what I say, yes."

"Won't get anything out of him dead."

Hippolito dismissed the comment and pointed to MacRaghnaill's blade.

The soldier shrugged in an almost carefree manner, pulled out his dagger and stood over the near lifeless body as the remaining prisoner gaped at the scene.

"You bastards," he screamed. MacRaghnaill pulled Skinner's head back to expose his neck. "You rotten, cowardly bastards," the other captive called out. "God will never forgive you. Never."

In a right-to-left movement MacRaghnaill sliced deeply into Skinner's neck. More blood spilled out onto the floorboards. Skinner's body offered up several quick jerky motions and ceased living.

Tears of rage flowed down Cadman's face.

Hippolito stepped over to him.

"You have information."

The pallid Englishman's chest heaved with his sobs.

"I do."

The words offered great solace to Hippolito. Finally. Cooperation. The captive promised to reveal what he knew. Hippolito could bask in the satisfaction of recovering from his previous mistake. Even better, the information would go a long way to making amends for Alejandro's death. It wouldn't bring him back; nothing would, but Alejandro would rest in greater peace knowing his brother had avenged his death.

Hippolito returned to his task. "You tell me, and it goes better for you."

"Yes," Cadman sniffled. "What do you want?"

Hippolito asked for a chair and set it opposite the captive. He couldn't believe his good fortune.

Cadman gave up everything. Hippolito at first doubted his truthfulness, but after further questioning changed his mind. The prisoner told him he and others fell behind their main party near *Rain am Lech*, "where your cavalry found us. Didn't expect to get captured."

He told Hippolito word in the Protestant camp had it the king intended to cross the Lech south of the city and lay siege from there. "He's just waiting for reinforcements from Saxony."

Hippolito probed for inconsistencies in the story.

The captive repeated the details in the same order.

Satisfied he had everything of value, Hippolito rose and walked to where the soldiers stood in a small circle. He gestured MacRaghnaill over to him. "I have what I am needing."

MacRaghnaill pointed to the prisoner with his chin. "What about him?"

In reply Hippolito said, "Kill him also."

MacRaghnaill answered with a fast nod. Without a word he approached Cadman with his dagger. At once the captive recognized his fate. His body trembled as MacRaghnaill stepped behind him.

Cadman moved his shoulders sideways in a last-ditch effort to avoid the unavoidable. His executioner clamped a forearm over his eyes, yanked back his head, and brought the blade around. It sliced deep into the Englishman's neck.

An indifferent Hippolito watched. *For Alejandro.*

Blood flowed from the Cadman's neck and filled his mouth. He didn't die at once; it took two violent convulsions before MacRaghnaill released his hold and let the body crumple to the floor.

Hippolito's eyes moved from the body to the room itself before they again settled on MacRaghnaill. He pointed to the dead men. "Take them away." The words spoken, he crossed the room, opened the door and left.

The soldiers turned to each other, unsure what to make of the man and the evening's work. MacRaghnaill pointed to the bodies. "Let's toss them somewhere and then go have ourselves some ale."

Hippolito hurried to find von Durin. He forced himself to remain calm while he passed on what he learned.

"Wonderful, Father," the slack-jawed von Durin said when Hippolito finished. "Wonderful. I had faith in you. You have no idea how happy the Field Marshal will be. *Rain am Lech*. Hah. The Swede means to take it from the south? For sure the Field Marshal will prevent his scheme from succeeding."

He grinned at Hippolito. "You've provided a valuable service, Father, and I expect you'll be rewarded for it."

Chapter 21

IN the false dawn Imperialist troops with and without rush lights raced around the camp with an air of excitement. Everyone heard the tidings. *We're off to Rain am Lech. The Field Marshal's got a new plan. We'll show those Protestant sons-of-bitches.*

With cannons hitched to horses, tents knocked down and horsemen in their saddles; all waited, ready for the Field Marshal to lead them into battle.

A day and a half later his advance guards gazed at the city of Rain as a heavy stream of foot traffic poured out the main gate.

"Amazing," a dragoon said to one of his comrades, "how they know."

"Quite," the other agreed. "Sometimes I think citizens have better information than the military."

Tilly's forces rode into Rain without opposition. He chose to camp outside the city walls.

Two days later, a reconnaissance unit returned and reported sighting an advance unit of Protestant cavalrymen.

Tilly called his staff.

"Gentlemen," he said as he paraded in front of them; "the Swede is close at hand. We will be ready for him. He will not find this an easy hen house to take. We can and will outwit him." He pulled his sword from its scabbard and raised it high. "Victory will be ours."

His generals unsheathed their weapons and bellowed, "Victory."

Tilly waited for silence. He pivoted and pulled a priest forward. "We have the good Father Costello to thank for intelligence about the Swede's intent."

Hippolito blushed while everyone clapped. When all fell silent, Tilly said, "Give us a prayer, Father; a prayer for victory."

"Of course, My Lord." Heads bowed. Hippolito gave hiss benediction.

Advance Protestant platoons arrived south of Rain early in the afternoon.

Catholic forces stared across the river and listened to whoops and hollers. Cannon fire silenced the Protestant invaders.

"Laugh at this, you devil worshippers," a heavily mustached Croat cried out. He fired his six-pound cannon.

The enemy failed to respond. "Hah," he shouted across the water. "All bluster. Tremble at our might, you dogs."

More enemy troops arrived and crowded near the river. Under fire from the right bank, Protestant soldiers felled trees and moved cannons forward.

Tilly lowered his spyglass. "God in Heaven, they keep coming. Fire the cannons again."

The two sides engaged in an artillery duel reminiscent of Breitenfeld. The guns at last fell silent.

Later in the day a thick white smoke rose for miles along the Protestant side.

A puzzled and nervous Tilly stroked his chin and stared across the water. "What's he up to?" he mumbled. "He's up to something, but what?" He looked around at his entourage. "Does anyone have any ideas what this is all about?"

No one offered a satisfactory explanation.

Tilly shook his head and stared across the water. "Let's stay extra alert, especially for anything from the south. The attack will come from there."

Smoke continued to waft into the sky and unnerve the Imperialist forces, but nothing more happened.

The following morning, a courier, out of breath and sweaty, rode up to the Field Marshal's pavilion and dismounted. He begged for an immediate audience with the Field Marshal.

"What, what is it?" Tilly demanded. "Speak up, man."

"My Lord, the enemy has breached our lines and crossed the river."

All eyes turned to the Field Marshal. Colour drained from his face. He pulled air sharply into his lungs. In an almost-whisper he said, "Where to the south?"

The courier shook his head. "No, sire, the north."

"The north!?"

"Yes, My Lord. They built a floating bridge in the night, at the narrowest point. Under our noses. They came across at first light. They have a foothold on this side. It's not secure yet."

Tilly barely heard. Again, he thought. The Swede, ever the master of surprise, had again bested him.

He blinked several times and cursed himself. The Swede had never intended to attack from the south. The smoke was part of the ruse intended to disguise his plans. *Fool! What a fool I've been. Well, nothing to be done about it now. Time to get going.*

He turned about. "Wecelo."

"Behind you, Herr General."

Tilly spun around. "Wecelo, sound the alarm."

Von Durin rushed off as Tilly called for his armour. His attendants hurried to make him ready. One tightened his cuirass; another put the belt and rapier around his waist.

The Field Marshal's eyes danced around the tent and then fell on Hippolito. "Once more you've failed me, priest," he snarled. "I'll deal with you when I return."

The rebuke delivered, Tilly rushed out of the tent.

Hippolito's legs felt leaden. He had trouble breathing. The world crashed around him. He so craved Tilly's good opinion. He thought he'd won back more than a measure of redemption after the interrogation. True, the iciness hadn't fully thawed, but Hippolito saw redemption for himself. Now this…

Hands clenched by his side, he recalled the prisoner's words. Lies, all lies. *You fed me heinous lies, and now see what you've done. May you suffer the deepest, scorching fires of hell.*

He came to a fast decision — he'd join the battle. *Yes,* he'd die for Christ, for Alejandro, for papa, for righteousness.

Full of piety, romantic notions of martyrdom in his head and tears streaming down his face, Hippolito ran for his horse. It took time to find and saddle his horse, but once he did, he turned and made for the river.

Tilly charged northward, his officers behind him. He kept his composure as everything around him fell apart. Close to the river he heard the fearsome Haakaa Paalle. Those deranged Finns and their war cry. He shuddered at the sound and remembered it from Breitenfeld.

Pike men, cavalry, and musketeers — both sides struggled to advance or hold valuable ground.

Tilly rode closer, intending to rally his men. Musket balls flew every which way; one careened from Tilly's breastplate and singed his collarbone. He winced. Rapier in hand he hollered instructions at the top of his lungs and paid scant attention to the blood on his lace collar.

"You're hit, sire," an aide called out as he rode beside Tilly. The Field Marshal didn't care; he only cared about stopping the enemy. "It's nothing. I'll have it attended to later."

At the same moment he spun his horse around to shout out a fresh set of orders, a new artillery barrage opened from across the river; Protestant artillerymen lobbed cannonballs over their troops and at the enemy. A Finnish gunner rammed the one-pound cannonball down his small Falconet barrel while another rushed his pole to jam powder and cannonball as far back as possible.

"One more left after this one," the loader said.

"Fine by me," the gunner replied. "We'll send it off and wait for them to bring us more ammunition." He put the slow match to the touch hole. Both men stepped back, aware of the carriage's unpredictable and dangerous leap when the cannon discharged its round.

The cannon boomed and sent off its iron ball of fury.

With great ferocity the round shot tore across the river and by chance struck both Tilly's steed and the Field Marshal's right leg. It hit with great force and knocked horse and rider to the ground. The result shattered Tilly's leg. The terror-stricken animal attempted to scramble back up on its legs, but only made matters worse for its trapped rider.

Men rushed over to lend aid and comfort to their commander.

Hippolito arrived in time to find the Field Marshal in excruciating pain, his leg a pulpy mess.

With great care Tilly's generals pulled him away from his horse. Tilly's condemnation still ringing in Hippolito's ear, he stared after the Field Marshal, uncertain whether he should follow the departing men or stay. The enemy took the decision away from him. More horsemen and foot soldiers raced across the river.

A musket ball flew past Hippolito's ear, so close he felt its breeze. All earlier thoughts of derring-do abandoned him. In haste, he turned his horse and headed back to camp. He dared one final glance at the bridgehead. The enemy continued to pour over the river.

By late afternoon, full panic set in among the Catholic League. Behind them came the heavy shouts of "God with us."

"Flee, priest," a Catholic hussar advised as he climbed into his saddle. "The Protestants are in no mood for prisoners, and don't much like Catholic priests."

"But what of our camp and weapons?"

"You're a man of God," the petulant officer said. "What is it to you? These are military matters." He turned his horse. "All the same to me what you do."

He galloped off.

Hippolito stared at his back. *He's probably right,* he thought. There wasn't any point in remaining behind. He wondered briefly where they had taken the Field Marshal.

Wild yells from behind demanded his attention. *They're not far away. I better go.* Afraid of capture, Hippolito followed in the general direction of the lieutenant.

By dusk he'd caught up with remnants of the retreating army. He found Tilly's generals huddled in a field. They at last reached some decision, mounted their animals and rode off.

Hippolito followed. A wind from the east picked up strength. Clouds thickened. A storm would break soon.

He caught up to one of Tilly's attendants whom he recognized. "Where is everyone, do you know?"

"*Oberdorf am Lech,* Father," the attendant said. "Not far from here. We heard they're taking the Field Marshal to *Ingolstadt.*"

"And after....?"

"Treatment, of course."

The man's words made Hippolito's decision. He'd go to *Oberdorf.*

The skies thickened and darkened, so much Hippolito swore it was night. A fat plop of rain landed on his shoulder, followed by a second one. The rains came. In the open it proved almost as dangerous as facing the enemy. Every so often a bolt of lightning lit up the darkness. After a particularly sizeable bolt, Hippolito's horse bucked in terror and threw him. It galloped off as rain pelted downward and sideways on the terrified priest.

He felt certain he might be struck by lightning at any moment, and kept as close to the cover of trees as possible. To his relief, he at last spotted lights from the village. Drenched, the terrified Hippolito plodded on in the darkness. Flashes of lightning helped him make out the church spire. He breathed a sigh of relief when he made it safely to the rectory doors, where he found Wouters and other clergy inside.

The storm took all night to spend itself.

The following morning, Wouters rushed off to get what information he could. When he returned, he called the other priests to him.

"My brothers," he said; "leadership is, at the moment, in the hands of His Majesty, Duke the Elector of Bavaria. Our beloved Johann Tserclaes, Count of Tilly, is in the most serious of conditions. Let us pray with all our might for his full recovery."

All dropped to their knees and offered appeals to the Almighty Jesus and Blessed Mother Mary. When they rose, Wouters said, "You may have heard the Count is being removed to *Ingolstadt*."

Heads nodded.

Wouters bore on. "We are charged with staying with the army. The good Duke Elector assures me our forces will regroup, and we are needed now more than ever."

The comment won a round of quick applause.

"To close," Wouters said, "we will follow the Elector to *Ingolstadt*. What comes next, well, God will direct us."

In *Ingolstadt*, they found lodging at a nearby seminary.

Word of Tilly's condition proved troubling. Infection had set in; doctors were unable to do much to help him. Bells everywhere pealed for the Grand Field Marshal. Churches held healing masses. Each one ended with, "I am the Lord, your Healer."

Hippolito participated as Wouters led the priests in mass. All of them watched and waited for any tidings of the Field Marshal's health.

A new rumour spread: the Protestant king offered his personal physician to Count Tilly.

More rumours flew about — the Protestants were advancing, Spanish forces were arriving, a new front would open, the Elector would soon sue for peace.

The rumour about a Protestant doctor in their midst proved to be genuine, though the Field Marshal refused the offer of assistance. Two days later he died. The town mourned, along with Bavaria and Catholic Christendom.

Chapter 22

Along line of empty supply wagons headed north to Peenemunde. Ainslie suffered the rattles and shakes, the unforgiving seat, and the petulant waggoneer.

Nothing else to do, he took greater interest in his surroundings than he had on the march south. The land and people appeared even worse than he remembered. Only crickets, field mice and ghosts inhabited the villages now.

Ainslie couldn't wait until they arrived back in Peenemunde.

A few days later, stiff from the journey, the Scot jumped down from the wagon, glad to be done with the punishing journey.

He hurried off to find whatever ship he could. When he reached the pier he introduced himself to the first mate of a ship laden with grain and bound for Glasgow. In broken Swedish, he told the sailor he had leave from the King's army. By decree of the Royal House, all members of the army and navy were granted free passage anywhere a Swedish ship sailed.

"To Scotland," an eager Ainslie said. "I'm off to Scotland. Can you take me?"

"Ja. What is your name?"

Ainslie gave it.

The first mate sounded it out. "All right, Ainslie Souter. I will inform the captain. You stay out of the crew's way, eat what we eat, and sleep wherever you can. Got it?"

"Got it. When're you leaving?"

"Tomorrow morning."

"I'll be here."

He thanked the seaman and returned to town, delighted with his luck. He might have been stuck for days in the town, without a room. Since the war the population of Peenemunde doubled in size. Rooms couldn't be had for gold.

Eager to be on the ship, Ainslie stood ready to board at dawn. He noted a few other passengers ready to board as well.

The first mate recognized him.

Once on board Ainslie watched everything as the three-mast fluyt prepared to sail. Early morning rays shone on the Sommar as she made her way out to sea.

A thrilled Ainslie stared into the far distance. *I'm bound for home. I've left the battlefields, no worse for wear. I've money in me purse, and I'm bound for home.*

The sailing master turned the cargo ship into a stiff breeze. The first mate hollered out, "Windward." The captain, feet spread apart, stood next to the sailing master, and ordered to have the ship swung starboard.

Ainslie watched with keen interest as sailors yelled the wind direction. *We'll have the wind behind us soon.*

Her sails now full, the ship handled herself well. Sailors hurried along the deck, readied the sails and tended to the rigging.

The winds calmed as they entered the Strait of Oresund.

A sailor climbed the main mast to the crow's nest. He shouted warnings as the ship made her way through the strait.

"Water's deep; straight ahead. Shallow, shallow. Swing port side. Steady. Steady. Little more to port."

Passengers and crew applauded as soon as the Sommar again reached open water.

It surprised and pleased Ainslie he didn't get seasick from the rolling motions of the ship this time. She pitched a bit in the strong winds, but Ainslie didn't mind. He watched the sea and took his fill of the clean, salty air. He even managed to sleep on deck without trouble, bothered more by the hard surface beneath him than the ship's motion.

"Land," a young female passenger shouted into the wind. She pointed. "Land."

Ainslie and others moved close to her. "Scotland," someone cried out. He gazed across the water. Yes, a small bit of land. He felt his heart skip a beat at the first glimpse of his homeland.

The ship drew closer and the Scottish shoreline came into better view. Sailors scurried up the mast to roll up the sails as the ship made for the Clyde River.

Ainslie couldn't stop staring at his homeland, a place he left a small lifetime ago. He paced with eagerness while the Sommar dropped anchor just outside Glasgow harbor. *Back on the Clyde. Same river I left wot seems ages ago. Fabulous.*

He leaned over the railing and gaped up and down the Clyde and at the scores of small and large ships tied to wharfs. *Unbelievable. I...am...back. I cannot believe it. I am back...in Scotland.*

Rowboats arrived and collected passengers.

By mid-morning Ainslie stepped onto the wharf. His walked past the empty shop where he signed up to fight in the German lands. He didn't slow down but glanced in the window and saw men in conversation. Their clothes gave them away. Swedes. *So they're still in business, still reeling in fools the likes of m'self.* He scolded himself. Maybe he wasn't fair. Those men didn't mislead him. He signed on of his own free will.

He continued on, eager to get out of the tumbledown area known for its hooligans, criminals and roaming press gangs. One hand on his dirk, his eyes moved about as he made his way back to the city center. No one accosted him.

The streets widened. Soon he saw shops open, housewives moving about with their daily routines and farmers bringing livestock to market. He allowed himself to relax and drink in the experience of being home again.

Different this, he decided as he studied the streets and buildings. Different, Glasgow was, from Stockholm and the German lands. The narrow streets were the same, but Glasgow had more factories, tanneries and foundries, and wasn't quite as pleasing to the eye. *Maybe it's just me. Maybe I've turned into some kind of right snob.*

Hunger struck. He'd soon give in to a good Scottish feast, but first he found his way to the London Exchange branch and deposited his money. It delighted him everyone spoke English and understood him.

His money secured, he headed to the *Rose and Anchor*. The serving girl, Elspet, served him. She smiled down at him; he returned the smile. "Here, I 'member you. Been away or something?"

He nodded. "Ay, something. Anywho, me stomach's ready for a good Scottish meal and a brew."

"So, speak up. What's your fancy?"

"You've any bubbles and squeak? Have a taste fer it." He referred to the popular dish of leftover cabbage, fried potatoes, and meat.

"Lot of it," he said, "and a good slice of lamb to go with it. I'll pay extra."

"Well now, you're the hungry one, ain't ya?" She laughed. "I'll see what I can do. Anything else?"

"Course. Good stout."

"Comin' up."

"Glad to hear it. Throat's ready; stomach to follow."

She turned and walked off. He followed the exaggerated sway of her hips in their full-length black skirt. *Pretty. Probably spoken for.*

He inspected the room. No one he recognized, but other characters took his interest. Again, it pleased him to listen to his brand of English, but he found the Glaswegian accent stronger than he remembered.

He watched a table of prosperous merchants in fine blue, mauve, and black doublets, hose, and ornamental sabers. Money there, he thought, as they roared at one man's witty comment or joke. He doubted any of them could use their swords though.

Elsewhere two men in yellow and black kilts leaned close to each other in deep, quiet conversation. Every once in a while one would glance up and glower at the room. *Wonder what mischief those two are up to?*

He finished his drink and tasty meal, wiped his mouth with the back of his sleeve, and left Elspet a nice tip. A pony, he decided; he'd like to have a pony beneath him for his trip to Mosstone. A fine Scottish pony. Make him feel at home again. Been tramping foreign lands far too long.

Glasgow had stables on every other block. Ainslie visited five and decided to do business with the last one. He chose a dun-colored, spirited Highland pony with a flowing mane and tail named Deri.

He indulged in a considerable bit of haggling. The price agreed, he left a hefty deposit for the use of Deri. He set out and rode along a path close to the sea. Twice he dismounted at a cliff overlooking the sea and took in his fill of the view.

Deri nudged his arm. He turned. "You're a good one, I'll give you tha'. It's a treat you're wantin', is it?" He opened one of the pouches of the saddle bag and pulled out a withered apple. He moved in front of her and held it in his palm. She accepted the gift and ate with pleasure. Done, she nosed him for more.

"Sorry, lassie," he said. "No more. You don't wanna be getting fat."

He approached Mosstone. A few people whose features he couldn't make out appeared in the distance. As he drew closer he passed the cemetery and noticed a new plot next to his mother. His uncle; they'd brought his body home.

Ainslie wanted to stop, but sensed village eyes on him, and thought it best to keep going. Two boys ran to Cormag's.

More than a handful of villagers met him in front of his grandfather's house by the time he rode up. He made out Cormag and Edine. Both wore welcoming smiles.

Cormag stepped forward. "You're back. Our prayers ha' been answered."

Ainslie climbed down, handed the reins to one of the boys. "Make her safe, willya. I'll be thanking you." He moved forward to embrace Cormag, certain the old man had shrunk.

They pulled apart. "Lovely to be back, granda. Thought about all of you many's the time."

"And good to have you home, laddie." Cormag directed a thumb toward his wife. "Go give your grannie a kiss."

Ainslie obeyed willingly. Edine wrapped her arms around Ainslie and squeezed. When they separated she said, "Come, come." She guided him to the door of the cottage. Cormag followed.

Inside, Edine spoke first. "We bin watchin' for ya all day."

Ainslie raised his eyebrows. "Zat so, nana? Why? I never told no one 'bout comin'"

"Mitchy Selby, your cousin."

"Ay. Wot of him?"

"You remember he's got the Second Sight?"

"If I did, I forgot, nana. Wot then?"

"Not even your granda can remember when we last had someone in the village with the Second Sight. Rare gift."

Cormag interrupted. "Woman, you've a point to make?"

Edine raised her eyebrows toward the roof as if beseeching a higher power to help with her husband. She returned her attention to Ainslie. "Young Mitchy come round yesterday to tell us you was comin' back. An' here you are."

"Mitchy told you? No. Wot else he give up?"

"Nothin'."

"You're right, nana. It's some amazin,' the gift."

"Ay."

"Can I ask you more 'bout it? Maybe at another time?"

"Course. Dinna know ya had the interest."

He hadn't — until he went off to war. Now he found himself interested in the likes of anything supernatural.

Edine reached for a clay jar of whisky. "Your granda'll have some of this too," she said, winking. She set down the whisky on the table and followed with three shot glasses.

Cormag pulled the stopper and poured. "I expect the third one's for you," he said to Edine without meeting her gaze.

"You're the wise one, Cormag. The prodigal son's come home and you'll no toast him alone."

Cormag filled the glasses and grinned at Ainslie. With the stopper back in the jar Cormag raised his drink in a salute and said, "Here's to us; what's like us, damned few, and they're all dead."

Edine and Ainslie honored the traditional toast and lifted their arms. Ainslie tossed his drink back; Edine sipped hers.

The whisky surprised Ainslie. It didn't burn as it once had.

Cormag smacked his lips. "Wonderful to see you again, laddie. You've much to tell us no doubt."

Edine finished her drink and agreed.

"Militia still looking for me, granda?"

Cormag shook his head. "No more. Gave up some time ago. No one'd tell them nothing. You're safe now, laddie."

"Glad to hear it."

Cormag's eyes moved from the three empty glasses to his grandson. "Us too." He thumped the table with his palm. "One more for such a chance." He poured before the other two could protest. Glasses filled again, he raised his and said, "Health."

Once again grandson and wife raised their glasses. "Health," they echoed.

Ainslie drained his glass and set it down a second time.

Edine reached forward and lightly slapped Cormag's arm. "We've him back, Cormag, young Lee."

"An' we have," Cormag agreed and turned his eyes on his grandson. "Ya notice who's lying beside yer ma, did ya?"

Ainslie perked up. "Ay. Glad ya brought it up, granda. It's splendid, is what it is. Hard to miss. Did ya have trouble getting eme back?"

"Och, ay, we did. Cost us more'n a bit of bother an' money, but he's back where he belongs."

"And the others, granda — them too?"

Cormag closed his eyes for a moment, opened them and said, "No. They'd no let us have 'em. Said it'd be a lesson to others."

The three retreated into a melancholy silence. Edine at last broke the silence and said, "Oh, oh, oh." She wagged a finger at Ainslie.

"Something we've got to tell you." Her eyes moved to her husband. "Go ahead, tell 'em."

"Och, ay," Cormag said and grinned at Ainslie. "Your auntie Skeena's to be married."

Ainslie craned his neck. "Ya've to be kiddin.'"

Cormag offered a crooked smile and a fast shrug. "It's the bald truth."

"Anyone I know?"

Cormag leaned back and tossed an arm in the air. "Not one of us. Comes frum Perth way. Down to visit Seamus Macfie outside the village. Seamus brought the man and your auntie together. Keith's his name; Keith Maculey."

"What's he do, this Keith?"

"Publican. Wants to set up a Public House on the Oglivie Road."

Once more Ainslie shook his head in wonder.

"A Public House, here, in Mosstone? What's happened to this place since I left?"

The other chuckled in reply. "Changes comin'" Cormag said. "Even here in Mosstone."

"Suppose. And he's reliable, this publican?" Ainslie asked.

"He is, ay," Edine said.

Ainslie could barely believe what he heard. "It's too much. Glorious for auntie Skeena. Pity his Public House isn't open yet. Be lovely to..."

The door swung open and denied him a chance to finish his sentence. Skeena entered. Ainslie rose and turned to greet her as Cormag said, "And speaking of our lovely Skeena..."

Skeena smiled at Ainslie, who quickly moved into her embrace. She kissed his cheek and broke away. "Wot're you saying about me?" she asked her parents.

"Telling Ainslie your good news, is wot," Cormag answered.

"Ay," Ainslie added. "Wonderful, auntie. You're to be complimented."

Skeena's smile grew wider. "Thank you. Queer as it is, but it's a lovely state of things. I never thought this'd happen to me again and..." She stepped back and considered her nephew. "Ya've bin away more'n a spell, laddie, so now let's have a proper look at ya." Her eyes studied the Ainslie before her; this was a more muscular, yet leaner young man than she remembered. She took in the noticeably dull, puffy eyes, the faint worry lines and the hard set mouth she didn't remember. Or the bits of gray at the sides of his head.

"Ya've changed, "she said.

"Had to expect it, auntie. I'm older."

"Course, course." *No, it's more than age. You're different — outside and in.* She kept the thoughts to herself.

He ate dinner with his family that night, barely able to engage in a lasting conversation before the townspeople, one after another, knocked at the door, wanting to greet the sole survivor of Carlisle Gaol.

Ainslie's annoyed grandfather at last mumbled, "If folks are so happy to see young Lee, least they could do is bring their own drink."

Edine slapped his arm with her fingertips.

"*Wheesh*t, hush Cormag; someone's bound to hear ya."

"Doesn't stop it from being true," he grumbled.

When the last guest finally removed himself, Cormag turned to Ainslie. "I've kept me promise. Your eme's cottage is the way you left it. Clean and everything's ready for ya when you've a mind to rest your head. We've left a fire for ya, and ya can use the embers to light the candles."

"Thanks, granda, thanks. Still catching up on me sleep. I'll bid the three of ya a good night, and see you in the morin'."

He rose, kissed each of them and made his way to his home.

His relatives remained seated, eyes on the door. Skeena studied her parents. "Go on, then; say it."

"Say what?" Cormag asked.

"Lee, da. He's come different."

"What'd ya expect? Laddie's bin off to war. Bound to change any man."

"You're not listenin' to the lass," his wife said. "It's more than just marching off to war. First glance'll tell ya he's good enough, but ya've to see past. Somethin' deeper. Maybe it's only the womenfolk who feel it, but there's a roughness in our laddie's heart. I think he hides it, but it's there."

Cormag waved them both off.

"You're making much out of little. He's alive, our Lee, and he seems fine. You know our saying: 'happy while you're livin', cuz you're a long time dead.' Lee's alive, an' I've no more to say on the subject."

Ainslie lit several candles and studied the interior of the cottage. Full of nostalgia, he walked around and touched and smelled his mother's and uncle's belongings.

I used to live here. In this cottage. Now it all seems so...small. How is did it get so? But then almost everything seemed smaller since his return — especially his grandparents.

He gave himself a quick wash and climbed into his uncle's bed. *Strange being here in eme's bed. I can only remember bein' in it once or twice.*

His mind reviewed the day's events, the satisfying homecoming and conversations with Cormag, Edine and Skeena. It felt almost like like old times. Almost, but not quite, back in his grandparents' home, the place of fond gatherings and happier times. If only his mother and uncle were alive.

A new thought came to him — Mitchy. He recalled the brief conversation with his grandmother about Mitchy.

Second Sight. The Scots, Welsh and the Irish were reputed to be gifted with the Second Sight, or as some called it, *the Sight of the Seers.*

Among the Gaels, the gift of Second Sight was considered rare and revered, Ainslie knew.

It baffled and vexed Pastor Wallace to see villagers bring gifts of food and comfort to Mitchy, to ask his help, yet worry Mitchy knew something private, something personal, about them.

Before sleep claimed Ainslie, he made up his mind to visit Mitchy.

For a few days Ainslie became something of an important man in the village. Everyone yearned to hear about his adventures. He on the other hand preferred not to speak of them. He couldn't understand the attention he received, and voiced it to his grandfather.

"Ay," the old man said, "you grew up here, lived here, and you know wot the village's like. They wanna hear your story, they do."

He caught a glimpse of the roughness Edine spoke about as Ainslie struggled to push his annoyance down at this imposition. Won't cost ya much," he advised his grandson, "ta give 'em what they're wantin.' No point in goin' off your head 'bout it. Do ya no good. Take the drink. Enjoy your time, and they'll tire of ya soon enough."

Ainslie agreed he'd try.

His grandfather's advice proved sound. He made the rounds of the village. He lost track of his stories, of Protestant victories and derring-do against papists. The first few times he gave factual accounts, but too much drink and spurring-on lent the stories a different hue. Protestant victories somehow became grander; Catholics became more loathsome.

As Cormag predicted, soon enough the shine left Ainslie, and he again became but another villager.

Ainslie visited his mother's and uncle's graves frequently. He looked on with approval at Raeburn's headstone and inscription, *Here lies Aiken Raeburn, a truer son of Scotland never existed.*

Skeena's wedding took place at the end of May. Ainslie met Keith a few weeks beforehand. Heavy and a bit shorter than Skeena, the thick-bearded Keith had an easy laugh and a generous heart. He adored his bride-to-be.

"Like 'em," Ainslie told his grandfather at the reception held on the grass knoll in front of the church. "He's every inch the publican. Why do they all have the same build?"

Cormag chuckled.

"It's true, but of no matter. He'll make a fine husband. Loves Skeena, and soon we'll have a place where we can all go to drink."

Ainslie grinned at the last part of his grandfather's statement.

By chance he spotted Mitchy in conversation with his grandmother and her neighbor, Aileen Carrick. He didn't at first recognize his long and lean cousin with his scraggly red beard.

He approached. Mitchy watched him draw close.

"Lee," Mitchy said and smiled. "Bin a while."

"It has, Mitchy," Ainslie said and offered his hand. "Dinna recognize ya at first."

Mitchy took the extended hand. "Can't say the same. Seen you walkin' 'round the village."

"So, wot're you up to these days, Mitchy?"

Mitchy gave him a crooked smile. "Not a lot, Lee. I'm both cursed and blessed with the gift. Know wot I mean?"

"As much as I'm able. Go on."

"I live well enough," the other man said. "People want to know things 'bout the future, and they pay me. I don't always get it right. And then there's Pastor Wallace." He turned his head and gazed at the round-shouldered clergyman in conversation with Skeena and Keith.

Ainslie followed his gaze as Mitchy said, "Surprised he hasn't had me burned at the stake."

"From wot I'm hearin' the village would rise up in revolt."

"There's fine news," Mitchy replied and laughed. "See? Even I dinna know."

"So how's this all work?"

"Not always sure m'self. You understand?"

"No."

"And tha's the hard part — explainin'. I touch things people have touched, and I can see into the future. Not always. Visions, like."

He stopped and gazed at Ainslie. "Are ya wantin' to know about yourself?"

"Yes and no. I do, but afraid to ask. And I've seen some powerfully awful things, Mitchy. Made me start asking more 'bout me life and wot's on the other side."

"I can't answer the second part, but I can do a reading if you want."

Ainslie shook his head. "Dunno, Mitchy. Like I said, I want to know, but..."

"Well, if you change your mind, I'm no hard to find."

Ainslie never worked up the nerve to meet with Mitchy, but he thought about it at least once per day.

On the wedding day, he looked around at the villagers. Most he knew by name, but not for the first time he wondered if he still belonged. He'd never have voiced this to his grandparents, but he felt he'd become an outsider. *If I really don't belong here anymore, then where? Who do I attach to?*

The more he thought about it, the clearer the answer became —his comrades in the German lands.

July arrived before he knew it. Taeberries and pears appeared. Evenings grew shorter and cooler.

Restlessness grew in Ainslie.

In a private moment Edine told her husband, "Laddie's away in his dreams. Got leaving on his mind. Soon, Cormag; you mark me words, soon he'll tell us."

Ainslie did; he surrendered to the impulse and advised Cormag and Edine he intended to leave at the end of the month.

Word spread, and on his last day the villagers held a communal feast for him at Dermid Raeburn's cottage.

Ainslie briefly chatted with Mitchy, but again couldn't bring himself to ask about his future. Maybe its best, he told himself.

In the early morning before the darkness surrendered to the light, when the ground mist gave everything a mystical feel, Ainslie readied Deri.

"You're sure you'll no change your mind and take some food with you?" Edine whispered as she hugged her woolen shawl to her shoulders.

"Thanks, nana, but I won't," he replied in a low voice. "I'll be fine. Glad I came back, and gladder yet I was here for auntie Skeena's wedding. You've both done me better than I've a right to ask. I'm beholden to you for everything."

Ainslie opened his arms wide and swept up his grandmother. When he pulled away, she raised her hands to hold his face, and at last dropped them. Her eyes remained dry but Ainslie saw the sorrow.

He turned to Cormag. After a long embrace, much back-slapping and a jest or two, they disengaged.

Ainslie swung himself into the saddle and stared down at his aged family.

Cormag spoke.

"We'll say it again, laddie; it's no too late. No one'll think the worse if you stay. Better future here than at war."

"Nothing you tell me I've no thought about, granda, but I have to go. Thank you again for all and everything. I'll be fine, and I'll write. But one more thing before I'm off ...." He told them about the bank. "If anything does happen to me, you're to go and get the money. I've left it in your name."

"We've no need for it," Cormag countered. "Bring yourself back is wot we're wantin.'"

"I'll be doing so, granda, but all the same, use it any way you like."

Cormag promised he would, which caused his wife to sniffle and say, "We'll pray fer you, you lovely boy."

Ainslie turned Deri, threw his grandmother a quick kiss, and spurred Deri on, not trusting himself to look behind.

"We'll not see him again, Cormag," Edine sobbed.

"Stop it," Cormag warned as he watched his grandson ride along the path. "You're gonna sound like Mitchy soon."

In his heart the old man secretly agreed.

Ainslie stopped at the cemetery and offered a fast prayer before climbing back in the saddle. "I've no joy you're both buried, ma, eme," he whispered. "None. I can never see or feel you again, but I'm thankful you're here together."

He broke off and swallowed.

"I'm leaving again. Ya likely knew, I'm bettin'. Have to return to something I said I'd no quit. I'll miss you both. I carry nothing but good memories of you. If you spare me a moment, say a prayer for me. I love an' carry you both in me heart."

Chapter 23

DERI wanted to run. Ainslie indulged her and rose in the stirrups. Soon enough she raced across a stretch while he concentrated on keeping his balance. When they reached an incline, he slowed her to a canter. Both caught their breath. He patted her neck. "Wee bit of fun there, eh, lassie? Got a feel fer the race, you have."

The activity allowed him to take his mind off his sadness. *Best to focus on the present.*

He reached Glasgow the following day. Soon enough he found himself in front of St. Kentigern's and recalled when he stopped there last with Blane and Conan. *So many changes since then,* Wistfulness settled on him as he stood there. *No point mopin' here again.*

Alert, Ainslie made his way down to the water. He saw ships anchored at pier four. None appeared to be English. Good — no press gangs.

With his dirk ready and his eyes taking in all activity, he arrived safely at the pier where he found two vessels readying for the open sea. The first flew a Swedish flag; the other a Dutch flag. He discovered the Dutch vessel intended to sail to southwest France, and the Swedish one to Stockholm.

Yes, the captain told him in perfect English, he could sail with them, but only to Stockholm. From there he'd have to find another ship to Peenemunde. "Shouldn't be hard. Ships go almost every day."

Ainslie thanked him. "Can't ask for much better."

"Glad you think so. We sail at first light. Find your pleasure in town if you like, but remember to be back before we cast off."

"No fear. I'll be be well on time."

Ainslie thought it best not to tempt fate, so he hurried into town for a bite to eat. Darkness found him on the ship with six other passengers, standing idly on deck. Ainslie wondered where they were bound.

Once out of the Clyde River they picked up a strong wind. Ainslie moved to the railing and gazed out onto the water. Whitecaps were unmistakable but he felt confident he could master the sea this time.

During the trip he talked to a few passengers but not an irascible giant named Drystan Hoskins. The man had crazy eyes.

His first encounter with the forty-something Welshman and his rat's nest of yellowish, dirty hair warned him to keep his distance. *Wouldn't wanna ever be on his bad side.*

He didn't get a choice. The two tangled at sea near the head, when Ainslie accidentally blocked Hoskins way.

"Outta my way, you," a glowering Hoskins rumbled. "A man's gotta use the head, you get out of his way, got it?"

In reply, Ainslie shook his head. "I'm not wanting trouble, friend, and there's no need for you to be so cruddy."

Hoskins narrowed his eyes further. He stepped closer and stabbed his forefinger into Ainslie's chest.

"Cruddy, is it? How's this for cruddy. I don't like you."

"Zat so?" Ainslie said and stepped back, away from the giant. "Well, since you brought it up, I've no taken a fancy to a blockhead th' like of you neither."

Hoskins bunched his fists and moved threateningly toward Ainslie. In turn Ainslie pulled out his dirk and waved it at Hoskins. The other man pointed to the weapon.

"You threatenin' me with yer little knife? I'll take it and shove it up your arse."

Ainslie held his tongue and waited. Mutual aggression in their stances, neither man backed down until Hoskins snorted. "Better not ever have your guard down when I'm around."

"Count on it," Ainslie assured him.

Hoskins offered another snort and walked past, careful to avoid the arc of the blade.

"Couldn'ta bin in too much of a hurry," Ainslie mumbled under his breath, "if he wasted time nettling me."

It seemed queer being in Stockholm again. Ainslie wandered off in search of passage to his next destination. In short order he found a ship bound for Peenemunde.

He took a room at an inn for the night. In the streets he thought about stopping by Stina Andreasson and her children's place for a visit, but talked himself out of it, and played the idle traveler instead. For old times' sake he visited the grounds of Jönköping Castle and watched a new batch of recruits go through their drills.

It's exactly the same like when I was here. Then again, he reminded himself, why would it be any different?

For dinner he indulged himself in Swedish waffles.

In Peenemunde Ainslie made enquiries as to his destination.

"Best guess is your unit's probably in *Nürnberg*," a sergeant told him. "Things are heating up. If they're not there, then someone's bound to know where they are. Just ask around when you get there."

"Thanks, I will."

The Swede nodded in approval. "There's a convoy leaving this afternoon. Go make arrangements now."

A quick conversation with a waggoneer resulted in a ride. He hoped this one would be friendlier than the last when he climbed beside the driver.

The man, Tomas Frick, didn't disappoint.

"It might be the last supply for Nürnberg in a while," he offered as the wagons moved out.

"Why?"

"They're getting ready for a big push from the Catholics. You'll have more excitement than you can stand."

A mile from Nürnberg, a platoon of Saxon horsemen rode up and accompanied them into the city. "Odd," Frick commented, as the cavalry moved to both sides of the column of wagons. "They didn't do this the last time we came." He called to the horseman beside him. "What's going on?"

"Protection," the soldier said.

"From?"

"Those damned *Landsknechte*."

"'Landsknechte,'" Ainslie repeated, aware he likely mispronounced the word. He turned his gaze on Frick. "Wot's this thing you...?"

"It's not what, it's who, and you've never heard of them?"

Ainslie shook his head. "Can barely get my tongue around the word. So who are they?"

"Mercenaries, foot soldiers like you, but different."

"Different how?"

"They mostly fight with the pike and the halberd, you know, with the cutting blade. And you'd spot their kind the moment you set your eyes on them."

"Oh, yeah. Why?"

"Because they all have beards and wear showy, puffed out, patchwork clothing of different colours, one uniform different from the next. Like nothing you've ever seen before. But don't be fooled by appearances. They can fight."

"So who do they fight for, these what-do-you-call-them?"

"Landsknechte," Frick answered, "they fight for anyone, but mostly themselves nowadays. They're worse than our side and the Catholics put together. The peasants hate them, and live in fear of them."

The column travelled the better part of the morning before it slowed and at last stopped.

Both Frick and Ainslie rose and stared ahead. Blocking the road stood forty or fifty armed pike men in an assortment of colours — reds, greens, blues, gold. In the middle a man held out his arm in a do-not-advance gesture.

Frick hadn't joked, Ainslie thought as he stared at the fierce men, their pikes held in the thrust position.

The Saxon lieutenant bellowed an order to his men. In reply, the men withdrew and readied their pistols. All spread out in a line, prepared to do battle.

The lieutenant rode forward and spoke to the leader of the Landsknechte. Fast enough, both men's voices rose, followed by considerable gesturing.

"What do you guess?" Ainslie asked as he watched.

"They're demanding some kind of toll," Frick said.

"And by the looks of it," Ainslie replied, "our lieutenant's refusing to pay. Pretty brave or brazen, these Landsknechte. Comes to a fight, my guess is we'll come out on top."

"Hope they see it the same way."

A few long tense moments passed before the Landsknechte nodded and the lieutenant turned his horse.

The Landsknechte mercenaries moved to the right, to the left, and back away from the column, thus allowing passage. All the while nervous Saxon riders kept firm grips on their weapons, their eyes alert.

Ainslie exhaled. "Could have done without the excitement," he said as he tossed a final glance at the mercenaries behind them. "Come to a fight, the only thing I have is me dagger."

"At least you had something," Frick said.

"Well, we got through, but this is the strangest thing I've ever seen in war."

"I told you."

They stopped to rest and water the horses. "Any news about the war?" Ainslie asked one of the Saxon riders.

"Papists coming."

"They are, eh?"

The man nodded. "Not exactly a big surprise; been expecting them for some time. They've raised a new army and are forcing us to retreat or defend what we have."

"Why doesn't the king bring reinforcements?"

The soldier considered the question. "He's tied up, is what we're told. Thinks we're strong enough to hold off any assault for now. Be a while before you'll be coming back here."

"Guess you're right; no big surprise. Good luck to you."

"Thanks," the man said. "We'll need all the luck we can get."

Ainslie noticed a line of civilians make its way to the main gate as they neared Nürnberg.

Frick nodded with his chin. "Refugees. They're fleeing the Catholics. Hope the city can feed them all once the gates are locked."

Outside the city walls pikemen and foot soldiers went through drills, unconcerned about the crush of civilians. Farther away, horse cavalry practiced charges and cannoneers fired practice rounds.

Teams of engineers busied themselves inspecting the walls for weaknesses.

You didn't have to be a Mitchy to know the enemy would arrive at the gates soon enough, a hot, dusty and bone-tired Ainslie thought as he jumped down from the wagon.

"Good traveling with you, Tomas," He shook Frick's hand.

"You too," Frick said, "and good luck and stay safe."

Ainslie turned. By chance his eye caught the hot-tempered Hoskins. *Och, god; I can't get away from this fool. As if our side dinna have troubles enough.*

Hoskins glowered at him. Ainslie returned the glare. Nearby soldiers caught the staring match. Ainslie didn't want the attention and decided to move on. *Enjoy your victory,* he silently said to Hoskins. *Hope I've seen the last of you.*

He asked a soldier where the headquarters were.

The man pointed. "In the Council Haus."

Ainslie found the ornate building. Soldiers were everywhere. He recognized a few, and tossed a casual wave. I'm in the right place, he thought, glad to be back in the familiar. Men jostled and shouted as Ainslie made his way down the corridor.

It took a while before he found someone to report to — Lieutenant Maki. The man's English proved better than Ainslie's Swedish, so they conversed in English.

"Come with me," Maki said and marched off to find Captain Pierson.

Maki's conversation with his superior lasted a short time. Ainslie couldn't keep up with their fast-paced exchange. A few quick ja-jas, and then Pierson dismissed the lieutenant and Ainslie.

Out in the hall, Maki turned to Ainslie, "You heard — Catholics are coming?"

"Heard, ay, sir."

Maki waited a moment, drew in his breath and said, "You took training — in shooting?

"I did, sir, yes, with lieutenant Geiger."

"Ah. In any event you are now no longer a pike man, but a musketeer. I have the authority to promote you. We've lost some men, and you've had the training."

Ainslie's eyes widened with pleasure. A promotion.

"Thank you, sir. I'll do you proud."

"I am sure you will. Onto the next thing. Go to the *kvartermästare*. Do you know this word?"

"You're meanin' the stores for clothes and weapons and the like, sir — the quartermaster?"

Maki nodded. "Good, good. Yes. The quartermaster." He sounded out the word again. "Now, go there. It is across from the *Frauenkirche* — the church."

"Ay, sir."

Maki pointed. "The Frauenkirche — you cannot miss it."

"Right, right. I think I passed it."

Maki carried on with his instructions. "Ask for a leather coat, bandoleer, powder flask, and of course your musket. If you have trouble with them, send them to me." He stopped and peered at Ainslie. "Good so far?"

"Perfect, sir."

"Next, your living quarters... From the church, go to *Westlicher Stern 43*." He repeated the name and number. "43. There and the next house, 45, is where your men are. Do you understand?"

"Ay, I do, sir."

"Everything in order then?"

"You mean are we done? Ay, we are, sir. Nothin' else."

Outside a light rain fell. Ainslie glanced up at the sky; the clouds weren't threatening. A good sign. The rain would probably stop soon.

He found it frustrating at the quartermaster, with its beehive of activity. Soldiers marched in and out, shouting orders. It seemed like forever before anyone bothered with him.

Back on the street with his arms loaded, it took him a while to get organized. Too warm to don his new coat, he draped it over one arm and cradled his musket across the other. He walked the twisting streets and alleys — a few so narrow he thought a man could easily touch the houses on either side at the same time.

Almost everywhere he saw evidence of people readying for an up-coming siege. Men inspected or repaired shutters ready to be closed at a moment's notice. Others hauled supplies and water into their homes; sheds with animal fodder were filled to the brim.

Ainslie saw men inspect wells, and merchants carry barrels of cooking oil, potatoes, cured meats, vegetables and medicines down stairs to underground cellars.

The twisting, narrow streets confused Ainslie. More than once he lost his way and had to stop and ask for directions.

The click, click of his boots echoed against the slick cobblestones as he continued his aimless search for the right street — Westlicher Stern.

He at last found the street. Unlike many others this one allowed two carts or carriages to pass. Moneyed burghers live here, he thought as he searched for the address. Lace curtains fluttered, and curious eyes watched him pass.

Number 43 sat at the end of the row of well-kept, half-timbered stucco houses with gabled roofs. He opened the thick ornate oak door and let himself into a darkened and lofty hallway with blackened oak beams and a tiled floor.

Ainslie set his belongings down and flexed his arms, grateful to be rid of everything.

Male voices floated into the hallway — voices he recognized. They brought on a smile. He wanted to join them, yet his eyes delighted in the splendour around him. They settled on an impressive glass mirror in a gilded frame hung over a heavily lacquered cabinet. He stared with admiration at the gold leaf frame. By itself it had to have been worth a small fortune. Its very size.... He remembered his mother's small handheld one. His uncle had paid a lot of money for it. What would his mother make of this one?

Not finished with his inspection, he let his eyes take in the dark wood panelling and the stone fireplace with its large chimney. Unbelievable! The size of it would take up most of his uncle's cottage.

His eyes moved to the waist-high, glazed vases, one burgundy and the other black, in the far corners next to some dark coffin stools.

He had no idea what — if anything — the vases held. He considered peeking inside, but thought better of it.

A high-back hall chair with a turned spindle back completed the hallway furniture.

"Place is like a bloody manor," he whispered as he finished his inspection. "Better than wot Castle Shiveringford's got, I'd bet."

A soldier stepped into the hallway and gave Ainslie his profile. Ainslie made a soft noise in his throat. The stranger startled and recovered before turning to face Ainslie. He noted the small shoulders and sparse beard. In turn the other man gave Ainslie an overlong appraisal before he said, "Yeah what're you wanting?"

Ainslie couldn't place the accent; had to be somewhere in the south, he thought. He answered the question with his own. "Wot's your home, then?"

Whatever its intent, his question did little to invite conversation. The other man set his face hard, the brown eyes full of suspicion.

"The Toon. Why, what's it to you?"

The Toon — Newcastle.

Something in the other man's attitude grated on Ainslie. He took a deep breath.

"Wot's it to me? I'll tell you wot it's to me. I asked you a civil question and you give me a cart load of shit."

His voice hardening, Ainslie continued, even as he heard chairs scrape on a wooden floor nearby. "You've no cause to treat a veteran comin' back to join his mates like this."

Seven men spilled out into the hallway. Ainslie gave them a fast glance, kept his face hard and returned his attention to the other man. With chin and neck extended he said, "What're you called?"

Whether Ainslie's severe manner, the arrival of others, or both, the challenger immediately lost some of his earlier posturing. He turned his head to the others, as if in search of their support. His gaze settled on Gisis.

"Well, go on then," Gisis urged. "The man asked you a question."

Ainslie's eyes found Jigs', who winked at him.

"Declan Cross," the man said in a low voice.

Ainslie sniffed. "Well, Declan Cross, here's a tip. You've no lived long enough to be giving me your kinda lip."

For the briefest moment everything went silent. Then Cecil spoke. "Now there's a given in life— find a wrangle and you'll find a Scot in the middle of it."

The comment broke the tension. All but Cross let loose with rowdy laughter. He appeared both relieved and confused.

Gisis, Jigs and Cecil crowded around Ainslie, ruffled his hair and slapped his shoulder with great affection.

"You're back," Cecil said. "We've missed you. Weren't sure if you'd come."

Ainslie beamed at his mates.

"Have to tell ya — tough choice between all the lassies back home and you lot. Somethin's wrong with me. Somethin' seriously wrong, 'cause I chose the likes of you."

The joke resulted in more backslapping and jostling before Gisis said, ""You've already met Declan. Don't mind him much; he's not a bad sort."

Cross jumped in. "Sorry. Come off bad, I bet, but I didn't mean nothin' by it."

Ainslie dismissed the brief confrontation. "Right, then, Declan; the thing's done. We'll pretend it never happened. I'll get to know you soon enough."

"Fine by me. Been here a month now."

Jigs interrupted. "Care to look around, Lee?"

Ainslie waved his arm about to indicate the house. "Fine this; actually, more like splendid. How'd we find ourselves in here?"

"No one living here," Jigs said, "so they put us in this one and the one next door. Belonged to two families. Strong Catholic convictions from what we heard."

Cecil jumped in. "Yeah, we heard they tried to sell them, but couldn't get their asking price. When things got worse, they ran. Guess they decided saving their skin was more important. Can't say one way or another if it's true, but does make a good story."

Ainslie followed Cecil into the room the soldiers used. A large, dark, rectangular oak table surrounded by eight chairs stood in the middle.

Ainslie gaped at the chairs. Each one was padded and covered in a green upholstered fabric. He'd never seen anything like it. He walked over to the closest chair and felt the fabric.

"Something, isn't it?" Cecil said.

"It is," Ainslie agreed.

Cecil swept his arm around the room and did a mock imitation of a man of refinement.

"This is our dining room."

"Dining room?" Ainslie repeated. "Well la-di-da." He remembered tales of some of the Mosstone village women who had worked at Castle Shiveringford; they'd often talked about the elegance of the dining room mansions and the grand meals laid out. Imagine, he told himself, having a separate room in which to eat.

The table and chairs sat on a large, deep patterned oval rug. A brick fireplace and chimney sat beyond the table. Opposite the table sat a buffet sideboard with panelled doors and thick, spindled legs.

The friends gave him a tour of the rest of the main floor. Another impressive but smaller room held several cushioned chairs and a large spinning wheel.

"And this," Cecil said, "is where the family — I mean, we — receive visitors."

"Receive?" Ainslie repeated and followed with a smile. "Are you lot receiving me now?"

Jigs joined in on the fun. "Ay, we are. Nothing's too good for Scottish nobility. We'll sit and have us a dram or two before we retire to dinner and a fine evening of cards n' good conversation."

They moved to the second floor which held several bedrooms with polished wooden floorboards and ornate canopied beds.

"And where do we all sleep?" Ainslie asked as they walked back down the stairs.

"Well," Cecil said, "the sergeants here, Morison and Gis," he jerked his thumb at Lang and Morison behind him, "have rank seniority so they get the beds. The rest of us make ourselves comfortable wherever we fancy."

Ainslie stopped halfway down the stairs, turned, and stared past Cecil.

"What! You two are sergeants now? When?"

Cecil moved past him and answered. "After Rain — the city. Huge battle."

"And before you say more," Gisis said to Cecil, "you'd best tell him you coulda been promoted too, but turned it down."

Cecil dismissed the assertion with a wave of his hand. "I have my own reasons."

"Ay," Jigs shot back, "and you're not telling anybody wot it is."

"Right."

Ainslie creased his brow. "Hold on now. Everything's going too fast." He pointed to Lang. "So, you and Jiggy have been bumped to sergeant, and Cec here's staying put. Have I got it right?"

Gisis nodded.

"And wot of the rest — Cade, Dev and Podo?"

The other three at first rewarded the question with an awkward silence as their eyes flitted back and forth. Something passed among them before Gisis at last nodded to Cecil and said, "Go."

In turn, Cecil let out a plaintive sigh. "Podo's next door. "Cade and Dev..." His eyes turned to Gisis and Jigs as if to seek help.

Ainslie caught the meaning. "Wot?"

Gisis cleared his throat. "We lost Cade and Dev. Only thing we know is a bunch of our footsloggers broke off from the rest of us. Cade and Dev were among them."

He lowered his eyes and slowly shook his head. "None of 'em ever come back."

"Och, no," Ainslie moaned. "They were a howling pair together. Always at each other, but never meant it. Made you laugh. Dev had his ways but you had to like him, and Cade — a better man you'd no find."

"Ay," Jigs whispered. "We miss em sore. Like you said, Dev could come across difficult-like but his heart was in the right place. They had a good fondness for each other."

Cecil spoke again. "Hate saying this, but good chance they're dead. Papists don't like to keep prisoners."

"No better than us," Jigs said. "But worst is if they're dead, they'll no get a good Christian burial. It's wot troubles me most."

"One thing for sure," Ainslie tossed in. "If they're dead, you can bet they've marched into heaven in each other's company."

"Gotta agree," Jigs said. "And good old John Knox himself'll be there to meet 'em and show 'em around."

"But Podo's still living?" Ainslie asked.

"He is," Gisis answered, "but he's changed, our friend. Not the same from before. Better brace 'self for the change."

"Wot'ya mean?"

Jigs held up a hand in warning. "Keep your head. You'll find out soon enough."

Another sense of awkwardness fell over the friends, each unsure of what to say.

Ainslie found his voice and asked why Paolo lived next door.

"His choice," Cecil said. "You have to ask him."

"There's more to this than you're telling," Ainslie challenged.

"True, but for another time." Cecil gazed at Jigs. "Why don't you go and get Podo. See if he wants to join us. The five of us'll take off and get some beer. I'm sure Lee here's got a tale or two worth telling about his time away."

"Good plan," Jigs agreed.

"We'll wait for you."

Jigs returned trailing a reluctant Paolo.

"We're back," he said. "Took a little doing getting our friend Podo here to come with me, but I promised we'd leave him alone if he at least made an appearance."

He spun, stepped aside and trained his gaze on Paolo. "Right, Podo?"

Paolo didn't answer but simply glanced around the room, a man who gave the distinct impression he'd rather be anywhere than with them. Nervousness riddled his entire being. The man Ainslie last saw demonstrated an easy comfort in social situations; this man gave evidence of being ill-at-ease. His eyes moved constantly, but rarely settled on his friends. His feet wouldn't keep still; he shuffled about in a small area of the floor.

Ainslie noted the small tremor in Paolo's hands.

Gisis hadn't exaggerated. It took all of Ainslie's willpower not to stare at his good friend, Paolo. An angry, ugly scar ran down the length of the right side of his face, from eye to jawline. Its outline against his light brown skin gave him an almost foreboding appearance.

Ainslie tried to think what the outline called to mind. It came to him. A salamander; yes, the scar resembled the picture of a salamander he once saw in a book. He thought the name curious, laughed whenever he said it.

Feeling the compulsion to embrace his friend, he smiled and said with more spirit than he felt, "Sergeant Alberti, good to see you again."

The once cheerful Paolo kept a deadpan expression on his face and surprised him with his answer. "You are back."

Stung by the cold response Ainslie said, "Ay, I am. You think I wasn't coming?"

Paolo drew in air, ready to say something, but Ainslie went on. "Ready to get caught up with what I missed. How've you been?"

"I am as you are seeing me."

Ainslie quickly noted the voice; it lacked emotion. Once filled with pitch, volume and character, it now presented as flat and uninspiring.

He tried again. "It's all, Podo; all you're givin' me?"

"You are wishing more?"

"Yeah, course I am; it'd be good to see your old pleasantness, but hey, do what you think's best."

In reply Paolo simply turned his gaze to the floor.

Jigs worked his way behind and to the left of Paolo. He wiggled his forefinger to get Ainslie's attention and sliced the air sideways with his hand. *Let it be.*

With a slight nod Ainslie acknowledged he understood.

If Paolo noticed, he didn't let on.

Jigs stepped forward, beside the Italian. "Let's quit with the chit-chat and be off and fill our bellies with beer while there's some to be had. And while we're there, we'll have a go at the Fräuleins?" He gazed at Paolo. "Wot'ya say?"

Paolo rewarded the enthusiasm with a slow shake of his head.

"I am tired. Better you are going without me."

The others stood frozen in place as Paolo spun about and left the room.

The disappointed friends stared after him. No one said anything for a moment. Finally, in a low voice, Jigs said, "Took some doing to get him to come this far. Thought we had a chance there. Never been the same since Rain."

"Wot happened?" Ainslie asked.

"We got into a scrum with papists when we crossed a river. Friend Podo caught a pike. Shoulda seen the blood. I thought he was a-gone. How he come through the stitchin's a big mystery."

"True," Cecil added. "Healed on the outside maybe, but not in here." He made a fist and wacked it over his heart. "Not in here." He shook his head as if to give credence to his own statement.

His eyes found Ainslie's. "It's rough. Lee, and I take no pleasure in saying this, but you've lost Podo. All of us have. He's gone for good. Try not to take it personally."

Easier said than done, Ainslie thought, but kept the thought to himself as Jigs said, "Terrible sight, Podo, wot with all them bandages 'round his head, face all puffed up." He met Ainslie's gaze. "Like Cec's saying: healed, the outside, but the inside, och, mince. Keeps to hisself now. Doesn't much bother with any of us."

Cecil spoke up. "Let him be. Let's at least the rest of us go get some beer and celebrate Lee's return."

They found their way to a nearby tavern. Ainslie treated Paolo's rejection much like a man who suffered a death. His friend's change and the loss of Devin and Cade put him in low spirits. He did his best to hide his feelings, but he didn't fool the others.

On his second tankard, Gisis leaned across the rectangular table and said, "Friend Lee, if anyone gives meaning to the saying, 'lost his best friend,' it's you." He pointed. "Your face, if it gets any longer, it'll sink into your beer. Cheer up. Things are bound to get better. Just something Podo's going through."

The others agreed, smiled at and jostled Ainslie.

As a group the men behaved like men everywhere under the influence of drink; they grew noisy, argued, told bawdy jokes, bemoaned their current lack of sexual opportunities, and more than occasionally lifted cheeks to break wind.

Ainslie joined in the fun but the sting of Paolo's rejection hadn't diminished. Nor had the anger with it — anger he couldn't quite understand. He rose unsteady and stumbled to the back to relieve himself. Almost out the door, he bumped into Pierce Hand on his way in.

Neither man prepared for the collision.

"Oof."

"What the..."

Hand's face darkened at the sight of Ainslie. "Whyn't you walk with your head up instead of up your arse, you fucking shite."

Ainslie had trouble standing on his feet, let alone uttering a logical, sentence.

"Lemme tell ya som..." he started to say.

Hand stepped closer to the drunken Ainslie, pulled back his left arm and swung. The punch struck Ainslie's left eye and sent him staggering backward. His hands flew to his face. As it did, Hand drew closer yet and delivered his next blow to Ainslie's gut.

Ainslie collapsed onto the dirty floor. Hand moved forward and let his feet do the rest. At the mercy of the Irishman, the Scot could do little but curl up and protect his kidneys and head as kick after kick landed on him.

The intervention of a taverner prevented Hand from kicking Ainslie to death. The man's beefy arm struck Hand behind the left ear. "The fucker went down like a sack of potatoes," someone later said.

Blood seeped from Ainslie's forehead and nose; his left eye was swollen almost shut. His ribs hurt; pain, excruciating pain like he'd never experienced.

"Quick," Gisis said as he helped Ainslie to his feet, "let's get him out of here before something else happens."

The friends hurried their wounded comrade back to Westlicher Stern.

It took eleven days and several visits to the barber-surgeon before Ainslie's eye attracted little attention.

"Could have been worse," Cecil pointed out, as Ainslie's swelling subsided and the bruises turned from blue-black to yellow. "Much worse."

In no mood for an uplifting speech, a testy Ainslie glowered at the Englishman.

"Are you through? It's no helping — your speech."

"Come on, Lee; I'm on your side. Just saying be thankful he didn't kill you. Soon you'll be up, about."

Ainslie softened his response.

"Ah, sorry; I'm no me old self. You're right it coulda gone worse."

He didn't share his private thought. *I won't be forgetting this, Hand. If the chance ever comes I'll see to it you'll not die a fair straight death.*

For days he brooded about how he intended to take his revenge.

"Podo asked how you were," Jigs said to him one day.

Ainslie's eyebrows rose. "Did he now?" he replied in his best imitation of a blasé voice. "Good of him."

Chapter 24

TWO weeks later, a lieutenant on the parapet picked up the sound of distant strains of fife and drums.

"Oh, oh," he murmured. "They're here."

He pulled his spyglass from his shoulder bag and trained it on the far horizon. Yes, there they were, coming into view, pennant bearers who marched in crisp formation behind the fife-and-drum corps Cavalry rode behind the drummers.

The lieutenant turned and shouted down. "Enemy in sight. Sound the alarm and get the Colonel. Hurry." He again trained his spyglass on the enemy and took in the cuirassiers in all their finery. Posers, he thought as he watched. Posers; the lot of them. They've practiced this. They're after the grand effect. Still, can't argue. They got my attention.

The enemy fife-and-drums line spread out and halted.

"Come on," the lieutenant willed the enemy, "come closer and get a taste of our cannon fire."

Bells all over the city pealed and trumpets sounded out the *Extinction de Feux*, extinguish all fires, and called the ready to arms.

Men locked gates and strengthened them with the thick crossbeams. Artillerymen ran to their assigned stations.

The stone walkways on the parapet became overcrowded; everyone wanted the chance to see the papist enemy.

Commanders threatened to flog or imprison anyone without business on the wall.

At Westlicher Stern, the friends heard the call to arms. Ainslie bolted from his bed and made for his leather coat, musket, bandoleer, and powder flask. He rushed down the stairs along with the others. Outside, heavy boots thundered off the cobblestone.

He met up with Paolo carrying his pike. The two gave each other fast nods of recognition as they rushed forward, both focused on the immediate danger beyond the city gates.

Pike men and musketeers separated and hastened to their assigned posts by the wall.

Ainslie's group stationed themselves by the main gate. His eyes took in the soldiers around him. By chance they landed on Pierce Hand. *What the hell. I can't turn around without seeing this arsehole.* He wanted to, but couldn't tear his eyes from Hand. He waited until he caught the Irishman's eye and gave him his best venomous glare.

Hand met the challenge with a self-satisfied smirk.

Quiet rage filled Ainslie's body. His heart raced, sweat glistened off his forehead and soaked his tunic. He clenched his teeth, his muscles hurt. He wanted to spring forward, to beat Hand senseless, but couldn't — too many witnesses.

Pierson rotated his men. All took turns on the walkway.

"Sergeant Lang," Pierson ordered; "bring up your platoon. Morison, your turn next."

By late morning Ainslie and Declan Cross stared across the plain.

"How many, you reckon?" Declan asked as they considered the sea of cavalry and foot soldiers.

Ainslie exhaled and said, "A lot there, Deck. At a guess, I'd say thousands."

Declan whistled in reply. "Never seen so many in one place."

"Not a common sight," Ainslie agreed.

Pierson halted the conversation. "Riders approaching," he called out. "Three." He set down his spyglass and turned. "You," he ordered Declan. "Run and fetch Colonel Berjosen."

"Yes sir."

Declan hurried off. Pierson watched the four riders in polished cuirass approach.

"Coming to ask us to surrender, Captain?" Ainslie asked.

The Huguenot stared ahead. "Don't know what else it could be. We won't do it, but code-of-conduct says they are obliged to ask."

The riders stopped short of the city gate; one moved forward and bellowed, "We wish to speak with your commander."

The words were in German.

Pierson answered in the same tongue. "He will be here in a moment."

No sooner had Pierson spoken than the pudgy Berjosen huffed up the stone stairway.

To no one's surprise the envoy demanded the surrender of the city.

Berjosen refused.

"You are confident of your decision?" the cavalryman shouted up.

"We are," Berjosen returned.

"God have mercy on your soon-to-be-departed souls," the Catholic answered. He swung about, his escorts behind him, and returned to his men.

Imperialist activity started shortly thereafter. Hundreds of men with shovels dug a huge circle around the castle out of range of cannon fire.

"What're they up to, sergeant," Declan asked?

"Haven't the faintest," Jigs said. He turned his head and shouted along the walkway. "Anyone tell us what they're doin'?"

"Circumvallation," someone shouted.

"I've no idea what yer sayin', let alone how to say it."

"Come here and I'll teach you something new."

Puzzled, Jigs walked to the owner of the voice, one sergeant Vince Bayner. A few moments later he returned to his men.

"Right then; as best as I understand it, they call it a "line of circumvallation — from the sounds of it, some kind of froggie word." He sounded out the word with great care before he continued. "They'll dig themselves this circumvallation, ditch, and surround us to stop our men from galloping out of the city an' charging across at them. And from there they can dig closer to the city walls."

"You mean like sappers?" Declan asked.

Gisis gave him a suspicious look.

"'Sappers?' You know 'bout sappers?'"

"I know a few things."

"Sure you do, ay."

Chapter 25

IT unnerved Hippolito — the madness that stalked him. At first he gave it little thought but, bit by bit, he recognized something was wrong. *Is this it? Is this what's in store for me? I'm going to slide into a madness I can't escape? Please, please, Dear Lord; save me.*

It started with an inability to focus. In the past his training coupled with his natural disposition made it easy for him to concentrate on any matter at hand. Now Hippolito's mind gave him little rest; it raced in every direction at a horse's gallop.

In addition, he found himself more quarrelsome and suspicious of others. Three times he accused fellow priests of plotting against him. He apologized later but it cost him the last of his good name. Now most of his his equals shunned him.

The disease, he felt certain the disease affected his state of mind. What happens when madness takes over fully, and I don't know the difference, he asked himself?

He shouldn't feel like this, he told himself, especially since Count von Wallenstein had taken command and formed a new army. Things really had improved for him.

After Tilly's death Hippolito stayed with the remains of the Catholic League. Wouters left to take a teaching position at the University of Leuven, and no one new took charge of the clerical mission. Hippolito had never heard of the university but supposed it must be a Catholic institution.

His superiors wrote and reminded him his assignment to the Catholic League would soon end. They anticipated his return. He hurried off a response and begged for an extension of his mission.

They replied and insisted he make his case.

"I am needed," he wrote. "Our troops still mourn the loss of our Most Gracious General, Field Marshal Johannes Tserclaes von Tilly. Our new Grand Field Marshal, Count von Wallenstein, settles into his duties. The soul of the army cannot do without a strong conservative voice— who better than a Dominican, the true voice of Holy Mother Church?"

He read his embellished letter twice, affixed a seal and readied it for dispatch. His superiors — so far away — might as well have been on the moon. How were they to argue his claims?

Four weeks later he received his answer. They granted him permission to stay "for the time being."

He read and re-read the response, exhilarated, having learned he did not have to return. His loyalty to his brother demanded better.

Hippolito's health took a turn for the worst. It started with dizziness, which then affected his sense of balance. A day didn't pass without a spell or a tumble of some sort.

Other ailments followed. His muscles ached and he suffered hot flashes; his upper cassock clung to him, soaked from his sweat.

He prayed for relief but instead woke one morning to discover he couldn't see. He sat up and called for help. His brethren rushed into his room and found a confused and panic-stricken Hippolito stumbling around his rooms, with his arms out in front of him. They brought him to Brother Francis who encouraged the continuation of prayer.

A day later Hippolito's vision partially returned.

"One thing after another," a grateful Hippolito said as he spoke to the Augustinian. "You know, I almost think I'm cursed."

Francis shook his head in disagreement. "You cannot believe what you've said, Father. Ours is not a vengeful God. Christ Jesus proved so by dying on the cross."

"Yes," Hippolito agreed. "My eyesight did return after many prayers. But now I have this...this leaking. It comes on at any time or place and causes me the greatest embarrassment. I may only have sight in one eye, but I'm not blind; I see others wrinkle up their noses when I'm nearby."

At night he laid in his bed, stared into the darkness and whispered, "Father, why hast Thou forsaken me?"

Another visit to Brother Francis set him off. He expected words of comfort but instead received the bleakest of forecast.

"I fear, Father, your disease is progressing. I say this with great reluctance — it is now out of my hands."

The words enraged Hippolito.

"Out of your hands?" he shouted. "What do you mean, out of your hands? Who are you to tell me you are done with me?"

Spittle formed at the corners of Hippolito's mouth.

"I...." Brother Francis began, but Hippolito cut him off.

"You are given the task to heal, not to choose to give up. You mend; you cure until all hope is gone. .All hope is not gone with me, do you understand, you cow-patch excuse of a holy man?"

Brother Francis addressed the outburst with tenderness. He clasped his hands together and braved out the storm.

"You have every reason to be cross, Father, at what life has thrown at you. I ask you to believe I have not chosen to deny you. I only point out what training and experience tell me. The disease always grows and attacks its host. I wish I could say otherwise."

Hippolito's shoulders collapsed. He swiped at his eyes, drew in a breath of air and apologized. "I don't know what came over me."

"No apology is needed, Father; it is the disease talking, not you."

Hippolito nodded in an absent way.

"Now," Francis said, "let us again consider your situation."

The barber-surgeon reviewed Hippolito's ailments and promised to do whatever he could to moderate his pain and discomfort.

"Should your pain become too severe, I will get opium to help manage it."

Hippolito raised his head and peered at Francis. "Opium? What is opium?"

"A drug, Father; hard to obtain. Quite powerful against pain. It comes from the east. We trade for it with the Saracens."

"And you think I need it?"

"You might, yes."

"All right," Hippolito said. "What else do you suggest?"

"Well, there are other medicines, such as Jesuit's Bark for your muscles. Some swear by it for nervous conditions. I am told, too, certain little red berries from California do wonders for those who suffer urination problems. I cannot remember their name at the moment, but I will see about getting them. For your unsteadiness, we'll try having you inhale burnt feathers."

"A lot there," Hippolito said.

"Indeed, Father. We will have to rely on trial and error until we find what helps you the best."

Count von Wallenstein moved about in his chair and winced. This damnable gout, he thought. Painful beyond belief, and no cure. All the doctors ever subjected him to was the cursed bloodletting. His scars testified to all the blood he surrendered, and it had made no difference. He glanced at his arm. Doctors. Bah. Pack of charlatans.

He consulted the same map his predecessor once did. What would Tilly think, he wondered, if he knew I took over his tent? Probably toss and turn in his grave.

He returned his attention to the map. Things were beginning to show promise. Mindful of the Breitenfeld experience Wallenstein carefully avoided all out-in-the-open combat with Gustavus. No matter how much the Swede taunted or challenged him to stand and fight, Wallenstein knew better — he'd be mauled.

Be like the fox, he told himself. Pick and choose the time and place to strike.

He studied the map and whispered to an unseen enemy "When I do, you will know, and will wish you weren't born."

Wallenstein's strategy relied on harassing the enemy; a strategy he intended to continue. His forces were spread thin, but already he'd won victories in Bohemia. He knew more would come.

Much to be gained from victory. It released wonderful memories of Magdeburg. He savored each remembrance. *We brought those high-and-mighty to their knees, we did.*

He, along with most of the officer corps, enriched himself with considerable plunder from Magdeburg. It was his due. The spoils of war. Rapes and wanton killings, well, unintentional outcome of military operations. What could one do? No easy task being a soldier.

He reached for his wine goblet, took a long drink and then set it back down. His eye fell on the plate of roasted chicken. Food, yes; he'd eat something to keep up his strength. He tore off a leg and munched hungrily.

Unlike his predecessor, Wallenstein liked to eat alone. He didn't need the comradeship of his men. Let them do his bidding and nothing more.

His mind returned to his conversation with Captain Jorge Riojas. "Intelligence tells us the Swede's soon on the move, likely heading for Nürnberg with a sizable force, sire."

Wallenstein ran his tongue over his teeth, then picked up his glass of wine and drank deeply. He set it down and bellowed for von Durin.

"Sire?" von Durin said as he hurried into the tent.

"Summon my commanders. Now."

Von Durin saluted. "At once Herr General." He spun and left.

Wallenstein kept the War Council meeting brief; all agreed Imperialist forces could not match up well against the enemy.

"I need to both distract and create a victory against the Swede until I'm at full strength. Unless necessary I will not countenance flight; however, full head-to-head combat with the Swede is suicidal. The day will come when I can, but it hasn't arrived yet."

He gazed at the faces around him. "I'm open to suggestions for strategies. Anything?"

The elderly general Bernhard Gossens spoke up.

"I have something of possible interest."

"Let's hear it."

"I know a perfect place for us to stand."

Wallenstein twirled the ivory end of his cane. "You're repeating yourself."

Gossens told of an old run-down castle. "'*Alten Veste*,' the locals call it — Old Fortress. Out on the flat plain; you can see it miles away. Be a simple thing to defend. We dig in, waste the Swede's time, and make him use his resources to root us out."

Wallenstein took more interest in the general's account. He let Gossens finish and uttered one word, "Show me —on the map."

Where?"

Delighted he had the Field Marshal's attention, Gossens rose and approached the large table map. A moment later stabbed a spot on the map. "About three miles from Nürnberg; between there and Furth. The Swede has to pass it to get to Nürnberg." He nodded as if to approve of his own viewpoint.

"I want to see it," Wallenstein said. "Take me there."

The entire War Council visited the hill. It proved to be all Gossens had said, and more. A medieval castle long abandoned but for occasional lovers, outlaws, and wayfarers in desperate need of shelter. Thick vegetation of brush and trees covered everything on the slopes and almost hid the once-traveled path to the top.

"Perfect," Wallenstein said. "We'll fortify this castle and send a regiment or two to Nürnberg. The Swede will be forced to split his forces; yes, it will do exactly what I want —tie him down in two places."

The old castle became a fortification once again. Hundreds of men and dozens of wagons laden with food, water, and materials struggled in their journey up to the ruins as Wallenstein and his retinue made themselves as comfortable as possible in the castle's interior.

The Count oversaw much of the fortification from his sedan. Soldiers and civilians worked at a frantic pace to ready the hill for the arrival of Protestant armies. Wherever possible, trees and underbrush were cut or burnt to give defenders clear shots at any onrushing enemy, and deep entrenchments were dug. Engineers cut and embedded young, thin trees into the entrenchments, with points facing upward. Anyone unfortunate enough to fall into the ditch suffered a horrible slow death on the sharp stakes.

With the work completed, Wallenstein inspected everything a final time. "Perfect," he said, as his footmen struggled to carry him. "This will do nicely."

Hippolito dismounted and led his horse to the castle, grateful Wallenstein had included the clergy atop the hill. Along with the other six priests, he started out well enough but the climb exhausted him. Out of breath, he moved to the side of the procession with his horse and let the others pass while he bent and pulled air into his lungs.

"Having trouble, Father?"

Hippolito looked up to find Brother Francis. The friar sounded concerned as he guided horse and cart toward Hippolito.

"No," Hippolito insisted. "I'll be all right. You go ahead. I'll join you soon."

The choicest spots at the peak belonged to the Field Marshal, his generals, and their escorts. Cavalry, musketeers, and foot soldiers laid claim outside the walls. The rest made do with what remained.

Eight days passed and still the enemy hadn't arrived. Late in the afternoon, advance units of the Swedish army were spotted in the northwest. The alarm went out.

Wallenstein bellowed for his footmen. At once they arrived and bowed. He threw an arm over each man. They lifted the Field Marshal. After considerable struggle they made it up the crumbling staircase. Out of breath and sweating, they waited stoically until crutches were handed to Wallenstein.

The Count shifted to his good foot and brought his spyglass up, his generals behind him. He studied the advancing enemy.

"Can you make them out, sire?" one of his generals asked.

"Yes," Wallenstein said, his full attention given to the distant enemy. "Nording's Finnar Cuirassiers. Hard to miss."

Far in the distance, twenty cavalrymen spread out in a line. Moments later, a second line formed behind them; then a third. They rode closer.

"Gustavus'll appear at any moment," Wallenstein said. "He'll show himself."

Wallenstein's prediction proved true. A different group of riders in distinct blue uniforms moved up behind the Nordings.

"General Baner's Cuirassier Regiment," Wallenstein said, mindful of Gustavus' favourite.

When the barren field filled with cavalry the lines divided and a short man in a broad-brimmed hat rode through, followed by an entourage. He moved to the front line and halted. The lines behind him closed.

Wallenstein immediately recognized the monarch of Sweden. He watched the king retrieve his spyglass and scan the hill and the castle. He lowered it and spoke to the king on the plain. "Good, come. Bring your soldiers. We'll wait."

The following morning, Gustavus' cannons opened fire. Trees on the lower hill splintered and fell; rocks shot into the sky, craters formed in what had been solid sections of the earth.

"Wasting his ammunition," Wallenstein scoffed. "The cannonballs can't reach this high. You'd think he'd figure it out."

The defenders farther down the slopes held a different view. They scurried out of range of the artillery. None wished to die from cannon fire.

By late afternoon the barrage ceased.

During the night, the temperature dropped. The following morning a thick ground fog blanketed the hill. The defenders listened to the sound of horses' hoofs, snorts, bridles tinkling, and the jingle of harness movement.

The Herzog Wilhelm Regiment made its advance through the fog. The alarm sounded.

"They're here, someone yelled. A moment later, gunfire erupted. Human and animal noises mixed in with the sounds of musket shots.

As quickly as it began, the first foray ended.

"What happened?" an Imperialist captain asked as the fog began to lift.

"They sent in the horse, Captain, to see what they could do," a bleary-eyed Moravian said, pointing down past the trench.

The officer used his spyglass and studied the hill. Three riders and their horses lay dead. "Didn't stay long," he said. "Can I assume the rest of the enemy withdrew?"

"They did, sir."

"Good, good. Not as easy as they thought. The only choice they have is to send men to try and take this hill." He closed the spyglass. "We won't let that happen, will we?"

"No, sir," the man answered.

"Glad you agree. For our faith and our way of life, resist everything the Swede throws at you. God smiles on you and history will record your heroic deeds."

In reply, the men clapped politely. The captain waited for silence and made his voice rise. "This is the first," he said and pointed downhill. "There will be more — much more. The Swede is pig-headed, and in this regard I admit we will be too."

He received a round of polite but nervous laughter.

Satisfied, he returned to the castle.

Swedish horse cavalry attacked the hill for two days.

"Damnable thing, General," one of Wallenstein's commanders said by the close of the second day. "Their bodies are piling up, to say nothing of the horses, yet they keep coming."

Wallenstein chuckled.

"There's the beauty of it, don't you see? The Swede's Achilles heel is his vanity. He cannot abide losing. The more Protestants we shoot, the more he wants this hill. A better man would cut his losses and relieve Nürnberg. But Gustavus isn't a better man."

The cavalry offered up easy, large targets to the sharpshooters. Shot out from under their riders, horses toppled while the men scrambled to retreat from enemy fire.

By the third day Gustavus abandoned the use of horses and sent in foot soldiers. Every day they attacked. Scotsmen, Irishmen, Swedes, Finns, Danes and the English all struggled with the thick trees on the lower part of the hill, only to meet the same fate as the cavalry.

"This is too easy," Beppo Minzico from Frozinone said to his friend, Tobia Zalli, as he reloaded his musket and aimed it downhill.

"I know," Zalli replied. "I only wish they would take their dead with them when they run."

They didn't.

A terrible smell assailed the noses of the defenders. Those closest to the entrenchments plugged their nostrils with small wads of cloth or wore bandanas over their faces.

The body count grew and the smell worsened. At night sentries watched as a Dominican friar wandered among the fallen with a candle lantern and dagger. Crows and other carrion eaters barely moved for him. In the dark, those close to the entrenchments heard the sound of teeth tearing at flesh and the occasional weak moans of the barely alive.

Hippolito moved among the scores of bodies, most dead. A few managed to survive. Those he found, he hurried into the next life.

He set his lantern beside a young man who issued soft moans. Hippolito dropped to his knees and lifted the boy to a sitting position.

The soldier couldn't be more than eight and ten. "Mother, please," he moaned in German, the front of his tunic covered in blood. "I hurt so much. Take it away."

"Shh," Hippolito whispered in a soothing voice. "Shhh. Soon your suffering will end, my son. This life offers you nothing. Sadly I do not hold out much hope for you in the next, but I will say a quick prayer of intercession for you."

With a fast thrust he drove the dagger into the boy's midsection.

The boy's near-unfocused eyes stared at Hippolito in disbelief as he made a deep gurgling sound. After a quick jerk movement he collapsed in Hippolito's arms.

Convinced the boy had no life left, the Black Friar eased him to the ground, pulled out his short knife, wiped the blood on the boy's clothing and released his victim.

With hands clasped Hippolito modified a prayer with, "Grant this soldier eternal rest, O Lord, and let Your Perpetual Light come to shine upon him. May his soul be welcomed, eventually, to rest in peace through the mercy of God. Amen."

The prayer finished, he picked up his lantern and moved on.

Two sentries close to the entrenchment looked on as Hippolito walked past them to the castle.

One turned to the other. "Brainsick, you think?" he whispered.

"What else explains it?" the second answered and rotated his forefinger next to his temple.

Gustavus showed no willingness to abandon the fight — until the eleventh week. By then the king's water and supplies ran short.

A few days later Wallenstein's scouts rushed up with word the enemy broke camp.

"What? Are you certain?"

"Yes," the scouts assured him. "Already a third of the cavalry have moved out and more are getting ready."

Wallenstein smiled; something rarely seen. "Do my ears play tricks on me? We have done the impossible and stolen a victory from the Swede. Now maybe the emperor will see fit to take advantage of this stolen time." He broke off for a few seconds and then said, "Check; no, double-check to make sure this isn't some kind of Trojan horse."

His men reported back the enemy had slunk away.

Another report reached Wallenstein. Protestant soldiers had deserted for lack of food and pay.

The Field Marshal understood. He too had trouble with money and food supplies. But for now he wouldn't think about that; he'd enjoy his victory.

He felt giddy with pleasure. "We've won, gentlemen," he crowed to the Council. "We've won. Not one of those useless moral victories, but a real one. We drove the enemy away."

Thrilled, Wallenstein ordered his last keg of wine opened and toasted his generals. "Wait, gentlemen; wait until the emperor hears of this. We are on our way to total victory."

Three days later Wallenstein gave orders to break camp.

Hippolito's bizarre nighttime wanderings soon became the topic of much talk. Brother Francis and the aged Franciscan, Father Cerny, took it upon themselves to seek an audience with Wallenstein. They stood as he heard out their complaint and tossed a so-what shoulder in response.

"I have more pressing matters to attend to than an insane member of your fold — if he *is* insane. There's a war going on or hadn't you noticed?"

"Please, your excellency," Cerny begged. "You must do something."

Wallenstein studied the deeply wrinkled Franciscan's face.

"Must I? He's not killing my soldiers or any of your fold. Tell me then, why should I trouble myself with a deranged friar? Brainsick, perhaps, but they're enemy soldiers. Less Protestants to worry about."

Brother Francis took a step closer.

"Your Excellency, it is true we are at war with an iniquitous enemy, but what Father Costello does is beyond deplorable. It is the cold-blooded killing of a human being, and cannot be judged as an act of war."

Wallenstein gave him a dismissive shrug.

"We are going around this in circles. What do you wish me to do? You haven't exactly told me."

Cerny took a deep breath. "You must confine him, Excellency, until we write to his superiors to have him relieved of his duties. He is a danger to himself and may soon be one to others of us."

Wallenstein had tired of the subject.

"I will take your worries under consideration and keep an eye on the priest. We are soon on the move with no place to confine him. Should the situation worsen I will act accordingly. Now my dinner grows cold. There's nothing else to say. Good day to you, Father, Brother."

The audience done, both men bowed and turned to leave.

A fast, knowing glance passed between them. *We wasted our time.*

Chapter 26

W HYN'T we just charge out and have a go at them?" Declan asked as he stared across at the Catholics.

Jigs gave him a reproachful glance.

"Och, laddie; you showed such promise with the sapper thing, you did, and now you've gone and ruined what I thought of you. It's a...."

Cecil broke in.

"What our studious colleague here's about to say, Declan, is give it a thought—if we threw open the gates and, as you say, try to 'have a go at them' they'd cut us down before we reached the circumvallation. What's the sense of it? We're better off to wait this out inside the walls."

"And die of poisoning," Declan said, waving a hand in front of his nose. "It really stinks."

"What'd you expect?" a bad-tempered Gillis asked: "Roses? People die and we've few places ta bury 'em. You try piling on corpses like we've got here from the last few weeks and see what you get. Leastwise at Breitenfeld we could burn 'em."

Declan held up his hands.

"All right, all right. I get it, but the smell's driving me mad. Makes me wish the Catholics would storm the walls and get it over with."

"Wait long enough and something's bound to give," Cecil said. "Bound to. I mean, they won't come straight at us, and good chance their supply routes are cut off by our king. We'll hold out, you'll see."

The city entered its ninth week of the siege. Food and water rationing was in full effect. Soldiers, children, and the elderly had the largest rations.

Fast enough Nürnbergers identified hospitals with centers of dying rather than healing. At least half a dozen times a day carts hauled away corpses and laid them to rest by the northern wall; the city's four cemeteries were full with no space available for more bodies.

Worse, the city had already used up all its ground limestone for the cadavers. As a result clouds of flies and other insects buzzed over the more recent corpses.

Stories circulated of cadaver robbers and other sorts of hideous activities occurring at night. The city fathers ordered curfews and hired sentries to guard the mass of human stench. Anyone caught out after the last peal of the evening bell faced arrest and lashing. They also ordered all taverns shut — much to everyone's dismay.

Skeletal horses fell and died as they pulled carts. If one fell, people rushed out with knives and cleavers — anything sharp — and hacked away at the dying animal. The poor creature's horrible screams could be heard from blocks away.

An irritated Declan let loose again.

"The smell; God almighty, you can't get away from it. Even in my sleep I smell the stench."

"'Jay-suz,'" an irritable Gisis snarled. "Shut your hole. We all get it how you feel. You think your blathering helps? One more word from you about this and I swear I'll send you to join the dead."

Stung by the rebuke, Declan apologized. "Guess I am going on and on."

"Catch on fast."

Afternoon shadows grew long at the close of Ainslie's watch. Along with Gisis, Jigs and ten others he had the rest of the day to do as he pleased.

His friends returned to the house. Ainslie didn't join them. "Wander about a wee," he said. "Stretch me legs."

Unsure of where to go or what to do, he let his feet lead him. He still had coins to spend. Here and there black marketers offered to relieve him of the money with temptations.

The first came by way of beer. A man approached and asked him if he cared for a drink.

Ainslie hadn't had any in weeks. He almost salivated at the word. He followed the vendor on the unbearably hot and humid day to the back of a house. Under a shaded tree he laid eyes on a modified wheelbarrow with a copper can. A ladle and large drinking cup sat next to the can.

Ainslie tried to haggle, but the man refused. He reluctantly paid the steep asking price. The vendor accepted the coins, lifted the lid, and poured beer into the cup. Ainslie downed it in almost two swallows. It was a bit off, but in the sweltering day it tasted like liquid manna.

His second encounter came with a mother and her child; she introduced something he'd never tasted — marzipan, made with ground almonds and egg whites. Ainslie paid the asked-for price and took his time savoring the delicious treat. He licked his fingers a final time while he walked along, the memory of the sweet taste still on his mind. He hoped he might stumble onto something else to tempt him, yet kept an eye out for danger.

Careful, he warned himself. Criminal activities had increased with each passing week. Victims of crime, especially those inflicted with knife wounds, were commonplace in the back streets of the city.

Lost in a warren of streets, Ainslie chose to follow one capable of accommodating only the smallest of carts. Already nervous, he gripped his dirk, ready for anything.

The lane sloped and bent. Nothing moved; no sounds came from any of the houses. His heavy boots echoed off the cobblestones of the tightly packed houses on the empty, quiet street. His nervousness increased; the lane showed no signs of life.

Should he turn back, he asked himself? He decided against it when he came to a bend. The lane had to open onto to a wider street soon; it couldn't be much farther. Past the bend he did spy a wider street. It ran at an angle. He exhaled. Good; he'd take it, hopefully back to the city square.

Movement between two houses caught his eye. He stopped, cocked his head and stared, certain he saw something. He willed the image to come into better focus. The shadows played with his eyesight, but he made out the two beings — a male and a female tucked into the back of a slender passageway. No danger to him, he determined, and moved on.

The female voice reached him. Young by the sounds of her. A private matter, whatever they were up to, none of his business.

The distinctive second voice floated out and brought him to a halt — a male voice, one he'd recognize anywhere. Pierce Hand.

Excitement rushed through Ainslie. What luck. Pierce Hand — a one-in-a-million chance to get even. He'd not waste the opportunity.

On the tip of his toes, Ainslie moved out of the sunlight and glanced around at nearby houses. Were any prying eyes at the windows? No; all seemed quiet.

Dagger out, Ainslie slipped into the shadows of the passageway. The couple stood engaged in their activity. He crept forward and hoped the Irishman wouldn't turn. A few more well-placed steps and Hand would be at Ainslie's full advantage for a little Scottish justice.

Palms damp, mouth dry, he moved softly forward. He squeezed the dirk, afraid it might slip from his hand. A few more feet, he thought as he drew closer, ready to spring. Only a few more feet.

Hand gave the girl his full attention and she uncinched the half-apron from around her waist. Ainslie heard him croak out a deep lustful, "Gut, gut. Du tun fein."

The girl pulled off her apron and worked on the small wooden togs of her smock.

Hand continued his encouragement in bad German. "Schoen, schoen."

Flecks of sunlight shone near the two, but Ainslie clung to the covering of deep shadows.

Something warned the girl. Her eyes moved up and past Hand. Her forehead wrinkled as she focused and tried to make out an indistinct, moving object in the shadows. Her mouth opened. Hand took no notice as he reached for her.

Ainslie sprang. A shriek caught in the girl's throat as Ainslie clamped a hand across Hand's forehead. He pulled the Irishman backward and plunged the dirk up below Hand's left rib cage. He wiggled the weapon in malicious pleasure while he gritted his teeth. "We're about to be better than even now, you fuck," he whispered into Hand's ear. "Ol' Nick down in hell's, waiting on you."

Off-balance and caught by surprise, Hand waved his arms in the air as he tried to free himself. Ainslie held tight. With force he pulled out the dirk and jumped back.

Hand reeled and crashed against a wall. He stood for a long moment with his mouth open before sinking to his knees onto the packed earth. He pressed his palm against the wound, tilted his head, and gazed up at Ainslie. One word escaped his lips "No."

An expressionless Ainslie crouched to eye level and held his gaze. "Yeah. 'Fraid so."

With terror in his eyes Hand made an effort to return to his feet, but failed. Blood soaked his tunic as he gave up the struggle and fell onto his side. Ainslie and a terrified young woman stared at him for a length of time until he lay perfectly still, his life taken from him.

Ainslie's eyes moved from the body to the stone-like and blanch-faced girl. He ordered her to fix her clothes while he wiped his dirk on Hand's clothes.

"Please sir," she whimpered; "don't hurt me. I need the money."

"No one's going to hurt you," he said. "Fix yourself."

Nervous fingers fussed over clothing.

His dagger back in its sheath, Ainslie searched Hand's purse and found three gold coins. He spoke to the corpse. "Where've you come up with these, eh? You been doing things you rightly shouldn't, I'm guessing."

The corpse offered no explanation.

Ainslie straightened, stepped over Hand, and faced the girl. He held out the coins and switched back to German.

"Take these. No use to him. Mind how and where you spend them. People may think you stole them. Best not to draw attention to yourself." He glanced down at Hand and returned his attention to the frightened girl. "A bad man," he said. "He had to die."

With the coins still in his outreached hand he said, "Go ahead; take these."

Wide-eyed, the girl reached out and accepted the coins.

Ainslie nodded in approval. "Good, but keep in mind if you tell anyone you saw me, even if they arrest me, I have many friends. They'll come for you. Understand what I am telling you?"

She nodded with fierceness. "Yes, yes, I do, sir."

"Go. Find some good reason to explain how you came into the money."

Her head again bobbed up and down. She wiggled past him and hurried to the passageway entrance.

Satisfied the girl wouldn't give him away, Ainslie moved to the entranceway and peered out. The street remained empty. He waved the girl off. "Slow," he whispered. "Walk slow. You don't want anybody wondering why you're running."

"Yes, sir."

In the street she smoothed her apron and moved as fast as she dared. He gave her a few moments' head start before he left the passageway.

In front of the Rathaus Ainslie washed blood from his hand in the stagnant water of the fountain. He examined himself closer, and saw nothing to say he'd been in any kind of struggle.

He felt no remorse at Hand's death. The debt was paid in full.

Word spread about a soldier's unnatural death; waylaid and robbed, the story had it. Not the first soldier, some noted; maybe not the last.

A directive from the commandant advised everyone to be extra alert.

"Shame about Hand," Cecil offered when word came about the soldier's identity.

Ainslie caught both the look on his face and the hidden meaning.

"Ay, I suppose."

"Terrible," Jigs added. "Big shame." He turned to Cecil. "So you ready to teach me the dutchie card game you been playing with Declan?"

Ainslie bumped into Paolo.

The Italian stopped and waited for Ainslie to draw near. "You are hearing Hand is dead?"

"Ay," Ainslie said, holding the other man's gaze. "Ol' Satan no doubt come to collect his own."

Paolo held Ainslie's gaze for a long moment. "How is he getting in middle of houses?"

Ainslie offered his best indifferent response. "No idea. You'd have to ask him. He's no sayin'. Does make you wonder what he was up to."

The conversation finished, Paolo gave him a quick nod and moved off. Ainslie followed him with his eyes. The rejection no longer smarted as much, but he still missed his old friend. The few times their paths crossed they both strove to be polite and restricted themselves to the barest of social give-and-take.

Two weeks later a joyous roar came from the main gate. It grew and traveled into the city. In no time church bells pealed and people ran through the streets yelling, crying and giving blessings to God Almighty.

The lifting of the siege threw the city into a near-carnival atmosphere. For whatever reasons Catholic Forces had withdrawn.

In spite of the jubilation many remained suspicious the recent withdrawal might be part of a trick.

The commandant sent out a platoon of cuirassiers to investigate. Scores of eyes followed the riders until they were but little dots on the horizon, horizon and disappeared.

"Men," someone shouted and pointed.

True enough, riders came back into view; some waved. "They're ours .Yes. Yes. They're waving. It's not a trick. We've won. The enemy's gone."

Once again those on the wall shouted themselves hoarse.

The main gate opened wide to greet the cuirassiers like conquering heroes. Mobbed, they had great difficulty entering the city. Everyone was eager to touch them and hear their report.

Three days after the arrival of autumn a hastily assembled marching band stood outside the main gate while the army readied to leave the city. Crowds cheered and women blew kisses and held their babies up as the defenders trampled out.

The soldiers marched in a long column beside a river as they made their way to *Coburg*. Outside the town they re-formed in military rows and paraded into Gustavus' massive encampment.

Temperate conditions soon gave way to cold which, in almost predictable fashion, then gave way to Saint Martin's summer. Everyone suffered from the sticky heat.

Cholera struck.

For nine days nearly a third of Gustavus' camp yielded to the worst of the illness. The infirmary tent couldn't handle the scores of soldiers who sought help. Most suffered both stomach and bowel problems. Soldiers lay on the bare ground writhing in agony, begging for mortal or heavenly intervention.

The stink of the latrines and the swarms of flies encouraged Gustavus to order work details for new trenches.

Declan returned to the tent from such a detail.

"Jesus, even a maggot'd stay clear of those pits. Good idea we dug new ones, but how come I had to go and dig while the rest of you sat around?"

Gisis threw him an impatient look. "Och, you're always on about somethin'. Us bein' here longer than you is why."

Declan sniffed himself and wrinkled his nose. "I smell bad; real bad — being near all those men puking and shitting. Can't make up their minds which end to stick into the pit."

"Show a little pity, will you," Cecil chided. "They're your fellow soldiers. Be glad no one in this tent's caught anything. And by the way, what's with all this coarseness? You never used to talk like this."

Declan shook his head in rebuke. "It's simple — the war."

"Simple, all right," Gisis mumbled.

Declan only managed a scowl.

The camp fever ran its course past the end of St. Martin's Day. The cold returned; everyone rushed for warm clothing and collected kindling and wood. Frost covered everything. No one wanted to leave the warmth of his bed in the mornings.

The friends shivered in their tent while they hurried into their clothes, all lamenting the cozy house where they'd stayed in Nürnberg.

Jigs pulled on his boots. "Warm as an egg under its mother bottom, we'd be now, if we'd remained there. Not middle of November yet, and already me nose's running. I'm afraid to freeze me balls off when I take a dump."

Gisis inspected his own winter jacket. "Glad I didn't toss this in the summer; be paying the price now, I would." He stamped his feet for warmth as he turned to his friend. "Havin' a shit's the least of your troubles, Jigs, now winter's come."

Outside a sizable blaze rose beneath the cast iron pot under their tripod. The friends stood around and warmed their hands; none dared or cared to sit on the cold, hard ground.

Gisis crouched by a large rock and cut away thin slabs of meat from the frozen flank. He handed the pieces to Jigs, who tossed them into the pot. "Tiresome, but at least it's food."

"Be grateful for what we have," Cecil said. "Bread, cheese and meat. More than we've had other times."

"Course," Gisis agreed. "Didn't mean nothin' by it; just saying. The king's feeding us better than expected."

"Where's he getting it from?" Declan asked. He waved his arm in a wide arc. "Countryside's been picked clean."

"And there's another reason we keep our food in the tent," Gisis put in as he kept at his chore. "Ta be on the safe side."

Chubby-faced Gustavus Adolphus Magnus opened his sable topcoat to reveal his blue-violet and yellow satin doublet. A man in no decided hurry, he climbed onto his favorite warhorse. He fussed in his saddle and checked his pistol holster. Within easy reach. Good.

Done, he let his eyes travel over the impressive might of his forces. With an imperceptible nod of his head, Gustavus signaled to Major Aako Turppa, ahead and at a right angle to him.

Turppa, with his thick, drooping mustache, turned his horse and faced the column. He filled his lungs and bellowed, "Royal Swedish Protestant Union Army and her allies, move out." He saluted Gustavus and rode back into line.

A dozen hackapelites reconnoitered the road ahead. Heads up and shoulders squared, they led their king and his vast army of cavalry, infantry, cannons, munition, and supply wagons eastward through the slushy snow.

A grateful Ainslie studied the gray skies; the snows had held off. Half an inch, he told himself. Not much of a problem. It could have been worse — it could have been more snow and bone-chilling cold. He'd take what the day offered. So far, anyway.

"Heard any rumours?" someone shouted.

Ainslie turned and searched for the owner of the voice — Albin Holgate. The Englishman gave him a quick, friendly nod.

"Rumors about what?" a different voice asked.

"Bloody hell, Carter," Holgate hollered to the man in front of him. "What do you think? About whether the Spanish whore-queen likes it from behind? I'm asking about where we're going this time."

"Ah for cryin' out loud, Holgate," the other voice shouted back, "What fleas nibbling on your balls?"

A different voice joined the argument. "Will you two shut up! We all know the same thing — we're off chasing those bead-mumblers."

Holgate's voice rose. "Wouldn't have guessed."

"Don't be a jackass all your life, Holgate."

"Same for you."

The army moved at a relaxed pace as the snow melted away. Their footing became soft and watery.

"Make up your mind," Gisis grouched to no one. "Warm, hot, cold; how's anybody supposed to keep up with theses batty conditions?"

Once more the cold settled in as they camped in the evening.

Cecil turned to Jigs. "Happy now?"

Jigs wasn't, nor in the mood for levity. "Piss off, you fucking smart-arse. If I wanna complain, I'll do it, and not have some English tellin' me otherwise. Why would I be happy 'bout the cold? Told ya before I don't like us bein' out here in this."

The others smiled to themselves. The words were there but they lacked venom.

A hackapelite rider tore into camp the next morning, jumped from his steed in front of Gustavus' pavilion, and sought permission from the guards to enter.

Reports of his dramatic arrival immediately swept through camp. Rumours flew. No one knew what, but all waited for something — anything — to happen.

Soon enough drums and fifes called the soldiers to formation. All waited for Gustavus. His aides opened the tent flaps and let their monarch through, his coat open to the elements. His top commanders stood behind him.

A ripple passed through the troops as a swarm of officers appeared and formed a circle around the short and stocky king. He's ready; action's coming, everyone thought.

"Can you tell anything?" Someone asked Ainslie as they stood in formation.

He shook his head. "Nah. Can't see him. Wonder what they're saying?"

"Probably last-moment instructions I'd guess. Bet it won't be long before we're off."

The circle broke; the generals hurried away in different directions and left Gustavus with his aide.

In short order the aide brought the king's horse to him.

Gustavus studied the sky and removed his coat. He handed it to his aide and climbed into his saddle. Trumpets blared, drums beat out their metered roll, and barking voices called for order in the lines.

Chapter 27

SHORT and plump, a Moravian nobleman General Rudolf von Colloredo, often mistaken for Gustavus in appearance, sniffled and reached for the handkerchief he kept in his sleeve. Last night's chill still lingered; his bones ached and the head cold didn't help his mood.

Be the death of him, this cursed thing, he thought — unless a Protestant musket ball found him first. He gave up a deep, wet sneeze. *By all the saints in Heaven, will my head ever clear? Should have stayed in Leipzig.*

In truth Colloredo took pride in being a man of action and not some layabout with a title. The goddamned Protestants were nearby; soon the struggle would start again. He intended to be in the thick of things, but wished he felt better.

Two days earlier Wallenstein complimented him.

"You did a fine bit of work, Rudi, evacuating most of our boys from Weissenfells. The town's going to fall, you know?"

"I do."

"You've still got what, a hundred or so soldiers in there?"

"I do."

"And they're led by..." Wallenstein snapped his fingers—"this, this captain, um, um, Delabonade."

"Yes."

"We have to get those men out."

"Should have pulled out with the rest."

"Well, we didn't and now I'm talking to you. Take a company of dragoons and escort them back to Lützen."

Colloredo gazed at his commander, Wallenstein, whose foot rested on a cushioned seat as he reached for his wine goblet.

"Consider it done. Anything else?"

"No. Just bring them back."

Colloredo moved to leave when Wallenstein spoke again.

"Oh, and keep an eye out for any signs of the enemy. If you see anything at all, send a messenger as fast as you can." He stroked his chin hair and added, "No time to waste. You better move fast."

Colloredo offered a fast nod.

"You'll be all right?"

The Moravian's forehead creased. "All right for what?"

"The soldiers — bringing them back. You don't sound too good. Or look too good."

You're a fine one to talk, Colloredo thought, but only offered, "I said I'd do it, Albrecht." He placed particular emphasis on Wallenstein's Christian name. Like everyone else, Wallenstein had first-hand experience with Colloredo's brusque and discourteous style; unlike others, he didn't take it well. His eyes narrowed, his jaw clenched. He blew out his cheeks. If Rudi hadn't been married to his cousin, Dominika, he might have sacked him a long time ago.

He shook his head as he studied Colloredo.

"I'll remind you whom you're talking to, Rudi. I am Count Wallenstein, Imperialist Commander and Grand Field Marshal, your superior, in case you've forgotten. I don't like your tone. Use it on others if you like; use it on me again and I'll clap you in irons."

The threat had an immediate effect.

Colloredo's shoulders sagged and he turned his eyes to the floor. "Sorry, Albrecht." He pointed to his head. "The cold."

Wallenstein left Colloredo an honourable way out. "Quite. We won't mention the matter again, but I'd advise you to keep yourself under better control."

"Of course."

Wallenstein picked up his crystal glass filled with wine. "Upon your return I'll pair you with Isolano. He and his dragoons need more seasoning."

Colloredo held his tongue but made a face — a face his countryman noted and on which he felt the need to make comment. "You don't agree?"

Colloredo answered the question with his own. "I can speak freely?"

Wallenstein hesitated for a moment before he replied. "Yes."

The slight hesitancy caused Colloredo to hold back until his exasperated superior said, "All right; what's your objection?"

"The man's a philanderer, Albrecht. And he's undisciplined. Makes me wonder how disciplined his men are."

"Philanderer," Wallenstein repeated. "You know something I don't?" He waved the comment away. "No matter. I'm sure his men can fight, and if he needs it, you can instill discipline into him."

Flattery fell on deaf ears with Colloredo.

The two men gazed at each other. Wallenstein sniffed. "Good luck and keep an eye out for the enemy."

Colloredo gave a stiff bow and left the room. Wallenstein stared after him for a moment longer and thought about Colloredo's wife. *A lovely, sweet creature, Dominika; hell of a thing though, bearing a cross like Rudolf.* He pushed the thought away and returned to the upcoming battle. *I'll win this round too,* he thought as he remembered Alten Veste.

Never one to shy away from bragging about his successes, he had sent off a detailed dispatch of the battle to the emperor. *Man's sure to hear it from other sources,* he told himself, *but it won't hurt to hear it from me as well.*

To his delight the emperor opened his coffers after reports about Alten Veste. Wallenstein now had new weaponry and a larger army. This time the Swede would feel the full force of full imperial wrath.

He moved his leg about and winced as he tried to find a more comfortable position. He'd give anything to be free of this pain.

Now less than five miles from Lützen, Colloredo led the dragoons and the remaining foot soldiers along a secondary country road which was in sore need of repair.

His deputy was the deep-eyed and big-hearted Austrian, Wolfgang Heider, who rode beside him. Heider proved to be a good subordinate. Twelve years younger, the clean-shaven Heider bore insults and injuries with ease. He accepted Colloredo and tried to make the best of his situation.

He glanced at his superior's profile. Head cold: who wouldn't be out-of-sorts? "Making good time, General,"

"Mmpf," Colloredo grunted, honking into his handkerchief.

Let him be, Heider thought; probably more taxing for him to engage in conversation.

Before long they made out the distant silhouettes of cavalry riding hard south of them on the open plain.

Heider spotted them first.

"Sire."

Colloredo turned his way. "What?"

Heider pointed past the general's chest. "Over there." Colloredo's eyes followed the arm. He found the distant figures, reached into his saddlebag and pulled out his spyglass. A moment later he lowered it and said, "They're here and coming fast."

"The Swedes?" Heider said.

"Who else? Dragoons. Advance party, my guess." He turned his head away from Heider and let off another deep and wet sneeze. Once more he cursed his cold, inhaled through his mouth, and said, "Quick; send someone back to Leipzig and let Count Wallenstein know Gustavus' arrived."

"At once," Heider replied and called one of the riders forward. He laid out quick instructions, followed by a demanding, "Go."

Heider returned his attention to Colloredo. "What now?"

Colloredo's eyes locked in on a small bridge by a fast-moving stream to their left as a "God is with us" battle cry reached them. He pointed. "There, bridge...make for it. On the other side we have a chance. If they get there before we cross, we stand and fight."

His horse responded to its master's familiar clicking noise and left the road. Heider followed but not before he turned and shouted, "Infantry double-time. Make for...."

His foot soldiers needed no prodding. Each man bolted for the bridge, aware of the oncoming riders. Their swords held in the locked-arm position, blood-curdling screams filling the air.

The foot soldiers arrived at the bridge first.

Colloredo, Heider and the Croatian cavalry found the going harder. The horses' weight worked against them. Each sunk to the top of its hooves in the soft, watery soil. The mushy ground not only slowed the animals, but also caused them agitation. As a result the cavalrymen's attention focused more on their horses' spirits than on the onrushing cavalry.

The Croatian dragoons dismounted and gathered around their leader, who drew his sword high and bellowed, "Zaa Boga I krscanstva." *For God and Christianity.* They retrieved their pistols, pulled out their swords and repeated the rallying cry.

If not for death and destruction the Rippach clash might have been little more than a ridiculous tale told over ale.

At first, the Protestant cavalrymen took delight at the near-helplessness of their opponents. Full of blood lust, they too left the road, only to find themselves in the same soggy mess.

All cavalrymen prefer dry ground and grassy fields — even hard, winter soil is better. This sponge-like field denied advantage to both sides.

Urged on, the horses grew stubborn. Some stopped and others simply sat like dogs to rid themselves of their riders. Still others hurried back to the road.

Denied the backs of their horses, Protestant dragoons were likewise forced to dismount.

Swordplay proved ridiculous; both sides therefore relied on their five-pound flintlock pistols to carry the day. Firing and reloading, firing and reloading, the Catholics retreated while the Swedes advanced, bit by bit. The gap narrowed until the two sides met on the bridge itself.

Swords, knives, pistol-butting and even wrestling and fist-fighting ensued.

Two Saxons threw a Croat to the ground and ran him through A Croat and Finn left their feet and rolled around on the wooden planks. In less than a moment the Croat's upper-body strength won the battle as the tip of his dagger pierced the Saxon's rib cage.

"Come on, come on," Heider shouted, as more Protestant cavalry arrived. "There's too many of them. Over to the other side! We'll get covering fire from over there."

Shouts of anger, desperation and pain competed with the discharge of firearms and the unmistakable cries of the dying.

"My eye. A musket ball. Help me."

"Maria! Maria. Remember I love you."

"Lars. Too late. Move it. You can't save him."

Heider's composure saved the Catholic side from annihilation. A musket ball smashed his upper right arm. Blood soaked his tunic. He remained on the far side of the bridge and bellowed out careful instructions, even as dizziness became his primary enemy.

"Don't panic. Order. Cross in orderly fashion. Are you not listening?"

"Come; we're almost across."

"Leave it. It's only a piece of cloth. We'll get another. Keep moving."

In small stages the Catholic side broke free and made it across the tributary and reorganized itself into two defensive lines. The enemy chose not to challenge, and retreated.

Two soldiers carried the weakened Heider onto soft grass as their comrades stood guard on the bridge.

Taunts, counter-taunts and the odd musket ball flew across the river, but the skirmish ended as fast as it had begun.

Chest heaving from exertion and his cold, Colloredo tried to assess the damage. Heider. Where was Heider? He spotted a circle of men with their full attention given to something on the ground. The men made way as he moved into the circle and found Heider, his head propped on someone's tunic.

A soldier knelt and elevated Heider's head. Colloredo dropped to his knee. An unmistakable glance passed between general and subordinate; both knew death hovered close at hand. Heider's lips moved but Colloredo couldn't make them out. The nobleman placed his ear closer to the dying man.

"Water," Heider begged. "Please...water; so thirsty."

"No." Colloredo shook his head. "No, Wolfgang; not just yet." An awareness came to him — he'd never used Heider's Christian name.

Worry on his face, he appraised the circle of men before he returned his attention to his deputy. "Don't trouble yourself," he lied. "We'll get you the help you need." He took hold of Heider's hand and squeezed. "You'll be fine."

Heider offered up a weak smile and directed his eyes past Colloredo. His chest expanded once; he then let out the air and yielded his life. Unseeing and unblinking eyes stared up toward a heaven they could not find.

Wallenstein received Colloredo's courier. He listened and made him repeat each word.

Satisfied the cavalryman had nothing else of value, Wallenstein dismissed him and used his crutch to hobble to the map. "Damn this pain," he muttered through clenched teeth. He tried to ignore it and give his attention to the map beside him.

"So, Gustavus; thought you'd sneak up on me, did you? Wipe me off the face of the earth and the whole thing'd be over? Surprise. Not the end game for you. Middle game's not yet begun."

Wallenstein sat in his chair and drummed a forefinger on his map. He had bested the Swede once already; he'd do it again and win outright. His resolve strengthened, he called for his aide. The floorboards creaked as the heavy captain hurried along the hallway.

"Sire?"

Wallenstein picked up his large glass of wine. "Von Durin, is Field Marshal Pappenheim ready to spring back into action?"

"He only arrived from Cologne yesterday, sire."

"And Gustavus only arrived on our doorstep today," Wallenstein snapped back. "I didn't ask you about his travel plans or to be his apologist; only if he's ready."

Big-headed fool, von Durin thought, but said, "Of course; pardon me, sire."

Wallenstein accepted the apology as his due.

"Pappenheim needs to get moving again," he said. "Have him saddle up. Also, Holk's horse; I want his battalion ready but kept back until the right time. Then we'll throw them at the Swedish sonovabitch."

"Jawohl, Herr General. Anything else?"

"No...Yes. Are our artillery units ready?"

"I believe so, yes sire."

Wallenstein arched his eyebrows. "Hmm. I'll go see for myself. Have my litter ready. In the meantime, those trenches on the Lützen Road..."

"Yes, Herr General..?"

"Musketeers," Wallenstein said. "I want musketeers in every one of those godforsaken trenches, ready to fire the moment the enemy comes down the road. I know the Swede. He intends to roll the dice. Let him have his way, and I vouch his horse cavalry will fly down to Vienna."

Hippolito grew more certain his death was at hand — if madness didn't claim him first.

Please, he prayed. *Please, dear Lord, let me finish my important mission. Give me enough time and then do with me as You will.*

He needed his wits if he intended to strike a blow for his brother and his faith. Dispirited, he trudged to a bridge with a group of Austrian musketeers.

The sun had set on the flat Saxon plain as Hippolito mulled over his vague plans. God called on him to engage in a task; no ordinary task, but a great and noble one. The task hadn't yet revealed itself, but it would. He felt certain of it.

Now he wrapped a blanket around himself and sat with a small group of soldiers around a campfire. By the way they studied him he sensed their reserve and worked hard to charm them with amusing accounts of clerical life. His efforts paid off; they settled back into their everyday conversations.

"Wonder what they're doing over there?" a soldier asked as he stared across the Rippach stream.

"Not much different than us, I'd wager," a comrade answered. "Warm fire, cold ground. Not like the high 'n mighty in either camp."

The remark earned a chorus of agreement before conversation fell off.

The men stared into the fire when a different voice said, "Think our artillery's set up?"

"Probably work on it overnight," a soldier suggested as he joined the fire. "For when the enemy comes at first light."

"No point worryin' about it 'til it happens," a third man said.

Hippolito thought about his day as the men continued their conversations. He'd fled the rectory when he discovered the other priests intended to seize and restrain him until they received further directions from Spain.

By chance he overheard their plan.

"Mad, I tell you," Father Alvaro Santos said to Father Amadej Skorupa. "He cannot be left alone."

"I agree, Father," Skorupa returned, "but what will become of him, do you think?"

"An asylum. What else?"

Hippolito heard enough; he didn't dispute he stood on the precipice of madness, but the madness had purpose — a calling. He'd answer the calling with his life.

It nettled at him they dared to question him, his task. He rounded the corner full of anger. Both men jumped at his sudden appearance. Santos turned crimson; Skorupa offered up an uncomfortable smile.

Hippolito's eyes moved from one man to the next as he spoke.

"At least in the asylum, Fathers, I can be certain I won't suffer nasty, inelegant remarks from those who purport to be men of God."

"I...we...," Santos sputtered.

Hippolito held up a hand.

"Enough! Never speak to me again — either of you." He stomped off. *Donkeys. They judge too easily and cannot understand what I am called to do.*

Incensed, he hurried to his room, stuffed the necessary items he needed into his small, cotton shoulder bag, and made for the livery.

He found a mule and rode the beast onto the street. Where should he go? The answer came fast enough —somewhere in the middle of this final battle — a battle to mark the end of the world. Somewhere he could do the most damage to the iniquitous.

It came to him: the bridge where the enemy first appeared. Armageddon will arrive there and he, Hippolito, will know his great undertaking. Whatever it would be, he felt certain it would have something to do with striking at the Protestant evildoers and winning glory for the Costello name.

Thick fog covered everything on both sides of the Rippach. Men could barely see more than four feet in front of themselves, let alone the stream.

Hippolito shivered as someone tossed more wood onto the fire. He felt and moved like an old man. How would he get through the day without help?

Feeling pressure on his bladder, he rose and joined a soldier making his water. He raised his cassock. With his mouth agape, the soldier stared as a powerful stream escaped the priest.

Hippolito finished, shook himself and offered his best smile. "Yes, even men of the cloth have to go." He let his cassock drop and returned to the fire, aware the man's eyes followed him.

The warmth of the fire cheered him, yet his body ached, although not so much from the cold.

The soldiers paid him no mind as Hippolito reached for his small cotton shoulder bag, picked it up, and moved off. Behind the cover of a horse, he opened the bag and rummaged among his things; sacramental oil, candles, bits of bread, a bell, a small crucifix and a jar of holy water. Those held no interest; the tiny ceramic jar did.

He drew out the cork stopper. With care, he tapped the jar and shook white powder onto his palm. Shivering, he brought the drug to his mouth and licked his palm clean. He made a face at its bitter taste and swallowed. Terrible tasting. Terrible, but essential.

He stoppered the remainder of the powder. There can't be much left, he guessed; maybe enough to get him through the next day-and-a-half.

A sneeze followed his sniffles. Hippolito returned to the fire and borrowed a tin cup. He drank and rinsed the harsh taste from his mouth. He thanked the soldier for the loan of his cup, already feeling his body's soreness melting away.

His thoughts returned to his heroic mission. God would find favour with him. The fire warmed him as he imagined his new life of eternity in heaven. What would it be like; how would Alejandro welcome him?

He smiled at the images. Ah, how blissful. His wonderful brother and blessed father; they'd be reunited and together and wait for Mama and Iniz to join them.

The fog lifted not long after noon. Both sides waited for the signal to attack. It started with a military drum roll from the Protestant side. The drums at last fell silent. Moments later Swedish cannons opened and fired round after round across the stream.

A solid four-pound steel ball crashed into an empty supply wagon close to Hippolito and sent it tumbling violently onto its side. Everyone dove for the ground.

"There's the answer to your earlier question, Ambroz," someone near Hippolito yelled.

"Where the fuck are our cannons?" Ambroz hollered back as other cannonballs came closer with each round.

The men quickly bolted in search of better cover.

Terror-stricken, Hippolito couldn't force his legs to move. He remained on the ground, his insides ready to let loose as a cannonball struck and toppled a small tree nearby. He pressed his face into the crook of his arm and shook with fear. The boom of cannons and the eerie howls of round shots rushing past him forced him into action.

Hippolito spied an overturned wagon. There, he told himself. Make for the wagon. Get under it for cover. He knew it wouldn't offer much protection, but still better than being left exposed.

He summoned up the willingness to move, and scurried to the wagon. Hippolito wasted little time dropping on his stomach and slithering underneath it.

Cannonballs whooshed and hissed over and past the terrified priest. Some landed nearby. He'd been at war long enough to identify the distinct sounds of light and heavy cannonballs.

He quickly regretted his decision to use the wagon for cover. Not enough protection. He should have moved farther back. Too late. If the wagon gets hit, he thought, let my death be instant.

A heavy ball whizzed past him. He squeezed his eyes shut. Another cannonball passed. A light, time-released explosion, he judged, packed with fuse, gunpowder and musket balls. Please, please, not me, he prayed.

The cannonball exploded in mid-air and sent a shower of musket balls in every direction. Some tore into the sides of the wagon and caused Hippolito to scream. He didn't think it possible for the male voice to reach such a pitch. His bladder gave.

Chapter 28

THE barrage stopped as fast as it began. With caution the Imperialist soldiers at the bridge raised their heads and stared at the ugly landscape of shattered trees, craters, body parts and death.

Nerves frayed, few at first took notice of the hackapelite riders who led their horses to the stream, re-mounted and made their way across the narrow bridge. An impassioned "God with us" fell on each man's lips.

"Take a look, you lazy good-for-noughts," an Imperialist sergeant hollered and pointed. "They're here. Get up and fight. I'll strangle you with my own two hands, damned if I won't. Drive them back."

The threat had little effect. Panic set in as Finnish cavalry whooped, hollered and made their way toward the foot soldiers. Imperialist soldiers abandoned their weapons and ran.

A trembling Hippolito prayed as the sounds of battle rang close by. Coward, he berated himself. Coward. He should have been out there fighting to complete his task, and for Alejandro. *You're a coward is what you are, crouching like a frightened rabbit beneath this wagon.*

Protestant foot soldiers followed the cavalry over the bridge. The juggernaut seemed unstoppable until fog rolled in again. Men could barely see beyond the reach of their arms.

Vexation replaced Gustavus' glee. Even-tempered and highly devout, he worked to keep his emotions in check as he addressed his commanders.

"The Lord, gentlemen, in His wisdom, brought back this fog. For reasons He deigns not to share, we are left to be patient and wait."

On the Catholic side Wallenstein blessed the fog; it gave him time to regroup. He squirmed in his sedan chair and roared order after order.

"Get the sharpshooters into the ditches," he demanded at an emergency meeting of his generals. "The fog'll lift. When it does, the Swede'll come charging this way. Let's give him a warm welcome."

None questioned the wisdom of the decision as he bore on. "Cannons. The cannoneers are not to leave their post. Leave their post and

I'll have them shot. They must be ready to spring into action the moment they see the enemy."

Well past midday the fog lifted once more. The delay changed everything.

As Wallenstein had hoped, his forces stiffened. Imperialist musketeers stationed in the previously dug trenches on the Lützen-to-Leipzig road picked off enemy cavalry.

Protestant losses mounted. With no other option available, Gustavus recalled his cavalry. By nightfall his forces slowed their journey southwest of Lützen, unending open land all around them.

Glow from both of the campfires, Catholic and Protestant, pierced the darkness.

A chilled and mud-caked Dominican, his heart full of hatred and revenge, shivered and brooded beside a fire. Imperialist soldiers found him a blanket and a bowl of stew. He ate with frenzy and the men tried not to stare.

Warmed by food and fire, Hippolito returned to his brooding. He would have his place of honour, he vowed as he pulled the blanket around himself; God wished it and the Costello name demanded it. But he needed to ease his body from the terrible aches that beset it.

He prayed to the Virgin Mary. Blessed Mary Mother, guide me and steady my hands while I take this drug to do the work I am anointed to do.

Little of the precious dose remained, but his aching body pleaded for assistance. He hurt, and sleep would deny him.

He rolled to one side, propped himself on his elbow and searched for his jar. A quick glance told him the soldiers were taken up with their own matters.

His hands shook as he fumbled for the jar, uncorked it and tapped out the remainder of the powder onto his palm. He had enough; enough to soften his pain.

He licked the powder from his palm and then made a spear with his tongue. He pushed it as far into the neck of the jar as he could. It offered nothing more. He pitched the jar away, settled back under the blankets and waited.

Once more the drug dulled his pain and gave him the temporary respite for which he longed. A sense of calm settled on him.

Hippolito thought of his childhood again, of those early, uncomplicated years with his mother and father. A fitful kind of sleep at last found him. Those nearby glanced at the holy man who gnashed his teeth and whose body jerked sporadically.

He woke with a start and took in his surroundings. Time to go. But where? It didn't matter. The Lord would guide him. Like a drunkard, he rose unsteadily to his feet, lifted his bag and moved into the darkness. Twice he tumbled into a ditch. His lower cassock and socks soaked up the water. The sudden bitter shock of cold sent him into a spasm of shivers. He knew he couldn't do anything about his discomfort. *Soon, soon it all wouldn't matter,* he told himself as he marched along aimlessly.

The first rays of the eastern sun revealed themselves as Protestant drummers beat out a rhythmic sound to signal the approaching attack. Soldiers ran to fall into formation. A few moments later the first field piece opened on Catholic positions again.

The Imperialists followed with their opening round until a terrible bombardment shook the earth.

The duel ran shorter in duration than at Breitenfeld, yet it still shook the earth and unnerved soldiers on both sides.

Imperialist cannonballs hit Protestant artillery pieces as the latter hurried to take up new positions. Trees crashed and broke in two. Cannonballs, hurled back and forth to do their utmost damage, tore open the ground, creating craters.

The duel ended; neither side certain of what it achieved, yet hopeful for great devastation.

For a few long moments an eerie silence replaced the clamorous noise. Not a bird chirped, not a spur jingled. Time and the world stood still.

Ainslie reveled in the silence. His ears still rang; he hoped he would never again hear such thunderous, vexing noise.

Proud and perched, back straight, on his white warhorse, his sword in its scabbard and a blood-red vest worn over his yellow buff-leather coat, Gustavus rode past his front line and reined in his steed. With his eyes trained on the enemy positions, he sat perfectly still.

Generals Baner, Lowenstein, Bernhard, De Knyphausen, Balach, Horn, Ohm, Brhae, and Henderson moved up beside him. A second line composed of majors and captains formed behind the Grand Council.

The horse cavalry came next, followed by legions of foot soldiers. In all, this was a grand fighting force intent to trample its enemy into the dust.

Only the front few ranks saw Gustavus pull out his spyglass and study the open plain to the east. A moment later he closed the field glass, turned his head and considered his officers.

His glance landed on De Knyphausen. "Doden," he said. "We have every reason to assume the enemy's sharpshooters are still in place. They are a bother. Can you get rid of them?"

"I can, your Highness," De Knyphausen said. "They won't fool us a second time. It will take longer to make our way to Lützen, but so be it."

"Agreed," the king said. "We anticipate your success."

In reply, De Knyphausen gave a half-hearted salute, turned and bellowed, "Infantry, move forward. Finlander Horse, follow."

A roar of "God with us" filled the air as hundreds of musketeers moved past the hackapelites.

Lieutenant Maki glanced over his shoulder at his men, turned and shouted, "Our turn. Vasa platoon, forward." He heel-kicked his horse and followed the advancing cavalry.

The lines ahead of Ainslie picked up their pace and ran at double-quick time. He drew in a lungful of air and ran with the rest.

The bugle at last sounded; the infantry stopped. All were glad for the pause and sought to catch their breath.

The unmistakable sound of hoof beats, followed by creaks of saddles and the jingle of bits, reached Ainslie.

Ainslie turned to Gisis and said, "Cavalry's ready, waiting for us." The other man answered with a fast nod, "Reading me thoughts."

The strident call came for the infantry to move forward.

Maki turned in his saddle and shouted, "Keen eye, men; keen eye. Don't leave any sharpshooters in the trenches."

De Knyphausen's strategy worked to perfection. Swedish, Dutch, and Saxon dragoons no longer bunched together or tore down the road in the most reckless way, only to be picked off by Catholic sharpshooters.

Trench by trench, musketeers and pike men cleared the enemy and allowed their cavalry and light cannons to advance.

"As soon as a head appears, Vasa," Maki shouted to his men, "make certain it disappears — forever."

"Yeah, yeah," Declan muttered. "What do you think we're gonna do?"

Ainslie and his line approached the next trench. The bodies of fallen dragoons, stiff and in unnatural positions, only heightened their resolve to kill any enemy in wait.

The alarm rose "Sharpshooter."

Ainslie saw long muskets rise out of the trench. By the time Catholic musketeers brought their twenty-pound weapons up, Ainslie's line already had its prop staffs jammed into the ground and trained at the trench. The unified crack of musket fire followed by the distinctive harsh smell of match-cords. Small cloudlets filled the air.

Catholic sharpshooters failed to find their marks, but three Protestant shooters found theirs.

"What're you waitin' for?" Gisis shouted. "Let's go get 'em."

Ainslie and the others raced to the trench. A roar of aggression erupted from each man as they jumped into the ditch, and were followed by backup troops.

Not a single defender survived; all died from the ends of wooden stocks or knives. Suffering no loss from their ranks, the men moved on to the next trench.

With the last trench cleared the advancing Protestant army stared across the wide, flat open spaces and made out the knoll on the distant shore with its windmills and enemy cannons.

Gustavus called for a pause as he met with his generals. His men took the opportunity to take what nourishment they had and mingle as they saw fit.

A magnificent, welcoming sound reached Ainslie's ears.

Cecil thought otherwise. "It's like listening to a tomcat's guts being pulled out," he said.

Ainslie's spirits refused to be dampened by the comment. "Och," he answered; "you've no appreciation for fine music when you hear the bags. Jealous is what you are, and there's a fact."

The men bickered good-naturedly while Ainslie wandered over to listen to the four pipers. He grew sentimental as he heard "Fair Fa' The Minstrel Hills."

A sudden, terrible nostalgia for home settled on him. He tried to dismiss the matter. Bein' soft is all, he told himself. Seeing all those dead riders put him in the wrong frame of mind. He turned and intended to rejoin the others when he saw Paolo head his way.

Both men's eyes searched for an escape. It proved impossible with the throng of other soldiers around.

Paolo spoke first as he stopped and adjusted his pot helmet.

"I am giving you a greeting," he said. He followed up with a no-teeth-visible smile.

Ainslie tried to find something clever to say and settled for, "How're you, Podo? It's gonna heat up now. Nuff action for all of us in a month of Sundays."

"You are right."

Ainslie couldn't think of anything else to add.

Both men fell silent, feeling ill at ease in each other's presence while a cacophony of noise swirled around them. "I best be on me way, then," Ainslie said, eager to free himself from the exchange.

"It is the same for me."

Following quick farewells, the two veered off in different directions.

Ainslie kicked himself and wondered why he let the chance pass to ask the question, what happened to their friendship? Then again, no point, he told himself. What broke couldn't be repaired.

On his white steed, his generals to either side, Gustavus lowered his spyglass and called out, "Gentlemen, their cavalry awaits us." He filled his lungs with air and bellowed, "This day God calls us to triumph for the cause of liberty and our Protestant faith."

A thunderous "God with us" answered in response rose from the front rank of the hussars, and followed in a wave of sound from those behind.

Gustavus signaled with a nod to Duke Bernhard. Ramrod straight, Bernhard faced the enemy with his wrist locked on his cavalry sword. He tore away from his king. Hundreds of cavalry followed while thousands of infantry cheered themselves hoarse and watched the drama unfold.

Mad, Ainslie thought; they're pure decent mad. Yet the sight of the cavalry charging the enemy still sent chills up his spine.

Croatian and Polish cuirassiers, equally keen to find glory on the field of battle, met the rush with a countercharge and their unmistakable *Jesu-Maria* battle cry.

Gustavus' left flank crashed into Wallenstein's best horse cavalry.

Ainslie again listened to the sound of steel against steel, of pistols discharged, of cries that made blood run cold —the shrieks of horses in sheer pain.

He turned to Declan. "It's now, laddie. By the end of the day only one of us'll be standing, mark me word."

"By 'one,' Declan said, "I hope you're meaning us, not them."

"Ay."

Declan kept his eyes on the battle. "Be nice."

Crazed with bloodlust the two sides flailed away at each other, neither able to maintain a consistent level of intensity.

Fatigue set in fast enough. Slashes and blows no longer came with the same strength. Sweat coated heads, necks and chests. Sword hilts grew slick and weapons heavy.

Each downward blow and each forward thrust used up speed and strength. Chests heaved as lungs sought to pull in much-needed air.

A Finnish hussar, exhausted and red-faced, dropped his sword and seized his chest just as he readied to slash at his opponent; a heart attack. He ejected the contents of his stomach as a dumbstruck enemy cuirassier stared in surprise.

Brute force made way for defensive measures as both sides searched for any advantage. Horsemen parried and evaded slashes and thrusts, hoping to cut the opponent, waiting for him to lose blood, searching for the all-important opening to defeat the enemy.

Unable to declare victory, Bernhard pulled back.

Swedish light cannons opened up.

Gustavus watched for a considerable time before he turned to Count Brahe. "Time to see what you can do, Nils. Bring them to their knees."

Brahe replied with a fast two-fingered salute, drew his cavalry sword, and spurred his horse forward. His cuirassiers did likewise.

The barrage stopped as Brahe charged. He relaxed his shoulders and moved off at a trot. In no hurry, his cuirassiers rode behind in perfect formation, with hundreds of infantry running up from behind.

Ainslie and his friends, held in reserve, watched on.

"So, what's his plan?" Jigs asked. "He's no intending to repeat Duke Bernhard, is he — not with the infantry, unless me eyes are no working right."

"Your eyes are working fine," Cecil assured him. "They're heading for those low stone farmer's walls. Wouldn't surprise me if there aren't snipers behind them."

"And the general's leadin' them?" a surprised Ainslie asked. "You'd think he'd be the first the papists would have a go at. Not meaning disrespect but it's mad, ridin' out so."

As predicted, Imperialist marksmen rose from behind the wall as the riders drew closer. They had an easy time of it at first. Five cuirassiers took lead balls; all toppled to the ground. The fifth bent forward in his saddle and his skittish horse trotted around in confusion before it came to rest in the middle of the field.

A musket ball caught an animal in the chest and pierced its heart. It trotted on a few steps farther, unaware, before it crashed and fell on its rider's left leg.

More of Brahe's men arrived, as well as pikemen.

Imperialist musketeers faced a furious and vengeful enemy. Cuirassiers' horses leapt the wall and wheeled about as Protestant pikemen rushed up to engage the enemy. Hacked at by swords from the rear and skewered by pikemen from the front, the Austrians died horrible deaths.

Brahe approved the results. "Well done," he told his officers as he glanced down at the dead Imperialists. "Stay alert. More papists will come. They won't give up easily."

Farther back Gustavus sensed victory as he moved nervously in the saddle. He marveled at his army, stretched over a mile. Win this, he told himself, Win this and the Roman is crushed. God favours us. He patted the neck of his horse, Ares, while he spoke to his nephew. "We engage the enemy again, young Kjell, and we intend to be a part of it."

Kjell shared the quiet view of his generals — the king's recklessness might yet cost him his life.

To the horror of his generals and advisors Gustavus often charged into battle, at times ahead of the cavalry. Worse, he shunned body armor. "It chafes," he'd say when asked, "and impedes free movement."

Gustavus bore his wounds with pride and felt certain divine providence watched over him.

Kjell learned to hold his tongue in his uncle's presence, but recognized the signs — excitability, the speed of his uncle's words and his hand playing with the hilt of his sword. No holding him back now, Kjell thought. He can barely contain himself.

Wallenstein sat upright in his sedan and focused his spyglass on the battle.

"Dammit all to hell, where is Gottfried? There's no reason for him not to be here. It's vital he leads a countercharge."

He's talking to me, von Durin thought, and moved closer.

"General von Pappenheim should be in the battle. To the best of my knowledge his cuirassiers are out there. I cannot imagine them without the general's good leadership."

"Right, right. Never mind, I see him. He's in the thick of it, all right. If anyone can give the Swede his comeuppance, Gottfried can. Hah. He thought he had us on the run, but no; I'd say we're beginning to come out on top."

With his sedan chair perched on the hill next to cannons, Wallenstein observed the developments and commented.

"Rudi's doing a fine enough job of maintaining the right; it's the center, von Durin. It's got to hold. Send more reinforcements to stabilize it."

"At once, sire."

Von Durin rushed off to deliver Wallenstein's order. He returned to find his superior brooding in thoughtful silence, mumbling to himself. The mumbling grew louder until he lowered the field glass and yelled, "Unbelievable."

Uh-oh, von Durin told himself. I don't like it when he gets like this. Experience taught him if something didn't go Wallentsein's way, he, von Durin, suffered the repercussions.

"What, sire; what is unbelievable?"

"Are you blind?" Wallenstein snapped. He pointed. "The fog's returning. Godammit, why does this always happen to me?"

Because you believe you're the center of the universe, von Durin silently answered and moved closer to his superior's chair. No doubt you think the sun needs your permission to rise.

He directed his attention to the battlefield. A ground fog, dense, white and shapeless moved in from the east and approached the field of battle. "Not good, sire."

Wallenstein shook his head in contempt. "No geniuses in your family, are there? No, not good at all. Sometimes I wonder why I keep you on."

Von Durin chafed but let the remark pass. *Go ahead and hurl insults. The day will come when you get yours; I hope I'm around to see it.*

Wallenstein spoke again. "You know what might make it worse, von Durin?"

"What, sire?" his fed-up aide replied, bracing for another insult.

None came. Instead Wallenstein cursed the fog and followed it up with, "One side or the other may win because of it. The winner won't stand because of determination, stealth or ability, but because of luck."

His voice weakened. "Luck — the one thing you can never control or predict."

In silent agony he kept an eye on the fog as it blanketed the field.

Less than a mile away, with his light cavalry behind him, the king of Sweden was also concerned about the fog. He drew his cavalry sword and made ready to charge.

"Please, your Majesty," Duke Lauenberg begged. "If we cannot keep you from battle, then at least don't rush ahead of us."

"We will be all right, good Duke," Gustavus insisted. "There is a war to be won today and we intend to inflict great damage before this fog blots out everything."

He goaded Ares to run.

"This cannot do, Majesty," General Hoffkirch shouted after him. "The fog's grown thicker and the dar..."

Gustavus paid no heed. He let Ares charge across the flat ground as the fog wrapped itself around him. At last he slowed, only to find himself alone. He strained to make out sounds dulled in the vaporous cold air.

Fear and second thoughts seized him as he realized the possible danger he found himself in. "What have you done, Gustavus?" he whispered, as he patted Ares for comfort.

Hoof beats; had his ears deceived him? He didn't think so, and strained to hear. Definitely hoof beats, but from which direction? He pulled out his pistol as he took himself to task for his recklessness. *I should have listened to Charles He warned me. Why do I always think I can survive anything?*

Unsure of what to do, Gustavus offered up a quick prayer.

Ares shook his head, snorted and pointed his ears forward. "You know something's out there too," Gustavus whispered, and wondered if he should turn around. But which way. The fog confused his sense of direction.

Unknown to Gustavus, Major Agapito di Colonna and twenty Imperialist cuirassiers were likewise swallowed up by the fog. Forty yards separated them from the Swedish head of state.

As with Gustavus, Colonna also halted and tried to determine his position. His second-in-command, Captain Nazario Rago, readied to say something to his double-chinned superior when Colonna stilled him with his hand held up, followed by a finger at his lips.

Colonna's horse pricked its ears. There was someone ahead; friend or foe?

The captain reached for his pistol and followed Colonna. Ahead they made out a sole, recognizable figure on a white steed; a man who waited for them to approach. Colonna took in the blood-red vest that held back a ponderous girth. He couldn't believe his eyes — the Protestant king.

Colonna didn't wait. He raised his arm, locked his elbow and fired. The lead ball hit Gustavus' steed in the neck. The animal beneath him shrilled and weaved sideways while Gustavus did his best to stay on the beast.

Rago, aware of Colonna's action, goaded his horse past Gustavus, turned, aimed his pistol and fired. The ball struck Gustavus in the spine. He arched his back but remained in the saddle.

Ares convulsed. His neck red with blood, Gustavus failed to remain in the saddle, and toppled to the ground.

The cuirassiers formed a circle around the prone but still breathing king. Colonna pointed down.

"Here lies the Lion of the North, the servant of Satan."

None felt pity for the helpless king.

Colonna lifted his eyes. "The fog's thinning." He again turned his attention to Gustavus. "We cannot take him with us. The enemy is close and may catch us. Pity. Time to be away."

"Sir."

Colonna turned in the direction of the voice. Rago.

"What?"

"Sir, can we at least take a few souvenirs? My children will have a keepsake forever of this notorious man."

Colonna considered the request. "All right, but make it quick."

Rago and a lieutenant dismounted and undressed the still-alive Gustavus. They removed his buff coat, vest, his sword and pistol. With keepsakes in hand they re-mounted.

Colonna led his men eastward —or so he hoped.

Stripped of his clothing and a death rattle in his chest, Gustavus clung to life when Hoffkirch's search party came upon him.

"Cover his body," the general shouted, livid at the discourtesy the vile enemy had shown a sovereign monarch. His face could not conceal his worry and anger. He could do little for his king but watch Kjell drape a buff coat over his uncle and elevate his head.

Everyone around the sovereign bore either a bleak or mournful face. Their majesty fought with valor. He couldn't remain here. Something had to be done.

Men shouted conflicting orders. "A wagon Get His Majesty a wagon. We have to take him to a hospital."

"No!" a competing voice insisted. "He won't survive the ride. He's losing too much blood. He needs help now. The doctor. Where's the doctor? Somebody get him. Hurry. Hurry."

A junior officer hurried to fetch the king's physician as the rest stared down on the man who singularly caused such disquietude and fear in his enemies.

With a white face and dry lips, Gustavus tried to swallow and to focus on those around him. The simple acts proved too much for him. He made gurgling noises and wet coughs with blood and phlegm on his lips. One final time he tried to speak and managed a weak, "My God."

The fog lifted as quickly as it arrived. With it, Adolphus Gustavus, friend and champion of Protestantism, surrendered his life. His men stood immobile and continued to stare at the king as Kjell gently lowered his uncle's head, rose, mounted his own horse and rode off to fetch the Royal Pastor, Jakob Fabricius.

A few moments later the Pastor arrived and cited prayers over Gustavus' body. He opened his bible, thumbed through the pages until he found what he sought, raised his head and took in all those who surrounded the king.

"My brothers in Christ," he said, as his eyes returned to the open book. "The Word of God tells us 'the Lord is compassionate and gracious, slow to anger and abounds in love.'"

Fabricius spoke in a clear, rich and strong voice; all the same. He at last finished with, "Psalm one hundred and three; verse eight through seventeen."

Men sniffled. A few wept openly while others fell to their knees and stroked the dead king's arm or cheek. One or two prostrated themselves and kissed their monarch's forehead.

The battle of Lützen raged on but few around their dead monarch noticed.

Chapter 29

WORD of Gustavus' death spread fast through both Protestant and Catholic ranks.

"Fallen," a jubilant Wallenstein cried out, wincing at the sudden movement of his foot on the thick, cushioned footrest. He waited for the pain to lessen before he spoke again. "Wonderful!" He studied his aide. "Von Durin, care to show a little more enthusiasm? I'll say it again. Gustavus, endless thorn in my side, is dead."

"Yes, sire," his weighty adjutant said. "Wonderful, indeed."

"More than wonderful," Wallenstein corrected him, somehow feeling miffed by von Durin's tone. "The Dark Angel no longer vexes us."

Gottfried Pappenheim, the Butcher of Magdeburg, had mixed reactions. One part of him took pleasure in the tidings, yet another lamented he would never meet the king on a field of battle.

"There you go, Filip," he proclaimed to his second-in-command as he placed his foot in the stirrup and climbed onto his horse; "God's mill grinds slowly but surely. It took time, but the sonovabitch is at last dead. Hope he burns in hell."

He broke off and thought about his words. "Dead...I can't believe it. Good for us; not good for them; they'll be leaderless now. And you know, Breitenfeld — we should have won at Breitenfeld."

He climbed into the saddle and gazed at his second-in-command. "Hell welcomes the Swede, Filip. Now, let's make his army follow."

Much like Gustavus, Pappenheim outpaced his officers.

Across the battlefield a team of Swedish cannoneers covered their ears as their artillery piece bounced on its large wooden wheels. Another four-pound ball flew from the cannon. The shot gone, one man hurried to dampen and clean the barrel of residual smoldering material while his mates readied themselves for the next shot.

The cannon fired again. The metal ball flew across the field and narrowly missed Pappenheim, yet both horse and rider suffered its most serious effects. The force of the rushed air from the projectile turned out to be mighty, and knocked Pappenheim's animal off its legs. The animal fell in a most unwieldy manner and tossed its owner from the saddle. He rolled and hit his temple on an embedded rock.

At first it appeared Pappenheim and his steed appeared to have had suffered only minor bruising and nothing more. It fast enough it became clear neither could rise without assistance; both in the most agonizing pain. Further, each suffered from torn skin and bleeding from their eyeballs.

In haste Pappenheim's officers lifted the dazed and confused man to his feet and set him on another horse.

They moved to either side of the horse to brace him and then guided him off the field. Another officer studied Pappenheim's favorite war horse. Nothing for it, he decided, but to destroy the beast. He readied his pistol and sent a ball into the animal.

Brother Francis examined his patient at the field hospital. His eyes took in the rising bumps on Pappenheim's skin. He bent, looked closer and didn't like what he saw. Something had built up beneath the general's skin, he reasoned; something he didn't quite understand. He guessed the general suffered damage to muscle and tissue not visible to the naked eye.

Finished with his examination, he spoke.

"Your highness, I can do no more. Most of your injuries are beyond my abilities. I strongly recommend you be taken to a hospital in Leipzig."

Even with his eyes bandaged and barely able to balance himself upright, Pappenheim remained stubborn. He bristled at the friar's recommendation.

"Nonsense," he growled, as his fingertips probed the bandage over his eyes. "There's too much at stake for me to leave. I have to return...somehow."

Francis spoke again. "There is much to admire about your gallantry, highness, but I must ask in what capacity will you lead the fight? You cannot see, cannot stand, and I regret to say you will die if you do not get proper medical attention. Tomorrow is another day."

It took considerable persuasion before Pappenheim relented.

His men settled the once-vigorous warrior onto a cart and made for Leipzig. If not for the medicine Francis gave him, every jostle and bump in the road would have made the trip even more unbearable.

The cart never reached Lützen. On the way, the man who lived for nothing more than meet the king of Sweden in battle, the man whose name became synonymous with butchery in the German lands, died from his injuries.

To Wallenstein's delight, his army stiffened and counterattacked. The once-vaunted Swedish juggernaut broke and pulled back. Better still, word reached Wallenstein's Grand Council hundreds of the enemy's mercenaries had deserted.

A brief lull occurred.

On the Protestant side, Royal Pastor Jakob Fabricius did something to become legend by day's end. Near a small wood he stood alone and broke into "A Might Fortress is Our God."

His voice, loud and clear, carried some distance. Soon enough junior officers joined, followed by commanders, and then rank and file raised their voices and joined in too. The hymn lifted men's spirits and called to mind a beloved king who lay at rest in the royal tent while preparations were made to return his body home for burial.

Field Marshal Bernhard, never one to let an opportunity slip by, seized on the uplifted morale. In haste he gathered his officers around him. Filled with great emotion, Bernhard reminded everyone about the need to finish what had been dear to their king's heart — the defeat of the enemy.

"We are not shrinking violets," he declared. "Nor did we come all this way to sacrifice so much blood in vain. Our monarch did not die so we could hang our heads, turn and retreat."

He brushed his beard with the back of his hand, cleared his throat and proceeded. "No, never, Faith is our virtue, and victory our destiny."

The speech won favourable reception.

"The Field marshal's got it right," someone shouted.

"Listen to him," others proclaimed.

What began as a polite circle of officers willing to give an ear to their leader turned into a roused collection of men eager to return to battle.

More than pleased with the response, Bernhard let his eyes sweep the circle. He'd reinvigorated his officers. He filled his lungs with air and roared, "Our great-hearted King Gustavus and justice demand you check the evil-doers who wish to force the yoke of Roman papism back on the peoples of Europe."

Again men whooped and cheered with wild enthusiasm. Again Bernhard waited for the cheering to die off. He drew his sword and raised it high.

"Bring the King's spirit back; we will offer a new plan and a new battle. This day will be ours."

"Hear him. Hear him" men called out and raised their own cavalry swords as Bernhard shouted, "Gustavus, Gustavus. Avenge the King. Avenge the King."

The chant grew in volume until at last the circle broke; in ones and twos, the officers dispersed, intent to repeat Bernhard's message to their own men.

Bernhard returned his sword to its sheath and pulled General De Knyphausen aside.

"We've held back our reserves long enough, Dodo."

De Knyphausen remained silent and waited for more.

Bernhard didn't disappoint. "I'm sure Wallenstein thinks we're done. We're not; far from it. Let's pay him back in a different coin."

"Our reserves?"

"Nothing else, Dodo. Why bring them if we won't use them?"

De Knyphausen stared long and hard at his friend. "Only proper. His Majesty's smiling at you right now, Johann. You're right. Let's set them loose."

"Exactly. Protestant steel will rule this day." He beat his gloves into his hand. "What do we know so far?"

De Knyphausen thought about the question before he answered.

"They still hold a superiority of cannon. I'm sure we can neutralize them. As for their cavalry, Holck and Piccolomini are in charge of the Papists. They're far from Wallenstein's best men."

"Good. I have faith in you. Wipe out the cannons. Run the swine over. After, we'll deal with their cavalry."

De Knyphausen offered a fast nod.

For his part Bernhard gazed at the man he'd known for forty years. "Know this, Dodo; we will triumph today. My speech to the men wasn't idle talk."

"I hope so; I pray so."

Bernhard placed both hands on De Knyphausen's shoulders.

"I will say it one more time. We will win. Now say after me, 'This day will not end until we send the last of these blackguards beyond Lutzen."

De Knyphausen repeated the declaration, this time with enthusiasm. Bernhard slapped the man's arms with open palms.

"Good. You have the king's spirit, the Swedish spirit."

Lieutenant Maki gathered his men. "We're to move out. The fight of our lives is here. Give your all."

Give our all, thought Ainslie. What did Maki think they'd been doing so far?

Not privy to the Scot's inner thoughts, Maki continued.

"We have not yet proven ourselves superior. The day is far from over. We will accept nothing but total victory."

His eyes swept over the faces. He drew a breath and spoke again. "You'll be with the Scots and Hendersson Brigade. God guide your hand and return you to safety."

He kicked his horse and left them. Moments later a bugle sounded.

Ainslie bent, picked up his fourquettes, hefted his musket and joined Declan.

Ahead, full of fervour and eager to return to battle, Colonel Renke von Brünnhof's cuirassiers mounted. The riders waited for the signal from von Brünnhof. Ever the military man, the tall and long-shanked von Brünnhof, with his sloping shoulders, moved to the front. He turned his horse toward the enemy, drew his sword and raised it high. He filled his lungs and bellowed out Bernhard's rallying cry. "To Windmill Hill. To victory. Take the cannons. Avenge the King. This day belongs to us. God with us."

Hundreds of voices took up the refrain as they drew their own weapons and readied for the charge.

Von Brünnhof drew in another lungful of air, kicked his horse and rushed off toward the enemy cannons with his battle-crazed men behind him. The ground shook under the large warhorses as the riders howled their murderous battle cry, "God with us."

The bugle blared again as sergeants called out, "Infantry. Make ready"

"Come on. Come on. Get ready."

"Into formation. What are you waiting for, an invitation? We haven't got all day."

The first line of pike men gathered, followed by the next.

Hundreds of men assembled. Fife, two drummers, and the standard bearer moved to the front. Pikemen and musketeers tightened their ranks.

Ainslie clutched his musket with greater tension.

"J'hear?" Gisis said softly as he stood to the left of Ainslie.

"Nah, Gis; hear wot?"

"We're going against the *Infantería de Marina*. Up ahead." He used his chin to point.

"The wot," Ainslie asked.

Gisis repeated the words and sounded out each syllable. "Spanish marines; whatever they are. Supposed to be the cream of the papist crop."

"No kiddin'? Where'd you get this?"

"Jigs. Don't ask me how he learned it."

"Cream of the crop, eh? Guess we should be honoured. No matter to me if it's cream of the crop or foot sloggers. Either way I'll do me best to stay outta their way."

"Amen. Stay safe and when all this is done we'll go into town and get blind drunk somewheres."

"Luck, Gis," Ainslie said, "and same to Jigs if I don't see him first."

"Right. Luck yourself. Gotta go."

Morison hurried farther up the line.

Ainslie let his eyes wander on the off chance he might catch a glimpse of Paolo. He'd offer a fast wave and a good luck sign. He couldn't see his old friend, but hoped they would both come out of this all right. His mind took him back to Jönköping and recalled with fondness their days in training camp. Hard, but they both still managed to have fun; they'd go into town and visit the taverns at the end of the day. Along with other trainees they often found themselves in a few street brawls with students from the university.

He sighed. So much had happened since then.

"Soldiers," Colonel Henrik Almquist shouted. "Forward to victory."

The musicians played the opening strain of a martial tune as eight companies advanced across the field. The fife player finished and fell silent. The drummers continued their ratapan as the tramp, tramp, tramp, tramp of the infantry's feet adjusted to the drumbeat.

It surprised Ainslie he didn't have his habitual dry mouth or knots in his stomach.

Two Catholic Tercio squares in perfect formation, flags aflutter, and cavalry behind them, awaited the Protestants at a farmer's field.

Ainslie couldn't help but be impressed. *Something, them standing so still, all glorious-like. Must have ice running through their veins. Wonder what they think of us? Too bad our cannons can't cut them to pieces. Now's I think of it, how come we're no using them?*

His eyes never left the Tercios, especially the cavalry. They worried him. *Hope none of those riders get close enough in this fight. Counting on our pikemen to keep 'em away.*

The man beside him also noticed the plumed men-at-arms in their mustard breeches and reddish-blue cassocks. "Buncha fops, ya ask me. Nothin' to be scared of."

Ainslie wasn't convinced. Showy or not, he didn't want any hussar bearing down on him. "Be dead brilliant if they get a taste of our cavalry right now."

"Them and our cannons," the other added.

Chapter 30

THE infantry came to a halt and stared across at the Catholics. Neither side moved for a few long moments until a bugle was sounded from their side.

Ainslie watched as both Tercio formations changed shape — and lengthened. Catholic foot soldiers started their forward tramp, tramp, tramp.

Protestant sharpshooters placed their weapons firmly in their prop staffs and waited.

Without warning Ainslie's stomach turned into knots, his mouth went dry, his muscles tensed, his heart pounded and his arms tingled. He might have continued to focus on the sensations in his body; instead his and almost everyone else's attention turned to something farther away — the sudden silence of the cannons on Windmill Hill, followed by hoarse and high-spirited shouting.

Protestant forces stared toward the commotion, particularly at the waving of cavalier hats. All knew. Victory. General Brahe, with help from Colonel von Brünnhof, had somehow captured the formidable enemy cannons. The advantage shifted to the Protestants.

Drawing comfort from the sounds of celebration, Ainslie allowed himself a quick smile. Meanwhile, the Catholic pike men drew closer — the distance now less than four hundred yards.

"Make ready to fire," Almquist called out in a shrill voice. Ainslie tore open his pouch. He held the musket ball between his teeth and ignored the awful, bitter taste, too focused on his task.

Catholic musketeers fired first. The strong, sharp smell of freshly burned powder and smoke filled the air. Protestant drummers and a pennant bearer fell. Next, five Protestant musketeers likewise dropped.

The command came from Almquist, "Fire!"

The first line discharged its weapons and made way for the second. A Catholic line responded. Both sides fired, re-loaded and fired again with frenzy.

Catholic commanders waited for the perfect moment to release their favored Tercio Espanola formations. A deep voice from the Imperialist side shouted a command. The enemy marched closer.

A captured Spaniard dragoon later shook his head as he recalled the experience of both sides crashing into each other.

"Mobs," he told his captors through the interpreter as he worried an imposing bump on his forehead with his fingertips. After another deep breath he continued. "No, worse—mobs with no regard for military tradition. It all came apart. Unheard of, this kind of thing."

He blinked and searched the faces of his captors. "What is the point of an army, of military discipline, if we all behave like charging Vandals and Visigoths?"

His fingertips pressed too hard on the bump. He winced before he gave his captors his best disapproving look.

His mind returned to a comrade surrounded by packs of Protestant soldiers, and how he had slashed away at those who tried to unseat him. Three had stabbed his terror-stricken horse while a fourth held it by its reins.

Mad with fear, the horse kicked and caught a Cossack from the Black Sea in the face. The Slav left his feet and flew into a rush of Protestant mercenaries, eager to get at the cuirassier.

Smoke still in the air, Catholic pike men raised their twelve-foot staffs high and ran at the enemy, "Jesu-Maria, Jesu-Maria" on every man's lips. They narrowed the gap.

Protestant musketeers waited for the order to fire. Their commanders at last gave it. A moment later lead balls tore into the charging Imperialists. One caught a Spaniard in mid-step. He dropped his pole as a crimson stream gushed from his throat. A hand flew up to staunch the flow even as he fell to his knees, eyes wide with terror, desperate for help that would never arrive.

Those behind trampled him, eager to get at the enemy.

More Catholic pike men fell. Gaping holes appeared in their formation, yet they continued until they crashed into the Protestant lines. Catholic pike block collided against Protestant pike block. Spike staffs raised to the sky, both sides determined to push the other back.

Commands in Swedish, English, Spanish and German filled the air.

"Push, push, goddamn it. Push. They fall, victory's at hand."

"Hacerlos dar tierra; ganamos, este es nuestro."

"Klopfen sie zu ihren knien, männer, und die weise ist unsere."

Inches mattered. Each side sought to collapse the first few ranks and then rush in with spears and swords to finish the enemy.

The battle might have taken a more determined course but for the unforeseen arrival of Finnish hackapelites. Fresh from their victory of Windmill Hill, they turned their horses and charged into the Catholic lines from behind. All heard the chilling war cry, "Haakaa Paalle, Haakaa Paalle."

Enemy horses behind them, the Protestant infantry in front, discipline broke in the Catholic ranks; the pike men fought but not as orderly units. Eager to escape being cleaved or run over, they rushed for the Protestant ranks, each man for himself.

Catholic musketeers, for their part, spun and trained their weapons on the hackapelites. White smoke again filled the air.

A Finn clutched his chest and toppled sideways. A second cavalryman took a hit to his right thigh. He acknowledged the wound with a scant glance and continued to hack down at the enemy.

A lead ball caught a horse in the chest. Its forelegs gave way as it summersaulted and snapped its rider's neck.

Field Marshal Don Fernández de Córdoba viewed the battle through his spyglass. He scowled.

"Mother Maria's apron, am I cursed this day?" he said to himself. "This is not the battle plan I gave these fools."

Nothing followed his beloved well-planned strategy— throw the enemy into confusion and then pick him off.

He winced as he watched discipline give way to confusion and disorder. His musketeers were supposed to give covering fire to his pike men, not turn their weapons on the horsemen. The cursed Protestants were now having their way. Those dogs of northern riders were supposed to be tied up at Windmill Hill.

Face grim, Córdoba ground his teeth in frustration. By the blessed saints, could anything else go wrong? If he didn't release his dragoons and rescue his foot soldiers, this would soon lead to a rout.

He squeezed his eyes shut, opened them and ordered his hussars to enter the fray.

The command given, they issued their own war cry, spurred on their horses and made for the hackapelites.

The Finns turned with glee to meet their opposites.

Horses reared, charged and spun, threatening to upend foot soldiers. Order disappeared. Pike men, musketeer, foot soldier, horsemen, it didn't much matter, both sides found themselves pulled into a chaotic vortex. Those on foot scattered and did their best to get out of the way; they pushed against the outward press of men.

A noisy, riotous and even more dangerous outcome followed — all in a crowed space. In the panic of the moment, men no longer fought for king or emperor, for ideals, for each other. All fought to free themselves from the violent confusion and disorder.

Ainslie didn't understand how it happened, how he found himself pushed into the middle of a large mob, squeezed from behind, the sides, and the front. The crowd grew so thick it pinned his arms and jostled him back and forth. He'd never known this kind of terror.

He struggled for air and to stay on his feet. A man beside him fell. He screamed, but no one paid him any heed.

Get out! Ainslie ordered himself. *Out, and fast. You'll die here. You'll be crushed.* He dropped his musket; it served no useful purpose. Animal fear took over.

With great effort he managed to free his dirk. "Outta me fucking way," he snarled, the threat issued to everyone in his immediate vicinity. "Now."

He made good on his threat with a fast slash. The arc of his blade cut into the upper arm of a large man to his right. The pike man let out a deep howl and turned a livid eye toward Ainslie.

At once recognition came to Ainslie — Drystan Hoskins, the wild man from the ship.

"Ya fucker!" Hoskins yelled. "Come here! He swung at Ainslie but the press of men prevented him from doing so.

Ainslie managed to move away. His dirk in front of him, he waggled between two men, Hoskins in hot pursuit.

"Ya fuck," Hoskins shouted after him. "Get back here. If I get you, you'll get worse than any papist."

Ainslie almost lost his footing twice. Once, twice, three times he tossed a glance over his shoulder, anxious to know whether the giant had managed to gain distance. He never doubted Hoskins would make good on his promise.

Drenched in sweat in the cold afternoon, Ainslie untangled himself from the worst of the crush. Dozens of soldiers lay on the ground, trampled by others. No one bothered to challenge the wild man with the knife. He hoped the mob would thin even further as he pushed, dodged, swore, threatened, and escaped both.

A Soldier Far Away

With a little more breathing room around him, he stopped to catch his breath. His chest heaved with exhaustion as the riotous crowd changed shape.

His eyes flitted about. He couldn't remain here; it wasn't safe. Somehow or other he'd be pulled into a fight with papists, or maybe even his own side. But where should he go? Not ahead — and worse yet, not the pressed mob from which he'd disentangled himself, the one with Hoskins.

Small battles raged on. Foot soldiers on both sides used whatever available to afflict damage and death. Pistols quickly became clubs. Knives proved themselves invaluable. Fist fights and wrestling matches were everywhere. A few with enough upper body strength swung muskets about like latter-day Samson.

Two Bavarians set on an already bloodied Silesian before they realized the man fought on their side.

Ainslie forced himself to think more clearly. What about his friends; what about Paolo? He'd abandoned them in order to save his own skin. *Nothing I can do about it now. I can't go back. I'll die.*

The excuse didn't sit well. His friends were somewhere else, away from him. He had to find them. Like it or not, he had to return up to the front.

He spied a dead Spanish pike man staring up at the sky. He approached and stood over the body. He bent and felt the man's cheek. Still warm; he couldn't have been dead long.

Ainslie unbuckled the corpse's sword belt. "You'll no be in need of this as much as m'self." He rose and cinched belt and sword around his waist. It offered some protection among the insane, life-threatening confusion around him.

He placed his dirk back in its sheath, then pulled the sword out and bounced the blade in his palm. Nice feel, good weight; better than the cheaper pieces handed out in Stockholm. But then, weren't Toledo swords said to be the best?

Aware he'd been daydreaming, he pressed himself to keep moving, to find a way back to the others. His shoulder muscles bunched, Ainslie tightened his grip on his sword, ready for anything.

To his right, he spied three Protestant pike men with swords drawn, circling two Spaniards, their backs against each other, one with a sword, the other a dagger.

Following a deep pull of air into his lungs, he rushed over to join the fight. All five battlers glanced his way.

"Friend," he called out in Swedish.

"One of us?" a bullnecked Swede asked in his native tongue while he continued to direct his sword at the two men.

"Yes," Ainslie answered in the same language. "Better hurry and finish this."

His sudden arrival caused greater dread in the Spaniards. The taller of the two with the knife wet his lips as his eyes darted about for any sign of help. Both men took careful, small steps while they made their own circle, watchful for any lunges.

The knife-wielder said something. "Maria Madre!, the other answered and crossed himself.

A moment later the knife-wielder spoke again. "Uno, dos. Ir."

Both men sprang to their right and rushed the soldier farthest from Ainslie. He sliced the air with his blade and missed the taller man's chest by inches.

The Spaniard bolted past. His comrade suffered a different fate. He didn't make it. Legs apart, feet braced, knees bent and blade ready to hack, a Swede denied him escape. *Try it,* his bearing said, as he held out his blade. *Do your best. You won't get past.*

The Spaniard hesitated. The pause cost him his life. In his moment of indecision he took his eyes off the others. The brawny Swede who earlier spoke to Ainslie moved with speed. He came up from behind the Spaniard, bent and slashed downward and across. The blade cut deep into the Spaniard's muscular shank and freed itself as the soldier screamed with pain. His knees buckled, blood soaked his hose and he collapsed.

The Swedes hacked him to death. A weak "Madre," and a moan escaped the Spaniard who used his arm to fend off the blows.

The Swedes huffed and puffed while their blades cut into a now lifeless body. Ainslie shook his head in disgust. *Daft. Plain daft. You're turning the body into bloody pulp. Wot's the use? Dead's dead.*

With care, Ainslie continued to make his way forward. The earlier, noisy riotous, panic-strewn struggle had broken up, replaced in places with haphazard independent struggles. To his left, more horsemen clashed. *Won't bother me, them busy with each other.*

He spied something long and narrow on the ground. Could it be? Excited, he hurried forward until the object came into clearer view: a musket.

Once more he searched for immediate sings of danger. Nothing. Good. He'd use the musket as a replacement for the one he'd tossed away. He returned his sword to its sheath and hefted the musket. His eyes searched the ground for a prop staff. None he could see. The weight? Hard, but he might manage.

He bounced the weapon. Nice feel. A closer inspection told him the weapon had powder in the firing pan. Excellent, but what about the match-cord? Ainslie couldn't be sure; he raised the weapon and blew on the wick. An ember. Still alive. He blessed his good luck.

Feeling more secure with the firearm, Ainslie cradled it and moved on. Horses and men lay dead or near-dead; men. Ainslie gaped at the carnage in disbelief. *Bad, but no as bad as Breitenfeld.* He shook his head at the thought. *Give it time. Bad's bad, an' the day's no done.*

He approached a dead horse and rider. For some unaccountable reason he decided he to take the saddle blanket.

As before, he scanned the area for immediate danger before he bent and spoke to the dead animal.

"Oiy, beasie" he said, as he undid the saddle strap. "You've done glory for yourself I'm bettin', an' I'm sorry it come to this. I may need the blanket. Hope you'll forgive me for taking it. I'm sure you're in heaven now, running and visiting with your friends and mathair."

It took considerable effort to pull the lilac-blue blanket from under the horse. He freed it at last and tucked it under his bandolier.

Carrion crows had arrived with their harsh caws as the violence lost much of its strength. The sight of the birds disturbed Ainslie. He furrowed his brows and thought about his friends. Where were they? No sign of them; but death, everywhere.

He heard horses at an easy run. He turned toward the sound. Four red-plumed men-at-arms, their cassocks trailing behind, white crosses emblazoned on their tunics, rode perpendicular to him and made their way across an open plain. They paid him no mind and rode on with determination.

Whether the musket gave him false courage, Ainslie didn't know, but without thinking he raised it to eye level. *A clean shot. Let them come closer, and hope they don't spot me.*

Don't be daft, an inner voice cautioned. Don't draw attention. Where will you run if you miss? Keep still; hope they ride by. Better a live coward than a dead fool.

What would Aiken have done, he asked himself. The answer came fast enough. He readied himself. "Better act fast 'fore they're off and gone." He checked the match-cord again, pushed it into the charging pan. The smoldering end made contact with the gunpowder there. He held the heavy weapon as steady as he could and aimed at the last rider. He squeezed the trigger, held his breath and waited.

The weapon failed. In disgust Ainslie lowered and stared at it, aware all sorts of things might cause it to misfire, including dampness. Even so, with a chance like this....

He never knew if his sudden movement caught the eye of his target, but the dragoon, sword held at downward angle, broke away from the others and made for him.

Fear seized Ainslie; he had no chance of outrunning the horse.

Ainslie's feet refused to move as the horse drew closer. He caught the smug look on the dragoon's face.

"God Almighty himself" he whispered as he braced himself to blunt the sword strike with his musket.

No blow arrived; no injury or death. The Spaniard rode past. Ainslie felt the rush of air. The man intended to toy with him like a cat does with a mouse.

The Spaniard turned and made ready to come at Ainslie again, his sword held high across his body. Ainslie recognized this position from his days at Jönköping — lean forward and then strike downward.

His brain worked furiously as his eyes sought escape. A solution — an obvious one — came to him as the war horse galloped toward him. He dropped the musket, pulled out the blanket and tore off his bandolier to better free his arms. He unfurled the blanket.

From canter to full gallop, the animal came on, extra confidence evident on its rider's face. Ainslie swallowed, braced his legs, and flapped the horse blanket with all his might as he made whooping sounds.

Years of love and experience with Highland ponies served him well. Massive, this war horse, compared to ponies, but in the end a horse was a horse no matter its size...even a war horse. They all acted the same; they all spooked.

The horse behaved true to form. It took fright from the saddle blanket and veered away from Ainslie. Its rider tried to bring his beast under control. He pulled hard on the reins and shouted. It made matters worse. The animal ran about twenty yards, stiffened its legs and jumped vertically as if possessed. It arched its back, kicked the air with its hind legs and spun.

The cavalryman's sword slipped from his grasp. He did his best to stay on the horse but it threw him, ran forty yards and stopped.

The drama ended as fast as it began. Winded, dazed and bruised, the dragoon lay on the ground, defenseless. Ainslie rushed over, behind the dragoon, seized him and lifted him to a sitting position.

A knee braced against the dragoon's back, Ainslie cooed, "There now; everything's gonna be fine in a moment. You'll have peace, you will."

Able or not, the Spaniard offered no resistance as Ainslie steadied one hand on the man's forehead. With the other he lowered the dirk and slid it up into the soft tissue below the man's chin. A medium-sized yelp came from the dragoon, followed by three quick spasms. Following a final escape of air, the Spaniard stilled, forever. Ainslie eased him down, withdrew the blade, and wiped it on the man's cassock.

The sky grew colder, the air more damp as sounds of battle diminished. Twilight wasn't far away.

With his head down, Ainslie stepped over and around dead bodies, scouring the field for his friends. Lost in his task, he gave little attention to the shouts of excitement as men rushed past him.

"We've won, we've won," someone whooped as Ainslie neared a large collection of bodies.

Ainslie ignored him, unbuckled his sword belt and stared at the bodies, certain he'd located the spot where the initial crush of bodies began.

He found few signs of battle wounds but plenty of contorted, mangled faces, all bluish in color. Sightless eyes held horror. Bones were broken or pierced the skin; other bodies lay twisted and crushed. They probably weren't all trampled, he guessed as he stared at the dead men; some were likely crushed standing upright. He remembered his own panic when the crowd squeezed him; he could barely get air into his lungs.

What about his friends? Where were they — had they escaped? It'd be dark soon. He had to find them.

Distant cheers and shouts reached his ears but he took no interest. He turned bodies over, expected the worst, but hoped for the best.

He found Cecil first, his skin bluish-red in color and his limbs twisted at an odd angle, mouth ajar as if ready to shout something.

"Och, no, no, no," Ainslie moaned as he gazed down on his friend. He bunched his fists and beat the side of his thighs. For several long moments he stood over the body and emitted a low moan.

With effort he bent down, picked up the lifeless body and carried it to a clearing. He laid it down with care. "I'll come back in the morning," he said, as he closed his friend's eyelids and folded Cecil's hands on his chest, "and give you a proper burying. You deserve tha' an' more."

He hoped no scavenger would come and assault the body before then.

"It's me honour to stay and keep you company, Cec, but you understand I've got to see if any of our other friends are here."

His gloomy search continued as the sun slipped below the horizon.

Ainslie's hunt turned up Declan and Jigs not far from each other. A strange feeling, something he'd never experienced, came over him as he stared down at Jigs. Ainslie had an unusual sense he'd split in two; he'd simultaneously become another person — someone who stood outside of his body and looked down on this horrid scene.

Awareness came to him — he'd stopped drawing air into his lungs. He pulled in a lungful of air. *Get a move on*, he scolded. With care he struggled but managed to carry Jigs and Declan, and lay them beside Cecil. After taking in several more deep breaths, he set off again into the cold evening air.

He at last discovered Paolo. His body face down, its form familiar to him. He turned it over and saw the distinctive scar on the face. Ainslie let his eyes roam down to the stab wounds; there were deep gashes where the cloth had ripped and dried smeared the front of his tunic.

Full of unspeakable sorrow, Ainslie knelt over the corpse and whispered, "Your troubles are spent. No man can say you didn't conduct yourself proud. You died a warrior."

He wiped his nose with his sleeve. "I'm sorry, I am, Podo, for what happened to us. I'll never know why, but remember this, old friend, as long as I'm walking the earth, you'll live on."

With effort, he lifted Paolo, laid him beside the others and vowed to return at first light. Gisis — he'd search for him in the camp in the hope he might have survived. If not, he'd come back in the morning. As for the four bodies — he'd say something...a prayer...anything, once he laid them in the ground.

Chapter 31

IT grew dark, so the young Scot turned and headed across the plain for Windmill Hill with its many lights, wild bonfires and happy noises.

Absorbed in his own grief, he didn't take notice of a man who crept up on him, or the distant silent figure in the distant who studied them both.

"Got ya, ya bastard," a grating voice said, as a heavy punch landed behind Ainslie's left ear and sent him toppling. "Thought you'd get away from me, didn't ya?"

Hoskins rushed forward to deliver a kick. "Wasn't sure you were dead. Glad you're not, cuz I'm gonna send ya there. Cut me? Nobody cuts me and lives to see the end of the day. Especially not the likes of you. Gonna be one useless, dead Scot on this field 'fore I'm done."

Kick after solid kick crashed into Ainslie's ribs, shoulders and head. He rolled and tried to get away but Hoskins wouldn't have it. Determined to have his vengeance, he made sure every kick landed in a vulnerable spot.

Blood poured out of Ainslie's nose and mouth. The assault continued. His right eye swelled shut. He felt certain he'd lose awareness when Hoskins stopped to catch his breath.

Wait, Ainslie warned himself. *Wait for a chance — any chance. It's your only hope. He won't let you on your feet.*

Hoskins took in noisy gulps of air as he gazed across at the lights on Windmill Hill.

Ainslie used the opportunity to free his dirk and hide it behind his lower hip. The simple move brought a spasm of pain. With mouth open, he tried to breathe the pain away.

He moved slowly to his right side and rasped, "I've to tell you something..."

"Oh, yeah?" a fatigued but overconfident Hoskins demanded, as he gazed down at his victim. What've you got ta tell me, ya worthless shit?"

In a soft voice, Ainslie spoke to the ground. "Something before you kill me." He spit blood and waited, hoping Hoskins would be curious enough to move closer.

Hoskins bent his knees and crouched over him, his weight on his toes.

Ainslie sensed his tormentor wouldn't get any closer. He had to strike from where he was.

With a malign expression on his face, Hoskins began his taunt, "I seen ya rolling on your side. Think you're gonna get up, do ya? Well, lemme tell ya, you'll..."

Hoskins never completed his speech. Ainslie bunched his muscles, pushed off on his elbow and barely succeeded. The giant saw the blade as Ainslie let out his war cry.

The awkwardness of his position almost worked against him. He aimed for the chest, but Hoskins' sudden shift caused the blade to veer upward toward the man's face. The tip slipped off the bone beneath the eyebrow and slid into his eye without effort.

Ainslie pushed deeper.

Both men screamed; Ainslie from the withering effort, and Hoskins from the violent intrusion into his body.

Ainslie plopped to the ground as Hoskins rolled on his back and screamed, "Get it out, Get it out!" In a panic he yanked out the dirk. Blood, copious amounts of blood, followed. Hoskins moaned and pressed a palm over his eye.

They remained in the grass, Ainslie facedown and Hoskins facing up.

Ainslie didn't trust himself to move. The pain; he'd never known such pain. It hurt just to pull in the smallest amount of air. He ignored Hoskin's moans and pleas for help. His moans weakened and Ainslie's attacker at last lay still.

With his face in the wet grass, Ainslie smelled the rich, cold earth. Get up, he told himself. You have to get up.

He rolled onto his back and attempted to draw in air. Each breath brought a new spasm of pain. He forced himself to his knees, holding his right hand over his cracked ribs. His ear was wet. He raised his hand to examine it. Blood; it seeped down his neck.

His eyes searched about for his dirk. He found it at last, wiped it on Hoskins and rose, slowly.

Unsteady, he staggered for the distant lights. He felt tired, so tired. If he could just rest for a moment — a little while — it might help. He let himself down on the soft soil. Wave after wave of pain flooded over and through him. Everything told him he wouldn't make it to dawn.

Six beautifully groomed horses stood hitched to an elaborate gilded carriage in Lutzen just as the last rays of sun found the earth. Their warm breath clouded the cold air as they waited for their driver. He, in turn, waited for his sole passenger, Albrecht von Wallenstein.

Moments later, two grooms carried Wallenstein to the carriage while a footman held open the door. It took considerable time before they settled Wallenstein under a horse blanket, his leg propped up to rest on the opposite bench. A footman closed the door and nodded to the ten buglers in front of the inn. With great fanfare they announced Grand Field Marshal von Wallenstein's departure.

The driver climbed into his seat, fed the reins through his fingers and flicked them. The horses started upon their long journey to Vienna.

Wallenstein's gilded, extravagant carriage led the cortege of baggage, generals, chamberlain, aides, courtesans, cooks and servants. Those unable to ride in a carriage followed on horse along with seventy-five men-at-arms.

Inside his carriage, Wallenstein brooded. How could he have lost? He pounded the seat. Unbelievable. Victory had seemed so certain at the beginning. He shook his head in disgust while he stared at the dark countryside. He'd have a hard time explaining this loss to that milksop, Ferdinand, who didn't know up from down. The man couldn't lead sheep through a field, let alone run an empire.

With great theatrics, Wallenstein exhaled. The Swede was dead; maybe he could claim credit for his death. It had to count for something. Yet he knew it wouldn't be sufficient.

He could almost hear the emperor's reprimand: *We gave you money, men and supplies, more than our hated enemy has, and yet you threw away this pivotal battle. We have lost full confidence, Field Marshal.*

To his very core Wallenstein believed himself a survivor. He'd met disappointment before; he would again. The war had been good to him. It helped him increase his wealth and estate. No, he told himself, he'd get through this; he'd find a way to stay in the game. War was nothing more than a game. Few matched his skills at playing it.

He winced again as he moved about the carriage. Cursed gout! He'd be glad to get home to Prague and take the thermal baths. Why wait until then? He'd stop at Karlsbad.

His mind wandered back to the war.

If Ferdinand held him accountable for this loss, he'd run and switch sides. Those bothersome Protestants, they'd likely win the war. They'd certainly have use for a man with his experiences. He prided himself on being a survivor, on the winning side. One way or another he'd find himself on the right side when the war ended.

The more he thought about it, the more he liked the idea of taking his talents to the Protestants. It might work out quite well.

Near mad with pain, a cold, hungry and anguished Hippolito prayed. *Heavenly Father, Please, I beg You, announce Your task and call me home. I cannot take any more.*

He sniffled as he walked along, his eyes accustomed to the dark. Every once in a while he turned to the lights radiating from the town. They were there, the vile Protestants, but at least they'd left him here, undisturbed.

A few moments later Hippolito made out a distant figure, its head bent. He watched. Would the man see him? No, he decided; the man showed no interest in glancing about.

Something else caught Hippolito's eye —another man, larger, coming up on the first. Hippolito saw the blow and watched the first man tumble. He heard modest noises, snorts, yells, moans. Small-scale sounds continued.

Against his better judgment Hippolito moved closer, eager to make better sense of what he heard. Protestants maybe; he couldn't be certain. Soldiers for sure.

Words floated toward him; English words. Hippolito immediately felt intense hatred, yet transfixed by the level of violence, he moved closer to watch the giant repeatedly kick the prone man. Would they spot him? Unlikely. Too taken up with hatred. Besides, his black mantle made him almost undetectable in the near dark. Even so, he stood ready to bolt should either spy him.

The kicks stopped abruptly. The aggressor said something to his prey. A few moments later he bent his knees and squatted on his toes. The massive body shielded his victim from view.

Faint words passed. Hippolito couldn't make them out. A sudden movement startled Hippolito. The giant fell backward with a scream and threw his hands to his face.

Hippolito's mouth opened in horror. He thought he saw a long dagger protrude from the giant's face. It must be lodged in the eye.

The giant wailed and pulled the dagger out. The screaming increased as he rolled on his back. The other man fell on his stomach and hugged the earth.

The two stayed so for a long time; only the giant's soft moans reached Hippolito.

No chance for him, Hippolito thought as he kept a watch on the giant. He'd bleed to death. Good.

Earlier in the day Hippolito wandered about dizzy, weak with hunger and thirst. A long, cold night drained him of much of his earlier fervor. Exhausted, he longed for relief from his misery. He wanted death; he wanted to join Alejandro and his father. *Vengeance,* he told himself. If he could have one chance at vengeance he'd be happy. Then he would willingly surrender to death. The Lord God would call him home.

"Psalm fifty-eight; psalm fifty-eight," he whispered. "'The righteous shall rejoice when he seeth the vengeance: he shall wash his feet in the blood of the wicked.'"

From the distant trees he watched the armies battle as he moved from foot to foot, to stamp out the cold in his feet. He prayed for a Catholic victory.

By the time the light grew more subdued his heart sank. Nothing left to do but wait for darkness.

His stomach growled its protest as he left the safety of trees and headed south across a field. He might get lucky and find shelter somewhere.

By chance, he came upon the two soldiers, stared and waited as both remained still. *Neither is moving,* he told himself, and built up his courage to advance.

The smaller man stirred. Hippolito froze. The soldier sat and crawled over to the other. Hippolito watched him pick up a dagger and wipe it on the giant. He placed it back in a sheath and rose. Unsteady and clutching his side, he hobbled off.

He's wounded, the Dominican thought. Hurt badly. A few steps later, the man dropped to his knees and again rested on the grass, his back to Hippolito.

With his eyes on the wounded soldier, Hippolito approached the giant cautiously. He raised a foot and pushed the shoulder. No response. Certain the man was dead, he bent and searched for food. Nothing. Disappointed, he rose and stared in the direction of the other man. His body now lay in the grass but offered up slight signs of movement.

An idea came to Hippolito, one he'd been after all along. His chance. He'd send this unredeemable follower of the Antichrist to hell, and then return to the bosom of the Divine Lord.

But how, he asked himself? How would he do it? The answer came as fast as the question: the man's dagger, the one he used to kill the giant — Hippolito would use the very same weapon.

Hippolito moved with stealth toward the injured soldier. He detected the smallest flickers of movement. This enemy had to be too weak from loss of blood and injuries to resist, he assured himself.

With care he approached from behind, bent his knees and let his fingertips touch the weapon on the man's hip. With one hand on the sheath, the other on the handle, Hippolito slowly guided the weapon out of its protective covering. His heart beat at a furious rate; what if the soldier woke and challenged him?

Go slow, he told himself. Very slow. Yes, almost there. The dagger's yours.

The tip had almost cleared the sheath when the soldier moved with speed and startled the priest. The man's hand reached across his body and yanked Hippolito's cassock.

Surprised, the Dominican screamed and released his hand from the dagger.

The soldier matched Hippolito's scream. He offset his clumsy efforts by only sheer will and strength. His rolling motion brought the two face-to-face. Hippolito worked to scramble out from under the soldier's grasp. The man wouldn't let go and pulled him closer. His fingers found Hippolito's neck. He pressed hard even as he coughed blood.

Only a few short moments earlier, Hippolito yearned for death; in an instant he fought savagely to stay alive as the soldier squeezed life from him. He raked and punched at the man's face. His strangler held firm.

Hippolito's lungs begged for air. None arrived. His vision blurred; his efforts to defend himself grew more and more feeble. He felt himself slip from awareness. A long agonizing moment later, his assailant crushed Hippolito's windpipe.

Ainslie tried to get more air into his lungs. The effort brought on a violent spasm of pain and coughing. He let go of the other man and toppled onto his back, where he remained for a few moments, emitting noisy wheezes. After one long, deep breath he whispered a sorrowful word: "Eme." He slipped into a state of shock, unaware of his surroundings, even as his body jerked in spasms of pain.

The next morning a soldier approached Gisis.

"Something for you to see, sergeant."

"Wot?" a downhearted Gisis replied, intent on finding his friends.

"Easier for you to see than for me to explain."

"Show me."

Together the two marched across the field.

The soldier continued, "We found them this morning when we piled up the bodies."

His jaw stiff with emotion and suspecting the worst, Gisis didn't ask any questions.

They arrived at the near-frozen bodies. The private directed his sergeant's attention to the orderly placement of four bodies and pointed. "Those are your friends, right sergeant?"

Gisis moved closer, studied the bodies, closed his eyes, then opened them and gave a fast nod. A deep sadness washed over him. "Ay."

"Very strange, don't you think?" the young man asked.

His eyes wet, Gisis nodded. His voice broke.

"They dinna die like tha'," he insisted. "It's clear someone's fussed and put 'em there."

"I think you're right, sergeant. Something else I want to show you. Can you follow me?"

Gisis did.

They walked another fifty yards and stopped.

Gisis gazed down at two bodies. He recognized Ainslie at once but not the priest. His shoulders collapsed as he gaped at the Scot, his mind unable to explain what his eyes took in.

"Lee; how'd you get here, and wot've you done?" he whispered as he crouched over Ainslie. "Biggest mystery in the world, wot I'm seein.'"

Ready to rise, he stopped himself — he caught the slightest of tremors in Ainslie's right hand. He bent closer and brought his ear to Ainslie's mouth.

Surprise and joy washed over his face. He turned and glanced at the other soldier.

"He's no dead. Not much life in him, but he's no dead. He may not make it. Run and get some blankets and a stretcher. Come back quick-like, and hope he doesn't die before we git him some help. Off!"

The soldier turned and raced away as Gisis searched for covering to keep Ainslie warm.

"It's a wonder the cold dinna kill you, Lee," he said, in soft hushed tones as he crouched over the inert body. "Let's hope you're a strong one and will pull through. Time'll tell, laddie. For now, you 'n me, we're the last of us."

Gisis rose, wiped at his eyes, turned and said. "I've our friends to attend to, so you'll be understandin'. We'll shove soil on 'em yet afore they have a proper Christian burial."

Four men lifted Ainslie and carried him to the infirmary.

Gisis supervised the burial of the others. With his face etched in pain, he watched as soldiers wiggled a makeshift cross into the disturbed soil of a common plot.

Gisis sent for the piper and requested a Gaelic favourite, "Piobaireachd Dhomhnuill Dhuibh," certain the dead would approve.

Prompted by Cecil's fast nod, the pipes struck up the tune.

None who participated in the burial sensed the unseen animated forces still close to the earth. They lingered, not joyful, not joyless, but certain of their purpose. They responded to a greater bodiless principle, separated from the earthly forces and passed to their manifest undertaking.

Eight-hundred miles away in Mosstone, Mitchy Selby awoke early in the morning and sat up in bed. He blinked in the darkness of his little cottage, put his feet on the cold ground and rose. With eyes unfocused, he stared at a distant place and remained still. At last he blinked again several times and then dressed.

He lit a candle and reached for his bagpipe.

Outside in the cold morning air, he walked away from the village and toward the church. The bagpipe firmly under his left arm, he filled the bag with air, tapped the chantler, released the air, blew into the mouthpiece and offered up the mournful tune, *Piobaireachd Dhomhnuill Dhuibh.*

The rest became part of Mosstone lore.

www.ingramcontent.com/pod-product-compliance
Lightning Source LLC
Chambersburg PA
CBHW070309260626
47160CB00003B/776